# THE MARQUESS CLUB KILLINGS

A gripping Welsh murder mystery

# GAYNOR TORRANCE

*Jemima Huxley Crime Thrillers Book 5*

JOFFE BOOKS

Joffe Books, London
www.joffebooks.com

First published in Great Britain in 2023

Cover art by Nebojša Zorić

ISBN: 978-1-80405-724-7

# PROLOGUE

*Early that morning*

Having completed his warm-up routine, Emyr Trevelyan-Goode locked the front door before setting out on his run. With the key safely zipped away, he turned his face skyward. He closed his eyes and inhaled deeply until his lungs filled with morning freshness, making his nostrils tingle. The air was noticeably crisper at this time of day. Especially when dew pooled on the greenery, as it did that morning.

With barely any traffic, or other hazards to avoid, it was safe to pop in his AirPods. It was a luxury exclusively reserved for early-morning runs, when he'd fill his head with whatever music suited his mood. This was his time. A short period when he put aside responsibilities and concerns to enjoy just being. He'd always start at a reasonable pace, picking up speed as he got into his stride. He pounded the pavement with confidence and determination. As far as he was concerned, this was the best part of the day, and he was on a high.

As usual, there was hardly anyone about, apart from the odd dog-walker and occasional like-minded runner. Emyr welcomed the solitude. It gave him time to clear his mind.

Flood his body with endorphins and get himself on track so that he would be ready to face whatever the day would throw his way.

He'd followed the same weekday routine for many years, no matter the weather. Up at six o'clock. Out by twenty past. Home by seven at the latest. Hit the shower. Dress. Breakfast. Grab his briefcase. Lock up. Set off for work. Weekends were a more relaxed affair, as he allowed himself an extra hour in bed.

He was aware that his friends sometimes ridiculed him. Called him mad. An obsessive. A fitness fanatic. But Emyr ignored them. While they languished in bed, he embraced the challenge. There was no way he'd ever become a couch potato. He relished the buzz of knowing he'd pushed himself to achieve his goals. Every morning, he timed himself, hopeful of shaving off a second here or there. Testing his muscles to move faster. Stretch further. Work harder.

With the final cluster of houses behind him, there was only a short distance until Emyr reached the footbridge that would take him over the bypass. From there, it was on to the cycle path and the homeward stretch. It had been at least ten minutes since he'd last seen someone, a woman who regularly walked her Samoyed at that time of day. They must have passed each other on thousands of occasions, but never spoke. Though, they always acknowledged each other with a cursory wave.

That morning, Aerosmith blasted into his ears and its energy invigorated him. He could feel the beat reverberate through his body, its power spurring him on. As the AirPods blocked out extraneous sounds, he was caught by surprise as a car swerved, mounted the pavement and screeched to a halt in front of him.

Emyr drew up sharply, but, propelled by forward momentum, it was virtually impossible to stop so abruptly, and he collided with the vehicle. His hands landed flat on the bonnet. His arms took the strain as he did his utmost to remain upright. 'What the—'

The couple were out of the car before he had a chance to say anything else. And his anger was short-lived as the fist to the face was delivered with such speed and impact that he was sent sprawling. His AirPods skidded across the asphalt and, as his head connected with the kerb, everything went black.

\* \* \*

It was autumn, and the landscape had lost some of its greenness to golden and reddish hues. Some leaves had already fallen. In a matter of weeks, the branches would be bare. Every day, the air became slightly cooler, and that morning the sun had risen to reveal a blanket of light cloud spread out across much of the sky. Here and there were dashes of the palest blue, but you had to look hard to find them. The previous night's weather forecast had suggested it would be overcast but dry. So when the storm struck, it took everyone by surprise. The wind picked up. Powerful gusts buffeted everything in their path. And as the cloud cover thickened, it turned ominously dark.

Shortly after seven o'clock the first drops landed on the saloon car. Moments later they were slamming against the roof with alarming force and increasing regularity, sounding like a coordinated attack of a thousand arrows unleashed by an unseen medieval army.

Even with the windscreen wipers set on the fastest speed, swishing and clunking like a manic metronome, the rubber blades were no match for the volume of water hitting the glass. It was treacherous to drive at speed, as headlights were ineffective and visibility poor. Fallen leaves covered drains, making it all but impossible for the large volume of water to run off. Surface water sprayed from passing vehicles and carriageway markings all but disappeared.

Having faded in and out of consciousness numerous times, it took a while for Emyr to appreciate that something was seriously wrong. His thoughts were woolly. Sporadic. Confusing. It was like being trapped in a loop. A nightmare, where you think you've woken up, only to find yourself facing the trauma again. He didn't know what was real. Or what was just his imagination.

His predicament became clearer when he noticed that his head hurt. As he tried to reach out to touch it, he realised that he was unable to move freely. And it was at that moment when panic took hold. With his hands tied behind his back and his ankles trussed together, there was little he could do. He swallowed hard. He'd been gagged, tied up and placed inside some sort of vehicle. He had no idea why anyone would want to do this to him.

Emyr's body had been dumped into such a tight space, being over six foot tall meant little room for him to move. His knees were virtually touching his chin, and his head was jammed against something hard. There was insufficient space to allow him to do anything other than to pound his feet against the closest surface. And despite doing his best to cry out, he knew his attempt at attracting attention was futile.

All he could do was keep trying, keep hoping that someone would hear him and get him out of there.

As for the people who had snatched him from the street, they were feeling the pressure too. The abduction had gone smoothly. It was the transfer that wasn't going to plan. Negotiating the traffic on the A470 was stressful at the best of times, but the extreme weather conditions had turned what should have been a relatively straightforward operation into the journey from hell. Instead of being the ones in control, following a carefully thought-out plan, they had been suddenly forced to improvise. Which, when you were abducting someone, was not a good thing. But they'd done it now. He was tied up in the boot of their car and there was no going back. Their only option was to brazen it out and get him to their destination. But it didn't help that the bastard was doing everything he could to draw attention to himself.

When they'd come up with the idea, there had never been any doubt in their minds that they were taking a massive risk. But they'd both agreed that something needed to be done. Something drastic, which made people like him think twice before they casually ruined another person's life. There was something wrong in society when you couldn't rely on justice running its course. And it was up to them to step up to the plate.

Traffic eased as they passed the queue for the M4 turn-off. Now the main concern was not to break the speed limit as they headed down Manor Way, with its various speed cameras primed to catch out unsuspecting motorists. As they approached the city centre it was important not to attract any unwanted attention. Any such mission would have been problematic under cover of darkness, but for what they had in mind, they'd had no choice but to execute it in the build-up to morning rush hour.

Having successfully negotiated a stream of traffic filtering into their lane as they came off the flyover onto North Road, they were taken by surprise when the van directly in front of them screeched to a halt. They braked sharply. Unfortunately, the driver of the vehicle behind them had not reacted so quickly. As metal hit metal they were shunted forward into the rear of the van. And if that wasn't bad enough, their boot popped open.

As he glanced in the rear-view mirror, his heart missed a beat. 'Shit! We've gotta get out of here now!' He was already unfastening his seat belt and reaching for the door handle. At first it didn't budge, and he quickly realised that the damage to the vehicle had affected the door.

'Move it. Mask on. Hood up. Head down and leg it. We can't salvage this,' he growled. He grabbed his Declan Donnelly face mask and slipped it on without any hesitation.

The man in the passenger seat was shaking and swallowed hard as he struggled to fix the mask in place. He hated taking risks. Especially ones that had the potential to end his career and result in him having to serve a prison sentence. After all, he wasn't a bad person. Just a desperate one. Not having planned for this he had to trust that this was the best course of action. As long as no one saw his actual face he had

5

a chance of getting out of there. Though he knew that if he looked up and caught anyone's eye, they would be shocked to see a rubber-faced Ant McPartlin staring back at them.

They forced their respective doors open, the driver first to make it out of the vehicle. He was already running along the pavement, head down, trusting his instincts, by the time the occupants of the other vehicles had had a chance to react.

It didn't take long for horns to blare as drivers demonstrated their mounting frustration. Knowing the layout of the road everyone realised that drivers headed towards the city centre would be stuck for quite some time, unable to continue with their journey until the vehicles involved in the collision had moved. It inevitably added to everyone's annoyance to see that the carriageways heading north remained free-flowing.

At that time in the morning there were few pedestrians. But give it another hour and the pavements in this area would be heaving with parents and children on their way to St Joseph's Primary School. As it was, there was only one woman and a child on foot in the vicinity of the crash.

'Mummy, look at that man!' shouted a boy. He tugged his mother's sleeve to get her attention and pointed at someone struggling to get out of the saloon car.

Moments earlier, as the vehicles collided, Emyr had taken another knock to the head. His ears were ringing. He was disorientated, nauseous and extremely dizzy. But despite all this, fear had made him determined to free himself. It helped that he was physically fit. He bucked, writhed and somehow managed to manoeuvre himself into a position where he could tumble out of the vehicle.

With his arms restrained behind his back and his ankles tied together, he couldn't manage his landing and tumbled straight into the path of an oncoming truck. The driver gritted his teeth as he slammed on the brakes and tried unsuccessfully to avoid the inevitable. Moments later, the vehicle jolted as the tyres crushed the life out of Emyr.

# CHAPTER 1

*A few days earlier*

Jemima raced across the carpet on her hands and knees as she played hide-and-seek with her young son. There were very few places the toddler could hide, and she already knew that he was behind the sofa. In recent months they'd played this game hundreds, if not thousands, of times before. It was his favoured hiding place. He was at an age where he thought that if he couldn't see you, then you couldn't see him. It was an endearing innocence she delighted in, and wanted to maintain for as long as possible. She could see his feet sticking out and could hear his uncontrollable giggles. 'I'm coming to get you!' she called. The well-used phrase elicited even more laughter and the youngster kicked his feet rapidly as his excitement reached fever pitch.

Finlay Luke Huxley, or Fin as everyone called him, was a delightful child. He had the sweetest of temperaments, boundless energy and displayed an inquisitive fascination with all things new. Seeing the world through his eyes had brought peace and contentment to Jemima's world. There wasn't a day that went by when she didn't thank her lucky stars that she was his mother.

'Is Fin hiding under this cushion?' she said, as she tossed it off a nearby chair. 'No, he's not. Oh dear, I don't know where he could be.'

Fin giggled in delight.

'I know . . . Perhaps he's behind the curtain?' She headed towards the window and gently pulled the fabric away from the frame. 'Oh no, he's not there.'

There was more laughter as Jemima crawled over to the sofa and poked her head behind it to come face to face with her son. 'There he is! What a clever hiding place, Fin. But now I've found you, it's tickle monster time!' She reached out and pulled the boy towards her. Moments later she was tickling his tummy, taking pleasure from Finlay's squeals of laughter as he wriggled and writhed in her arms.

That morning's game of hide-and-seek was tinged with sadness, at least for Jemima. It would soon be Fin's first birthday, and a year since she had started her maternity leave. The clock was ticking, and she was due to return to work in three days' time. The happiness Jemima had experienced in the last year was something she could not have anticipated. She was reluctant to have to step back into work mode — being a detective inspector was frequently stressful and often dangerous. But being a single parent to two boys meant that she had no option. They needed the money and Jemima doubted she could find an alternative job that paid a similar amount.

Jemima's domestic set-up was an unusual one. As well as Fin, she was mother to her adoptive son, James. She'd been a stepparent to the boy for a number of years, having married his father, Nick Huxley. But shortly after James's birth mother was killed in a traffic collision, Nick had discovered something that turned his world upside down, and he'd walked out on James and Jemima, leaving her to pick up the pieces.

With Nick gone, life had been hard for the two of them. It hadn't helped matters that he had fallen apart so spectacularly in front of James's eyes. When the boy had needed him most, Nick had wallowed in his own self-pity and ignored the needs of his grieving child. With Nick no longer contributing to the family finances, Jemima had found it hard to manage on her wages alone. There were mortgage payments and extra childcare costs as she'd struggled to balance her home life with a career that, at best, often meant that she worked long and unpredictable hours.

Jemima had done her best to save money wherever she could. James was a growing lad and there weren't many weeks when she didn't need to buy him new clothes. Indeed, it was a conscious effort to save money that had ultimately led to events surrounding Fin's conception. It was something she hadn't foreseen and had changed her life in ways she couldn't have imagined. If the conception hadn't been traumatic enough, the birth had been equally stressful too.

For the last eighteen months, Jemima had been living with her sister, Lucy, in a large house on the outskirts of a small village in the Vale of Glamorgan. It was an arrangement that Jemima had entered into reluctantly, but one that had worked out well.

Lucy ran a successful business from home, where she sourced products for inclusion in bespoke corporate hampers, which were distributed to clients all over the world. The business had grown rapidly and was extremely lucrative. In fact, Lucy readily admitted that she had more money than she could ever spend. Her husband often worked away, returning home for a handful of fleeting visits. Their marriage was unconventional, but one that Lucy seemed happy with.

As Lucy, herself a mother of young children, led a busy life, she employed Eloise, a live-in nanny. It was one of the reasons she suggested that Jemima move in with them, as Eloise would help take care of James and also look after Fin when Jemima returned to work. Eloise was great with James, and the boy clearly enjoyed being part of a large family group.

The knowledge that her adoptive son was happy and thriving in this new environment had been a weight off Jemima's mind. She was still reluctant to return to work, though, as she would miss the daily interaction with Fin. She would be his mother regardless of whether she was at home or at work, but it was inevitable that she would miss out on some of his important milestones.

As the doorbell sounded, Jemima felt a flutter of excitement. She glanced at her watch and smiled, knowing exactly who had arrived. 'Who's that, Fin? I think it could be Mason. Shall we go and take a look?' She stood up and held out her hand for the toddler.

'Hi there,' Mason said, before moving in to kiss her.

Fin let go of his mother's hand and held his arms up to the vicar. The boy's eagerness was clearly apparent.

'Well, I've got a great big bear hug for this little cub!' Mason bent down and swept the toddler up into his arms. Fin shrieked with delight as Mason held him close and bounded up and down while growling like a bear.

Jemima laughed watching the two of them clearly enjoying a game they had long since made their own. She loved her life at the moment. Before Fin's birth it had been inconceivable to think that she could ever feel so happy. Those feelings were things other people experienced. Whereas Jemima's joyous moments tended to be short-lived and invariably came with a high price.

It was these past experiences that made Jemima reluctant to give in to her emotions. It wasn't that she wanted to be stand-offish. She was just unable to shake the feeling that something would inevitably go wrong and she would lose everything that was now good about her life. Deep down, she couldn't bring herself to believe that she deserved to be happy. It was something she'd had drummed into her from a very young age. When thinking about things objectively, she knew that the idea made no sense whatsoever. But logic did little to overcome the result of years of insidious emotional abuse inflicted upon her by her own mother.

Jemima had shared these fears during her counselling sessions. She'd initially been sceptical about the value of talking things over in such a setting, but had been forced to do so a couple of years earlier. It had come about when Nick had discovered her unconscious on the bathroom floor, having lost a lot of blood when self-harming. At the time she had been at a low point of her life, regularly cutting herself in an attempt to feel in control.

Nick had betrayed Jemima's trust by informing her boss, Detective Chief Inspector Ray Kennedy, who in turn had insisted that she attend counselling sessions before allowing her to return to work. Knowing that others were now aware of her self-harming had been a difficult and humiliating realisation. It was something she could never fully forgive Nick for. Though she had ultimately come to accept that his actions had saved her from the self-destructive path she had been following.

Jemima knew that there would be no quick fix for her mental health issues. Her intrusive thoughts and bouts of low self-esteem would resurface at times of extreme stress. But talking about her troubles helped her to manage her feelings and keep the negative thoughts under control.

It was immediately apparent to those who saw them together that there was a special bond between Jemima and Mason. Their mutual affection was undisguised and they obviously cared deeply for each other. There had been much speculation about their relationship, though no one had dared ask either of them to confirm the suspicions that they were romantically involved. If it had been anyone other than Mason, someone would have undoubtedly asked, but to the other villagers, Mason Roy was their vicar, the man they turned to in their hour of need, and who in return strived to help people regardless of whether or not they were members of his congregation. As such, the villagers kept any such speculation to themselves. Or at least to within small friendship groups.

Apart from official occasions, Mason dressed casually, with a clerical collar the only evidence of his profession. In a village where a Welsh accent was prevalent, his Canadian one was another striking feature. Little was known about his life before he had become the incumbent at the village church. Even Jemima had ascertained only sketchy details of his background and was not inclined to press him for more information. The reluctance they both displayed to pry into each other's lives was a major factor in what had cemented their fledgling relationship.

# CHAPTER 2

On the eve of her return to work, Jemima poured herself a large stiff drink to combat her rising anxiety. It was a strange feeling, having spent so many years in the job. Before Fin's arrival it had been the inevitable maternity leave that she'd dreaded. But with the events of those final hours of the case, combined with the trauma of the birth, she had ended up welcoming the break.

At first, her head was all over the place. Unsurprising perhaps, given what her body had just gone through. Perhaps more astonishing was her initial reluctance to see any of her colleagues. Even Dan Broadbent, who, despite being her sergeant, was a close friend and someone she thought of as a brother. But those feelings had faded and within a week or so, with so many other things to occupy her mind, she had settled into her new role of stay-at-home mother. She had enjoyed the fact that she was free to do normal things, to spend time with her family and cherish every moment she had with both James and Finlay. It was without a doubt, the happiest she had ever been.

Whenever Dan had spoken about life at the station, it had seemed as though she had little connection with what he told her. She'd smile and comment on a few things because it was the polite thing to do. But she'd had no real interest in what was going on there. It was as though she had put her work life in a box and firmly closed the lid, refusing to even think about it unless she had to.

Now, with the return to work imminent, she lay in bed longing for sleep. Yet no matter how hard she tried to relax, it was impossible to settle. She could sense the clock counting down. Feel the darkness pressing in around her, making it hard to breathe. The hard-won contentment that had fortified her throughout the last few months leached from every cell of her body, as fast as blood from an open vein.

The thought of spending less time with her children was heartbreaking. Finlay was at an age where he was changing by the day. Each new discovery and achievement brought a level of joy she had not appreciated could exist. It was delightful to watch his face light up whenever he was around her and other family members. Hanging out with the children was like immersing yourself in innocence and wonder, where simple pleasures became cherished experiences.

She had always known this moment would arrive but had somehow managed to put it to the back of her mind. But in the morning, there would be no avoiding it, and that knowledge saddened her. These relationships, which meant so much to her, would never be the same again. She would always love her children and hoped they felt the same way about her. But as the job inevitably took up so much of her time, she wouldn't be there for important occasions. It was as though something was about to die.

Jemima knew from personal experience that policing was a dangerous and exhausting career. The job chewed you up and spat you out. Over the years, it had affected her physically and emotionally. Some of her colleagues had already paid the ultimate price, sacrificing their lives in the line of duty. Every officer went on shift knowing that this was a possibility. It was a reality that as a police officer, the threat of physical harm lurked around every corner and behind every closed door.

Having thought long and hard about the sort of career she wanted to follow, Jemima had joined the force straight from university. Her decision had been guided by a desire to make the world a better place. But that idealised enthusiasm seemed like it belonged to a lifetime ago. She was fortunate that her own squad were trustworthy, which was down to DCI Ray Kennedy being highly selective when bringing a new officer onto the team.

What she hadn't initially appreciated was that the force had its own criminals and thugs. Thankfully they were in the minority, but they were there. Operating in the shadows. Hiding in plain sight, while they did everything in their power to normalise their beliefs and actions and form networks of like-minded people. It was only a few weeks ago that Broadbent had informed her of two officers who had been suspended on suspicion of taking bribes. And shortly after going on maternity leave, she'd seen a news report about another officer who had been accused of sexually assaulting a female while transporting her to the station.

And then there were the office politics, which was something she'd never managed to get used to. Prejudice and bigotry were rife in every police force throughout the country. Yet it was brushed under the carpet, as it was too uncomfortable and embarrassing to address. And as an individual, if you dared complain or try to do something about it, you might as well kiss your career goodbye.

As a female Jemima had fought hard to gain respect and claw her way up the ranks. She'd had to prove herself every step of the way. Put in more hours. Work harder. Be smarter. Give more to the job than many male officers would ever be prepared to give. But over the years she'd seen many of those less capable men rise swiftly up the ranks into roles where they would perpetuate the inequalities. And it wasn't just women who were treated less favourably. If you weren't white, male, or straight, the odds were stacked against you.

Throughout her maternity leave, Dan Broadbent had been a frequent visitor and had kept her apprised of what was going on at work. Not the nitty-gritty of individual cases, but the general mood, station gossip and changes that would affect the squad. Over the years, their bond had become far more than that of colleagues. After a rocky start to their partnership, they'd looked out for each other. And there had been occasions when they'd each put themselves in harm's way to protect the other. They were so in tune that they practically knew what each other was thinking. Their families socialised outside of work. Jemima was godmother to Dan and Caroline Broadbent's son. Despite having no blood ties they were, to all intents and purposes, family.

They had often discussed the tragic events at West Winds, both feeling the need to unburden their guilt, which neither of them was under any illusion they would have to live with until the end of their days. An inquiry had absolved them of any wrongdoing. There was only one person to blame for the loss of life, and that person was currently serving a long prison sentence, having stood trial and been found guilty of murder, among other things.

Still, knowing that one of your own had lost their life in such a cruel way was a heavy burden to bear. It was a catastrophe none of them would ever forget. No matter how long they lived.

Dan had told her that the squad had increased in size over the last few months. Gareth Peters, who was already part of their team, had been promoted to the rank of sergeant. Though it was a bittersweet recognition of his dedication and hard work, as he had slotted into the post made vacant by Finlay Ashton.

There were three new officers, who Jemima was yet to become acquainted with. DC Nancy Chen had joined the squad six months ago having completed a successful undercover operation with another police force. Given the dangerous nature of what she had done it had never been an option for her to remain in that force.

DCI Kennedy had already been aware of DC Aadi Patel as he was a serving detective in another Cardiff police station.

He had a good reputation as a hard worker and a team player, but a restructuring of the force meant that his squad was being disbanded. Kennedy had wasted no time in snapping him up before he was approached by someone else.

The most recent recruit was PC Victoria McCarthy. Having been a uniformed officer for three years, she had been assigned to the squad five weeks earlier, after expressing a desire to progress her career. And so far, it appeared that she was shaping up nicely. As far as Kennedy was concerned, if Jemima was happy with McCarthy, Victoria would be offered the post on a permanent basis and would become a detective constable.

Jemima tossed and turned, getting increasingly frustrated as she struggled to sleep. Despite being mother to a young child, it was not something she had experienced for quite a while. Fin had long been sleeping through the night, and tonight he continued with this trend, oblivious to the imminent change that the following morning would bring.

With the arrival of daylight, Jemima knew that she had reached the end of this phase of her life. Finlay's cot was at the side of her bed, and the youngster was already sitting up and playing with his toys. Her heart lurched, and she swallowed hard, determined not to cry. She didn't want to upset the children, so she plastered a smile on her face and spoke to Finlay in a sing-song voice, jumped out of bed and scooped him up into her arms. Her lips feathered his skin as she covered his face with kisses. He returned the affection in an unsophisticated manner and laughed as he slobbered across her cheeks.

So far so good — she'd made it seem as though everything was normal. Having changed Finlay, she carried the toddler on her hip as she popped her head into James's room. The lad was still asleep, curled on his side, with only his head visible above the duvet in which he was cocooned.

'Ja-Ja! Ja-Ja!' squealed Fin. His eyes lit up with excitement at seeing his sibling, and he writhed relentlessly, making it impossible for Jemima to keep a firm hold of him. It was his only way of communicating the fact that he wanted her to put him on his brother's bed.

To all intents and purposes, things were normal, in this crazy set-up of her sister's house. Breakfast time was as chaotic as ever. Cereal was munched, milk slopped, beverages drunk, and toast crunched. By the time everyone had finished, the table looked as though a bomb had hit it.

Lucy glanced at the kitchen clock. 'Shouldn't you get going?'

Jemima was well aware of the time. She had practically been counting down the seconds until the inevitable moment arrived. The trouble was, she didn't want to leave all of this behind. She could picture each of their days, piqued that those images would not involve her. While she was on duty, facing scenes that would make most people want to turn tail and run for the hills, their days would most likely be filled with fun and laughter. It was reassuring to know that they would be safe and happy, but she wanted that for herself too.

If there was any way around it, she would walk away from the force without a backwards glance. But she knew that she would not find another job that paid as much as her police inspector's salary. Over the last year her savings had taken a significant hit, and that was with Lucy subsidising them to a large extent. She couldn't thank her sister enough for everything she had done for them.

Realistically they both knew that she would never be able to pay Lucy back. With only her wage to rely on, it would take every penny to keep herself and the two boys afloat. The house she had shared with Nick was being rented out. It had been the only viable option as the mortgage still needed to be paid. But as she hadn't seen or heard from Nick since he had failed to turn up to his court hearing, she had felt obliged to keep half of the rental profits in a savings account, as she didn't want him accusing her of stealing what was his. Having seen a ruthless side to his character, there was no way she was prepared to be backed into a corner by him and forced to make any decisions that would ultimately have a detrimental effect on her and the boys.

The only realistic option available to Jemima was to continue as a police officer. Whether she wanted to or not, they needed the money.

# CHAPTER 3

As Jemima locked the car and walked the short distance to the entrance of the police station, she steeled herself for what was to come. She was surprised to feel butterflies in her stomach. It was as though she was the new girl, and this was her first day on the job — instead of someone returning to familiar surroundings where she had spent far more time than she would have liked.

But as she stepped over the threshold that feeling changed. It was the smell that settled her nerves. A fragrance so subtle, yet familiar. Anodyne. Neither pleasant, nor offensive. It was reassuring, like discovering a favourite old cardigan that had been shoved to the back of a drawer. It confirmed she belonged there.

Squaring her shoulders, she stood a bit taller. With each step she took, Jemima's confidence continued to grow. There were smiles and greetings from people she knew, which quickly made her feel as though this was just like any other workday.

Jemima hesitated. Should she head for the DCI's room, or go straight to the squad room? She had spoken to Ray Kennedy a few days ago, but as she had not seen him recently, she thought it prudent to get their reunion over and done with. He was usually busy, so it would most likely be a quick in-and-out. But as he was her boss, it was the polite thing to do. And unless he informed her of something urgent that needed her attention, it would leave her free to spend more time settling in and getting to know the newer members of the squad.

The entrance to his room was in darkness. If true to form, the DCI would have been at his desk for at least the last hour. Which must mean he was either attending a meeting or was in the squad room. So, she turned and headed back the way she had come.

She fully appreciated that everyone had had plenty of time to adjust to the absence of DS Finlay Ashton. Kennedy, Broadbent and Peters would have worked numerous cases while she was on maternity leave. But for Jemima, this was the first time she had set foot inside the station since Ashton's death. Wherever she looked, she could still feel his presence and half-expected to bump into him at any moment.

Jemima appreciated that things had changed. The sudden death of any member of a group inevitably altered its dynamic. An entire year had already passed. More than enough time for everyone to settle into a new routine. Yet Jemima's absence throughout the collective mourning process meant that they had all moved on without her. They had been there to support one another as they worked through their grief. Having missed out on that harrowing time, she would be out of kilter with the rest of the team. There was a lot of catching up to do. She needed to get the lay of the land as there were a lot of changes to come to terms with.

Through the door's glass panel, she could see that the others were already at their desks. She took a deep breath, opened the door, and stepped into the room.

Broadbent looked up. 'Hey, it's good to see you.' The welcome was warm, and Jemima returned his smile. Before she had a chance to say anything, Gareth was on his feet, his arm outstretched to shake her hand.

'Great to have you back, guv. You've been missed.'

'It's good to see you, Gareth.' Jemima meant it. She'd only been in the squad room for a matter of minutes, yet it was as though she had not been away. She knew Finlay Ashton would not be there, but found herself unable to stop glancing across to the desk that had been his.

'It'll take a while, guv,' said Gareth, as though reading her mind. 'Even now, I'm sometimes caught off guard and half-expect Fin to be here.'

'Come and say hello to everyone,' said Dan.

Jemima turned in his direction and saw that the three newest members of the squad had gathered at her desk. Each of them looked eager to make her acquaintance. There was no denying that things had changed in her absence. It was slightly unsettling. She plastered a smile on her face and closed the gap between them. 'Wow! So many new faces.' As she uttered the words, she wondered if she sounded resentful or concerned.

'I'll do the introductions.' Dan was acting like the host at a party. 'This is DC Nancy Chen.'

'Good to meet you, Nancy. How long have you been part of the team?' Dan had already filled her in on the new recruits, but asking the question was a way of breaking the ice.

'Must be about six months, but to be honest it feels like for ever. Dan and Gareth made me feel so welcome.'

'I know what you mean.'

'This is DC Aadi Patel,' said Dan.

'You seem familiar,' said Jemima. She cocked her head slightly as she tried to recall where she had seen him before.

'I used to work at Cardiff Bay. I was assigned to this station for a couple of months, following the riot,' he replied.

'Ah, yes, I remember.' The memory was etched upon the minds of any serving police officer working in Cardiff a few years earlier. It had taken everyone by surprise when a teenage girl had whipped up a rampaging mob by calling for support on social media, claiming that the police were trying to fit her up. The result had been swift. Shockingly violent and senseless. Some city centre business premises had been destroyed. Their station firebombed. The eyes of the world had been trained on Cardiff as the army was called in to bring peace to the streets and re-establish order. Rioting that had lasted less than a day had caused millions of pounds' worth of damage to the city centre.

'And this is our newest addition, DC Victoria McCarthy.'

'I'm on secondment to this squad. Been here five weeks.'

'I've seen you around the station,' said Jemima. 'You were a PC?'

'That's right. But I so want to be a detective,' she gushed.

'So, what case are we working?' Jemima dropped her bag on the desk and took off her coat.

'Lucky for you, we're just finishing the paperwork on a case we closed at the end of last week. There's nothing that needs your immediate attention, so you've time to settle back into the swing of things,' said Dan.

'That's where you're wrong, lad,' said the DCI, who was heading in their direction. Even though she hadn't seen him for a while, Jemima knew something serious had happened. Ray Kennedy was walking so fast that he was almost jogging. His face was red, and there were beads of sweat on his brow. Kennedy didn't do anything quickly. Slow, steady, method-ical, calm — these were the adjectives that best described the DCI. Yet as he closed the gap between them, he was display-ing none of these attributes.

Something was up, and Jemima was in no doubt that she would soon be informed of her next case. Feeling an unexpected lump in her throat, she swallowed hard. In the past, she had taken things in her stride, but that was before she had appreciated that she had so much to lose. Well and truly settling into family life had given her a new perspective on things. And she, more than the average person, knew how quickly life could be upended.

# CHAPTER 4

Having arrived at the station less than quarter of an hour ago, it suddenly felt as though she had never been away. It was business as usual. Which meant only one thing. Something bad had happened.

'Good to have you back, Huxley. You've been missed. However, no time for easing yourself back in gently. You're going to have to hit the ground running on this one. Right! Gather round, I need everyone's full attention.' As he spoke, Kennedy levelled his gaze on each of them in turn. There was no hint of softness in either his expression or his voice. Whatever he was about to say was deadly serious.

'There have been some worrying events this morning, and I expect everyone's A game on this one. I've just come from a meeting with the top brass. At seven o'clock this morning, Judge Rory Lawson kissed his wife goodbye and got in his Jaguar to make his usual journey to the crown court, yards away from this building. This is a commute he's undertaken day in, day out for decades. Today was different. He didn't make it in. His car was found abandoned a few miles from home with his mobile phone still inside.'

'I take it there's no sign of him?' asked Jemima.

'None whatsoever. Tyre tracks at the scene suggest the vehicle skidded to a halt. Whether that was to avoid something, caused by a mechanical fault with the vehicle, or he was forced off the road has yet to be established. We've a couple of PCs at the scene and a forensics team are on their way there. As far as I'm aware, there wasn't any obvious damage to the vehicle. The only thing we know for certain is that Judge Lawson is nowhere to be found.'

'Does he have any known health issues?' asked Jemima.

'I've no idea. But I've just been advised by the chief constable that this team is tasked with finding him.'

'I thought you investigated murders, not missing people?' said Victoria.

'We're not talking about some random missing person here,' snapped Kennedy. 'This is a high court judge who's seemingly disappeared off the face of the earth. He's currently presiding over a murder trial. This is as serious as it gets.'

'Sorry, I didn't mean . . .' Victoria lowered her head, her cheeks burning with embarrassment. Everyone knew that the young officer was wishing that the ground would open up and swallow her.

'Yes, yes, I know, lass. I'm sorry, I appreciate you're here to learn,' said Kennedy. 'It's just that there'll be a lot of pressure on us with this one.'

'Any chance it's linked—'

Broadbent hadn't finished asking the question before Kennedy shot him an irritated look. 'Yes! Thank you, Daniel. I was just about to get to that. Now if you don't mind . . .'

'Sorry, sir,' muttered Broadbent. He stuck his hands in his trouser pockets and shuffled his feet, looking like an overgrown schoolboy who had just received a telling-off from the headmaster.

'Huxley, as Daniel was about to say, earlier this morning there was a very disturbing incident on North Road.'

'I remember hearing the news report, sir. A young man tumbled out of a car boot straight into the path of an oncoming vehicle.'

'That's right. He'd been tied up, gagged and blindfolded. Bottom line is that it's not our case. I've no idea whether it was a college prank gone wrong or something more sinister. But as Judge Lawson seems to have vanished without trace only ten miles or so from where that occurred, it's possible the two cases could be linked. I'll follow up on that inquiry. Find out if they've made any progress and establish who's been doing what. I'll let you know if I believe it to be linked to Lawson's disappearance.'

'Right you are, sir,' said Jemima.

'As far as I'm concerned, you're more than capable of dealing with this, Huxley. Now, this is the location Judge Lawson's car was found.' Kennedy spread out a map and pointed at a location. 'And these are all the personal details we have on him.' He handed Jemima some handwritten notes. 'I appreciate you haven't had time to draw breath, but I don't need to tell you that speed is of the essence. So, get to it and be sure to keep me informed. You know how this'll go. I'm going to have the powers that be breathing down my neck, as if I haven't got enough to worry about. It's not good for my blood pressure. Not good at all.' And with that, Kennedy turned and walked out of the room.

'Well, welcome back me,' muttered Jemima. She sighed as she quickly gathered her thoughts. It would have been nice to have had a couple of hours to settle in, catch up with Dan and Gareth, and acquaint herself with the newer members of the team. Instead, she had to kick off a serious investigation this very minute.

'Right, let's get organised. Dan and I will visit the scene to see if we can get a better sense of what might have happened. We'll also go to the judge's home, speak to his wife, and get a more detailed sense of what her husband's really like.

'Gareth, I want you and Victoria to head across to the court. Speak to anyone who knows the judge. Facts. Gossip. Anything and everything. And find out if he's ever received any threats. Someone like him must have numerous enemies.

Get a list of past cases and details of the one he's currently presiding over. I don't need to spell it out to you. You know the sort of information we need.'

'Will do, guv,' said Gareth. His chest puffed out, and he stood a bit taller as he took on board the implied confidence that Jemima had in him. He was determined to demonstrate to her that he was up to being a sergeant.

'Aadi, Nancy, I want you both to concentrate on obtaining and viewing any CCTV footage. Check out what's available in the vicinity of where the car was abandoned. This would have been Lawson's start point.' Jemima drew a cross on the map to highlight the location of the judge's home. 'And according to the DCI, this is where the vehicle was found abandoned.' She drew another cross. 'So, it's safe to presume that he took this route.' She used a highlighter to illustrate it. 'By my reckoning, he'd have driven through this village. It's safe to presume traffic would have been light. My best guess is that at that time in the morning it wouldn't have taken him more than five minutes to get from his house to that village.'

'It'll take a quick call to check on the location of traffic cameras,' confirmed Aadi. 'Though I wouldn't be surprised if there aren't any in the vicinity. They tend to be located in urban areas.'

'I think you're probably right. But as you've already pointed out, you'll know for certain by making one call,' said Jemima.

'We can go door-to-door along that route to see if any of the properties have security cameras covering the road. We might get lucky and pick up VRMs of any other vehicles travelling along there around that time,' said Nancy.

'Excellent. Let me know immediately if there are any developments. Otherwise, we'll meet back here at midday to pool the information. Let's get moving.' Jemima hadn't even had the opportunity to sit at her desk, let alone log on and catch up with her emails. But as she passed the desk that used to be Ashton's, she thought that perhaps it was best to be thrown in at the deep end. At least it meant that she wouldn't have time to sit and reflect on the fact that her colleague was no longer a part of the team.

As they reached the car park, Jemima tossed Broadbent a set of keys and headed for the passenger door. 'You can drive.'

'That's a turn up for the books.' His eyebrows arched in surprise.

'Don't go thinking I was oblivious to the fact that you hate being a passenger whenever we're together. I know my driving scares you.'

'Well, you have to admit that sometimes you take unnecessary chances. After all, you're a bit of a speed freak,' said Dan.

'Oh, come on! In all the years we've been together, we've only had one accident. And that certainly wasn't my fault.' Jemima was referring to an incident when a drunk driver ignored a red light and sideswiped them at a major intersection. The timing couldn't have been worse. They had just arrested a suspect and were taking him back to the police station. The crash had allowed the prisoner to escape and had set off a series of devastating events that would impact people's lives for many more years.

'I think motherhood has calmed you down.' A wry smile played across his lips. Dan was baiting her to get a reaction. He knew that he was the only person who could get away with speaking to Jemima in such a way.

'I've missed this,' she said.

'What?'

'Us. Together. The banter.'

'I know what you mean. It wasn't the same without you.'

They sat in comfortable silence for a while as they headed out of the city. The traffic became lighter, until they could travel at a more consistent speed. 'What's up with Kennedy?' asked Jemima.

'What d'ya mean?'

'I dunno. He just didn't seem himself. I think he's aged since I've last seen him.'

'Haven't we all. It's hardly surprising given everything that happened.'

'I s'pose. Though I think it's more than that. I got the impression something was bothering him.'

'Can't say I noticed. Then again, he's not someone I spend much time with.'

'Umm . . . yeah, I'm probably reading him wrong. After all, it's not as though we've spent much time with each other in the past year. Add to that that I'm also out of practice. My intuition's probably a bit off at the moment.'

'That'll be it,' said Dan.

Jemima jumped as her phone pinged with the arrival of a text. Until that moment she hadn't appreciated how uptight she was feeling. As she glanced at the screen and discovered that the message was from Eloise, her stomach lurched. Like every new parent on their first day back at work, she had done her best to forget about home for a while, but the feeling that something could be wrong with Finlay was suddenly too much to bear. Her hands shook as she opened the message.

Her fear soon proved to be unfounded. Rapidly scanning the words, a sense of relief washed over her, and she quickly sent a reply as she let out an audible sigh.

'Everything OK?' asked Dan.

'Yeah, it's just Eloise letting me know that she's taking Fin to soft play.'

'First day back's a bitch, but it'll get easier,' said Dan.

They approached the turning for the minor road along which the judge's car had been abandoned, where there was a lone uniformed police officer charged with directing traffic. He stood next to a sign stating that the road was closed due to a police incident. Broadbent stopped the car to identify themselves and after a brief exchange, the officer allowed them to pass.

At first, there was no sign that anything was amiss. Natural topography prevented the road from being straight and plentiful hedgerow restricted what little view they would otherwise have had. After negotiating a series of bends the road straightened, and they got their first view of the potential crime scene.

Up ahead, a forensic van was blocking the entrance to a field. A short distance away, a couple of forensic officers, whose white suits stood out against the bucolic background, were already processing the scene.

'Looks like Jeanne's hard at it,' said Jemima. The person she was referring to was a scene-of-crime officer who often attended the same cases as them. Over the years, Jeanne Ennersley and Jemima had cultivated a good working relationship.

When Broadbent brought the car to a halt, they opened the doors and put on their shoe coverings and a pair of protective gloves in case they touched anything at the scene.

Jeanne stopped what she was doing and straightened up. 'Hey, Jemima. It's good to see you. Your sidekick's been like a lost puppy without you.'

'Thanks for that, Jeanne.' Broadbent reddened at the woman's unexpected words.

'Just telling it like it is.' She laughed.

'It's good to see you too, Jeanne. So, what've we got?' Jemima was keen to get on with the job, find out if this really was an abduction or if the judge had merely gone walkabout for some unknown reason.

'On first sight, it could've been a case of braking hard to avoid something in the road. You can see the tyre marks on the asphalt. He slammed on those brakes and skidded to a halt. But on closer inspection you can see signs of a struggle. The vehicle's virtually pristine. Nice cream leather upholstery, which for our purposes are a godsend. Now take a look at the passenger seat,' instructed Jeanne.

'Specks of blood?' asked Jemima, though she already knew the answer. There was no mistaking the dried spatter of rust-coloured spots.

'That's right, and they weren't caused by an accident. His head didn't impact with any fixtures inside this vehicle.

The rest's as clean as a whistle. I'd put money on it that the driver was punched in the face.

'In my opinion, the most likely sequence of events was that someone ambushed him, forced him to stop. Before he had time to react, they'd opened the driver's door and punched him in the side of the face. The impact would've shoved his head sideways, hence the blood spatter onto the front passenger seat and a small amount on the side window.'

'There's no apparent damage to the vehicle and the airbag hasn't deployed, so we can rule out any form of collision,' added Jemima.

'Precisely. I see that your time at home hasn't dulled your deductive powers. Anyway, I've found more evidence to back up my theory. Take a look here.' She pointed at the driver's doorsill.

'Scuff marks, and a fair few of them too,' said Broadbent.

'Suggesting a struggle,' continued Jeanne. 'Take a closer look.'

'There's quite a few on the inside and one on the outside . . . Someone dragged him out of the car. His feet were flailing about as he tried to stay inside the vehicle and his attacker had one foot on the ground and the other on the outside of the sill to steady themselves as they hauled him out,' said Jemima.

'Oh, you are good, Inspector, but you've still missed something.' Jeanne's voice was smug as she watched Jemima's reaction.

Always one for a challenge, Jemima found herself caught up in the moment. Finding evidence, discovering its importance in making sense of a crime scene, and tracking down criminals were all things she loved. It was exhilarating to be back in the fray, exercising that part of her mind once more. It was what she excelled at, and it gave her a real sense of achievement — at least when things worked out the way she hoped they would.

'Don't tell me . . .' Jemima bent down to take a closer look, squinting at the area immediately in front of her face.

31

There was nothing obvious low down, but as she straightened her legs, she spotted what Jeanne had alluded to. 'Fibres snagged on the side of the frame.'

'Yep. Give the girl a biscuit.' Jeanne laughed at her own quip. 'There's a rough patch of metal there. It's possible that if those fibres aren't from the judge's clothes, they could have come from the clothing of whoever dragged him out of the vehicle. I was just about to bag them up when you arrived. Oh, and I should have mentioned that we found a single shoe on the road. I'd guess it worked its way loose during the scuffle. Most likely the judge's, otherwise the owner would have retrieved it.

'But I think this may interest you. I believe there was more than one vehicle involved in this abduction,' continued Jeanne. 'See those marks on the road surface about five yards away? Suggests to me that someone was following the judge's car.'

'They blocked him in,' said Dan.

'I'd say so.'

'So we're dealing with a premeditated abduction. They knew his routine, which means they'd been following him for a while,' said Jemima.

# CHAPTER 5

Due to the narrowness of the lane, Broadbent had no choice but to turn the car around and head back the way they had come. It would take the scene-of-crime officers hours to thoroughly examine the area. And during that time the road would remain sealed off from traffic and pedestrians.

'As there's no choice but to follow the diversion, it'll add the best part of half an hour on to our journey time. Still, it'll give me time to contact Aadi and Nancy. Any CCTV footage we can get our hands on could help us crack this case. If Jeanne's reading of the scene is correct, there should have been a vehicle tailing him, and if we can get a registration mark . . .'

Nancy picked up on the third ring and confirmed that they had just arrived at the village and were about to start canvassing the area. Jemima quickly relayed the findings at the crime scene and emphasised the importance of identifying the vehicle that had tailed the judge's car.

Jemima and Broadbent eventually reached the Lawson home to find a family liaison officer already there. The property was large and imposing, set back behind substantial electrically operated gates, which would make it very difficult for anyone to gain access if they were uninvited. An intercom with a video screen was clearly visible, but there was no need to use it as the gates were open and a uniformed police officer stood guard.

'Stunning-looking place.' Broadbent nodded in approval.

'I s'pose so.'

'I guess it takes a lot to impress you these days.' Dan was referring to the fact that Lucy owned an exceptionally large property on the edge of a picture-perfect village. It was a far cry from the poky modern house Jemima had previously shared with her husband. Though the village that Jemima had once thought of as being a perfect place to live had turned out to be a hotbed of crime, violence, and secrets. It had been hidden well until a young woman's body had been discovered inside the church only a few hundred yards away from Lucy's house.

'This place is like a fortress.' Broadbent pointed at the security cameras fixed high up on the property. 'They'd be safe enough inside. I bet the entire gaff is wired up to the local nick.'

'We both know there's ways to circumvent security measures. But I agree — since whoever's behind this was determined to snatch him, they went for the less risky option. That stretch of road minimised the chance of being spotted. Especially at that time of the morning. This house would've been more problematic, and they'd have had to deal with whoever else happened to be inside. There would have been too many unknown factors, making the outcome less certain.'

Jemima pressed the doorbell and they were let inside by the family liaison officer, who identified herself as PC Anita Formby.

'How's Mrs Lawson bearing up?' Jemima kept her voice low as she didn't want any family members to overhear their conversation.

'Surprisingly well, given the circumstances. Though it's barely ten o'clock and she's hitting the Campari at an alarming rate.'

'She's had a shock. I suppose it affects everyone differently. I just hope she's not too far gone to answer our questions.' Until she'd had time to make up her mind, Jemima was prepared give the woman the benefit of the doubt.

'I think she's a regular drinker, ma'am. Given the number of empties in the kitchen, it's a wonder she can function at all.'

'Great.' Jemima sighed. The last thing they needed was to have to try and get information out of someone who had plied themselves with alcohol. As this was a fact-finding mission, they needed Mrs Lawson fully compos mentis. It was a given that under the circumstances the woman would most likely be emotional, which in itself had the propensity to cause problems when endeavouring to establish facts. But with a copious amount of alcohol added to the mix, the chances of them finding out anything useful was negligible.

'Any other family members present?'

'No. They've three adult children. None living at home.'

'Any other close relatives living nearby?' pressed Jemima. She was keen to establish whether there was someone else who knew Lawson well enough and had seen him in the last few days. Someone who could answer their questions without being hindered by the effects of their Campari habit.

'Apparently not. Come in, I'll take you through to the kitchen.' PC Formby led the way to the rear of the property.

Jemima had a sinking feeling about how their encounter with Mrs Lawson would go. She noticed that the interior was light, airy and welcoming. Everything appeared scrupulously clean. It made a pleasant change from some of the properties it was necessary for them to enter. In the kitchen, her eyes were drawn to an array of empty spirit bottles, clearly meant for recycling. She hoped for the woman's sake that the couple did a lot of socialising at home. If she had consumed even half of this amount, then she was drinking far more than was good for her.

Emilia Lawson stood, phone in hand, speaking slowly and deliberately. Even so, there was a detectable slur to her speech. She had been married to her husband for thirty-nine years. They had met at the law firm where she had worked as a clerk. Back then she was young, pretty, and self-aware enough to appreciate that the only way she ever stood a chance of living the sort of life she dreamed of was by marrying a man with good prospects.

The moment she laid eyes on Rory, she had set out to make him her own. Flirting. Flattering. Making herself useful. At first, he had appeared immune to her charms. But Emilia had had no intention of giving up, and after five excruciating months of ingratiating herself, Rory finally succumbed. Emilia finally had what she wanted and had kept piling on the pressure until she wore him down and got the all-important ring on her finger.

At sixty years of age, she had gained about fifty pounds on her pre-wedding weight. It now seemed so long ago that she could barely remember the days when she had cared about being stick-thin. Her weight had crept up with each of her pregnancies and had leaped even further with the onset of the menopause. She couldn't recall the last time they had been intimate. There was no one to impress. No one to make her feel desirable.

When the children came along, Emilia had resigned from work. It had been an easy decision, as she had never been career-minded and had only ever done the bare minimum to get by. But since her offspring had grown up and moved away, she had felt trapped. The world had moved on and she didn't have the right skill set for any employment suitable for someone of her social standing.

With so much time on her hands, she had grown to hate their home, despite it being the house she had begged Rory to buy. There was no denying the fact that it was a desirable property fitted out to the highest specifications. Yet as far as she was concerned, it had become nothing more than an upmarket prison cell.

With Rory rarely home, she spent much of the time alone. It was the reason she so frequently sought solace from her favourite tipple. She was very particular about how it was made. Heavy on the Campari, light on the soda. And always with three ice cubes. Their weekly Waitrose delivery always included two bottles. Another favourite indulgence was a daily box of Lindt chocolate, which she munched her way through every afternoon.

Over the years, Emilia had lost the handful of friends she had socialised with. It didn't help that she had no real interests. Or that those who knew her had become wary of her growing reliance upon alcohol. What had once been thought of as the mildly amusing behaviour of someone who was tipsy had soon been recognised as something more serious. No self-respecting woman of her age wanted to be associated with a lush. Especially as when Emilia had a few drinks inside her, she was prone to revealing embarrassing secrets.

The lowest point of her life had occurred almost a year earlier, when she had crashed her car in the middle of the afternoon only yards away from a primary school. There had been no other vehicle involved, and thankfully no one was hurt. When the police arrived, she claimed that she had been dazzled by the sun. But Emilia wasn't fooling anyone as it had been easy to smell the alcohol on her breath. She was arrested at the scene and was found to have been more than twice the legal limit. Already having six points on her licence, she had been banned from driving.

The incident had caused a rift with Rory as she had slapped the arresting officer across the face, telling him he had no right to treat her in such a disgraceful manner as she was the wife of a judge. Rory had been forced to apologise to the officer and call on a favour from the Assistant Chief Constable, who was a personal friend. After a substantial amount of grovelling, Emilia had avoided being prosecuted for assaulting the police officer.

'Pick up the phone, Anthony. Something's happened to your father, and I need you to come home.' Emilia disconnected the call and turned unsteadily, tossing the phone on the kitchen work surface. She sighed loudly, making no attempt to hide her sense of despair. She was still staring out into the garden as she reached blindly for a glass and greedily drank the remainder of the vivid liquid.

Jemima and Broadbent exchanged a worried look. As his wife, Emilia was likely to be privy to all sorts of information that other people would not know. It was quite possible that she might be able to point them in the direction of the person responsible for her husband's abduction. Ideally, they needed her stone-cold sober. But the way the woman had downed that drink, Jemima knew that wouldn't be the case. She just hoped that Mrs Lawson's senses were still sharp enough to recall any potentially useful information.

Jemima was about to speak when Emilia caught a glimpse of them in the corner of her eye. As she quickly spun around, the movement proved too much for her and she stumbled towards them. Broadbent caught hold of the woman in time to break her fall.

'Who the hell are you?' Emilia's antagonism was undisguised, and her face unnaturally flushed — though whether from alcohol, embarrassment or annoyance was anyone's guess. The smell of alcohol oozed from her pores. It soured her breath as she spoke.

'I'm Sergeant Broadbent and this is Inspector Huxley. We're investigating your husband's disappearance and need to ask you some questions.' It was all Broadbent could do not to wrinkle his nose in disgust.

'Well, I've no idea where he is. In fact, I've no idea where anyone is. I've been trying to get hold of my children. But no one's answering their phones. People say that blood is thicker than water, but my family are nowhere to be found when I need them most. Pour me a drink, dear. Heavy on the Campari, light on the soda. It's purely medicinal. I've had such a terrible shock.'

Jemima's hands were at her side. She clenched her fists, digging her nails into her palm as she attempted to combat a rising wave of frustration. It was quickly becoming apparent that Emilia Lawson was inebriated. It was understandable that following the shock of learning that her husband had been abducted the woman might have drunk a moderate amount of alcohol to steady her nerves. But there was no doubting the fact that she had consumed far more than was good for her. It was selfish and irresponsible, given the circumstances, as it significantly reduced her chances of telling them anything useful.

As far as Jemima was concerned, PC Formby had messed up big time. As an FLO, she would have known that they would need to speak to Emilia. And as such, she should have ensured that the woman had only consumed a small amount of alcohol. There would be an inevitable dressing-down for the uniformed officer once they were out of earshot.

'Under the circumstances, we need to speak—'

Jemima didn't have a chance to complete her sentence before Emilia Lawson interrupted.

'Whatever you have to say will have to wait until I've had another drink. My house! My rules!' The woman's expression darkened and there was no mistaking her belligerence. 'Now pour me that drink!'

Jemima ignored the demand and instead turned to face PC Formby. When she spoke, her words were icy. 'Make Mrs Lawson a very strong coffee. Put plenty of sugar in it. I need her sober. And once you've done that, you can remove every bottle of alcohol from the premises.'

'Y-yes, ma'am,' she stuttered. The young officer dropped her gaze and immediately set about the task. Her hands trembled as she clattered about, searching through the cupboards. She knew that she should have stopped Mrs Lawson from drinking. But the woman was formidable and clearly upset. The role of FLO was a balancing act. Supporting the family, while being the eyes and ears for the investigation. Often the family were completely innocent. But there were occasions when they knew more than they were letting on. If an FLO could gain their trust, there was a chance that they would let their guard down and let slip some important information.

'Who the hell do you think you are? I don't want coffee. I want a Campari and soda!' demanded Emilia.

'Well, you'll be having coffee. I need you sober. Your husband's life could be—'

'I said—'

'Don't test my patience, Mrs Lawson.' Jemima's voice was hard and uncompromising as she quickly closed the gap with the woman. 'Now, I suggest you sit down, sober up and cooperate. Else I'll have no alternative but to arrest you for being drunk and disorderly and failing to cooperate with a police inquiry. You have a choice. You can either answer our questions, or you can sober up in a police cell.' As she spoke, she reached into her back pocket and extracted a set of handcuffs. It was all a bluff, but it had the desired effect.

Emilia's shoulders slumped and she began to cry. 'I-I'm th-the v-victim here.'

'No, you're not, Mrs Lawson. You've just had far too much to drink and you're feeling sorry for yourself. Your husband's the actual victim, and he needs your help. Pull yourself together and drink this cup of coffee. It'll help sober you up.'

'I haven't eaten anything today,' said Emilia.

'Make Mrs Lawson some toast, and keep the coffee coming,' said Jemima.

PC Formby was beginning to feel like nothing more than a glorified waitress. Nevertheless, she did as she was told. After all, it was partly down to her negligence that Emilia Lawson was in this state.

'I'm going to check in with the rest of my team. You've got ten minutes to get that down you and sort yourself out. Otherwise, you can sleep it off in a cell.' Jemima nodded at Broadbent and they headed towards the front of the property.

Emilia Lawson watched as they disappeared from sight. She wasn't used to being spoken to in such a manner. Usually, when she threw a hissy fit, people backed down. Especially when they realised that her husband was a judge. But this female inspector was different. She wasn't going to be messed about, and Emilia knew she had met her match.

# CHAPTER 6

As far as Jemima was concerned, it was hard to believe that only a few hours had elapsed since she had walked into the station worrying if she had made the right decision about returning to work. It already seemed like a distant memory. Being landed with a high-profile abduction moments after returning had allowed her no time at all to settle back in. Her hopes of reacquainting herself with some familiar faces and getting to know a little about the newest members of the team had been nothing but a pipe dream. This new start was a baptism of fire.

She was already questioning the wisdom of having returned to such a stressful and dangerous career. Certainly, the camaraderie was great. And there was the feeling of satisfaction when you solved a case and got justice for the victim's family. But tracking down murderers, getting inside the head of psychopaths and dealing with all sorts of other violent crimes was a soul-destroying experience. And there was no denying the fact that even with right on your side, you ended up paying for it emotionally, physically, and in some instances with your life.

Over the years there hadn't been many occasions when she had questioned her choice of career. But she'd settled in surprisingly quickly to spending her time with the children, finding it a rewarding experience. Enjoyable. Fun. And she could hardly say the same about her first morning back at work, where she was having to track down whichever dangerous person or persons had abducted a high court judge and, if that wasn't bad enough, to pussyfoot around the victim's wife, who was a belligerent, self-entitled drunk.

It made Jemima question why she was continuing to put herself through this. Surely there were better ways for someone with her educational background to earn a living? Having recently spent so much time with the children, the possibility of training as a primary school teacher seemed appealing.

Feeling jaded, she closed her eyes and tilted her head to face the sky, inhaling deeply to fill her lungs with clean country air. She picked up on the smell of freshly mown grass, and there was also a hint of the aroma of livestock coming from nearby fields. The Lawson house smelled fresh enough, but Jemima had found the alcohol fumes given off by Emilia cloying and overpowering.

'You'd have thought, what with Lawson's job and the amount of money he earns that they'd have it all. But she's far from happy. Her drinking's obviously not just a one-off. She's a right old lush,' said Broadbent.

'Yeah, I got the impression she hadn't just reached for the bottle because of what's happened to her husband. Those empty bottles and the speed with which she downed that Campari and wanted another said it all. It makes me wonder what's so awful in her life that she'd choose to see it through the bottom of a glass.'

'I guess money doesn't buy you happiness. Just as well for the likes of us, eh? So, you gonna touch base with the others?'

'No point. They've already got their work cut out. I'm sure they'd let us know if they come across anything useful. I just wanted to give Mrs Lawson a few minutes to sober up. If she can manage to keep the toast and coffee down, it should mitigate some of the effects of the alcohol. The main thing is that we get her talking. Gareth's more than capable of getting the lowdown on the official side of the man. After all, everything to do with the court cases he's presided over will be a matter of record,' said Jemima. 'We've got the difficult task of trying to find out what makes the private man tick. He might be a judge, but when it comes down to it there'll be aspects of his life he won't want to be made public. Everyone has something they're ashamed of. Let's face it, even though she hasn't told us anything yet, it's obvious that his wife's got issues. She's an alcoholic. Something's made her turn to the bottle. And who knows, it could be the very reason why her husband was abducted.'

'My money's on this being down to one of his cases,' said Broadbent.

'You could very well be right. Given his job, it's the most likely scenario. But we still need to look at his personal life. If it doesn't throw up anything useful, then we'll know where to concentrate our resources. But for now . . .'

They had barely been standing outside the house for ten minutes. Yet, when they went back inside there was a noticeable improvement in Mrs Lawson's demeanour. She had taken Jemima's threat seriously and appeared to have made the effort to sober up sufficiently to be able to answer their questions.

The woman was perched on a stool, which appeared uncomfortably small for someone of her size. On the countertop in front of her was an empty plate littered with an array of crumbs, and there was a smell of burnt toast in the air. She was raising a cup of steaming liquid to her lips when she spotted their arrival. 'I've done as you asked, Inspector. This is my fourth cup. If I have any more caffeine, I'll be bouncing off the walls. I'm sorry you had to see me like that. I don't react well under pressure. But even I acknowledge it's far too early in the day to reach for the bottle. No matter how tempting it might seem.'

Jemima noted that Emilia Lawson was speaking more coherently. Despite this, her speech was still slurred, though it was evident that she was making an effort to concentrate and engage in an appropriate manner.

Jemima dragged out a stool on the opposite side of the breakfast bar. As the legs screeched against the tiles, Emilia winced. Jemima sat down and looked across, noticing that the woman's eyes were bloodshot, but the glazed expression that had been there when they first arrived had all but disappeared.

'I'm sure you must appreciate that this is a fact-finding exercise, and you may be upset by what I'm about to say. As things stand, we suspect that your husband was made to stop his car a few miles from here. An examination of the vehicle suggests that he was forcibly removed from it. As yet, we've no idea who is responsible for abducting your husband, or, indeed, why he was taken. I have officers at the crown court gathering information about trials your husband presided over. However, we can't rule out anything at this stage, which is why we are here. We need to find out as much as we can about your husband's personal life,' said Jemima.

'This surely has to be down to his work. You don't get to be a judge for as long as Rory has without making some enemies along the way,' said Emilia.

'As I've said, I'm not prepared to rule anything out so early on in the investigation. I agree that your husband would have made enemies through his work. It's an occupational hazard we all face. But it's quite conceivable that his apparent abduction has nothing to do with him being a judge. In order for us to target our resources effectively, I need to learn everything I can about your husband. So, tell me about him. About your family. Your friends. And especially about anyone who might hold a grudge against him,' said Jemima.

Emilia sighed. 'There's not much to tell. Rory's . . . Rory's just Rory.'

'What exactly does that mean? That statement doesn't tell us anything.'

'My husband is a man who lives for his work. He enjoys what he does. It was one of the first things I noticed about

44

him. He's got a sharp intellect. It's not easy working your way up the ladder in his profession. It's a cutthroat, competitive business.'

'But he obviously has a home life, Mrs Lawson. He married you. You have a family together.' Jemima was doing her best not to show her irritation. The woman must be in shock, though she wasn't acting in the manner Jemima would have expected. 'The court doesn't sit on the weekends. Surely you would spend time together. Perhaps meet up with friends or family?'

'Let me tell you about my family, Inspector. My children don't give a damn. They had a privileged upbringing, private education, the lot. Anthony is a GP, Tristan an architect, and Tilly's a captain in the British Army. They wouldn't have become what they are today if they had been born into another family. But there's no acknowledgement of our role in their individual successes. They rarely visit.' Emilia huffed. 'Of course, I don't blame Tilly. The British Army comes first. Months away on tours of duty. Her time's not her own. But the boys . . . Well, you can't tell me that they're unable to find time to visit. Yet there's been no thought of FaceTime, WhatsApp, Zoom, or whatever else is out there. They barely pick up the phone. I've left messages this morning to tell them about their father, but neither of them has called back. It's disrespectful and extremely disappointing.'

Jemima made a mental note to contact each of the Lawsons' children. There were many reasons that adult children avoided contact with their parents. She knew through her own experience with her mother just how toxic some familial relationships could be. It was possible, though perhaps unlikely, that one or more of the Lawson children could reveal information about their father that might be pertinent to the case. Information that they, as police officers, might not become privy to from other sources.

'When we arrived, we overheard you leaving a message for one of your sons. Has he not returned your call?' Jemima knew it was possible that if he were busy, he might not have picked up his messages. Conversely it could also suggest that all was not well in the Lawson household.

'No, he hasn't, which isn't unusual. He's a GP so he's exceptionally busy.'

'I'll need contact details for each of your children,' said Jemima.

'Why? They'll have nothing to do with Rory's disappearance.'

'I agree it's unlikely, Mrs Lawson. But in cases such as this, we need to speak to all family members. And you also need to tell us which regiment your daughter serves with.'

Emilia muttered her discontent as her fingers fumbled with the keypad of her phone. She held it out so that Broadbent could make a note of the numbers.

'Does your husband ever speak to you about any aspects of his work?'

'Not at all. I've no interest, and it would be completely unprofessional for him to do so. No, he has a strict policy of leaving the law at the courthouse.'

'Have you noticed any recent changes in his behaviour?'

'Like what?'

'For instance, has he appeared withdrawn, preoccupied, or perhaps worried? Has he changed his routine? Have there been any new acquaintances?'

'No, no and no, not as far as I'm aware. Oh, this is all becoming too much for me. You should be out there trying to find Rory. Not here, upsetting me for no good reason.'

'Mrs Lawson, I assure you that we're doing everything possible to find your husband. But as we've no idea of who has abducted him, we have to quickly familiarise ourselves with every aspect of his life. I appreciate that this is an extremely upsetting time for you, but these first few hours are crucial.'

As a police officer investigating such a crime, pushing the spouse for information was a fine line to tread. Emilia Lawson was clearly on edge, and Jemima sensed that the woman wasn't the sort to pay much attention to whatever was going on around her. She seemed unnaturally self-absorbed and exceptionally needy. Any troubles her husband had, whether work-related or personal, were likely to go unnoticed unless they were things that directly affected Emilia.

'We'll need a list of names and contact details for all of your friends and extended family. Also, names of any events your husband attends, organisations he's associated with, clubs he's a member of. Anything at all that could point us in the direction of people he might have interacted with.'

'I don't have any other family. Rory has a sister. They're not close. Haven't spoken in years. The last I'd heard she was living in Cardiff.'

'What's her name?' asked Broadbent.

'Francesca Dubois.'

'Do you have a contact number?'

'No.'

'What about an address?'

'No. Like I said, we lost touch years ago.'

'Friends? Acquaintances?' pressed Jemima.

'He plays golf every Saturday morning. With one of your lot, if I'm not mistaken.'

'I don't suppose you have a name?'

'No.'

'In that case I'll need you to tell us which club he's a member of.'

Emilia sighed but answered the question.

'Do you have any domestic help?'

'Yes, Maureen Winkler. She comes in three mornings a week, but this isn't one of her days.'

'Do you mind if we look around the property? We'd like to examine your husband's personal effects. They're likely to be of no importance, but it's possible they could throw up new avenues for us to investigate. And as you seem to be unaware of the identity of your husband's associates, it might prove useful to us.'

'Be my guest. I've no objection. Though I doubt it'll help. Rory's study is on the top floor. I hardly ever go up there.'

'While Sergeant Broadbent and I are going through your husband's things, I'd like you to sit with PC Formby and compile a list of any potential acquaintances, organisations or clubs your husband has links with,' said Jemima.

'Do you reckon she's hiding something from us?' asked Dan. They had reached the first-floor landing and were walking towards the nearest bedroom.

'I'm not sure. Alcohol dulls the senses. It would certainly cause her to be less observant and affect her memory. But the few details that she's revealed suggest to me that they live separate lives. There was no implication that they do things as a couple. So perhaps Emilia genuinely doesn't know much about her husband. They've been together a long time. It's not unusual for couples to grow apart but continue living together.'

The bedroom was large and had a masculine feel to it. Everything was practical. A sober colour scheme. Dark, hefty furniture. Broadbent set about opening cupboards and drawers. 'Looks like separate bedrooms to me,' he said. 'No sign of any of her stuff here.'

'No paperwork, either. It's probably in his study,' said Jemima.

Further investigation confirmed that the Lawsons did indeed sleep in separate bedrooms, though there was nothing of interest in either of the rooms.

Jemima took the lead as they climbed the stairs to the second floor. There were three doors at this level, and Jemima felt a flutter of excitement when she noticed that unlike any of the other internal doors, one of them had a keyhole.

'This looks promising.' She pressed down on the handle. It barely moved. 'It's locked.'

'I'll ask Mrs Lawson for the key,' said Broadbent.

'No need. She'll most likely say she doesn't have one. It'll just waste time we don't have. I only need a couple of minutes. I'm a bit out of practice, but I'm perfectly capable of opening this.' Jemima extracted some small metal implements from a zipped compartment inside her bag.

'Here we go again,' muttered Broadbent. He was well aware of Jemima's so-called party trick. It wasn't the first time she had picked a lock while they were investigating a crime. 'I'm not looking. If it comes to it, I'll say the door was unlocked when we got here.'

Jemima was already on her knees determinedly jiggling the thin implements she always carried with her. 'I'd expect nothing less,' she said.

The lock mechanism yielded. 'And hey presto, we're in.' She pressed the handle once again and the door swung inwards.

'Oh, I'm good,' she said. 'Looks like his study. And since it was locked, I'd guess there are things in here he doesn't want anyone to see.'

They stepped inside the spacious room. Jemima's eyes were drawn towards a bookcase covering an entire wall. She examined some of the more interesting titles. Apart from a plethora of law books there was an abundance of old, possibly valuable first editions. It seemed that the judge had eclectic and expensive tastes, and the collection seemed a valid reason for keeping the room locked.

'Are you gonna help or what?' asked Broadbent. He was already rummaging through the top drawer of the judge's desk.

'In a moment.'

'Dammit!' snapped Broadbent.

'What?' Jemima turned to face him.

'Paper cut.' It was difficult to understand what he had said as he was sucking his finger.

'Don't worry, I've got a plaster.' Jemima rummaged frantically through the contents of her bag. To an outsider it might have seemed like a ridiculous response, as it was only a paper cut. But Dan had a phobia of blood, and the last thing she wanted was for him to keel over or vomit. In recent years he had worked hard to try to overcome this severe reaction, as he knew it could be an impediment to career progression within the police force. He was fortunate that Jemima was so supportive — he was certain that other serving officers would not be so accommodating.

'What's this?' Jemima picked up a key card. It was black with the initials *PM* embossed on one of the surfaces, while on the other side was a figure 1.

'I dunno. I found it in this drawer in a small leather pouch beneath his paperwork. Looks like the key to a hotel room. But I've not come across any with those initials.'

'Me neither. It might be of no relevance, but we won't know until we've established what it's for. I s'pose it's possible it could be linked to the court, which should be easy enough to establish. Though as a first step, when we go back downstairs, we'll ask Mrs Lawson about it.'

As she turned to face the bookcase once again, Jemima noticed a shelf about level with her eyeline where three books, clearly part of a series, were out of alignment. Their spines were proud of the others by no more than a quarter of an inch. It was likely that a casual observer wouldn't even have noticed the difference. But as they were here to search the place, Jemima had paid far more attention.

She tried to push the books back into line, but they wouldn't yield. It had to mean that there was something behind them. She removed the books from the shelf and found the locking mechanism of a safe, which was built into the wall.

'Well, I wasn't expecting that.'

Broadbent stopped what he was doing and moved closer to get a better look. 'That was well disguised. Nine times out of ten they locate them behind a painting. Don't tell me you're gonna try to open that?'

'No way. My skills don't go beyond lock picking. As this is a keypad, we could be here all week and still not come up with the right combination. I'll ask Mrs Lawson if she knows what it is. Otherwise, I'll inform Kennedy and ask him to arrange for someone to open it up.'

Eventually satisfied that there was nothing else of relevance, they headed back to the kitchen. Emilia Lawson looked up eagerly. 'Did you find anything useful?'

'Possibly. Firstly, I was wondering if you have the combination to the safe in your husband's study?'

'What safe? I don't know what you're talking about. You shouldn't have gone into Rory's study. He'll be furious if he finds out. He doesn't allow anyone in there. Not under any circumstances. Not even to clean. It's his work, you see. He's so busy that he sometimes has to bring home sensitive documents and work on them late into the night.'

Jemima couldn't help but raise her eyebrows in surprise. She could fully accept that Lawson might have to put the hours in at home. But if his wife's assertions were correct, then he would bring the documents home with him and take them back to the court on the following day. If they related to active cases, it made no sense for him to keep them at home while he was not there.

There had to be more to it. She couldn't imagine what Rory Lawson was so keen to protect. His wife's assertion that he didn't want anyone else going in that room because of his need to protect documents relating to his work seemed too far-fetched. Admittedly, she didn't know the workings of the judiciary, but instinct told her that it would be highly irregular for Lawson to remove sensitive documentation from the courthouse. With a lock on the door together with a hidden safe that even his wife knew nothing about, it seemed that the man had something he was determined to hide. But was it the reason he had been abducted? They had no way of knowing until they saw for themselves what was inside that safe.

'Anyway, you've got it wrong,' said Emilia. 'The safe's not in his study. It's in the drawing room. Behind the copy of the Matisse.'

'In that case, do you know the combination for that safe?'

'Of course I do. It's where we keep important documents. I'll open it for you, but I doubt you'll find anything useful.'

They followed Emilia towards the drawing room. 'I'd like you to wait outside until I've opened it up. I don't want anyone seeing the combination.'

They did as she asked and moments later she called them both into the room. It soon became apparent that the woman was correct, as there was nothing of interest. Just the usual passports, insurance policies and house deeds.

'Thank you for that, Mrs Lawson. I'm sorry we had to put you to the trouble of opening it up. Any idea what this is for?' Jemima showed the woman the key card.

The woman's eyes widened. 'No, I've never seen it before. What do you think it's for?' There was a note of concern in her voice, as though it had suddenly occurred to her that there were things going on in her husband's life that she was unaware of.

'We've no idea. Do the initials "PM" mean anything to you?'

'No.' The woman shook her head and began to cry. 'You think he's having an affair, don't you? That must be the key to some hotel room.'

'Our only concern is to find out what happened to your husband this morning,' said Broadbent. It had suddenly crossed his mind that his wife, Caroline, would be distraught if she were to discover that he had been abducted, which had made him feel more compassionate towards the woman.

'You should know that I'll be arranging for some other officers to call around later today,' said Jemima. 'They'll need access to your husband's study. You don't need to concern yourself about that, as PC Formby will deal directly with them. She'll remain with you while we continue with the investigation.'

'A word, please, Anita.' She nodded in the direction of the hallway.

'Ma'am.'

'You messed up big time this morning,' Jemima said in a low voice once out of earshot of Emilia Lawson.

'I'm sorry.' Anita's cheeks burned with shame. She knew that she should have taken the alcohol away from the woman, and wished she'd taken the initiative and done something about it.

'Save it. You let yourself down and you cost us time we don't have. You have a job to do. All I'm asking is that you get on and do it.' Jemima fought to keep her sense of frustration from spilling over into her voice. She needed Anita be their eyes and ears inside that house, and for that to happen, it was important to keep her onside. There was a fine line between reasonable and excessive criticism of the junior officer. And Emilia Lawson was a difficult woman to manage.

'I know you've got an unenviable task, Anita, but we need Mrs Lawson sober in case we need to question her again. So make sure she doesn't have access to any more alcohol. And while you're keeping an eye on her, I want you to call everyone on that list of contacts. Establish when they last saw or spoke to Rory Lawson.'

Anita nodded. 'I can do that.' She was keen to make up for her previous mistake.

'Good. As for the golf club, get a list of members, along with their contact details. You'll need to speak to all of them and establish if they know Rory and what contact they've had with him recently. His wife's already told us that he regularly plays with one of our lot, so find out who that is and get back to me. This is my mobile number.' She handed Anita her contact details. 'Your role is crucial. We're up against it. So far, we don't have any viable leads, so I need you to work through that list as quickly as possible. I'll have a word with the officer outside and get him to come in to help you.

'Oh, and when you get in touch with her kids, tell them I need to speak to them immediately.'

# CHAPTER 7

Jemima and Broadbent arrived back at the incident room to find Kennedy with three unfamiliar officers.

'Good, you're back,' the DCI said. 'Given the nature of the case, I've organised reinforcements. For once, the powers that be didn't quibble about it. This is DS Steve Morgan, DC Gaynor Lane and DC Rick Chapel. They work together out of the Barry station and come highly recommended. I've been assured you won't need to babysit them.'

With the clock ticking, Jemima appreciated that they needed all the help they could get. But still, these latest recruits were yet more officers that she was unfamiliar with, who may or may not turn out to be good at their jobs.

Kennedy was clearly unaware of Jemima's concerns. 'I suggest you hold a briefing in five. Get everyone up to speed and allocate tasks. But don't start without me.' He headed out of the room.

There was no sign of Gareth and the others, which was unsurprising, as they were all tasked with gathering information, something that would take a significant amount of time. Meanwhile, Jemima and Broadbent had spent a few hours at the Lawson house, and Emilia had not told them anything useful. It was frustrating given the seriousness of the situation. She just hoped that the FLO would come up with something useful as she worked her way through the list of contacts.

When Kennedy returned, Jemima began the briefing session. It was a task she had carried out routinely over the years, though having spent a year as a civilian, it suddenly seemed a little daunting. It was the second time that day that she felt a flutter of nerves, but she cleared her throat, smiled, and got on with it. After introductions were out of the way she revealed that morning's findings.

'Jeanne Ennersley from Forensics has informed us that there's little doubt that Rory Lawson was abducted. Her initial assessment is that the abductors used two vehicles. One followed Lawson's car and most likely communicated with the driver of the other vehicle, which ambushed him and brought his car to a halt. There's no doubt that this was a planned abduction. It was carried out early enough in the morning for there to be little chance of other traffic. It's safe to presume they'd scoped the area and selected a section of road that was narrow enough and sufficiently remote for no one to observe what was happening. Dan, get the images up on the board.'

'Sure.' He arranged a series of photographs as Jemima continued talking.

'That's Lawson's abandoned vehicle. You'll see how narrow the road is. They hijacked him just after he came around the bend. He had no option but to slam on his brakes — you can see the skid marks. But if you look closely, you'll spot tyre marks from another vehicle that stopped abruptly in the middle of the carriageway, preventing Lawson from reversing. He was trapped. There was no available exit route.'

'How can you be sure that the rear vehicle was involved?' asked DC Lane. It was a reasonable question.

'We can't be certain of anything, but it's highly likely. To intercept the car at that point in the road, they had to know when it was going to arrive. Otherwise, they could have stopped the wrong vehicle.'

'And the only way they could do that is if there was communication between the occupants of the two vehicles,' said Kennedy.

'Precisely.' Jemima noticed some of the new arrivals nodding and looking impressed. 'There was a small amount of blood spatter across the front passenger seat and on the passenger side window but no blood elsewhere in the vehicle, suggesting that whoever abducted the judge probably punched him in the face. The impact would have forced his head round. There were scuff marks on the driver doorsill and some cloth snagged on a rough section of the car's bodywork.'

'Torn from the judge's clothes,' interjected DC Chapel.

'Either that, or from the abductor's,' said Broadbent.

'A single shoe was found in the carriageway a few yards away from the car. It most likely belongs to the victim. Probably came loose in the struggle as he was being transferred into the other vehicle.'

'Has there been any ransom demand?'

'No contact whatsoever. It's possible that could come later. But if they don't make contact and this isn't about money, then we're into a whole different ball game and it makes it more dangerous for Lawson.'

Kennedy took up the narrative. 'Which is why we need to get a handle on this as quickly as we can. I don't need to hammer home the importance of what we're all here to do. I expect one hundred percent commitment from all of you. Judge Lawson has sentenced numerous lowlifes throughout his career, which places a huge target on his back. It's our job to figure out who's taken him and get him back safely. But the clock is ticking. Every second he's out there increases the chance that he's hurt. Or, worst-case scenario, killed. Back to you, Huxley.'

'Thank you, sir. After visiting the crime scene, Sergeant Broadbent and I visited the judge's house, where we spoke with his wife. Unfortunately, she wasn't very forthcoming. From what we observed, I'd say it's likely the Lawsons are living separate lives, but she's put together a list of contacts

— extended family, possible friends, and the name of the golf club where he's a member. I've tasked the FLO and the other uniformed officer at the property with contacting everyone on that list.'

'Excellent,' said Kennedy.

'Also, when we searched Lawson's study, we found this.' Jemima held up an evidence bag containing the distinctive key card.

'What is that?' DS Morgan moved closer to take a better look.

'Looks like a hotel room key card. We showed it to his wife, but she claimed to have no knowledge of it. As you can see, it's embossed with the initials *PM*. Though, as far as we're aware, there are no local hotels with that moniker. The underside also shows the number one, suggesting it's for room one.'

Jemima was about to continue when the door opened so forcefully that it banged against the wall. Constable Victoria McCarthy raced into the room. Her cheeks were flushed and she was clearly out of breath. 'S-sorry. I've just come from the courthouse. Gareth asked me to give you this.' She thrust sheets of paper into Jemima's hands.

'What's this?'

'A list of names of guilty defendants in the most recent cases the victim presided over. It also contains details of defence witnesses and known associates for each case.'

'Why not email it to me?' Jemima was surprised that Gareth had wasted time writing things out instead of forwarding them electronically. He knew the way they worked and was aware that time was of the essence.

'Their database was corrupted. The only access to the records is by going through paper files. It's like stepping back into the Dark Ages.'

'Surely they've got a backup?' asked Jemima.

'That was the first thing we asked. Put it this way, they should have. As far as we were able to establish, it was written into the contract that the external developer should do weekly backups. But—'

'Let me guess, no one bothered to check that the contractors were fulfilling their obligations.' Jemima sighed. There seemed to be so many people in public service who didn't do their jobs properly. Most of the time they got away with it. But when something went wrong and their negligence came to light, it inevitably meant that the knock-on effects were bad. Sometimes catastrophic.

'Got it in one,' said Victoria.

'Are we talking weeks or months since the last backup?' Jemima held her breath as she hoped for the best.

'Ten months.'

'You've got to be kidding!'

'Afraid not, and they won't agree to us taking the paper files out of the building.'

'Well, if they want to get pissy about things, let's see how they like having three of our officers camped out in their office space. Do you think you'd be able to get some night-shift officers to continue going through their records? This is going to be labour intensive, and we'll be progressing at a snail's pace. What could have been done in an hour, we'll be lucky to achieve in a day,' said Jemima.

'I'll make it a priority to sort that out,' said Kennedy. 'If the abduction is down to one of the cases he presided over, these delays could cost Lawson his life. Let's face it, we're six hours in and there's been no ransom demand. The longer they keep him, the greater the risk of us finding them. They wouldn't have transported him far. They'd want him at the destination point as soon as possible. So I'd wager this isn't any ordinary kidnapping.'

'I know,' said Jemima. 'OK, DC Chapel, I want you over at the crown court. You'll assist Peters and McCarthy. Morgan and Lane, you're to remain here. You'll both help us sift through this data. If we find any likely suspects, Lane can arrange for them to be brought in for questioning.'

Jemima split the list into four. 'Take your pick and get cracking,' she said to the others. She picked up the remaining list.

'Before you start, you need to know that when we examined the transcripts of the court proceedings there were three trials where threats were made to the jury, prosecution counsel and Lawson,' said McCarthy. 'I've highlighted those references, so you should've no problem spotting them.'

'Good work, Victoria.' Although this setback was frustrating, Jemima was impressed by Gareth and Victoria's efficiency. They were clearly making the best use of time and the limited resources at their disposal, and with an extra person to help, things should speed up. 'Right, get to it, everyone. We're up against it.'

'Huxley, hand that key card over,' said Kennedy. 'You've got your hands full. I'll see what I can find.' They were all so focused on their tasks that no one noticed the concerned look on his face. Or the fact that it was an effort to keep his voice sounding as though it was just business as usual.

'That'd be helpful, sir. Oh, and before I forget, we found a hidden wall safe in Lawson's study. It's a keypad combination. According to his wife, no one apart from Lawson is allowed in that room. Even the door was locked. We know for a fact that it's not the main safe, so it's definitely for his personal use. Under the circumstances I'd say we need to get it opened. There could be something inside that could give us an actual lead.'

'I agree. I'll arrange for someone to go over there with specialist equipment and get the thing open.' Having placed the key card in his shirt pocket, Kennedy headed back to his office.

# CHAPTER 8

As they each concentrated on their allocated task, the silence in the room spoke volumes. For a part of the station usually alive with voices, the only sounds were of paper being turned, keyboards being tapped and biros scratching as notes were made. Such was the assiduous collective determination of these four people that it would have been easy to mistake the officers for students sitting an examination.

The tension in the room was palpable. Everyone was concentrating hard, determined to sift through their batch of information as efficiently and thoroughly as possible. It was grunt work, boring but essential. No one wanted to be the person who overlooked some link that could turn out to be the vital clue they were looking for.

As things stood, there was nothing to go on. No clue. Obvious or otherwise. They needed to identify a viable lead soon. The only thing they knew for certain was that the prospect of Rory Lawson being found alive was diminishing with each passing second.

It was a lot of pressure to heap on everyone's shoulders. The understanding that even a momentary lapse in concentration could result in a man dying was an effective way of focusing the mind. But what made it even more daunting was the fact that this could be a complete waste of time. Without knowing who had abducted the judge, they were unable to establish a clear motive. There was the possibility that his abduction might not have been linked to his job. In other words, they were blindly searching for a proverbial needle in a haystack.

Morgan and Lane had set themselves up at the far end of the room while the others were at their usual desks. They had a monumental task ahead of them as the list of names they were working through was only the tip of the iceberg.

'What a welcome back, eh?' Dan's voice was no more than a whisper. 'Trouble always seems to follow you around.' They had been working steadily for at least twenty minutes and he needed a break.

'I know what you mean. I was hoping to ease myself back into the swing of things. It already feels as though I haven't been away.'

They continued working, until Jemima turned the page and her eyes landed on one of the highlighted entries. It was as though time stood still. She couldn't move and was unable to speak. All she could do was stare.

Most of the defendants meant nothing to her, but at the name 'Joseph Waverley', she broke out in a cold sweat. She had never met the man, but she knew of him, as did Kennedy, Broadbent and Peters. Joseph was the youngest son of Leonard Waverley, who headed up a vicious crime family located in the north of England. The Waverleys had gone all out to expand their criminal empire and Joseph had moved into people trafficking. He had seen it as having a double benefit. Firstly, it helped to replenish the stock of girls in his expanding chain of brothels. Secondly, it was a bold move he felt sure would impress his father.

Joseph had eventually been arrested by the National Crime Agency for his part in an operation linked to a murder Jemima and her team had been investigating. A young woman's body was found inside a church no more than a few hundred yards from Jemima's sister's house. She had been shot in the chest with a bolt fired from a crossbow.

The case had been excruciatingly complicated, with so many lies and deceptions that nothing had been as it seemed. And with the NCA breathing down their necks, it had often felt as though they were having to work with their hands tied behind their backs. It had been the last case Jemima had worked on before going on maternity leave and had resulted in the most devastating moment of her career.

From the corner of his eye, Broadbent picked up on a change in Jemima's body language. 'You all right there?' It wasn't like Jemima to be so still. When she didn't respond, he got up and rushed to her side. 'What's wrong?'

Still unable to speak, she merely pointed at Waverley's name.

'Shit! I wasn't expecting that.' Broadbent felt the strength drain from his legs and he slumped onto the nearest seat. 'It's highlighted. Which means he threatened Lawson.'

Neither of them had first-hand experience of Joseph Waverley. But they knew he was a nasty piece of work. On his own he was nothing more than a jumped-up wannabe. A young man who, to all intents and purposes, was desperately trying to win his father's approval. He had spent his entire life being the butt of his elder brother's jokes. Though instead of proving himself to be as capable as the rest of his family, he had allowed his desperation to get in the way of his decision-making. Things rarely seemed to go right for him, and when they went wrong, they went wrong big time.

Leonard Waverley was a man of means. Not only financially — he had contacts too and the muscle to back up anything he set his mind to do. Even though Joseph had let the family down, he was still Leonard's youngest. And the Waverleys looked out for their own. Crossing any of them placed a target on your back.

There was no record of Leonard having attended his son's trial, which had been held in Cardiff Crown Court. But there was no doubting that he would have sent a representative in his place, someone to lift his son's spirits and show him that his old man was thinking of him.

'Are we ever going to be able to move on from that godawful time? It's hard enough coming in here every day, knowing how Fin died. I still have nightmares. Deep down, I know it's not my fault. After all, it could just as easily have been me. But it doesn't stop the guilt . . .' Broadbent's profound sadness was etched across his face. It seemed that in a matter of seconds, he had aged a few decades.

Jemima reached out and touched Dan's arm, but he flinched. 'Don't be nice to me. I don't deserve it.' His voice trembled and he couldn't even look her in the eye.

'You did nothing wrong, Dan. I distracted you. We all made decisions that night, and it was the culmination of those decisions that led to Fin's death. Even if you'd been with him, there's no guarantee that things would have played out differently. As dreadful as it is, Fin's actions cost him his life. We can't go back in time. It happened. It's tragic, but each of us has to carry on and learn to live with it.'

It broke Jemima's heart to see Dan like this. In the immediate aftermath of Fin's death, Dan and the others had had to continue as serving police officers, answering numerous questions to establish that they were not directly to blame for what had happened. And finally, when things began to calm down, it was down to them to clear out their mate's desk and look on as someone else sat in his seat.

Of course, Dan, Gareth and, to a certain extent, Kennedy could turn to one another for support, whereas Jemima had gone on immediate maternity leave. But despite the abrupt change to her personal circumstances, something that occupied most of her waking moments, she still acutely missed Ashton and had regrets over what had happened.

Broadbent shook his head. 'I know it's ridiculous. It's not as if the Waverleys killed Fin. But Joseph played a part in the events leading up to that night, and just hearing his name is a trigger. It opens the floodgates and allows those awful memories to get inside my head again. I can't afford to allow myself to think about that bloody awful time, because if I do, I won't be able to focus on trying to find Lawson. I spent weeks, months even, where I was just going through the motions. I was fuck-all use in this place. And how Caro stuck with me, God only knows. I realised afterwards that I was married to a saint. The shit she's had to put up with . . .'

'I know where you're coming from. I feel it too. It already felt raw, coming back to this place for the first time today. I obviously knew that Finlay wasn't going to be here, but I still couldn't stop myself from glancing across to his desk when I walked through the door. It's as though my mind won't accept what I know to be true.' She felt her throat tighten with emotion but continued speaking. 'I had the same visceral reaction as you when I saw Waverley's name on that list. But we've got to rise above it. Lawson's out there somewhere. His life is in danger, and if we don't come through for him, he might very well die. This is the first possible lead we have, and we need to follow it up if only to rule it out. It's got to be worth taking a look at the Waverleys. They're hardcore villains and more than capable of snatching Lawson. Though I doubt any of the family members have done it themselves. They'll have plenty of lackeys for that.'

She strengthened her resolve. 'Find out which prison Joseph's in, and I'll make some calls to see what his old man's been up to.'

When she came off the phone almost thirty minutes later, she was pleased to see that Broadbent was looking more like his old self.

'Looks like something's going our way,' he said. 'Joseph should've been in a Category A, but what with the over-crowding, he ended up in Cardiff.'

'Well, at least that makes it easy for us, and goes some way to explain what I've just been told by someone in the know at the North-East Regional Special Operations Unit.'

'Which is?'

'NERSOU have got eyes on the Waverley operation, among others. Apparently, Leonard and his wife have taken a break. Len and Jackie are staying at a hotel in the Bay. They're booked into a suite for three weeks. Come to visit their little boy. Seems that Jackie's missing him.' Jemima could fully appreciate how a mother could miss her child, even when they were an adult. Though how anyone could feel maternal towards a scrote like Joseph Waverley was beyond her comprehension.

'The word is that the Waverley clan's been involved in a turf war. We'd already heard that they were looking to expand their business. It was one of the reasons Joseph ended up on our patch. But things have heated up in recent months. There's been inevitable pushback and the Waverleys have taken some heavy losses. The inspector I spoke to said it's been like the Wild West up there, with three crime families fighting it out.'

'If it wasn't for the fact that innocent people could find themselves caught in the crossfire, it'd be a result if scum like that took one another out,' said Dan.

'I get where you're coming from.' Jemima sighed. 'Anyway, it seems Jackie's had enough of the macho bullshit. She's at the end of her tether. Threatened to walk if Leonard didn't allow her to spend some time with their youngest. So they've come to Cardiff and have brought protection. A couple of meatheads are staying at the same hotel. I doubt they'll be in a suite, but Leonard's taking no chances. Apparently, these days he doesn't take a piss without a bodyguard being present.'

'Wonderful. So there'll be inevitable aggro with the muscle just to get to talk to the main man.' Broadbent already had a bad feeling about how things would go down.

'Most likely. I've requested images of the four of them, so we'll know who to look out for. Should be emailed through in the next few minutes. I'll arrange for a team to pick them all up and bring them in for questioning. It won't do them any harm to let them stew in the holding cells until we're ready to interview them.

'In the meantime, give the prison a call and tell them that we'll be there within the hour to interview Joseph. From what I've heard about him, he's not the brightest and he's got a reputation for letting his mouth run away with him.'

'With someone like Joseph we've just got to push his buttons, sit back and see where it leads us,' said Broadbent.

'I agree. This could turn out to be the break we've been looking for.' Though even as she said it, Jemima had a feeling that this would turn out to be misplaced optimism.

# CHAPTER 9

HMP Cardiff was a Category B facility located within a stone's throw of the city centre. From the outside, it was an imposing yet depressing sight. For visitors it wasn't the most welcoming place, even less so for the prison officers along with the hundreds of male inmates, who were obliged to endure the place. But at least the former got paid to be there and could leave at the end of each shift.

Jemima hated having to spend time inside a prison. Even an hour or so seemed far too long. It was the thought of being locked inside a facility where so many people detested you. A place where even prisoners who were natural enemies would happily put their differences aside for a short while if it meant they had a chance of doing you physical harm. She was thankful it wasn't something she was routinely obliged to do. Their investigations inevitably required them to interview suspects and witnesses, but ninety-nine times out of a hundred, these people were not currently spending time at Her Majesty's pleasure. They both knew that there was minimal risk to their safety — security measures for such an interview were taken seriously — but even so, there was no denying the fact that once the doors closed behind them, they were in a dangerous environment.

Having had their identities verified, they were kept waiting at the reception area for what seemed like an inordinately lengthy period. Broadbent sat patiently, but Jemima preferred to pace back and forth. She reminded Dan of a caged animal.

When Broadbent had phoned up to arrange the interview, he had done his utmost to impress upon the prison official the urgency of their request. He had explained that a high court judge had been abducted, and his life was most likely in imminent danger. Yet it seemed that his words had fallen upon deaf ears. Either that, or they were playing silly buggers to demonstrate that when you were inside a prison you had to abide by prison rules, regardless of who you were, or the reason for your visit.

Jemima counted every step she took. It was the only way she could keep her frustration in check and stay sane in the process. As she was about to take her seven-hundred-and-thirty-fifth one, a locking mechanism on the door to the left of the seated area clunked loudly and a surly-looking prison officer walked in. The man looked as though he was carrying the weight of the world on his shoulders. His hair was cropped short, and he appeared to be dead behind the eyes. If it wasn't for the fact that he was wearing a prison officer uniform and was also on first-name terms with the person manning the reception booth, he could easily have been mistaken for a prisoner gone rogue.

'You're police?' he asked. There was no apology for keeping them waiting, and no attempt at social niceties. As he held his laser-like gaze on Jemima, she had to force herself not to flinch.

'That's right,' she said. The words had barely left her lips before he continued.

'Identification.'

She half-expected him to pin her up against the wall and threaten to strip-search her if she didn't comply.

'Detective Inspector Huxley and Sergeant Broadbent.' She thrust her identification so close to his face that he had to take a step backwards. She was in no mood to be treated so disrespectfully. Nevertheless, she battled to keep a lid on her rising frustration. As much as she would have relished the opportunity to demonstrate that he was no match for her, this was not the time to get into an argument. It would be counterproductive to get his back up. When it came down to it, they were all on the side of law enforcement. It's just that the man who stood between them and the person they needed to speak to obviously had a hell of a chip on his shoulder.

She suddenly decided to change tactics and instead gave the prison guard what she hoped was a disarming smile. 'Sorry about that. I'm just a bit stressed. You know how it is. The job gets to you sometimes. I apologise for having disrupted your routine, but I'd really appreciate it if you'd escort us to the interview room. We've got a high court judge who's just been abducted and it's possible your prisoner knows something about it. Truth is, this is our last throw of the dice, and we could do with a break. It's not going to look good for the police or the prison service if the judge dies on our watch and it turns out that we could have saved him if only we'd spoken to your prisoner sooner.'

Although said sweetly, the threat was unambiguous, and the guard was seasoned enough to know that he would be held accountable should he continue to waste their time and the judge ended up dead. He'd played his power games. Had his fun. Now it was time to let it go and do the right thing.

'This way.' He headed back the way he'd come and rapidly typed a code into a keypad, which in turn unlocked the door. 'Quickly.'

They were ushered into a narrow corridor. Ten paces ahead there was another locked door. This time the guard selected a key from a bunch he carried on a chain secured to his belt.

'Inside.' He stood aside, waited for them to pass, followed them in and locked the door behind them.

They found themselves inside a secure room with a table and four chairs. Every piece of furniture was bolted securely to the ground. There was another door, presumably locked, in the opposite direction from which they had come. This was a small space, not good if you happened to be claustrophobic. The air was different in here. It smelled strongly of disinfectant. It was so overpowering that Jemima's initial reaction was to wince. It hurt her nose and seemed to coat the inside of her mouth.

The guard was obviously anticipating this reaction. 'You get used to it.' His lips twitched at her apparent discomfort. He leaned against the wall, within easy reach of a panic button. Both police officers hoped he wouldn't need to use it.

'Where's Waverley?' asked Jemima.

'On his way. Take a seat. He won't be long.'

A few minutes later there was a clunk and the other door opened. They got their first look at the youngest member of the Waverley clan, and it was easy to imagine that he was the runt of the litter.

Joseph Waverley was in his mid-twenties. Yet in the outside world he could have passed for being in his late teens. At barely five foot six he could have weighed no more than eight stone. His complexion was blighted with acne, and his left eyelid swollen shut. A purple bruise covered almost the whole side of his face.

'What happened to you?' asked Broadbent.

'Slipped in the shower.' Joseph tentatively lowered his wiry frame onto the unforgiving plastic seat.

Jemima wondered what other injuries the young man had sustained. This prison was far enough from home for the threat of his family to hold little, if any, sway. And it wasn't as if he had an imposing physical presence. His puny physique would be no match for anyone, should other prisoners decide to give him a hard time. Growing up in a crime family meant that Joseph would have always had people on hand to look out for him and step in if he needed protection. But in this prison, he was bottom of the pile. He'd trafficked and exploited women, some of whom had barely reached the age of consent. They were crimes that many prisoners detested. Which meant that Joseph was fair game for whatever they decided to do to him.

'How's it going, Joseph?' asked Jemima. Not that she cared. But as he was clearly having a hard time it might be an effective icebreaker. Show a bit of compassion and who knows . . . He might let his guard down.

'You don't care one way or the other. So do us both a favour and cut the crap. What d'ya want?' His lips barely moved as he uttered the words, no doubt hindered by the recent injuries to his face. His voice was hard, and noticeably different from the local accent in these parts. His uninjured eye stared defiantly, emphasising the fact that he wasn't afraid of a couple of coppers. Especially one that was a woman.

'At your trial you made a number of threats.'

'Yeah! What of it?'

'Having read a transcript I can see that you threatened the jury, the prosecution counsel and the judge.'

'If you say so.' Joseph was beginning to look and sound more relaxed. He had quickly worked out that if they were asking him questions about his trial, it obviously meant that they didn't have anything else on him. He and his close associates knew that there were numerous things he had done. Things which, should the police become aware of his involvement, they would inevitably investigate. He was already serving time and had many more years to go before he was considered for parole, though, given the serious nature of his crimes, it was doubtful that it would be granted. As things stood, he had an end date in sight, albeit a long way in the future.

By the time he was released, he would no longer be a young man. And if his daily punishments continued, his arsehole would easily be able to accommodate a tennis ball without him feeling a thing. But at least he could hold on to the fact that he would eventually get out of this place. Whereas if the police brought additional charges against him and made them stick, he might never see the light of day again.

'When you made those threats, you implied that there were individuals on the outside who might take retaliatory action against anyone involved in your trial.'

71

'Yeah, well, it's a possibility, innit? But if someone's gone an' done it, you can't lay that on me. I've been in 'ere. There's no way I'm takin' the rap for anythin' someone else 'as done.'

'What about your father? Has he done anything?' asked Jemima.

'Don't be stupid. My old man's a law-abidin' citizen. Pillar of the community. Never broken the law in 'is life.'

'I've heard that he's currently in Cardiff.' Jemima studied Joseph's expression as she spoke. He wasn't giving much away, and his facial injuries made it all but impossible for her to tell if he was rattled. But when he replied there was a noticeable inflection to his voice. It made her think that perhaps he didn't know anything about the judge's abduction.

'Well, it's no secret. The screws'll tell ya me mam's comin' to see me. No law 'gainst that. She's down 'ere on 'oliday with me old man. Me mam's missin' me.'

'Very touching,' muttered Broadbent.

'You think what you like, mate. It 'appens to be the truth. Now if tha's all, I've got things to do. Take me back to me cell,' he said to the prison officer who had accompanied him into the room. 'I ain't got nuffin' more to say to these coppers.'

'Don't you want to know what's happened?' asked Jemima.

'Nah! Not the slightest bit interested. Now take me back to me cell. The smell of pig's turnin' me stomach.'

Jemima knew there was no point in trying to engage further with Joseph. Even if he knew something, he wouldn't say anything. They waited for him to be escorted from the room, then stood up to leave and made their way out of the prison.

'That was a waste of time,' said Broadbent.

'I dunno about that. His old man could be behind this. After all, Joseph didn't appear to be the slightest bit interested in anything we had to say.'

'So why didn't you tell him about Lawson's abduction?'

'Because we'll soon be interviewing Leonard, Jackie and their entourage. And this way, even if Joseph manages to get a message to them before we've picked them up, there's very little he can tell them.'

# CHAPTER 10

Jemima wished she'd had the foresight to bring a change of clothes with her. It was something she had routinely done in the past. But she was so out of the swing of things the thought hadn't even entered her head until now.

The visit to the prison and the encounter with Joseph Waverley had left her feeling sullied. Common sense told her that it wasn't the case. The areas they had spent time in and the seats they had sat in were as clean as anywhere else. It was more that the sight of Waverley had brought back a whole host of bad memories. Even though it was the first time they had set eyes upon him, the man was still linked to the events leading up to Ashton's death. Nothing would ever take that association away. It was far too painful and personal. And Jemima sensed that Broadbent felt that way too.

Ideally, she would have bagged up the clothes she was wearing and changed into a fresh set. But as she didn't have the option, or the time, she knew that she had to try to put the visceral disgust to the back of her mind. She thought there was every chance she would feel the same revulsion when she interviewed Joseph's parents and their henchmen. Though apart from the fact that their youngest son had set up and participated in the people trafficking operation that had ultimately led him to this part of the country, they had not been involved with those actual events.

Broadbent was uncharacteristically quiet as they drove back to the station.

'What're you thinking?' she asked.

'It'd be good if someone offed that little bastard. They'd do the world a favour.'

'Yeah, but there're plenty more of them about. I suppose we should take consolation from the fact that he's obviously having a rough time in there. That's some sort of payback. Not enough, but a start. And as bad as Joseph is, I reckon his old man's a hell of a lot worse. After all, word is he didn't rate his youngest, and if that's the case . . .'

They parked and walked into the police station to find that Jackie Waverley had been brought in for questioning. The woman had been in the hotel spa making the most of the amenities. Officers had caught up with her while she was having a massage. They'd had to ask a member of staff which customer she was, as Jackie's face had been caked in a bright green facemask, which had made her impossible to recognise.

Despite a thorough search of the hotel and the immediate surrounding area, Leonard and his thugs were nowhere to be found. Apart from an initial outburst, where Jackie had shouted, screamed and slapped the closest police officer, the woman wasn't talking. Given the colour of the facial treatment and the fact that she had subsequently remained resolutely quiet, some bright spark had quipped that she was the Incredible Sulk. It appealed to everyone's sense of humour and the moniker had stuck.

The desk sergeant took great delight in relaying this tale, and from his enthusiastic description of a scene he could not possibly have witnessed first-hand, Jemima was sure that it had been embellished many times over.

When they entered the interview room Jemima got her first look at the Waverley matriarch. It was immediately apparent where Joseph got his unfortunate looks. Jackie was as scrawny as a scarecrow, with bleached-blonde hair styled into an unflattering bob. Long strands hung limply over her sunken cheeks.

Jemima had seen more attractive crack addicts.

The officers' arrival at the spa had been unfortunate timing for Jackie. For a woman who routinely refused to leave her bedroom without applying an industrial covering of cosmetics, it was mortifying to be led away barefaced. However, they had afforded her the courtesy of allowing the therapist to remove Jackie's face pack and a female officer had stood there as she changed out of her robe.

Clad in baggy leisurewear, and devoid of her treasured mountain of bling, the woman looked more like loose change than the million dollars she usually strived for, yet invariably failed to achieve. With no Leonard to protect her, what had started out as a few hours of pampering had unexpectedly turned into an afternoon of humiliation.

Slapping the PC had been a visceral reaction and had felt good at the time. Though when her brain kicked in a few seconds later she had regretted doing it. Not because the officer didn't deserve it, but having struck a police officer in full view of numerous impartial witnesses, there was every chance they would charge her and make it stick.

Jackie's sole concern was that Leonard would be angry with her. She'd broken his number-one rule that family members never put themselves in a position where charges could stick. In the grand scheme of things, slapping a police officer was small fry. But all Leonard would see is that she had let him down, and there was no doubt in her mind that she'd suffer for it. She'd learned the hard way at the beginning of their relationship: defy Leonard and he'd hurt you. It was the way he kept everyone in line.

Leonard had drummed it into every member of his family that they mustn't disrespect or antagonise coppers, though he wasn't against having them killed. But that was different. He despised the filth. They made his life difficult. But he was clever enough to appreciate that you could still get things done if you were careful. There were people on his payroll whom he trusted to do his bidding. They took the risks and kept the family out of it. If by any chance they were arrested and charged, they knew the score: keep their mouths shut and do the time. As long as they followed the rules, he would ensure that their families were looked after, as they would be when they finished their stretch inside.

It was a tried-and-tested method that had worked well. That is, until his idiot youngest son had gone and got himself arrested for people trafficking. Joseph had let the family down big time. He'd given the filth a bona fide reason to poke their noses into the Waverley family business, and that had made life difficult.

Until that point, the Waverleys had been riding high. They had been muscling in on smaller operations, expanding their empire by forcing competitors out of business. The Waverley name meant something among the criminal fraternity. What's more, the police had nothing on them. Of course, they had their suspicions. They'd have had to be stupid not to. But Leonard's core team of enforcers were careful. There was nothing to lead back to the family. And then Joseph had gone and messed it all up . . .

With the preliminaries out of the way, Jemima began her questioning. 'Where is your husband, Mrs Waverley?'

Jackie ignored the question and examined her fingernails. Having had a full manicure before the police arrived, they had been sharpened, strengthened, and would have made effective weapons. They were painted a vivid shade of scarlet and reminded Jemima of talons caked in blood. It seemed to her that this woman employed someone to do the housework, that she cared about appearances and would buy expensive things, desperate to disguise the fact that she was nothing more than trash. She'd insist that everything in her life was nice and neat, just so long as someone else was putting the effort in to achieve that.

Jemima slammed her fist on the table. 'I asked you a question!'

Jackie said nothing and kept on studying her nails.

Jemima changed tack. 'We've just come from the prison, and I almost felt sorry for your boy. Joseph's in a bad way. He's taken quite a beating.'

The mention of her beloved son got Jackie's attention. She looked up, opened her mouth slightly, as though to say something, but thought better of it. Jemima immediately realised that this was Jackie's Achilles heel. This was the way she'd get her talking. To capitalise on the small breakthrough, she ramped up the pressure.

'Joseph looked so frail. He's in there with some real hard cases. Men that are physically *way* bigger than him. I'm talking about the psychos who think that nonces don't deserve the air that they breathe.'

'My Joey's no nonce! I won't have you saying that about him!'

Jemima supressed a smile. She'd scored her first point. 'Well, they all think he is. Still, if Joey makes it to the end of his sentence, he might come out a changed man. I wonder—'

'What d'ya mean, if he makes it to the end of his sentence?' Jackie's face paled noticeably until she was almost white with fear. The question was gabbled and her voice had risen a few decibels.

'Oh, didn't you know? We heard on the grapevine that he's having regular lessons on what it's like to be sexually abused. When we saw him, he was struggling to walk, and he was obviously in a lot of pain when he tried to sit dow—'

'Noooo!' wailed Jackie, as she gave up any pretence of trying to hold things together.

'I'm afraid so.' Jemima raised her voice to ensure Jackie didn't miss anything. 'I wouldn't want any son of mine in there. It's awful what goes on inside those prisons. It's a well-known fact that the guards are so busy that they can't watch over all of the prisoners, all of the time.'

'You've gotta help him. Make them stop. My Joey don't deserve that.' Jackie was sobbing now.

'I'm afraid we can't. Prisoners don't listen to the likes of us.'

'There must be something.' The woman looked and sounded desperate. 'I've got a visiting order to see him this afternoon.' She looked at the clock on the wall. 'I should be there now! I've missed the visit — my Joey's gonna think I don't care!'

'That's such a shame, but I'm afraid it's unavoidable. You could have been out of here by now if you'd answered our questions. So how about you cooperate? And we'll see where we go from there.'

'Will you ask if they'll make an exception for me? Explain that I was helping you? Tell them to let me see him outside of visiting hours?'

Jemima knew that the prison officials would not agree to such a request, but she also recognised that in her desperation, Jackie was overestimating the influence a police officer would have. It was something she could use as leverage. 'I'll make you a deal,' said Jemima. 'You cooperate fully with our inquiries, and I'll ring the prison and do my best to get you in there to see your boy today.'

'Anything. I'll answer any questions you put to me. Just get me in.'

'What's the real reason you and your husband have come to Cardiff?'

'I've already told you. So that I can see Joey.'

'Just you?'

'It breaks my heart, but Lenny's got no intention of seeing him. He's ashamed of the boy. Washed his hands of him as he brought trouble to our door. You lot have always had it in for Lenny. On his back any excuse you get. Trying to fit him up for things, and he don't deserve it. My husband's a businessman. We're a law-abiding family. No one apart from Joey has ever been inside, but he's not a bad lad. Easily led, that's all.'

Jemima was immune to the woman's lies. She had heard similar denials many times before. People trying to paint a picture of a perfect partner or child. It didn't mean that the person believed what they were saying. Just that they wanted the outside world to think of those close to them in a different way.

She was determined to push on. 'When did you arrive in Cardiff?'

'Late yesterday afternoon. Must've been about five. The hotel would have a record of when we checked in.'

'And how many of you made the trip?'

'Four of us.'

'Who? I need names.'

'Just family. Len's brother, Liam, and his wife, Tracey. We're down here for three weeks. Never been to Wales before, so we thought we'd take time out and have a proper break.'

No one had mentioned that Leonard Waverley had a brother. It was something that would have to be checked out. Either he wasn't part of their criminal empire, or he was smart enough to have distanced himself and pull strings from afar.

'Anyone else?'

'No. Why would there be?'

'Because we'd heard that some of your husband's so-called business associates had come along for the ride,' said Broadbent.

'Now you come to mention it, when we went down for breakfast this morning, we did see a couple of people we know. But that was a coincidence. I think Len had been bragging about our hotel to them. They had some time off and must've liked the look of it. I mean, it is an impressive place. But we had no idea that they'd booked a room. They're here independently. Last time I looked it was a free country.'

'So, where's Len at the moment? He wasn't at the hotel.'

'He's away for the day. Him and Liam's gone on a boat trip to some island called Steep Holm. You can see it from the hotel. Bloody boring if you ask me, but they were dead keen. It's some sort of nature reserve. Got birds and rare flowers. Sends me to sleep just thinking about it. I can think of far better ways of spending twelve hours.'

'Twelve hours?' Jemima was clearly shocked.

'Yeah,' interjected Broadbent. 'She's right. I've been there myself. There's only one company that you can book with. They're based in the Bay. The actual boat trip takes about fifteen to twenty minutes. It's the tide that constrains things. Second largest tidal range in the world. They've got to sail there and back over the two high tides. No way around it.'

Jemima suppressed a smile. She'd almost forgotten about Broadbent's love of nature. He'd once surprised her on a previous case with his in-depth knowledge of peacocks. And here he was again, knowing something that she didn't.

It'd be easy enough to check on the Waverleys' alibi, as the company would have recorded details of their passengers. Though even if the brothers had alibis, it didn't mean that Leonard's goons hadn't abducted Rory Lawson.

'What're the names of your husband's associates?'

'From what I can remember, I think they were Carl Bovey and possibly Mal Nevin. Then again, I might be wrong. You'd be better off asking Len about that. Now I come to think about it, I'm sure they were going on the same trip.'

Jemima sighed. This interview wasn't going the way she had expected it to. If Leonard's henchmen had visited Steep Holm today, then there was no way that they could have been involved in the judge's disappearance. 'And where's your sister-in-law?'

'Oh, Trace is doing what she always does. She's hit the shops. Heard all about the St David's Centre. She'll be giving Liam's credit card a right hammering.'

'Sit tight, Mrs Waverley. We just need to check some things out.' Jemima stood to leave.

'But you said you'd contact the prison and persuade them to let me see my Joey today.'

'And I will when we've finished questioning you.' Jemima headed for the door with Broadbent in tow.

'My Lenny always says you can't trust coppers!' shouted Jackie. The door had already shut by the time she had finished the sentence.

'What d'ya reckon?' asked Broadbent.

'It'll be pretty easy to verify what she's told us. Are you sure about the length of those boat trips?'

'Yeah, I'm positive. It's about a twelve-hour round trip.'

'Is there a way they could get on and off that island by any other means?'

'I s'pose it's possible they could have had a small craft come and pick them up and drop them back there. But I honestly can't see how that would work, given the tides. They'd be counted on and off that boat trip, and they're strict with timings. You have to be on time. I honestly think you're clutching at straws if you think that that's what they did.'

'Yeah, you're right. Whoever's abducted the judge would either have needed to stay with him, sedate him, or kill him straight away. And if they were going to kill him, they could have done that without dragging him out of the car. It would have taken only a matter of seconds. For either of the other scenarios, they'd have to have taken him somewhere secluded, and that would have taken time. If Jackie's telling us the truth, and those four men went out to Steep Holm today, then as long as all four of them return they couldn't have abducted Lawson.'

'So, what do you want me to do?' asked Broadbent.

'Get a team of officers together and head down to the Bay to meet that boat when it comes in. If they're on it, I want all four of them back here, so that we can question them. And whatever you do, don't underestimate them. Waverley hates cops, and his thugs are there to protect him. They wouldn't think twice about hurting you.'

'I thought you said that if they spent the day on the island, they couldn't have been involved in the abduction?'

'They couldn't have been there, but it doesn't mean that Waverley or any of the others didn't pay someone to do their dirty work for them. And that includes Jackie. She's really cut up about Joey being in prison. I'd say that that gives her a pretty good motive for having the judge abducted. The Waverleys are a violent family. I'm sure that Jackie hasn't been married to Leonard for God knows how many years without making a few contacts along the way.'

'When you put it like that . . .'

'In the meantime, I'm going to do some digging around to see what I can find out about Leonard's brother and his wife. When I spoke to my contact at NERSOU, there was no mention of Leonard having a brother. And from what I was told, they'd been looking into that family's business interests for a significant amount of time. Something's not quite right, and I need to get to the bottom of it.'

# CHAPTER 11

With Broadbent's departure, Jemima took a few minutes to check in with Eloise, to find out how Finlay was doing. Video chatting in an empty corridor, Jemima saw the toddler napping in his cot. Her heart lurched. Close to tears, she quickly ended the call. She hadn't been expecting this first full day of separation to be such a brutal experience.

Determined to put a lid on her emotions before she embarrassed herself in front of colleagues, Jemima returned to her desk. The room was relatively quiet as Morgan and Lane were still working their way through the lists of names from the court. Determined to make the most of the peace, Jemima set about her own tasks, knowing it was the ideal time to concentrate.

First off, she flicked through her emails and opened one from her contact at the NERSOU. It was a list of names and photographs of the Waverley family and their known associates. She quickly scanned the information, then went through it once again. It was as she had thought. There was no mention of Liam Waverley, and the text specifically mentioned that Leonard Waverley was an only child. There were three men named Liam on the list. Hardly surprising, as it was a popular name. Two were known enforcers. The other was Leonard's solicitor.

It was frustrating that despite being hours into the investigation, they had so far failed to find a single lead on Rory Lawson's whereabouts. It didn't help that they had no firm idea why he had been abducted. If it had happened to any ordinary member of the public, it would have been easier to narrow down the possibilities, as most people didn't have long lists of potential enemies. But given the nature of Lawson's career, there were hundreds if not thousands of individuals who could realistically hold a grudge against him.

The very fact that a ransom demand still hadn't been made increased the likelihood that whoever was behind this had no intention of allowing Lawson to walk away unharmed. If the reason for his abduction had been money, they would have made their demands by now. Otherwise the longer they kept him, the greater the risk that something would go wrong and lead to them being identified.

Jemima appreciated that because of Joe Waverley's tenuous link to Ashton's death, there was a very real danger of wrongly fixating upon that family. But until they could definitively prove their involvement one way or the other, the Waverley clan would be suspects.

She had been inclined to believe Jackie when the woman had claimed that they had travelled to Cardiff to enable her to visit her son. And if the four men had spent the day on Steep Holm, it would have been impossible for them to have carried out the abduction. Yet, on the face of it, Jackie's claim that they had travelled with Leonard's brother appeared to be a lie, and Jemima's patience was wearing thin.

It was time to speak to the Waverley matriarch again. Jemima walked to the door but was stopped in her tracks as Nancy Chen and Aadi Patel came bustling into the room. It was impossible not to notice that they were both in an upbeat mood.

'You found something?' asked Jemima. All thought of speaking to Jackie was suddenly put on the back burner.

'Sure did,' said Aadi.

'It wasn't easy, but we eventually found five different properties along the route with CCTV footage showing the road. To be honest, the quality of the various recordings isn't great, but we were able to identify Lawson's vehicle on each of them. The two nearest systems to Lawson's house showed two vehicles following, but the three other systems only showed one vehicle following him,' said Nancy.

Aadi took up the narrative as Nancy drew breath. 'The driver of that car was very close behind. All but tailgating him. It's obvious there was no intention of either losing sight of Lawson or allowing any other vehicle to get in the way. It fits with the theory that someone was following him and working in conjunction with another vehicle to ambush Lawson on a quieter stretch of road.'

'Great work, guys. How clear were the images? Did you get the vehicle's registration mark?' Jemima felt a glimmer of hope. It was the first bit of positive news in the investigation.

'We caught a break as it had just started to get light, which meant that the security systems recorded in colour. So, we know that the vehicle was a blue hatchback. But that's where our luck ran out. The angles of the cameras meant that none of the images captured a registration mark, make or model of the vehicle. Apart from guessing it's relatively new, we've no idea where to begin to narrow it down. So many of these vehicles look quite similar,' said Nancy.

'Show me the footage,' demanded Jemima.

A few minutes later she was standing in front of a monitor watching the blue hatchback follow Lawson's car, and soon concluded that Patel and Chen were correct. There was no visible indication of the make, model or registration mark of the vehicle. 'I agree. We've no way of working out what it is. So, it's time to call Kate Franklin.' Jemima picked up the phone and dialled a number.

'Who's Kate Franklin?' asked Aadi.

Nancy shrugged and looked at Jemima, who ignored her.

'Hi, Kate? It's Jem Huxley . . . Yeah, that's right. First day back. I've got a favour to ask. Could you pop up and cast your eyes over some CCTV footage my officers pulled off some home security systems? We've a vehicle we need to identify. Most likely tied to this morning's abduction of Rory Lawson . . . OK, thanks, Kate. See you in five.'

Jemima ended the call and turned to face the two junior officers. 'DS Kate Franklin is the force's resident expert on cars. The woman's amazing. I can guarantee that once she's seen these images she'll know the make, model and exact shade of blue. We still won't have a registration mark, but at least we'll have more information to go on.'

Kate Franklin's obsession with cars had begun at an early age, most likely encouraged by the fact that her father was a mechanic. She was the youngest of four children and being the only girl, with three car-obsessed brothers, Kate had decided to make it her obsession too. She had made it her mission to learn everything she could about cars, memorising a phenomenal amount of information most people would consider completely pointless. Soon the brothers who had laughed at her for being a tomboy were in awe of her. Especially when it became clear that Kate really did know her stuff. Her obsession had continued throughout her life and her encyclopaedic knowledge and rapid recall of facts about anything to do with cars had proved useful in many police investigations. Kate was a one-of-a-kind officer. Completely irreplaceable. She also happened to be Jemima's kick-boxing sparring partner.

'Hi, Jem. Great to have you back. I've missed our workouts. My fitness level has dropped since you stopped training.' Kate held her arms out to give Jemima a hug.

As Jemima embraced her friend she looked across and noticed Nancy frown. It seemed that the younger woman disapproved of this spontaneous show of affection in a work setting.

'I've missed our sessions too. We must get a definite date in the diary,' said Jemima, refocusing her attention on

Kate. Seeing her friend had made her realise how much she'd missed their twice-weekly sessions. It had offered a good workout and had also been fun. She'd love to get back into the swing of things, get back to where she'd left off. 'Though I doubt I'll present you with too much of a challenge.'

'Don't do yourself down, girl. You might not have trained recently, but you know you've got what it takes.'

'Nice of you to say so.' Jemima experienced a momentary warm glow. It felt good to be praised by someone as competitive and capable as Kate Franklin.

'Anyway, enough of the small talk. Let's get down to business. Where're these images you want me to look at?'

With a click of the mouse, Nancy started the footage.

'Freeze it there,' ordered Kate. She moved closer, squinting slightly as she cocked her head to one side. 'That's a ST-Line X Edition Ford Focus. Desert island blue. It's no more than a few months old.'

'Brilliant, thanks, Kate.'

'No probs. Happy to help. Anyway, better get back. Things to do. Email me and we'll set up a session. I'll soon get you back to peak fitness.' She left the room without a backward glance.

'Impressive,' said Aadi.

Jemima and Nancy shared a knowing look, each of them shaking their heads discreetly. It was obvious to both women that they had the same thought. Although he would never admit to it, Aadi Patel was clearly in awe of Kate Franklin.

'Aadi, contact the DVLA and get the names and addresses of anyone who owns a car of that specification. Start off with a twenty-mile radius of Lawson's house,' said Jemima. 'Nancy, a word.' She gestured for the DC to follow her.

'What's up, boss?'

'I noticed your expression when you saw Kate and I hug each other. You seemed uncomfortable.'

'Not uncomfortable. Just surprised, given the environment we're in. Even though there's supposed to be equal opportunities in the force, as women we still need to prove that we're not just up to the job, but that we're better than male officers. Yet you openly let your guard down.'

'I get where you're coming from, Nancy. Believe me, I've had to fight my corner against far too many misogynists, but I've learned something along the way. Being female gives you a different perspective on things, and that can be an advantage. A lot of people think that this is not the right sort of job for a woman. Whereas we both know that's absolute bullshit. What you need to understand is that you're not going to change people's minds by hiding your femininity.'

Nancy's eyes widened, as if she couldn't believe what she was hearing. She opened her mouth to say something.

'You can have your say in a moment, but let me finish explaining, because this is important,' continued Jemima. 'Whatever you're doing, be it in a work scenario or your personal life, you need to be true to yourself. Each of us is unique, with our own set of strengths, weaknesses, interests, hopes and dreams. And that is a good thing. Diversity should be embraced because it brings so much more to the table. Don't constrain yourself or waste your energy trying to conform to someone else's idea of what a good police officer should be.

'There are a significant number of male officers, especially the older ones, who believe that any affection is a sign of weakness. What they fail to appreciate is that it is the suppression of those feelings that makes people weak. In this job, compassion and empathy are useful tools. If you understand how others are feeling, you can anticipate their reactions and take action accordingly.'

'I think I get where you're coming from,' said Nancy.

'That's good, because it takes a lot of energy trying to supress your inner self. And doing this job, you need to conserve that energy, not waste it. You are here on merit. If you spend your time trying to prove that you can act like a man, you're basically siding with the misogynists.'

'I don't understand.'

'By suppressing your true self, your actions are affirming their belief that men are better than women. Why else would you strive to emulate them?'

'Wow! I never thought of it like that.'

'It took me a long time to appreciate it. I realise that you don't know me. You've only heard about me from Dan, Gareth and the DCI. But let me tell you, Kate and I hugged each other because we're friends and we haven't seen each other for a hell of a long time. Neither of us think that that simple act of friendship is a sign of weakness because we're confident about who we are. We're both as good as any male officer on this force.' She smiled. 'Out of interest, what has Broadbent said about me?'

The question took Nancy by surprise, and her cheeks reddened. 'O-only that you're the b-best DI he's worked with,' she stuttered.

'Would it surprise you to know that when I first joined the squad as a newly promoted DS, Dan gave me a hard time?'

'But he's always singing your praises.'

'Yeah. Well, a lot has changed over the years. It's not an exaggeration to say that he hated my guts when I first arrived. He wanted me gone and went out of his way to make things awkward for me.'

'Never!'

'Ask him yourself if you don't believe me.'

'So, what changed?'

'I put my life on the line to save his.'

Nancy's eyes widened. 'Really?'

'Yeah, I could have chosen to back off. There're a lot of men in this station that would have done just that, but I couldn't. I stepped up, took on his attacker and ended up in hospital. But it was worth it because it saved Dan's life.'

'So which case was this? What happened?' asked Nancy. No one had mentioned this incident and she was keen to know more. It seemed that there might be more to the DI than she had first thought.

'We don't have time to go into it. But once this case is over, perhaps Dan and I will tell you about it over a drink.'

Nancy looked disappointed but recognised that there were far more pressing matters that required their attention.

Jemima continued. 'Kate and I know each other because we're kick-boxing sparring partners. I've recently had a baby, so my focus has been elsewhere. I can't deny that I'm out of practice, but I'm going to start training again soon. Those skills saved Broadbent's life and mine too on numerous occasions.

'What I'm trying, very ineloquently, to say is that I'm not afraid to show the softer side of my personality. But when it comes down to it, I'm one of the toughest officers in this station. You ask any man here, and I doubt you'll find many who would readily take either Kate or me on in unarmed combat.'

Having only seen Jemima for a matter of minutes before being sent on an assignment, Nancy's first impression of her senior officer had been that she was most likely an unremarkable woman, someone who had worked her way up through the ranks and had possibly been given a helping hand along the way because she was easy on the eye. Yet after this brief conversation, the first they had had, she was starting to think that perhaps DI Huxley was someone to look up to, and whose qualities she might like to emulate.

'Anyway, enough of the pep talk. Go and give Aadi a hand.'

# CHAPTER 12

As Jemima set out on her way to speak with Jackie Waverley, she saw Broadbent heading in her direction. His cheek was bleeding. 'What happened?'

'Underestimated the length of the knuckle-dragging thug's arms. That and not being quick enough on my feet. Can't complain though. He came off worse in the end. He'd only just landed the blow when one of the uniformed lads had him with a baton. Brought the bastard to his knees, which allowed us to cuff him.'

'He'll face assault charges.'

'Too bloody right,' growled Broadbent.

'Did all four of them come off the boat?'

'Yeah. They're all waiting to be questioned. But what we didn't know is that Liam is actually Leonard's half-brother, and he's not a Waverley. His name's Liam Blakeman—'

'And he's Leonard's solicitor,' interjected Jemima. 'That explains why no one seemed to know that Leonard had a brother. They must have a mother in common and kept it quiet for obvious reasons. You up to interviewing them with me?'

'Just try and stop me,' said Broadbent.

The Waverley clan were taking up a lot of police manpower. With each of the men in a separate interview room, four officers were required to keep an eye on them. The station was at full stretch, which meant that they'd had to be pulled off other duties.

'We'll start with the meatheads as they're more likely to let something slip while they're still agitated,' Jemima said. 'And it'll be good to let Leonard and his brother stew for a while. They'll both be more guarded, and given their self-perceived high status, they'll be angry about being kept waiting, which could give us an edge too. If we're lucky.'

'I wouldn't count on it. Bovey and Nevin have been part of Waverley's crew since they came out of nappies. They're loyal foot soldiers. Grunts like that do as they're told, no questions asked.'

'Yeah, you're right. First day back. Misplaced optimism.' Jemima kicked herself for not thinking of that. It was blindingly obvious and demonstrated how out of touch she was. She was under no illusion that a year's maternity leave had made her soft and dulled her intuition. There was no doubting the fact that she had a lot of catching up to do, mentally as well as physically. Especially since she was leading a rapidly expanding team of officers, all of whom were relying on her to make the right decisions. The last thing she wanted was to not be up to the job and make a bad call that could cost either the victim or another officer their life.

As Jemima walked into the interview room to get her first proper look at Mal Nevin, she quickly concluded that he was far uglier than his mugshot. It made her wonder if the midwife had known which end to slap when he was born. His lank straggly hair reached below his shoulders, and it was impossible to tell whether the strands were greasy through lack of cleanliness or merely Brylcreem. Either way it was a repulsive look. A sweat-stained T-shirt stretched across his steroid-enhanced body, straining to accommodate biceps bigger than Jemima's waist.

Nevin made a show of looking her up and down. 'Now why couldn't they 'ave sent you to meet me off the boat?' he drawled. 'You're much more my type.'

From the corner of her eye, Jemima sensed Broadbent's cheek muscles tighten. Nevin had recently punched him, and he wasn't about to let the thug get away with disrespecting Jemima too. She discreetly moved her foot and gently tapped her partner's ankle. It was a signal to tell him that no matter the provocation, he should not react to anything Nevin said.

The duty solicitor looked young enough to be on work experience. She had repositioned her seat towards the far end of the table. It would have been impossible to move even a millimetre further away as her shoulder was already pressing against the wall. Her unease at having to be in the same room as this man was palpable. She sat bolt upright as though every cell in her body was on high alert. Jemima knew that if the woman had any choice in the matter, she would have a ten-foot wall between herself and her client.

Jemima ignored Nevin's remark and proceeded with the interview once the formalities had been completed. She scanned the information forwarded by NERSOU. 'You've quite the rap sheet, Malcolm.'

'Yeah! What of it?' Nevin leaned forward in an attempt to invade Jemima's personal space. Globules of saliva sprayed the table as he spat out the words, but the distance between them was too great for it to affect either officer.

'As you've just attacked Sergeant Broadbent, you'll be having another spell inside.'

'Bring it on. I 'ear Cardiff's prison is like a first-class 'otel. Whatever time I do will be worth it. Just to 'ave seen the look on 'is pretty face when I lamped 'im.'

Nevin's words were a light-bulb moment. Jemima realised why this lowlife had reacted so violently and thumped Broadbent, when there had been no need for him to do so. The man had wanted to be arrested. There would have been no way for the Waverleys to know that the police would meet them off the boat and bring them in for questioning. But Jemima would have put money on it that sometime within the next few days, Nevin or Bovey would have done something in front of plenty of witnesses to get themselves arrested.

Despite the official Waverley line being that Leonard had washed his hands of his youngest, it was clearly his plan to engineer a way to get one of his own on the inside of that prison to protect his son.

Jemima was determined that that wouldn't happen. As soon as she left the interview room, she'd have a word with Kennedy and make sure that Waverley was placed in a different prison.

'Why are you in Cardiff, Malcolm?'

'No comment.'

'Where were you at seven o'clock this morning?'

'No comment.'

It quickly became apparent that Nevin had no intention of answering any question put to him. The man wanted to be charged with assaulting a police officer, as his employer needed him inside Cardiff prison to protect his youngest son.

Carl Bovey proved to be just as uncooperative as Nevin, but as they had nothing to hold him on they had no option but to release him.

Next up was Liam Blakeman. As he was a practising solicitor, Jemima knew they were unlikely to get any useful information from him. When they walked into the interview room, the man looked up and smiled.

'At last. I was beginning to think you'd forgotten about me. So, what's this about? Why am I here?'

Jemima knew there was no point in being anything other than direct with this man. As Leonard Waverley's solicitor, he had successfully negotiated his way through numerous failed attempts at bringing his half-brother to justice. Liam would know every trick in the book. He'd probably written some of the chapters himself. It would be a waste of time trying to trick him into revealing things he had no intention of saying.

'You're here because of your connection to Joseph Waverley,' said Jemima.

'Well, I wasn't expecting that. Yes, I'm Joseph's uncle, but then again, you already know that. Surely Joseph can't be causing any trouble. He's safely locked up in this city's prison. Unless he's escaped? Is that it? Has there been a prison break?' As he uttered the words, Liam suddenly became more alert.

'Not as far as I'm aware. At the time of Joseph's trial, he threatened the lives of the jurors, the prosecution team along with their witnesses, and the presiding judge.'

'Let me assure you, it would have all been baseless bravado. Ever since I can remember, Joseph's always let his mouth run away with him. He was trouble from the moment he began to walk and talk. He's the bane of Len's life. Caused him no end of hassle. It's most likely because he was the youngest, and Jackie's favourite. Every time Len would try to bring him in line Jackie would go off on one. No one was to say anything against her little blue-eyed boy. It's the reason he ended up out of control and has paid such a hefty price.'

'Why have you come to Cardiff, Mr Blakeman?'

'A couple of reasons. Firstly, my wife and I wanted a break. Len and Jackie were coming here anyway, as Jackie wanted to see Joseph. We've not visited this part of the country, so we thought we'd tag along. Secondly, Len and I have always wanted to visit Steep Holm. Which, as you know, is what we did today. There're a few other places we'll probably visit while we're in this neck of the woods. It's a beautiful part of the country. Don't you think?'

Jemima marvelled at the fact that the man appeared to be so relaxed. He didn't appear to be annoyed at having been brought to a police station. It was as though he was happy to chat about his family and their holiday. 'No doubt you're wondering why you're here, so I'll get to the point, Mr Blakeman. Shortly after seven o'clock this morning, Judge Rory Lawson, who presided over Joseph's trial, was abducted. He—'

'Let me stop you there, Inspector,' interjected Blakeman. 'I don't know where you're going with this, but we had nothing to do with this abduction. I can understand why you might've jumped to the conclusion that we did. But I assure you, you've got this wrong. Leonard and I were already at sea, making the crossing over to Steep Holm. While we were on the island we were with other people for the entire time. If you don't believe me then ask the others that were on the same trip.'

'You have to admit that it's possible that Leonard could have arranged for the abduction,' said Broadbent.

'I admit no such thing! It's an outrageous suggestion. You say that Joseph threatened his judge during the trial, and I'm sure it's on record that he did. But the lad's serving his sentence. Why would Leonard, or anyone else in our family do anything that could risk Joseph's chances of getting parole further down the line? It doesn't make sense.

'It's broken Jackie's heart that her lad's in prison. She'd have Len's guts for garters if she thought he'd do anything to risk Joe getting out of there. It just wouldn't happen.

'And apart from that, do you honestly think I'd risk my own liberty or career by being party to such a thing? I abide by the law. I can understand that you could think that I might have questionable morals. It goes with the territory in my line of work. But let me assure you, everything I do is within the remit of the law. Yes, I do the utmost to protect my clients, but that's what I'm paid for, and everyone, no matter what they've been accused of, is entitled to have legal representation.'

As much as Jemima detested this family, she couldn't argue with what Liam was saying. It was the way the legal system worked.

'As well as being my brother, Leonard is also my client, and I can categorically state that he has had nothing to do with today's events. It's absurd to think otherwise. Leonard would have to have been out of his mind to arrange for this judge to be abducted while he was located in the vicinity of the crime. It's a ludicrous suggestion.

'I'm sure you'll agree that some professions are more dangerous than others. It's hardly surprising that a judge would make some enemies along the way. Newsflash! Criminals don't like being sent down.

'I know nothing of this judge, but I'd bet you anything that he has far more enemies than most people could ever imagine. And depending on the trials he's presided over, a lot of those people who have a grudge against him are not the sort of people you'd want to get on the wrong side of.'

Jemima silently agreed with everything Liam Blakeman was saying. She had nothing to hold him on, and so did the only thing she could do. 'You're free to go, Mr Blakeman.'

'Have you interviewed Leonard yet?' he asked as he stood to leave.

'No.'

'In that case, as his lawyer, I insist on being present.'

'There'll be no need,' said Jemima. Blakeman would not allow his client to incriminate himself in any way. And as much as she refused to believe in coincidences, she had to acknowledge that the Waverleys had a legitimate reason for visiting Cardiff. With the four men spending the entire day on Steep Holm there was no way they could have been involved in Lawson's abduction.

'Your sister-in-law is still at the station. She'll be released within the next few minutes. Perhaps you could pass her a message?'

'Yes?'

'Please inform her that I've spoken with a prison official but was unable to get special dispensation for her to see Joseph today. She'll need to follow the usual channel to obtain another visiting order.'

From the contemptuous look that Liam gave her, Jemima could tell that the man knew that she hadn't asked for any special dispensation for the visit. It was a petty victory which meant little in the circumstances. But it buoyed Jemima's spirits that she had done something to upset a member of the Waverley family.

# CHAPTER 13

With each passing hour, Jemima was regretting having returned. Were she still at home she could have spent time playing with Finlay, watching him discover something new and taking delight in his innocent view of the world. Instead, she had chosen to return to this godforsaken place, which had a way of grinding you down. In the space of a few hours any optimism she'd had had been sucked out of her. She was back on the treadmill, running as fast as she could but getting nowhere.

In the distance there was the sound of raised voices coming from somewhere within the station.

'All going on today,' muttered Broadbent.

'Guv, a word,' said DS Morgan.

'What is it, Steve?'

'Don't know if you heard the ruckus downstairs?'

'Yeah. What's going on?'

'I looked at the other two highlighted names on the list. Defendants who made threats against Lawson. A lowlife named Grant Templar was one of them. He was second in command of the VBs.'

'Who are they? And why did you say *was*?'

'The Valley Boys, or the VBs, as they like to be known. They're a gang that's come to prominence within the last year,' said Broadbent.

'Explains why I haven't heard of them.' It was yet another example of how quickly the world was changing, and it wasn't for the better. 'County lines?'

'Not as far as we know,' said DC Lane. 'They're a bunch of scumbags who to a certain extent have helped keep the influence of the county lines gang under control. There's a turf war underway. Probably not a bad thing as they're killing each other off. Let's face it we could all do with having less of those bastards on the street, preying on vulnerable kids. Trouble is that with the way things have gone, there have been instances when innocent bystanders have got caught up. Been in the wrong place at the wrong time.'

'The point is, they might be lowlife trash, but I don't think you can rule them out of pulling something like this off. Especially since, nine days ago, Templar got shanked. Bled out in the shower. Word is that the guards accepted a bung to look the other way,' DS Morgan continued. 'The head of the VBs is Grant's elder brother Jarvis, and those two were close. It's gone nuclear on their turf since Grant was offed. Jarvis is out for blood. Not just against those responsible for killing his little bro, but against anyone who had a hand in sending him down. He's got numerous people eager to please him, which makes the VBs a likely candidate for having snatched Lawson. Jarvis isn't looking for a payday. He'll want to hurt him until he can't take any more and then they'll finish him off.'

'Excellent work, Steve. I think you could be on to something. The death of his brother could easily have set Jarvis out on the path of revenge, and it'd certainly explain why there's been no ransom demand,' said Jemima. 'Is he among the ones they've brought in?'

'No. There's a team of officers out looking for him, but so far there've been no sightings. They've brought in his new number two, Paul Drake. He and Jarvis have been friends since they were kids, and Paul was one of the VBs from the get-go. So, if anyone knows where Jarvis is, it's him.'

Jemima nodded. 'If the VBs are behind the abduction, it's possible that Jarvis could be holed up with Lawson, doing God knows what until he's ready to finish him off. I'm coming with you to interview Drake. We have to push him hard. Find out if he knows anything about Lawson's abduction and get him to give up Jarvis's location. As he's got a long-term close relationship with Jarvis, it's unlikely he'll let anything slip, but as things stand, he's our only shot.'

'No problem, but before we go, you need to know that I'm waiting to hear about a nonce named Kelvin Baker,' said Morgan. 'His name was highlighted, so I've had officers out searching for him. He's a convicted paedophile, recently released. Goes without saying he's on the sex offenders register and it's part of his bail conditions that he reports twice weekly to his nearest station.'

'Let me guess. He's absconded?' Jemima knew the answer before she'd even asked the question.

It was the same old story repeated ad nauseum. With excessive pressures on the justice system, all sorts of dangerous prisoners were allowed to return to society. The assessment system was flawed. For those considered suitable for early release, conditions such as having to wear a tag and abide by curfew restrictions were routinely used, along with regularly reporting to police stations and attending meetings with parole officers. The theory was fine. Yet in practice it was often a disaster. There were some paroled prisoners who would follow the rules, but many prisoners were incarcerated because they either couldn't follow or had no intention of following rules, and it was not unusual for them to abscond shortly after their release.

'Not as far as I know. He's fulfilled his bail conditions. Just wasn't at his registered address when they went to pick him up. Got another hour or so before his curfew kicks in.'

'Did he threaten Lawson?'

'It's a strange one. Wasn't so much a direct threat against him. More of a general threat. Probably just bluster. But as he was being taken down, he looked directly at Lawson and shouted out that he knew a lot of things about a lot of people.'

'What does that mean?' asked Jemima.

'No idea. Apparently, Lawson didn't react and neither did anyone else.'

'Umm, right everyone, I know it's a big ask but you have to keep going. It might seem like we're on a hiding to nothing, but we can't afford to ease up or lose concentration. Don't dismiss anything you think might have legs. Lawson's abduction wasn't a random act. He was taken for a reason. We just don't know what that is. But somewhere in his life, there'll be something that caused this. We just need to find it.' She turned to the new officers. 'Aadi, Victoria, keep working your way through the DVLA data. Cross-reference it with names from the court cases. Gaynor, keep going through those lists. Ring Gareth and get him to send someone over with whatever they've managed to compile in the last hour. We need a regular feed of that data. Dan, give Gaynor a hand. We need to sift through the information quicker. When Steve and I have finished interviewing the VBs, we'll review progress. In the meantime, if any of you come up with a viable lead then be sure to let me know.'

She made her way to the interview room with Morgan. 'How do you want to play this?' he asked.

'This is no time to play nice. It's not as if we know whether the VBs are behind Lawson's abduction, and if they're not this could be a huge waste of time. But as he's a seasoned gang member we need to go in hard. Threaten to throw the book at him and see what spills.'

Jemima's first impression of Paul Drake was that this was a ferret in human form. The man was small and wiry. His complexion pale and pitted. His beady eyes kept darting about as though he was desperately trying to spot an escape route.

He nodded in approval. 'Not bad. Not bad, indeed.' But as his eyes didn't keep still, it was impossible to tell which of them the man was referring to.

Jemima was repulsed by what came out of his mouth. Not by Drake's words — they were the usual unimaginative garbage she'd heard countless times before. It was the man's breath, so foul, it suggested that he was rotting on the inside. She took a seat, swallowing hard as she fought the urge to gag. It was an incentive, if she had ever needed one, to make this encounter short and to the point. With the preliminaries out of the way, the interview began in earnest.

'I'll get straight to the point, Paul. You were arrested on the street with almost seven hundred pounds in your pocket.'

'I won it on the gee-gees, innit.' He smiled, pleased with his explanation.

'Show us your betting slip.'

'You what?'

'You heard me, so cut the crap. We all know you didn't win that money. You got it when you did your rounds, collecting off the dealers.'

'Dunno what you mean.' Drake shook his head and folded his arms.

'Your life as you know it is over, Paul. We've more than enough on you to not allow you to walk out of here a free man—'

'Ohhh man! I 'aven't done anythin',' he whined.

'Interrupt me again and I'll make sure you never see the light of day,' said Jemima.

'Stick to the facts, Inspector,' said the duty solicitor. Until that moment the woman had sat there with her eyes closed, and Jemima had wondered if she was using the opportunity to catch up on her sleep.

'We've had you under surveillance, Paul. We know the route you take. The collection points. We've photographs of you collecting the money.'

'I'd like to see those photographs,' said the solicitor.

The woman was beginning to get on Jemima's nerves. She ignored her and went to say something else. Sensing the solicitor was about to repeat her demand — a demand Jemima would be unable to fulfil as there were no photographs of Paul Drake — Jemima held up her hand to silence the woman. Surprisingly, it worked.

'As things stand, you're facing a long stretch, Paul. You might find it a walk in the park. Or you might get shanked like your mate, Grant. But I can make those charges go away.'

'Eh?' Drake was clearly confused. He looked blankly from one to the other, trying to make sense of what was happening. Until his solicitor spoke.

'They're offering you a deal, Mr Drake. You tell them what they want to know, and they'll drop the charges.'

'That's right, Paul. So, where were you at seven o'clock this morning?'

'In bed, innit,' he drawled.

'Paul, we all know you come from the Cynon valley. You've probably never set foot outside of Wales. So, stop putting on that fake accent. It's pathetic and makes you sound stupid. It might impress the kids on the street, but it doesn't work in here.'

'I's tellin' youse the truth. I was in bed.'

'And can anyone corroborate that?' asked Morgan.

'You what?' Drake's eyes almost disappeared completely as he wrinkled his nose.

Jemima sighed. It was already apparent that Templar didn't keep Drake around for his sharp intellect. 'Was anyone with you?'

'Nah! I was on me own like. I'd had a skinful and was sleepin' it off.'

Jemima believed the man was telling the truth. At least the part about his being alone. It was hard to imagine someone desperate enough to want to spend time with him in a confined space. 'Where is Jarvis Templar?'

'Dunno no Jarvis,' he replied. He did his best to make eye contact as he uttered the lie, but the effort proved too much for him.

'Paul, you have the letters V and B tattooed on the back of your hands. As does every member of the Valley Boys. We know that you're tight with Jarvis. You were in the same class as him at school.'

Paul's shoulders sagged. He had finally accepted that there was no way to convince these officers that he wasn't connected to Jarvis Templar. 'OK, I admit we hang out sometimes. But that's all.'

'I'll ask you again. Where is Jarvis?'

'I dunno. Look, he took Grant's death hard. He's gone off to get his head together. 'S'all I know.'

'Word is he was angry,' said Jemima.

'Yeah? Well, I don't blame him. He lost his little bro.'

'Believe me, Paul, I get it. I really do. The question is, is Jarvis planning to do anything about it?'

'Like wha'?'

'Like make people pay.'

'And 'ow's he gonna do that? 'Im that shanked Grant's cosied up inside, innit.'

'What about Judge Lawson? Is Jarvis going after him?'

'Youse've gotta be kiddin' me! The judge didn't shank Grant.'

'Well, someone snatched Lawson this morning. Forced his car to stop and dragged him from it into another vehicle. We're thinking it's down to Jarvis.'

Paul began to laugh, forcing even more foul air out of his lungs in the general direction of Jemima and Morgan.

'What's so funny?'

'Good on whoever took him, I say. But it's got nothin' to do with Jarvis, or the VBs. None of us have a vehicle. Me and Jarv can't even drive.'

'I'm returning you to the holding cell for now, Mr Drake.'

'You said you'd lemme go!'

'Not yet. We might need to question you further and we can hold you for a while yet.' Jemima headed out of the room without a backward glance.

'Lyin' bitch!' screamed Drake.

Steve Morgan followed closely behind Jemima. They were both glad to distance themselves from the putrid stench.

# CHAPTER 14

It was the second time that afternoon that Jemima had felt the urge to scrub herself clean. Yet, as with the previous occasion, there was no chance of that happening. She was determined it would be the first thing she did when she got home. But it was anyone's guess as to when that would be. The way things were going it was almost certain she, along with the rest of them, would be pulling an all-nighter.

'Did you believe Drake when he said that Jarvis isn't behind Lawson's disappearance?' asked Morgan.

The question broke through Jemima's thoughts and brought her back to the here and now. There was a moment of self-doubt as she questioned her fitness to lead this investigation. It was a huge responsibility for such a big case on her first day back at work. But a man's life was in her hands. She owed it to Lawson and his family to do everything in her power to find him.

'I don't know. I've not come across Jarvis before, so I've nothing to base a judgement on. That said, I wouldn't trust a word that comes out of Drake's mouth. Though if Jarvis has a similar level of intelligence as Drake, it's difficult to imagine them pulling off the abduction. Do me a favour and tell the others I'm calling an update meeting in five minutes.

Instead of narrowing our options, we're throwing up a hell of a lot of questions. It's inevitable most things will turn out to be irrelevant. But my concern is that while we're rooting around trying to find a viable lead, we'll miss the one thing that will break this case wide open.'

'I'll let everyone know.' Morgan turned towards the incident room.

Jemima continued along the corridor to Kennedy's office. Despite the DCI putting her in charge of the operational side of things, she knew that he needed to be kept informed. Part of her was grateful for his obvious confidence in her abilities. In normal circumstances she would have relished the opportunity, but as this was her first day back after such an extended period of leave it was like being thrown overboard, mid-ocean, without a flotation aid.

The relative silence in that section of the corridor was shattered as Kennedy bellowed from inside his office. Someone was receiving the full force of his anger. Jemima was unable to make out what he was yelling, but as she got within a few feet of his door she heard him roar once again. The sound was pure rage. It made her shiver. There was barely time to take her next step when something crashed. She could feel the shockwave through the floor.

Fearing what lay ahead, Jemima ran the last few steps, ready to confront whatever was happening inside Kennedy's office. As the blinds were closed, she listened intently as she reached for the door handle. It was disconcerting that there was no sound coming from inside the room. Taking a deep breath, she pressed down and allowed the door to swing open.

'What do you want?' Kennedy was sitting behind his desk with his head in his hands, not even bothering to look up to see who he was addressing.

A quick glance told Jemima all she needed to know and she allowed her muscles to relax. There was no one else in the room. But it was obvious that all was not well with the DCI. The office looked as though it had been trashed.

'You all right, sir?' In all the years she'd known him, she had never seen Kennedy like this. He had always been calm and approachable even though he was a stickler for the rules.

'I'm fine, Huxley. Don't you bother yourself about me. So, do you have anything to report?'

'We're following numerous lines of enquiry, but they seem to be throwing up more questions.'

'So why are you bothering me?'

Jemima was shocked. Something was clearly wrong with Kennedy. He always insisted on being kept informed. And as she hadn't seen anyone else in the corridor when she heard the ruckus coming from the room, the only conclusion she could draw was that the DCI had trashed the place himself.

'Just letting you know that I'm about to hold a briefing session. Have you got anywhere with that key card?'

'No, I haven't, and it's unlikely to be important. Get out, and do whatever it is you're doing, Huxley. I've made you SIO on this case. So go and do your effin' job! You don't need me to hold your hand.'

Jemima couldn't believe what she was hearing.

'And don't go opening your mouth about this,' he called after her, sweeping his arm in a wide arc at the mess. 'This is nothing. I'm just having an off day and I can do without any pointless tittle-tattle. If this gets out, I'll know it's come from you, and there'll be consequences.'

Jemima's brow furrowed, but she said nothing. Kennedy's behaviour was uncharacteristic and unwarranted. There was clearly something worrying him, but now was not a suitable moment to find out what it was. There would be plenty of time for that once they had found Lawson. Instead of saying anything that would undoubtedly antagonise him further, she took a deep breath and bit down hard on her lip.

If someone had spoken to her in that way under any other circumstances, she would have had it out with them there and then. But this was no ordinary day, and she was convinced that there were things going on with the DCI that she was unaware of.

With the scope of the Lawson case spreading like an oil slick, Jemima was faced with no other option than to dig deep and do everything in her power to ensure that the team covered all the bases. Their priority was to locate Lawson and get him back alive. Whatever was up with Kennedy would have to wait until she had time to deal with it. Though, the way things were going, she had no idea how soon that was likely to be.

Jemima entered the incident room to find that Gareth Peters had returned and was deep in conversation with Broadbent. When Jemima asked for everyone's attention, the room fell silent. 'I take it the others are still working through the records at the courthouse?' she asked.

'Yeah. It's a hell of a task.' said Gareth. 'I've brought the latest extracts with me, and I'll head back over as soon as the briefing session ends.'

'Has anyone got a lead?'

'I've come across something, but I'm not sure if it's relevant,' said Broadbent.

'What is it?' Jemima hoped that whatever Dan was about to tell her would be their much-needed breakthrough piece of information.

'I was going through the list and I noticed a defendant named Zach Trevelyan-Goode. He's not someone I've come across, but his name's quite unusual.'

'Spit it out, Dan.' Jemima wasn't usually short with him, but time was of the essence, and she didn't want a rambling explanation when bullet points would do.

Broadbent flashed her a look that told her in no uncertain terms that he wasn't impressed with her sharpness. 'You know what I'm like. Can't go more than an hour or so without eating. So, I popped to the canteen to grab a packet of sandwiches and that's when I heard the gossip. The deceased of that incident that occurred this morning on North Road, close to St Jo's Primary, was Emyr Trevelyan-Goode. And the list of trials I was working though had a Zach Trevelyan-Goode. And you've got to admit, it's an unusual surname,' said Broadbent. 'I've just left a message for Glen Buchannan to get back to me. He's the SIO on the Emyr case.'

'Great work. I've a feeling you're on to something, Dan. Given the surname, I'd say there's a good chance Zach and Emyr are linked. What's more, I can't recall there ever being two abductions within the space of hour or so, in this area. And we've got it in black and white that there's a link between Lawson and Zach Trevelyan-Goode. So if we can establish a connection between Zach and Emyr . . .' Jemima's mind raced ahead as she tried to join the jots and come up with a reasonable hypothesis as to why these two abductions had occurred in relatively close proximity and within such a short space of time.

'Buchannan's going to be up to his eyes on it, so he's unlikely to stop what he's doing and speak to us. Get back on the blower and chase up another officer working that case. Tell them there's a possibility that it could be linked to Lawson's disappearance, and that I need Buchannan to speak to me immediately.'

Dan nodded as he reached out for the phone. As usual, Jemima's decisiveness had buoyed his confidence. It was something he had missed over the last year. His gut instinct had told him he was on to something. Yet although he had gone some way towards following up on his hunch, he had hesitated at pushing it when the officer he had spoken to told him that there was no one available to speak to him about the case. He knew it was a lack of confidence, which was something he needed to overcome if he were ever to get promoted. Until the evening of Ashton's death he'd never been backward at coming forward. But the events leading up to that moment had made him wary. Especially since no matter what anyone said, he still believed that he should have somehow prevented the attack that had led to their friend and colleague losing his life.

He felt as though he'd been treading water since Jemima had gone on maternity leave. It was pathetic really. He'd missed her. They all had. But she was back now, and when this case was done and dusted things would return to normal. With Jemima there to guide him, he'd stop second-guessing himself and get his career back on track.

'Gareth, do you have the trial transcript for the Zach Trevelyan-Goode case?' asked Jemima.

'No, it's over at the court. We listed defendants' names, the charges they faced and the verdict. Give me a sec and I'll tell you what we have.' He ran his finger down the list, searching for the appropriate entry. 'OK. He was facing allegations of revenge porn. Two different women claimed he had uploaded intimate photographs and videos without their consent.'

'And the verdict?'

'Guilty, but Lawson sentenced him to community service,' said Gareth.

'I want those transcript papers on my desk in ten minutes. Don't take any bullshit off the court officials about documents having to remain in their building. Just tell them that Lawson's life is on the line.'

Gareth had barely made it to the door when Broadbent called, 'I've got Glen Buchannan on the line.'

'Transfer it to my extension.' Jemima hurriedly opened her drawer to take out a pen and paper. 'DI Jemima Huxley.'

'DI Glen Buchannan. Your sergeant explained the situation at your end. I'd heard that the judge was missing but with everything that's going on at this end I didn't pay it any attention. I didn't realise he'd been abducted. So I didn't make a connection to our case. Otherwise, I'd have got in touch. After all, what's the chances of there being two abductions on the same morning in an area like this?'

'My thinking exactly,' said Jemima.

'Have you made any progress?'

'To be honest we're just pissing in the wind trying to make sense of the little information we have. There're no witnesses, but Forensics suggest that Lawson was dragged from his car. We're confident that he was forced to stop his vehicle. It appears that there may have been another vehicle trailing him until he was ambushed. There was no significant blood loss at the scene, and we've been unable to locate him. So, we're looking into the possibility that he's been abducted.'

'And a man like Lawson would have a hell of a lot of enemies.'

'Exactly, which is why we're looking at cases he presided over. That's what led us to your case. We're not sure there's any connection, but a guilty defendant in one of Lawson's cases had the same surname as your victim.'

'Umm, that does sound interesting. Though, as things stand, I can't say for certain that my victim is actually Emyr Trevelyan-Goode. But I'm fairly confident it is, as he was wearing a medical bracelet.'

'I don't understand — are you saying he was a hospital patient?' Jemima thought Buchannan must be referring to the plastic band fitted around an in-patient's wrist.

'No, this is something people with certain medical conditions are encouraged to wear. It lists their name, any medical condition, known allergies, blood group and details for next of kin. Apparently, our guy had epilepsy. But as helpful as it is, I'm still trying to make contact with the next of kin in order to get a formal identification. Which, given the extent of the injuries, might not be as easy as it sounds . . .'

'In that case, I need to ask you a huge favour,' said Jemima.

'Ask away.'

'If the family member identifies your victim as Emyr Trevelyan-Goode, I'd like you to find out if he's related in any way to Zach Trevelyan-Goode.'

'I take it that this Zach was the defendant in the case Lawson presided over?'

'That's right. I know it's a flimsy connection between these two abductions. But it needs to be followed up asap. Especially since Lawson is still missing.'

'Leave it with me. I'll get back to you as soon as I know anything.' Buchannan terminated the call.

# CHAPTER 15

While Jemima sat at her desk perusing the transcript of Zach Trevelyan-Goode's trial, Broadbent had been tasked with familiarising himself with the police investigation that had led to the suspect being charged in the first place. Every so often she could hear his grunts of disapproval, interspersed by the odd 'Seriously!' or 'Oh, for fuck's sake!'. She knew exactly how he felt as the words on the page made difficult reading. She found them particularly emotive having herself been the victim of an horrendous sexual assault. And it was both shocking and disturbing that despite the jury unanimously finding Trevelyan-Goode guilty, Rory Lawson had not seen fit to impose a custodial sentence.

She did not doubt the courage it would have taken for both victims to come forward and report him and couldn't help but admire them. Their stories were different from her own experience. Neither of these women claimed to have been physically attacked by Trevelyan-Goode. Indeed, they openly admitted that their sexual encounters with him had been consensual, and the result of being in what each woman had initially considered to be a healthy relationship with him. Their problems began when those relationships ended, and they discovered that the man they had trusted had betrayed them in the most awful way.

The prosecution portrayed Trevelyan-Goode as controlling and manipulative. Having entered into a relationship with each woman, he had displayed a similar pattern of behaviour. What had initially been viewed as attentive, considerate behaviour eventually became overbearing, bullying and controlling. And when each woman found the strength to walk away, Trevelyan-Goode posted videos and stills of them online. The most intimate moments of their lives were out there for anyone to see. Nothing was left to the imagination. And when the police searched his home and examined his computer, they discovered that he was part of a network of like-minded individuals who took pleasure in sharing revenge porn and, in some instances, got paid handsomely for it.

Jemima felt for these women. Trevelyan-Goode's vindictiveness had sentenced them both to a lifetime of humiliation. He had treated them appallingly, as those images would be out there for ever. Shared, sold and viewed repeatedly. Never knowing if people they knew, or even random strangers, had seen them. It was the worst possible mindfuck.

It had taken guts to give evidence in court. Trevelyan-Goode's counsel had dredged through every aspect of each of their lives as she had set out to discredit them. They would both have known before entering the witness box that this would be the inevitable strategy the defence team would adopt. After all, they were not there to act as moral guardians. They were there to do everything in their power to ensure that their client got off.

There was no doubting the fact that Trevelyan-Goode was a reprehensible character. The picture painted of him throughout the trial was of a man with no moral compass. Someone who, even while on trial for his crimes, still apparently felt no remorse for his actions. It was no surprise that the jury had seen him for what he was and returned a unanimous guilty verdict.

But as Jemima continued to read the transcript, her eyes widened. She reached Judge Lawson's statement where he summed up the issues for the jury to think about as they retired to consider their verdict. If she had been at the court while he was making his closing remarks, she might have thought that his instructions were balanced and fair. But knowing that despite a unanimous guilty verdict, Lawson had failed to set a custodial sentence, it caused her to question his impartiality. And if this crazy thought had occurred to her, then what had the victims and their families thought? Had this been a subtle attempt to lead the jury into finding Trevelyan-Goode innocent?

*Ladies and gentlemen of the jury, you have heard the evidence presented by both the prosecution and the defence counsels. I will shortly be asking you to retire to carefully consider the evidence to enable you to arrive at a verdict upon which you are all agreed.*

*The prosecution has presented the case of how the defendant posted explicit images of these young women online. They have called upon witnesses to assure you that these images were uploaded by Mr Trevelyan-Goode and originated from material filmed by him for the purpose of making it available on the internet.*

*It is the prosecution's case that neither of the young women in question knew of or gave their consent for these images to be taken in the first place. However, it is not in question that the sexual activities in which Mr Trevelyan-Goode played a part were undertaken between consenting adults.*

*In your deliberations, you must consider whether these young women were unwitting victims or whether they were complicit all along, only to backtrack and deny their decision when ultimately faced with the implications of their actions and any subsequent shame they might have felt.*

*I ask that you approach your deliberations in an impartial manner. The subject matter is undeniably emotive. The thought of filming then uploading footage of such an intimate nature might make you feel uncomfortable. But if it was the case that this was done consensually, as Mr Trevelyan-Goode asserts happened, then you must find him not guilty. Do not allow your personal feelings to cloud your judgements. I ask you to let the facts speak for themselves.*

*When considering these matters, you must give weight to the burden of proof and bear in mind the premise upon which our justice system stands. In other words, it is down to the prosecution to prove beyond all reasonable doubt that the defendant carried out these acts with malicious intent and without the knowledge of the two women in question.*

*You will now retire, elect a foreman and consider your verdict.*

Ninety minutes later, the jury sent word that they had reached a unanimous decision. The speed at which they had arrived at this suggested that there had been very little deliberation, as they must all have been of a similar mind.

When the foreman declared they had found the defendant guilty, Judge Lawson instructed that the defendant be taken down and returned to court the following week to allow time for him to receive victim impact statements that would feed into his decision-making process for sentencing.

The written impact statement from the first victim, Merryn Andrews read:

*I entered into a relationship with Zach Trevelyan-Goode in good faith when I was a trusting, naïve and optimistic eighteen-year-old. He was four years my senior, and we were together for ten months. At that time, I had very little life experience and was excited about what the future had in store for me. At first, Zach gave me no cause for concern. I fell in love with him and thought that he loved me. That changed when I discovered that he had cheated on me and I ended our relationship.*

*I am a shy, conventional person. Everyone who knows me will tell you that I do not like to draw attention to myself.*

*That is why it is so devastating to have discovered that Zach posted those highly personal images of me online. He clearly thought nothing of it, but his actions have destroyed me.*

*It is no exaggeration to say that I feel as though my life is over. Before this happened, I had hopes and dreams. Now I am existing in a waking nightmare. I hate myself so much that I've even considered ending it all.*

*Before this happened, I would have described myself as successful, hardworking, and optimistic. I was ambitious and had a career with good prospects, but now I've lost my job as a trainee manager of a local supermarket. It was a demanding role and I used to look forward to going into work. I took pride in myself and what I was achieving, but now it's impossible for me to imagine carrying on. I had a public-facing role, and when those images were put out there, I was too scared and ashamed to go into work each day. I just couldn't face anyone.*

*Unless something like this has happened to you, you cannot imagine how debilitating and humiliating the effects are. I have no choice but to try to live with what he did to me for the rest of my life. It is beyond distressing to know that thousands, if not millions, of people have seen and will continue to see the most intimate parts of my body. It's brought shame on me, my parents, my brother and my grandparents. My granddad had a stroke brought on by the stress of what happened, and my mother just cries all the time.*

*Whatever sentence is imposed upon Zach Trevelyan-Goode, he will have the certainty of that coming to an end. He will have something to look forward to. I will not have that luxury, and neither will my family.*

*The moment Zach posted those images online, he saddled me with a life sentence, and I will never be free until the day I die. He has made me feel worthless, has turned me into something for men to fantasise about as they pleasure themselves. I'm terrified to leave the house, unable to make eye contact with anyone, and reluctant to speak to anyone. My body has been shared against my will, and it feels as if there's nothing left of me. There's nothing that's just mine.*

116

*The old me has gone. I'm just a shell, going through the motions. I've resigned myself to never finding happiness or even a basic level of contentment again. I can't imagine how I could, as Zach's left me incapable of trusting anyone.*

The other victim impact statement came from Kareena Daniels, who had been the woman Zach had hooked up with while he was still with Merryn. Theirs had been an on-off relationship, neither intending it to be a serious affair. Kareena's statement was less detailed than Merryn's, though there was no doubt that she was furious with Zach. She expounded upon her humiliating experience when discovering images of herself online. She explained that as an undergraduate in her final year at university, it was her belief that the emotional strain resulting from Zach's actions had prevented her from focusing upon her studies. She was afraid this would result in her attaining a lower grade than she had been predicted to get and was also fearful that it could negatively affect her future career prospects should potential employers find out about it.

Kareena demanded that Zach receive the maximum allowable sentence to send a message to anyone else tempted to post revenge porn online. There was no mention of any impact upon a wider family network or of her shutting herself away from the world because of what had happened. She just wanted Zach to pay for his actions.

As Jemima read the case file everything going on around her faded to insignificance. This case was fascinating and horrifying, and the implications for the victims were inconceivably awful. Having herself been the victim of a sadistic sexual assault, Jemima knew exactly how difficult it was to come to terms with what had happened to her. Yet what had happened to these women seemed even worse. They had not been subjected to a physical attack, but mentally and emotionally their own bodies had been used as a weapon to humiliate, even destroy them. And given the nature of the internet and how easily those images could be shared, their ordeal would never end.

As Jemima continued reading, she eventually reached the record of Lawson's decision when sentencing Trevelyan-Goode. Having issued the usual preamble, the judge went on to explain his decision. For someone who was generally thought of as reaching his conclusions in a fair and measured way, what he had said was possibly ill-advised and demonstrated a lack of understanding of the psychological implications for the victims of this particularly disturbing modern phenomenon. By not imposing a custodial sentence it could be seen as trivialising the act, giving the go-ahead for others to post revenge pornography online. Whichever way you looked at it, his decision sent out the wrong message.

*Zach Trevelyan-Goode, you have been found guilty by this court of law, and the evidence has shown that your actions have caused distress to the victims. I am aware of the seriousness of this crime, and in no way condone what you did. Be under no illusion that under normal circumstances I would have no choice but to impose a custodial sentence. However, it is my opinion that you too will undoubtedly suffer the stigma of your ill-advised actions. You are still a relatively young man. Given your age and the fact that you have no doubt been influenced by distasteful practices within modern culture, I trust that as you mature you will reflect and feel shame for what you have done.*

*Evidence suggests that you have previously been of good character, and this conviction might very well have a negative impact on your life chances. The role of our prisons is to reform not to punish. But given the lack of capacity in our prison system I see no justification for a custodial sentence. Therefore, I sentence you to two years' suspended sentence, during which restrictions will be placed upon your movements. In addition to that, you will undertake twenty weeks of community service, and you will have to meet with and abide by any rules imposed by your probation officer.*

*You will be required to make financial recompense to both of the victims. The amount will be determined by this court.*

*This is an opportunity for you to reflect upon your past behaviour, recognise the harm you have done and make better choices going forward.*

Jemima was sufficiently self-aware to recognise the fact that her own experience affected her impartiality when it came to crimes of a sexual nature. Yet, given the impact that the crime had and would continue to have on the two victims, the verdict seemed far too lenient and wholly inappropriate.

As she was about to close the file, her phone rang. She was pleased to hear Glen Buchannan's voice.

'Jemima, I've just finished the identification with the victim's next of kin, and I can confirm that he was indeed Emyr Trevelyan-Goode. But that's not the best of it.'

Jemima gripped the phone tighter as she felt her heart rate increase. She could tell from the tone of Buchannan's voice that he was about to impart some crucial information that would give them their first definite lead. Unable to stop herself, she interjected, 'He's related to Zach.'

'Not only is he related. They're identical twins.'

'You've got to be kidding me!' shrieked Jemima. Her voice shattered the relative silence of the room, abruptly breaking everyone's concentration. It was only natural that all eyes turned towards her in their eagerness to hear about whatever development she had just learned of.

Sensing that everyone's eyes were upon her, Jemima glanced up and gave a thumbs-up sign. 'There's a chance it's a case of mistaken identity,' she said, as she continued her conversation with Buchannan.

'I agree, but I need to carry out background checks on Emyr. After all, it's conceivable that whoever snatched him could have got the twin they were after.'

'I'll follow up on Zach since he's got a proven link to Lawson. We should keep each other informed.'

'Definitely,' said Buchannan, before disconnecting the call.

Jemima addressed the other officers in the room. 'You'll want to hear this.' She hadn't finished speaking before everyone had gathered around. 'We've recently established a link between Rory Lawson and a scumbag named Zach Trevelyan-Goode. Dan was the one to spot it. What I've just learned, and what has the potential to give us our first decent lead, is that at around about the same time as Lawson was snatched, Zach's identical twin brother was also abducted.'

There were audible gasps and a couple of expletives muttered as the implications of what Jemima had just told them hit home.

'How do you want us to play this, guv?' asked Steve Morgan.

'I want you and Gaynor to keep plugging away at your task. This is the most hopeful lead so far, but until we're absolutely certain that the abductions are connected you should keep looking through those lists of trials. Aadi and Nancy, you need to keep on doing what you're doing. We still need to identify the vehicle and its driver. Dan and I are going to speak to Zach's victims. Reading the transcript of Zach's trial has been an eye-opener. What that scumbag did was despicable. But Rory Lawson's actions are at best questionable. It demonstrates to me that he is not a man who is above reproach.'

'I agree,' said Broadbent. 'Zach's a right scumbag. It makes me sick just reading the case file. I can't begin to imagine what those two women must feel like. I just don't understand how he could've been given community service. We had a watertight case against him. He was found guilty, and it was a unanimous verdict. He should be serving time for what he did.'

'I can't get my head around it either,' said Jemima.

'As far as I'm concerned, Lawson failed those women. They put their trust in the justice system and they were let down spectacularly. It's unconscionable. It's basically saying they're worthless. I tell you now, if some lowlife had done that to Caroline, I wouldn't be responsible for my actions.' Dan was usually level-headed and easy-going, but his voice had dropped to an almost feral growl as he struggled to contain his anger.

'I'd say that's a perfectly natural reaction.' Jemima gently touched his shoulder and felt his muscles relax. 'It makes me wonder if someone close to those women felt the same way and tried to do something about it. After all, Zach and Emyr were identical twins.'

'Sounds reasonable. So, what's our next move?' asked Dan.

'I want you to find addresses for both victims. In Merryn Andrews's victim impact statement, she mentions how the incident adversely affected her family. Particularly her parents, grandparents and brother. I want names and contact details for all of them.' She turned to Gareth. 'I'd like you to do a background check on Kareena Daniels. There was no mention of any family or anyone else close to her. So, I want you to do some digging into her personal circumstances. Find out if anyone was likely to take the law into their own hands to seek justice for her. Then I want you to check out whether or not Kareena or any of her close associates could have had a hand in Lawson's abduction. Go and speak to her. But don't go on your own. Take a uniformed officer with you.'

# CHAPTER 16

It occurred to Jemima that if Lawson had given Trevelyan-Goode a suspended sentence, when the morally right course of action would have been to impose a custodial sentence, it might be worth looking closer at his sentencing of other prisoners. She wasn't aware of any rumours about the judge being particularly lenient and, knowing what station gossip was like, she was all but certain someone would have talked about it over the years, if that had been the case. However, it was worth checking out. If victims and their families felt that justice had not been served even after a jury had reached a guilty verdict, it could substantially increase the number of people who held a grudge against Lawson.

She glanced towards the two officers diligently working their way through the list of names supplied by Gareth's team and thought it was time to expand their brief. They wouldn't thank her for it, as the task was mind-numbingly boring and repetitive — they would have to have look again at every guilty verdict and make a judgement as to whether Lawson's sentencing had been appropriate.

The Trevelyan-Goode lead looked promising, but it was far too early to put all their eggs in one basket. There was a realistic possibility that someone like Lawson could have numerous enemies. And there was always the chance that the other abduction was a huge coincidence, which ultimately might turn out to have nothing to do with what had happened to the judge. As they still had no clear idea about who had abducted Lawson, they really needed to ensure that they identified everyone with a potential vendetta.

Everyone was in a sombre mood, aware of the need to find that elusive crucial link, yet at the same time trying to ignore the fact that they were nowhere closer to identifying the abductors, let alone finding the man, despite their considerable efforts.

Jemima's phone rang.

'Huxley,' said Kennedy. 'I've called in a favour. Two uniforms are heading in your direction. Use them as you will.' Kennedy cut the call before she was able to reply.

'Thanks, sir,' she muttered to herself. Before she had a chance to wonder about the DCI's uncharacteristic abruptness, two uniformed officers walked into the room. Jemima didn't recognise either of them. Then again, she figured that there must have been plenty of changes throughout her year of absence. Not least on her own team.

'DI Huxley?' asked the female officer.

'That's right. I take it you're the reinforcements I've just been told about?'

'Yes ma'am, we are. PC Anna Coveney and PC Connor Morten. You can trust us to get on with whatever tasks you set. Just tell us what you need us to do, and we'll make a start,' said the young woman.

Jemima was delighted. Anna exuded confidence, and Jemima sensed the couple would be an asset to this operation. And there was no denying the fact that her team could certainly do with the extra help. With the introductions out of the way, she set Coveney and Morten to work with the others, knowing that their input would be welcome.

As Jemima returned to her desk, Broadbent called her over.

'I've got Merryn Andrews's contact details,' he said.

Jemima grabbed her coat. 'Let's go.'

It turned out that Merryn had moved back in with her parents as she was no longer capable of looking after herself. And given the fact that she had been in a long-term relationship with Zach, it was extremely unlikely that she would have mistaken his twin for her ex. Jemima was almost certain that the young woman had nothing to do with the abduction, but she needed to see Merryn for herself, as there was always the possibility that her breakdown had been exaggerated.

The Andrews' address was outside the city and would take the best part of half an hour to reach, even with Jemima behind the wheel.

'This is going to be a difficult one. They'll already feel angry and let down, and we've no evidence to suggest they've anything to do with the kidnappings,' said Broadbent.

'Yeah, but we need to ascertain whether or not they're behind it. So, let's get on with it.' Jemima found a parking space and cut the engine.

The Andrews lived in a semi-detached house. There appeared nothing remarkable about the property — it looked much the same as every other house on the street. It was set back slightly from the pavement, with a low wall topped with metal railings that needed painting. A double gate, rusty over a large area where the paint had flaked, blocked the narrow driveway, which led to a garage. A Ford Ka was parked near the front of the property.

'No way they'd bundle someone into that. It'd be physically impossible,' said Dan.

Jemima ignored him, headed for the door and pressed the bell. A light was visible through the obscured glass panel, suggesting the occupants were home. Within seconds, a figure appeared at the entrance. A TV could be heard playing in the background.

The door opened slightly, as far as a safety chain would allow. 'Who is it?' asked a male voice.

'We're police officers, Mr Andrews. I'm Detective Inspector Jemima Huxley and this is Detective Sergeant Daniel Broadbent. We'd like to talk to you.'

'Let me see your IDs.' The man clearly had no intention of releasing the safety chain until he was certain that they were who they claimed to be. When he was finally satisfied, he opened the door. 'What could you possibly have to say to me? Is it about what happened to Merryn?'

'Not as such. Could we speak to you inside?' asked Jemima.

'I s'pose it's better that standing out there. These days the neighbours are always curtain-twitching. Don't want to give them anything else to gossip about. But keep the volume down. Merryn's upstairs in her room. I don't want her getting upset.'

'It's not our intention to distress any of you, Mr Andrews. It's just that an incident occurred earlier today and there's a small possibility it could somehow be linked to what happened to your daughter.'

'You mean that lowlife's gone and done it again? I'm telling you now, it's on that namby-pamby liberal judge if he has. They should have locked up that Trevelyan-Goode and thrown away the key. He's a danger to women.'

Jemima privately agreed but maintained a professional silence.

'Come into the lounge. My wife is in there watching the television.'

They followed Jim Andrews into the room, where Catriona Andrews sat on a sofa that looked far too big for the size of the room. She looked questioningly at her husband.

'They're police officers. Here to speak to us about something.'

'What's happened? Has he done it to some other poor girl?' Her eyes widened, and she pressed the palms of her hands to her chest.

'Not that we know, Mrs Andrews. We're here about Judge Rory Lawson.'

'You'll not persuade us to back down,' interjected Jim. 'Call himself a judge! That man made a mockery of the justice system. He was out of order and we've every right to do what we've done.'

'Do what, exactly?' asked Jemima.

'We're far from happy with Lawson giving that thug community service. So, we've written to our MP and engaged a solicitor to see what can be done about it. It's not right. That jury found Zach guilty. It was a unanimous verdict, for God's sake. He destroyed our Merryn. She'll never be the same again. She's a shadow of the girl she used to be. The animal should've been locked up. He's done it to two young women already. You mark my words, he'll go on to rape someone soon. The man's nothing but a pervert.'

Jemima's breath caught in her throat as Jim Andrews's words took her by surprise. Since her attack, anyone who knew her had purposely avoided discussing rape, or any form of physical sexual assault, when she was present.

She swallowed hard and forced herself to concentrate on the reason they were at the Andrews' house. But the unwelcome memory of that night in the alleyway had surfaced like a genie escaping its bottle. She knew she had to suppress these thoughts, but it was easier said than done. A man's life was riding on her not making a hash of things. It was essential to get back on track by focusing her attention on the here and now.

Broadbent surreptitiously glanced in her direction. He knew her well enough to appreciate that the word might have caused Jemima some distress. Determined not to show the Andrews that anything might be amiss, he took up the narrative. 'You're completely within your rights to engage a solicitor and contact your MP. I would have done the same if I was in your shoes. Tell me, have you ever tried to contact Judge Lawson or perhaps Trevelyan-Goode since the verdict?'

'Why the hell would we do that? They both make me feel sick to my stomach. I don't ever want to see either of them again.' The volume of Jim Andrews's voice increased with each word and the skin darkened on his neck and face. The question had obviously riled the man.

His display of anger was enough to focus Jemima's mind. It was the realisation that things could quickly get out of hand, and the appreciation that she needed to dial down the tension in the room, before things escalated further. 'Sergeant Broadbent isn't suggesting you would, Mr Andrews. It's just that something's happened to the judge, and we're speaking to everyone who may have reason to think badly of him.' Jemima's tone was calm and placatory, far removed from the maelstrom of emotions that had threatened to overwhelm her only moments earlier.

They still needed to establish if any of Merryn's family had acted upon their grievance or knew of anyone who would do so on their behalf. And to do that, they needed to keep the narrative going. This was always going to be a difficult conversation to have, but it was essential. Ideally, they would ask their questions, get truthful answers, and be out of there as quickly as possible.

'Take a deep breath, Jim,' said his wife. She reached out, took his hand, and squeezed it gently. There were tears in the woman's eyes.

It was difficult to reconcile Merryn's parents with the images displayed on a family photograph hung in pride of place over the fireplace. It showed the couple with their son and daughter and must have been taken at most a few years earlier at their son's graduation ceremony. But since then, they both appeared to have aged considerably. They could have been mistaken for decades older than they were. The Jim in the photograph was a handsome, robust man whose eyes twinkled mischievously. Now his cheeks were sunken, his arms lacked definition and his clothes hung shapelessly, as though they had once belonged to someone a couple of sizes larger.

Catriona's hair was grey and in need of styling. Her face was lined and her skin lacked lustre. She spoke slowly and deliberately, as though every word was an effort. Jemima wondered if the woman was on antidepressants. It was impossible to imagine that this couple would have the energy or the wherewithal to abduct anyone. Just looking around, it was obvious that they were barely keeping things together.

'How's Merryn doing?' Jemima addressed the question to Catriona.

'Oh, you know . . .' The answer was non-committal, but it wasn't a great stretch of the imagination for Jemima to understand how she must feel.

'And how are you both managing?'

Catriona's face crumpled. 'Bless you, you're the first person to ask about us.'

'I appreciate it's hard. You're trying to take away her pain, but you can't. She has no choice but to work through it, and it's heartbreaking to watch her suffer.'

'You sound as though you're speaking from experience,' said Catriona.

'Different circumstances. Profound impact. It changes you. Life will never be the same, but it doesn't mean you can't eventually go on.' The two women made eye contact and nodded their understanding, both smiling sadly.

The tension in the room lifted when Catriona next spoke. 'I apologise for our defensive demeanour. We're still reeling from the outcome of the trial. We'd hoped it would be a turning point for Merryn, but that wasn't to be. It's taken a toll on all of us as we're having to be strong for her. Hide our own feelings, try to stay positive. It's like constantly treading on eggshells.'

'It's perfectly understandable, and I'm sorry we've blundered in at this time, but we're up against it. So, if you could just answer our questions, we'll leave you in peace.'

'What do you want to know?'

'Is there anyone in your family who would physically confront either the judge or Zach Trevelyan-Goode?'

'No, absolutely not. We believe in the rule of law. For all the good it's done us,' said Catriona. 'Writing letters to get that beast's sentence overturned is as far as we'd ever go.

We've never been involved in physical altercations. We're not that sort of people.'

Jemima believed the woman was telling them the truth. 'What about your son and your extended family?'

'Oh, no. Our son, Peter, is a junior doctor at the local hospital. Of course, he's upset about what happened. We all are. But he's not the sort of person to do anything about it. He's gentle, kind-hearted and exceptionally busy. I can categorically say that'd he'd not do anything like that,' said Jim.

'And we've no extended family apart from my parents. They're both in their late eighties and my father recently suffered a stroke,' said Catriona. 'I genuinely can't think of anyone who would be capable of confronting either of those dreadful men. We don't move in such circles. It's not as though we socialised much before this happened. We've always kept to ourselves. Done things as a family.'

'I'll need an address for your son, as we'll still need to speak to him,' said Jemima.

'He's on shift until the morning,' said Jim.

As they left the lounge, they heard footsteps on the stairs. The sound was quiet, slow and deliberate.

'Who's there, Mum?' The voice was so high-pitched that it was easy to visualise the panic the speaker was experiencing.

'No one for you to worry about, darling. They're just going,' said Catriona.

Mrs Andrews accompanied them to the door, and as Jemima turned to say goodbye, she noticed Merryn standing halfway down the stairs. Her first thought was that she had seen corpses in better condition. The young woman before them was unhealthily thin and her complexion so pale as to be almost translucent. That is, apart from the section directly beneath her bloodshot eyes, where the skin was dark and puffy from lack of sleep and constant crying. As she reached up to distractedly brush a strand of hair away from her eyes, the sleeve of her loose-fitting top fell away to reveal a series of raw welts on her forearms. They varied in length and crisscrossed the skin in a random pattern.

It was hardly surprising that Merryn's fragility had led her to self-harm given the intense pressure she was under. No one mutilated themselves unless they were desperate and felt they had no control over their life. Jemima's heart went out to the young woman, as she had years of her own experience of cutting herself. It was a dark, dangerous and lonely road to travel.

'What's your take on them?' asked Broadbent as they pulled away from the Andrews' house.

'I think they were telling us the truth. They had nothing to do with either of those abductions. Next stop, the hospital. We need to speak to Peter Andrews.'

# CHAPTER 17

The short journey to the hospital seemed interminably long. The clock was ticking. Yet despite Jemima and the team throwing everything at it, they were no closer to finding Rory Lawson. She hoped that Glen Buchannan was having more luck at his end with the North Road investigation. It didn't matter to her if he would ultimately be the one to break the case, as long as they got Lawson back alive.

Jemima glanced sideways as they walked past the hospital's Accident and Emergency entrance. It seemed like the worst possible department to be assigned to in the hospital. The place was heaving. In her experience it was always the same, regardless of the time of day or night. Police officers moaned about the pressured environment of their job, but nine times out of ten it was a walk in the park compared with what these healthcare workers dealt with. It was high-stakes chaos with no let-up, juggling priorities, managing expectations and tackling one life-threatening situation after another.

The noise died down as they turned the corner towards the main entrance of the building. It was a different world at this time of day. Outpatient clinics were over, and the concourse was relatively quiet. The only people coming and going were visitors.

They checked at the reception desk to find out which ward Peter Andrews was on, then headed up the staircase to find him. In a short while they arrived at a paediatric ward, which was a marked contrast to other areas of the hospital. Here, vibrant-coloured walls and cheerful artwork lifted the mood in an attempt to distract those children unfortunate enough to have to spend time there.

As Jemima glanced around, she could see no obvious sign of any male doctor. A couple of nurses were gathered at the main desk huddled together, talking in low voices and occasionally laughing in a conspiratorial manner. Sensing the detectives' approach, they ended their conversation abruptly and the closest one asked if they could help.

Jemima showed the young nurse her warrant card. 'We're looking for Dr Andrews.'

'He's just gone on his break. He's in the staff room. I'll take you there.' The young man arched his eyebrows as he glanced at his colleagues. He knew better than to ask why they wanted to speak to the doctor. But there was no doubt in Jemima's mind that when he returned, speculation would be rife.

Peter Andrews was in conversation with a young woman of a similar age. As they approached the door, Jemima had spotted them through the side window. They appeared at ease with each other and were enjoying their downtime.

'Peter Andrews?' Jemima needn't have asked as his name badge was visible. She introduced both herself and Broadbent, explaining that they were there to enquire about a personal matter. 'You might want to find somewhere we can talk in private.'

'I'll make myself scarce.' His colleague's name badge told them that she was also a doctor.

'No need. Camille and I are close friends. We've no secrets. You can speak in front of her.' Peter gestured towards some free seats.

'You sure?' asked Camille. 'I don't mind.' She appeared to not want to intrude upon whatever discussion Peter was about to have.

'Stay. Please.'

'We wanted to talk to you about your sister's trial,' said Jemima.

'What about it?'

Jemima noticed Peter stiffen. She sensed he hadn't expected them to ask about this. 'How did you feel about Zach's sentence?'

'What do you mean? How do you think I felt? I was devastated for my sister. It was an absolute travesty. I don't know how that judge can sleep at night.'

Camille reached out and took Peter's hand. 'Don't upset yourself, Pete.'

'I can't help it. You warned me not to get my hopes up. Yet I was still stupid enough to hope that that scumbag would get what he deserved.'

'Why did you warn Peter not to get his hopes up?' asked Jemima.

'I was trying to manage his expectations. You might think I'm a pessimist, but I believe I'm more of a realist. If you were the victim of a sexual assault, would you go down the route of a court case?'

The question blindsided Jemima. She swallowed hard but held the woman's gaze as she replied, 'No.'

'Exactly. And why is that?'

'This isn't relevant,' interjected Broadbent. 'We're not here to discuss hypothetical situations. We're here to follow up on a line of enquiry.'

'That's it, I'm outta here.' Camille let go of Peter's hand and stood up. 'I've got patients to see.'

'With regard to what happened to your sister, have you ever considered taking the law into your own hands?' asked Broadbent.

'Are you for real? I'm a doctor, not some bloody vigilante. Yes, I'm pissed off at what that so-called judge did. And yes, it's had a detrimental effect on all of us. Especially Merryn. I've given my parents money to retain a solicitor. We're doing everything we can to try to overturn the sentencing.

We intend to shine a spotlight on Lawson, and show he's not fit to be a judge. My sister should have had justice, and what Lawson did was inexcusable. He snatched away any hope that Merryn had. By playing down the seriousness of Zach's actions, he gave a green light for any other sick bastard in this country to do whatever the hell they like.'

'I can understand your anger. But I need to know if you, or anyone you know, have approached Judge Lawson since the trial?' asked Jemima.

'No. It'd be a complete waste of time. The only thing we want is for Trevelyan-Goode to be incarcerated. A jury found the man guilty. He's ruined so many lives and should have been put behind bars. Yet that judge allowed him to walk free. It's a wonder he didn't pin a medal on his chest! Lawson isn't fit to hold that office.'

Jemima shared the man's sentiment but said nothing.

* * *

They returned to the station, frustrated by the lack of progress, which seemed to be the measure of the day. As they strode into the operations room, Steve Morgan glanced up and called her over.

'Glen Buchannan was on the blower about ten minutes ago.'

'What did he have to say?' asked Jemima, hoping that this would be the breakthrough they so badly needed.

'His team have delved into Emyr's background. Apparently, he was a local government office worker. Twenty-five years of age. Engaged to be married. A well-respected all-round good guy. In fact, no one had a bad word to say about him.' Steve relayed these facts from notes he had made while speaking to Buchannan. 'He lived in the village he grew up in. Bought a house with his fiancée, Cerys Jones. His parents' property is nearby, and that's where Zach still lives.'

While Steve continued to speak, Jemima's mind raced ahead. Buchannan's findings were pointing to a case of mistaken identity.

'There was a falling-out between the two brothers since Zach was arrested. Emyr was said to have been disgusted by his brother's actions. It also had a knock-on effect for Emyr's relationship with his parents. They felt the need to keep a roof over Zach's head. But Emyr was quite outspoken about what he considered to be their misguided support.'

Steve turned the page. 'Within the family, Zach's actions probably affected his brother most of all. As they were identical twins, they had spent their entire lives getting mistaken for each other. But what had once been a source of amusement became a worrying scenario for Emyr. People in the village knew him well enough, but when Zach's face hit the headlines, Emyr was sometimes subjected to a barrage of abuse from strangers who naturally assumed he was Zach.'

'I can imagine,' said Jemima.

'They hadn't found any witnesses to Emyr's abduction, but from the clothes he was wearing, Buchannan was certain it occurred when he was on his morning run. Unlike his brother, he was a fitness fanatic. Obsessive in his routine. No matter the weather, he always ran the same circuit at the same time in the morning. He'd done it for years, and when it all came out about Zach, I think it was even more of a reason for Emyr to stick to that time, as not many people were up and around.'

'Did he manage to establish the location of the ambush?'

'He thinks so. They found one of his AirPods, which he believes must've been dislodged during the struggle. It was at the edge of the village, about twenty yards or so from the nearest house. At that time of the day, it's likely no one would have seen or heard anything. Emyr would have been quite isolated. Buchannan reckoned it's a safe bet that they chose the ambush point because there'd be no witnesses.'

'Which suggests that if it was a case of mistaken identity, the abductors didn't know the village or that family well enough to realise that Zach and Emyr were identical twins. But abducting him was made so much easier since their target, albeit the wrong one, was a creature of habit,' said Jemima.

'Exactly. There's a lot to be said for varying your routine. Not being too predictable,' said Steve.

'Surely his fiancée would have noticed that he didn't return from his run?' Jemima thought that if only the young woman had raised the alarm promptly Emyr might still be alive. Though realistically, she knew that she was clutching at straws.

'Unfortunately, she spent last night away with work. Apparently, she confirmed that he was a stickler for routine. Always set out at the same time and followed the same route. Which has helped Buchannan narrow down the time of the abduction. It also suggests that if the two abductions are linked, they had to be carried out by different people.'

Jemima quickly thought through the implications. 'That's interesting. It's conceivable we could be looking at a group of vigilantes.'

# CHAPTER 18

Jemima glanced in the direction of Gareth's desk. He was talking to someone on the phone, having already returned from interviewing Kareena Daniels. Jemima asked everyone to take a break from their respective tasks and gather round. No one needed to be asked twice, as it was a welcome break from the intense concentration of the last few hours.

'Firstly, thanks for your efforts today. I appreciate everything you're doing and value your input. I realise that it's a hard slog, which might end up coming to nothing. But as we've not yet identified the people behind Lawson's abduction, your efforts stand the best possible chance of us finding out who's taken him. Has anyone managed to identify any potential suspects?' She looked around at the sea of tired faces.

'Vic and I are working our way through the DVLA records,' said Aadi. 'We're slowly narrowing it down, but so far, we've not come up with anything useful.'

'Keep at it for now. That vehicle was tailing Lawson. If we can identify the driver, we might stand a chance of finding him. How's it going with the court records?'

'Still working our way through them, but there's nothing obvious. It could be that Zach's lenient sentence was just a one-off. In my opinion, Lawson arrived at a reasonable sentence for every guilty verdict I've looked at today,' said Gaynor.

'Which could suggest that the Trevelyan-Goode link is important. But until we know for certain I want every one of those court records examined.' Jemima ignored the groans of the various officers engaged in that task. Every case involved an element of grunt work, and no one liked having to do it. But it was a fact that mind-numbingly sifting through records and checking data often exposed the elusive link that made sense of everything else. She just hoped for Rory Lawson's sake that they made some connections soon.

'Did you get anything useful from Kareena Daniels, Gar?' He'd finished his phone call and had joined the others.

'No. We spoke to her, but I'm pretty sure she's got nothing to do with any of this. She was pissed off with Lawson, but claimed she wasn't surprised. Referred to him as an over-privileged old fart. The embodiment of everything that's wrong with this country's justice system.'

'Sounds like a pretty serious grudge to me,' said Jemima. 'Why are you so sure she's got nothing to do with what's happened?'

'Because she's got a rock-solid alibi. After Zach humiliated her, she joined a women's group that aims to prevent anyone posting revenge porn. They're also lobbying for a change in the law to allow longer maximum prison sentences. Kareena was one of a handful of delegates from Cardiff who went up to London to speak at a convention to try to get the government to take this more seriously. She'd just returned and was getting out of a taxi when we arrived.'

'Which would put her in the clear for both abductions,' interjected Broadbent.

'Exactly. She's been in London ever since the verdict. Her MP also happens to be her sister, and Kareena stayed at her London pad. She's helping Kareena highlight the need to bring in legislation to make hosting companies more accountable for everything their users post. They travelled back to Cardiff together and showed us footage from the convention.'

'Sounds like a watertight alibi. I guess we can cross her off our list of potential suspects,' said Jemima. 'With regard to Merryn Andrews and her family, I don't think any of them are involved in acts of physical retribution. Right now, Merryn's hardly capable of putting one foot in front of the other. As for her parents and brother, they're already going down the route of trying to get a judicial review. They've given us the name of their solicitor, so we can check out the validity of that claim. If it proves to be the case, I can't see that they would risk vigilantism.

'We don't yet have any evidence to prove that Emyr Trevelyan-Goode's abduction and that of Rory Lawson are connected,' she continued. 'That said, it seems too much of a coincidence to ignore. The obvious connection between the two is the trial, and that is reinforced by the fact that Emyr was the defendant's identical twin. So—'

The door opened with so much force that it almost came off its hinges. Chief Inspector Kennedy's entire face was grey and slick with sweat. He looked like a man who was carrying the weight of the world upon his shoulders. Fast approaching his fiftieth birthday, he wasn't in the best of shape.

Jemima's first thought was that Kennedy might be having a heart attack. Having witnessed his earlier violent outburst, which had been so out of character, she knew that something was going on with him. He knew so much about her personal demons and instead of throwing her to the wolves had kept her secret and offered his support. As far as she was concerned, that level of loyalty was a two-way street. Yet here he was, clearly tormented and possibly ill. Instinct told her that it was something serious.

Yet with the day's events playing out in such a dramatic fashion, this was neither the time nor the place to try to get to the bottom of what was wrong with her senior officer. As soon as this was over, she would make it her top priority to get him to open up and help him in whichever way she could.

Kennedy took a deep breath before saying anything. When he spoke, he addressed the entire room, though failed to make eye contact with anyone. 'I know it's not the best timing, but I've got to go out and won't be contactable.' Leaving no time for anyone to respond, he walked away.

'Sir! Did you get anywhere with the key card?' Jemima's voice was more than loud enough for him to hear, but Kennedy just kept on walking.

Jemima was left open-mouthed. She couldn't believe what had just happened. Glancing at Broadbent she saw that he was as perplexed as her. Sensing he was about to comment on Kennedy's puzzling behaviour, she shook her head slightly to signal him to keep quiet. Dan took the hint. The others in the room were also clearly surprised by this recent turn of events and were speculating about whether a body had been found.

'OK, listen up!' Jemima had to get everyone's full attention. Kennedy's apparent dereliction of duty was shocking, and everyone, including her, was keen to know on what was going on. But for now, they had work to do, and she needed everyone to focus. 'The DCI has obviously got something important he needs to attend to. It's not the time or place to gossip about where he's going or what he's doing. I'm as perplexed as the rest of you. But I guarantee that whatever he's doing must be important. I expect everyone to continue with their respective tasks. Work quickly and be thorough. Remember, a man's life might very well depend on it. Keep me informed of any developments.' Jemima gestured for her sergeant to follow her out of the room. 'Dan, a word.'

When she was sure they were out of earshot she asked, 'What am I missing? What the fuck's going on with Kennedy?'

'Not sure. He's been acting oddly for the last few weeks.'

'Any particular event spark this?'

'Not as far as I know. Gareth's picked up on it too. There's clearly something up with the gaffer but he's not letting on. Gotta be something serious though, for him to walk out in the middle of this shitstorm. I mean it's not gonna play out well with the higher-ups.'

'What's that? I heard my name mentioned.' Gareth joined them.

'Kennedy. Acting strange,' said Dan.

'Yeah. Something's not right with him. No idea what it is. Can't really ask him what's up as he's never really confided in me,' said Gareth.

'I agree. His behaviour's so out of character. I'm worried about him,' said Jemima. 'I went to see him earlier and he was in a hell of a state. Quite aggressive and I think he'd trashed his office. He's not doing his job properly and has just buggered off in the middle of an investigation without any explanation.' There was a part of her that was angry with the way that Kennedy was acting. It was unprofessional and so unlike the man she thought she knew. He was someone she looked up to. An officer with an exemplary record. Someone who always did things by the book and went the extra mile.

'I've never known him to be like this. It's as though he couldn't care less about this case.' Broadbent shook his head in despair.

'He hasn't even told us if he's managed to find out anything about that key card,' added Jemima. 'It comes to something when even your own DCI seems to be throwing obstacles in the way of an investigation. Anyway, we don't have time to waste. Who were you on the phone to when we returned, Gar? Anything to do with the case?'

'Oh yeah. With Kennedy acting like that, it slipped my mind. It was Formby, the FLO. Lawson's sons have turned up. No sign of the daughter yet.'

'In that case we'll head over there and have a word with them. Hopefully they'll be a bit more forthcoming than their mother, and perhaps we'll find out a bit more about what Rory Lawson's really like.'

# CHAPTER 19

They arrived at the Lawson house to the sound of a heated discussion taking place inside one of the downstairs rooms near the front door. The altercation was between two men, but their actual dialogue proved to be more difficult to follow. Despite their tones being forceful and agitated, they were not shouting at each other, and it seemed they were doing their best to keep the volume down. Though whether that was so as not to upset their mother or to minimise the risk of the FLO overhearing was yet to be established.

Whatever their intention, Jemima's interest was immediately piqued. As far as she was aware, the only men in the house were the Lawsons' sons. If the family had secrets they were determined not to divulge, then this was an opportunity to discover facts and potential concerns they might otherwise not be made privy to.

She was reluctant to ring the doorbell as it would make their presence known. Instead, she stood and listened, but all she could hear was the odd word or phrase, such as: *'it's time'*, *'too damaging'*, *'suspicions'* and *'acknowledge it'*.

These were extremely stressful circumstances for any family to deal with. It was inevitable that emotions would be heightened. But the words she'd heard didn't seem to fit with worried family members. They were more in line with ensuring that damaging information didn't make it into the public domain than ensuring that the police were informed of anything that could potentially help them locate the victim. It didn't take a detective to work out that the family was keeping information from the police.

As the heated discussion petered out, they heard a door open then slam. Understanding that there was nothing more to be gained from eavesdropping, Jemima rang the bell. Within seconds, there was the sound of approaching footsteps.

PC Formby opened the door and stepped outside to speak to them. The strain of having been at the house for much of the day showed on her face. It was an exhausting and often underrated job, providing support to families at their wits' end, reassuring, listening, supporting, yet all the while surreptitiously looking for clues and trying to glean information that those closest to the victim might wish to hide.

To ensure they could speak freely, all three officers headed back towards the car.

'How's it going in there?' asked Jemima.

'You saw what it was like earlier. Emilia was a complete nightmare, but she's sobered up now. I had to be quite firm with her and she didn't take it well. Thinks she's a cut above the rest of us. Both sons finally turned up, though. Tristan, the younger brother, arrived first. Anthony less than an hour ago.'

'I got the impression there was some sort of argument going on when we arrived. Picked up on a few words that give cause for concern,' said Jemima.

'Yeah. There's noticeable tension between them. At first, I thought it was because their father's missing. That'd mess with anyone's head. But watching the interaction between them and their mother I sense there's a lot more to it than that. They've kept a lid on things whenever they've been in my presence, but it's obvious something's going on beneath the surface, though I've no idea what it is.'

'Has anyone suggested who might be behind Lawson's disappearance?'

'There's been no speculation that I've heard.'

'Any sign of the daughter?'

'No, and strangely enough, no one's mentioned her.'

'Is anyone else there? Any friends or extended family offering support?'

'No.'

'Not a close family then.'

'Definitely not. Given the circumstances, you'd think they'd put whatever differences they had aside. But this lot haven't. It makes you wonder what's gone on in the past.'

'Did you and the other officer get anywhere with those lists?'

'Yes and no. The golf club proved difficult. Didn't want to cooperate at first, even when I explained that Lawson had been abducted. So I called in a favour from a couple of uniforms. They went around there, read them the riot act, and eventually got them to print off a list of members. I couldn't believe it. There are more than a hundred names on that list, and most of them don't answer their bloody phones.'

'Emilia said her husband regularly played golf with a copper. Did you recognise any name on that list?'

'No, I've not come across anyone I've heard of. Then again, that just means that whoever it is doesn't work out of my station.'

'I suppose so. Has anyone been in touch with their cleaner yet?'

'What with working through those lists and keeping an eye on Emilia, I've not had any time. I've got her address though.'

'In that case, text it to me and we'll go there after we've spoken to the family. Give me a copy of the golf club membership list too. You never know, something may jump out.'

As they entered the house a man wandered distractedly from one of the side rooms. At first, he appeared oblivious to their presence. He held a phone to his ear, and they could hear a voice on the other end of the line. After glancing in their direction, he held his free hand up to signal that they keep quiet. 'I'll have to call you back. The police have just arrived . . . Yeah, OK . . . Bye, bye.' He disconnected the call and placed the phone in his trouser pocket. He offered his hand. 'Tristan Lawson.'

With the introductions out of the way, Tristan led them into the sitting room, where Emilia was slouched upon the sofa. Since their previous encounter the woman's demeanour had clearly changed. Instead of the recalcitrant drunk, she appeared lost and in need of moral support. It was such a marked contrast to when they had first encountered her. Jemima couldn't help but wonder how much of this was an act to get sympathy from her offspring.

'Have you found our father?' asked Anthony. He was sitting next to his mother, holding her hand.

Jemima could see that both sons resembled their father. Anthony to a far greater extent, having inherited his fathers' eyes and jawline.

'Not yet—'

'What do you mean, not yet? It's been hours since he went missing,' interjected Emilia. The woman's voice had lost the forcefulness of their initial encounter. It was now higher, weaker and crackled with emotion.

Anthony squeezed his mother's hand supportively. 'Try not to upset yourself, Mother. I'm sure the police are doing everything they can. Now, I really think you should try to get some sleep. This stress isn't good for you. As your son and a GP, I'd advise you to take this pill. It'll take the edge off and allow you to get some sleep.'

'I want to be awake when your father returns.'

'None of us know when that will be, and you can't possibly carry on like this. You'll make yourself ill. Tris and I are going nowhere until everything's settled. We'll be here to watch over you and liaise with the police. Take the opportunity to rest while you can. I'll wake you as soon as there's any news.' He handed the medication to his mother, who took it without argument, and then excused herself from the room.

Jemima went to say something. Anthony placed a finger on his lips to indicate that she should remain silent. She bristled at his haughty attitude, but did as she was requested. Having only been in their presence for such a short period of time, she was already irritated by Lawson's sons. She could understand Anthony's concern for his mother, but the way the brothers conducted themselves suggested that their needs and that of Emilia overrode any concern for their father.

Emilia's footsteps could be heard ascending the stairs. As they faded, Anthony spoke. 'Sorry about that, but if Mother remained, I guarantee the conversation would have been all about her.'

Jemima raised her eyebrows in surprise. 'Before we begin, you both need to know that I'll be recording our conversation. It's nothing for you to worry about, but it ensures that we have a complete record of all the information you give us, and it speeds things up as it means we don't have to take notes.'

The brothers exchanged a look, which lasted no more than a second or two. Anthony was the first to speak. 'That's fine. Please continue.'

Jemima took out a recording device and placed it on the coffee table in front of them. She activated the machine and gave the usual preamble before the questioning began in earnest. 'I'm sure you'll both appreciate that we're up against it. We still don't know who has abducted your father. Or why he was taken.'

'Surely you haven't just been sitting on your hands waiting for a ransom demand?' asked Anthony.

'I can assure you that we're doing everything we can to find your father. But he is bound to have made a lot of enemies throughout his career. When we spoke to your mother this morning, she was . . .' Jemima hesitated as she searched for a delicate way of saying what she meant. 'Umm, perhaps somewhat incapacitated.'

'You don't need to concern yourself with our feelings, Inspector. We're both astute enough to have realised that our mother is an alcoholic. She's been that way since we were teenagers. We don't like it, but there's nothing either of us can do about it,' said Anthony.

'Well, as you can imagine, she was unable to answer many of our questions, and was vague on those she did answer. It also didn't help matters that we were unable to speak to either of you, or your sister.' Jemima looked from one to other of the Lawson siblings as she made this remark. It was a fleeting reaction, but she was convinced that she noticed the slightest tensing of Anthony's jawline when his sister was mentioned.

'All I can do is apologise, Inspector. We lead busy lives. It isn't always possible to answer the phone or even pick up messages if we're in the middle of things. I, for one, had patients to see. They pack as many appointments in as possible. Every shift is like a treadmill.'

Jemima knew that Anthony was waffling, and sensed he was trying to deflect attention away from the mention of his sister. The question was why?

'Your sister — I believe her name's Matilda?'

'That's correct.' Tristan jumped in to answer before his brother had the opportunity to say anything further.

'Has anyone informed her about her father? Is she on her way here?'

'No and no.' Anthony's voice was firm and he held her gaze, as though to emphasise the fact that he had nothing to hide. Yet there it was again. The slightest tensing of his jaw.

Jemima knew she was right. This was his tell, something he was doing his best to control, but which had inevitably betrayed him. She needed to push the brothers harder about their missing sister. Find out why neither of them had contacted her. It was understandable that if she was on active duty, it would be impossible for her to drop everything immediately and get compassionate leave to come home. But there would be ways to get a message through to her about a family emergency at home.

'Where is Matilda's regiment currently deployed?' It was a reasonable question to ask.

'What is this? Why are you so concerned about our sister? You're wasting precious time instead of doing everything you can to find our father,' said Tristan.

'It's a simple enough question, and I'd like it answered. I have no hidden agenda. I just believe that every effort should be made to let her know what has happened.'

'Our sister serves in a special unit, Inspector. It's all very hush-hush. We never get to know where she is, and even when we get together, she never speaks about what she does. She's told us it's safer that way,' said Tristan.

That line of questioning was best left for now, but Jemima was determined that when they returned to the station, she would either task someone with contacting Matilda's regiment, or, if time permitted, do so herself.

'Fair enough.' Jemima smiled sweetly to emphasise that she had accepted the explanation. 'Moving on, I need you both to tell us everything you know about your father. We've enough information to build a picture of him from the work perspective. It's the private man where the details are lacking.'

'Surely his abduction is linked to his work,' said Anthony. From the tone of his voice, it was immediately apparent that this was a statement, not a question.

'We're not prepared to rule anything out at this stage — it would be negligent to take that approach. If we're to stand any chance of getting your father back alive, and soon, we need to know as much about him as possible. And we need to do that quickly to enable us to target our resources effectively,' Jemima said. 'If this were a kidnapping, we would have expected a ransom demand before now. But as no contact has been made, it suggests that this isn't about money. It's personal. Someone holds a grudge against your father.'

'What are the possible outcomes?' asked Tristan. 'Don't sugarcoat it. I want a genuine assessment of where this is headed.'

'In that case, it doesn't look good. We have evidence to suggest that your father was taken by force, and that his abduction was not a spur-of-the-moment event. Evidence suggests that more than one person was involved.'

'Christ! Whoever's behind it isn't messing around, then,' said Tristan. As the reality of the situation began to sink in, it was clear to see that the stress was getting to him. With his elbows on his knees, he cupped his chin and closed his eyes. His complexion had paled considerably.

'Breathe it out, Tris. Nice slow breaths.' Anthony placed his arm around his brother's shoulders. 'You can't afford to lose it. You have to be strong, for Mother.'

'Do you think they'll kill him?' It was Tristan who asked the question.

'It's a possibility, but until we know the reason for the abduction and have identified the people behind it, we've no way of knowing,' said Broadbent.

'Which is why we need you both to cooperate and answer our questions as quickly and thoroughly as possible,' Jemima added. 'Every second these people have him decreases the chances of him getting out of this without facing serious harm or even death. I'm sorry, I know that's not what you wanted to hear. But for your father's sake, we must push on.'

'What do you want to know?' Unsurprisingly, Anthony was the first to recover.

From the behaviour she had witnessed, Jemima was convinced that he was the dominant sibling. Though, in the outside world, both young men were probably used to calling the shots. A behaviour no doubt reinforced from childhood by having been brought up in such a privileged family. Status and the family name would matter to them. Which may very well make them reluctant to answer truthfully if there was some family secret that, should it come out, might adversely affect their social standing.

'I appreciate the fact that neither of you have lived at home for an extensive period, but you will both still have an invaluable perspective of Rory the man.'

Tristan shifted uneasily and began picking at the skin around his nails. Anthony remained upright in his seat, staring straight ahead at some elusive spot on the wall.

'Let's start with your father's interests.'

'He's always been quite self-sufficient. Not the sort to socialise excessively. He's a member of the golf club. Doesn't get to play as regularly as he'd like, as work commitments frequently get in the way,' said Anthony.

'Have either of you ever played golf with your father?'

'I haven't. Not my sort of thing. More of a squash man,' said Anthony.

'I've played with him once. It's a good way of making the right sort of connections. Especially useful in a business such as mine,' said Tristan.

'You played with your father and some other members?' asked Jemima.

'That's right.'

'Do you remember any of their names?'

'I'm sure one of them was a police officer. Davies? Denvers? Something like that.'

'Deavers?' asked Broadbent.

'Yes, that's it.'

'Anyone else?'

'There was William Parkinson. He and my father go way back. They were at school together. But the man my father wanted to introduce me to pulled out at the last moment. Which was a shame, because I'd rearranged my schedule, which, given my commitments, is a difficult thing to do.'

'Who were you hoping to meet?'

'A big-time property developer. But all wasn't lost. Fortunately, my father arranged a meeting for the following week. He booked a table in one of the private dining rooms at their club. I had to sign the register to get in. I didn't care where we met as long as I could pitch for the contract. This guy's a big player and the deal was huge.'

'Did you manage to land the contract?' asked Jemima.

'Yeah. I took along my portfolio and presented my ideas. My father was immensely proud of me. He told me afterwards that there were other architects bidding for that particular contract.' Tristan smiled as he recalled the moment.

'What's this property developer's name?'

'Edward Trevelyan-Goode.'

It took a great deal of effort for Jemima and Broadbent not to react. The revelation was huge. Shocking. Yet neither of Lawson's sons appeared to be aware of the importance of this information.

'Can you remember the date that you landed this contract?'

'Let me look at my phone. I'll have made a note of it in my diary. My entire life's mapped out in there.'

Jemima all but held her breath as the younger Lawson brother brought up the screen and finally responded. The date he gave them was a few weeks before the Zach Trevelyan-Goode court case. This was a huge and damning revelation, as it meant that Rory Lawson should not have presided over the trial. They had proof that he had conspired with Edward Trevelyan-Goode to pervert the course of justice. And the connection between the two men also explained why Rory Lawson had been lenient when it came to Zach's sentencing.

Broadbent was the first to renew the questioning, determined to find out as much as he could. 'Has your father been a member of this club for long?'

'Ever since I can remember. It's been a godsend for him. It's not unusual for him to come home late. Once court has ended for the day, he inevitably has other work-related things that call upon his time. People often make the mistake of thinking that a judge's entire workload consists of just sitting there watching everything play out, whereas I'm sure you'll appreciate there's far more to it than that. He frequently doesn't get home until ten o'clock or sometimes even later. Whenever he works late, he has dinner at his club.'

'Are we talking health club?' asked Broadbent.

'No, nothing like that. It's a private members' business club. Very exclusive. Exceptionally old-school. All high-back leather chairs, fine dining. Very stuffed shirt. It's where the movers and shakers of the business community hang out.'

'Was it only you that had to sign the register to get into the club?'

'Yeah, Edward's a member too. I think that's how they became friends in the first place.'

When she had been assigned the case earlier that day, she had been determined to do everything in her power to find Rory Lawson and return him to his family. But with this latest revelation, she was more determined than ever to find him — though not so that he could return home and continue with his life. Jemima wanted to find him so that he could stand trial for perverting the course of justice. The man had brought shame and ignominy on the entire judicial system.

'I've not heard of that club.' Jemima suddenly felt intensely angry, and it took significant effort on her behalf to prevent her feelings from playing out across her face. Rory Lawson had done a deal to benefit his youngest son and in return had denied Merryn Andrews and Kareena Daniels the justice they deserved. It was an absolute travesty, unethical and undoubtedly illegal.

'You wouldn't have. Father describes it as one of the last bastions of the patriarchy. The fairer sex is discouraged, and membership is by recommendation only. It's one of the city's best kept secrets. But under the circumstances, since it's such a huge part of his life, I'm sure my father would understand why I've told you about it. I just hope it helps the investigation,' said Tristan.

'I'll need the name and location of this club,' said Jemima.

'It's the Marquess Club just off the Boulevard de Nantes. I think that's why he favours it. A five-minute walk from the court and he's there. He phones his food order through so it's often ready when he arrives. Don't blame him really. It's probably a better option that eating here. Mother's always been a dreadful cook.'

Jemima was surprised and horrified to learn of this club's existence. Especially since she worked only a stone's throw from where Tristan had said it was located. The thought of there being such an establishment at the heart of her city, where the successes of the privileged few were facilitated, went against every value she clung to.

While inroads had been made over the decades, misogyny still thrived. There was a certain type of man who would always come out on top of any situation, regardless of whether they merited it. Lip service was paid to equal opportunities, but they were a myth. Processes were followed to adhere to the law and ward off potential criticism, but decisions were made by influential people with a vested interest in maintaining the status quo. Everything else was window dressing. It was the same old story — money talked. Birthright mattered. Those with the right connections got on. Meritocracy was nothing more than an unattainable pipe dream.

Even without the connection between Lawson and Trevelyan-Goode the entire set-up stank more than a week-old sock. If Jemima's hunch about potential networking alliances being formed and strengthened inside this private members' club was accurate, then it seemed wrong that any member of the judiciary could be a member. As a judge, Lawson was trusted to apply the law impartially to ensure that justice was served. Yet this seemed like an upmarket version of a Masonic lodge.

And as Tristan had already confirmed a friendship between his father and Deavers, did that mean the superintendent was a member of the Marquess Club too? If that were the case, it also placed a question mark over his ability to carry out his duties impartially, which in turn could compromise the entire police force. The implications were almost too awful to consider. It certainly explained why Lawson had gone easy on Zach. It was a trade-off. Each man doing a favour for the other's son.

As soon as Lawson was assigned Zach's trial, he should have declared an interest and recused himself from the proceedings. Instead, he had chosen to keep quiet and despite the jury returning a unanimous guilty verdict he had chosen not to impose a prison sentence. Until now, it was unthinkable that such a respected judge could have perverted the course of justice. What many would have considered to be a blip in an otherwise exemplary career might have been put down to a moment of incompetence instead of recognising it as a blatant act of corruption.

It was possible that if someone else had learned of the link between Rory Lawson and Edward Trevelyan-Goode, they could have decided to take the law into their own hands. As Zach's identical twin, Emyr could easily have been mistaken for his brother and ended up paying for it with his life. It was also a plausible reason for Rory's abduction.

'Thank you both for your cooperation. You've given us things we will certainly follow up.' As she ended the interview, Jemima switched off the machine and placed it in her bag.

A thought occurred to her, and she decided to ask the FLO about it on the way out.

'Has anyone from the station been around yet to open the safe in Lawson's study?'

'No.'

Kennedy had told her that he would sort this. There had been plenty of time since she had raised the matter for him to have arranged for someone to come out and get the contraption open. Yet for some unfathomable reason, he obviously hadn't done anything about it. This was another instance of him letting them down.

In a moment of frustration, instead of leaving as they had intended, Jemima returned inside to speak to Anthony and Tristan. 'Do either of you have the combination to the safe in your father's study?'

Having studied people's behaviour for many years, she knew from their surprised expressions that Rory's sons knew nothing about the safe. When they both confirmed that they were unable to help her, she informed them that an officer would be sent around to open it and transport the contents to the station, where she would examine them.

# CHAPTER 20

Jemima and Dan walked to the car in silence, each lost in their own thoughts. Despite the brothers' obvious intelligence, and even though they were possibly hiding something else from the detectives, it was apparent that they had no idea of the importance of what Tristan had just told them.

But their collective excitement about Tristan's revelation had been tempered by Kennedy's unprofessional behaviour. The DCI had failed the investigation by not arranging for an officer to come out and open Lawson's safe. Jemima just hoped for her boss's sake that when they finally got to find out what it contained, it would have no bearing on the case.

Jemima jammed the key into the ignition and started the engine. 'I can't believe Kennedy. He categorically told me to leave it to him! We need to get someone out here to open that safe now.'

'Yeah, there's one thing you can be sure of. If any of us had messed up like that he'd have had our head on a platter,' said Broadbent. He grunted and shook his head in despair.

'I get where you're coming from, but I think there's more to it. I know I've only been back for a few hours, so I'm not the best person to judge this, but I'm sure there's something seriously wrong with him. He's losing his grip.

You saw him earlier. He's not acting rationally. When have you ever known him to just walk out in the middle of a case? He didn't even attempt to give us an explanation. It's not like him. Something's up with him, Dan.' Jemima's frustration was tinged with concern. 'After this case is over, I'm going to sit him down and try to find out what it is. He looks as though he's carrying the weight of the world on his shoulders.'

'He won't thank you for interfering.'

'That's as may be, but it's a risk I'm prepared to take. He doesn't have to confide in me. But he needs to speak to someone. Even if it's the force's counsellor.' It worried Jemima that Ray Kennedy was going through some personal crisis. She knew all too well what it was like to feel out of your depth and not to have anyone to confide in. Secrets had a way of eating away at you. It was easy to start out believing that you were in control of things only to discover when it was far too late that if you'd shared your concerns at the outset, your problems would have been far more manageable.

'Anyway, buckle up, then get Gareth on the phone. We've things to organise before we get back,' she ordered. Broadbent was still fastening his seat belt as Jemima pushed the gearstick into first, released the handbrake and pressed the accelerator so forcefully that they all but skidded out of the driveway, causing a cloud of dust to rise as chippings were forced from their resting place.

Dan swallowed hard, knowing from experience that this would inevitably be a stomach-lurching journey. He wasn't one for taking risks, and even more so since witnessing what had happened to Ashton. One of his greatest fears was riding on rollercoasters, but when Jemima was hyped up and behind the wheel, he'd willingly agree to ride every rollercoaster in the country instead of having to sit in the passenger seat praying they'd reach their destination without incident.

They'd only been travelling for a matter of seconds and he was already petrified. Rogue greenery slapped against the side of their vehicle as they raced along the narrow lanes. Thoughts of hitting a pothole at speed or Jemima failing to judge a bend in time increased his certainty that she'd lose control and flip the car.

'Dan! I asked you to ring Gareth. We can't afford to waste time.'

Her voice brought Broadbent back to the here and now, and he pressed speed dial to connect them. Selecting the speakerphone option he placed the phone in the hands-free device. It was by far the safest method as he couldn't seem to stop his hands from shaking.

Gareth picked up within seconds. 'Guv?'

'Gar, send uniforms out to pick up Edward and Zach Trevelyan-Goode. I want them both at the station by the time we get back. We've just been told about another link between them and Lawson which could explain the abductions. They're to be cautioned and told that they're being brought in for questioning about an ongoing inquiry. At this stage I don't want them to know any more than that.'

'Right you are, guv.'

'I also need a couple of officers to go around to the Lawson house asap. There's a safe in Lawson's office that needs opening and the contents brought back to the station. Kennedy was supposed to have arranged for it to be done earlier today, but he didn't. Lawson's family claim to know nothing about its existence. And if they're telling the truth, it makes me think that Lawson has something hidden in there that he doesn't want anyone to know about.'

'So it could possibly be useful to the case.'

'Exactly. We need to know what it contains.'

'I know a couple of trustworthy lads, guv,' said Gareth.

'Thought you would. Tell them that they'll need to take cutting equipment with them. And I know it seems a low priority, but send someone out to speak to the cleaner. She's spent a significant amount of time at that house over the years. She could be privy to all sorts of useful information, and I want us to cover all bases. Dan will text you the address.' The list of things for Gareth to do just kept on growing.

'Right you are, guv.'

'Oh, and once you've done that, I want you to do some digging into the Marquess Club. But do it on the quiet for now.'

'I've not heard of that place.'

'Neither had we. It's a private members' club just off the Boulevard de Nantes, and it links Lawson with Edward Trevelyan-Goode.'

When they eventually left the narrow lanes behind them, Broadbent breathed a sigh of relief and stopped gripping his seat. The hair-raising part of the journey had only lasted ten minutes or so, but his fingers had cramped, and his heart rate had risen to an unhealthy level.

He wasn't a fan of the countryside. In his opinion, villages were all well and good but give him the city any day of the week. The lack of space in an urban area had its downsides. But at least the roads were better maintained, and you didn't have bloody great hedges obscuring lethal hairpin bends.

Jemima's eagerness to travel at speed seemed less reckless now that they were travelling along a better road. Having confidence that Gareth would organise things at that end, she appeared more relaxed. The implications of the information Tristan had readily revealed could be catastrophic for the justice system. It placed a question mark over every decision Lawson had made throughout his career. Not only as a judge — prior to that position, he had been a practising barrister.

Even if they managed to find Lawson and get him back alive, this information would ultimately bring about an ignominious end to the man's career. He would inevitably face legal proceedings, stand trial and, should he be found guilty, serve his sentence alongside many of those whose fate he had sealed. Whichever way you looked at it, Rory Lawson's future prospects looked particularly grim.

The unconscionable actions of this man who had sworn to uphold the law would result in a swathe of appeals. It wasn't inconceivable to think that ultimately some very dangerous criminals would seek to have their sentences reduced or even overturned because of Lawson's actions. Even if this turned out to have been the only occasion that he had manipulated a sentence, its uniqueness would be irrelevant. The fact that it had happened would open the floodgates. Any prisoner who had had contact with him could have legitimate grounds for appeal.

As these thoughts swirled through her head, Jemima became concerned that anger would get the better of her. If that were to happen, it could very well lessen her ability to make sensible decisions. The best thing she could do while she was driving was to think about something else, as there was nothing more she could do about getting to the bottom of this particular hornets' nest until they reached the station. So for the time being she decided to shift her attention back to the DCI's worrying behaviour.

'I know we've already spoken about it, but give me the full lowdown on Kennedy, Dan. I've been away for so long that I'm out of touch with everyone, but we both agree there's something seriously wrong with him. I've never seen him act like this before, and with everything we've just heard about Lawson, and the possible implications that Superintendent Deavers is a bent officer, we'll need Kennedy onside.'

'I agree. He's got more clout than us. I've been racking my brains about what's going on with him, but the truth is, I haven't got a clue. Recently when we've gone to the pub after shift, the DCI's been quiet. You know what he's like when he's got a drink inside him, he usually bangs on about the good old days. But there's been none of that. He just nurses a pint. Makes it last, and he's quiet too. It's as though his mind's somewhere else.'

'What about Sally?' asked Jemima.

'We haven't seen her lately. It's ages since she's come out with us. At first, I thought it might be down to her shift pattern. But now I don't know . . .'

'You think they're going through a rough patch?'

'Happens. I always thought they were well suited, but you know what it's like in this job. Not many couples seem to stay together.'

'Perhaps I'll give Sally a ring when we've put this case to bed. Ask her out for a drink. Sound her out on things.'

'Good luck with that. Can't see Kennedy being too pleased about it. He'll just think you're sticking your nose into things that don't concern you.'

Jemima knew Dan was right. It was one thing making pertinent enquiries linked to a case. But sniffing around a fellow officer's personal life for no good reason other than to find out if they were having problems in their relationship was completely inappropriate. She only had to think back to when her own marriage was breaking up. The last thing she would have wanted was for any of her colleagues sticking their beak in to matters that didn't concern them.

Traffic was light and they reached the station in record time. As they climbed the stairs, Jemima spoke. 'I'm going to see if the DCI's back. Check with Gareth and find out the latest and I'll join you in a few minutes.'

Jemima found Kennedy's room in darkness. When she opened the door and put the light on, she was shocked to see that the room was in a worse state than earlier. Either he'd continued to act irrationally after she'd last seen it, or someone else had come to finish the job. It made no sense.

At any other time, she would have tidied up. She hated the thought of a more senior officer coming along and finding the place like this — it would reflect badly on Kennedy. As it was, questions would inevitably be asked. He was acting out of character. Yet whatever was going on with him, Jemima didn't want it to have a negative impact on his career. Like anyone, Ray Kennedy had his faults, but he was a good police officer and he'd always had her back.

Jemima sighed, knocked the light off and closed the door. If Kennedy didn't return soon and sort it out, she'd do it herself the first chance she got. But right now, she needed to know if the Trevelyan-Goodes had arrived at the station, and whether there had been any other developments. As she made her way to the incident room, she wished she had delayed her return to work. What she would give right now just to have a cuddle with Fin, or help James with his homework.

Gareth and Dan were talking quietly in the far corner of the room, while everyone else was still engrossed in their respective tasks. When they spotted Jemima heading in their direction, they stopped talking and waited for her to join them.

'What's the latest, Gar?'

'Just had a phone call to say that both Trevelyan-Goodes have been picked up. They weren't together and are being brought in separately.'

'Excellent, and did you make any progress on the Marquess Club?'

'That's a different matter. I've managed to get the address. Contacted Companies House to get any registered information but they didn't have a record of it. Long story short, I've dug around and discovered it's registered in Panama.'

'That raises a red flag,' said Jemima. 'You'd only set up an enterprise like that if you had something to hide.'

'What're you thinking?' asked Gareth.

'Dunno. Shell company. Tax avoidance. Organised crime. Any number of reasons, but none of them good.'

'And Lawson's one of their members!' said Broadbent. 'Seems to me he's as corrupt as they come.'

'I've a feeling this will just be the tip of the iceberg,' said Jemima. 'Keep digging, Gareth.'

'Do you want me to get a warrant to search the building?'

'Not yet. We don't have any evidence that it's linked to Lawson's disappearance. See if you can establish any links to organised crime. Sound out the National Crime Agency. If you come up with anything, then come and get me. Dan and I will be in one of the interview rooms. We'll see if we can get anywhere with Edward Trevelyan-Goode. No matter how dodgy Lawson turns out to be, we must get him back alive. Make sure the others don't let up on their tasks. I need everyone to remain focused.'

'Who are we interviewing first?' asked Dan as they went down to the interview rooms.

'The father. He's the one pulling the strings in that family. I doubt Zach would know who's behind Lawson's abduction. Once we tell Edward that we know of his connection with Lawson, we might stand a chance of him telling us everything he knows. If Zach's sentencing is behind Emyr's death and Lawson's abduction, then Edward has his own son's blood on his hands. I'm sure he wouldn't have set out for this to happen. But it has and there's no going back.'

# CHAPTER 21

For a grieving man approaching his sixtieth birthday, Edward Trevelyan-Goode somehow managed to look suave. It helped that he had a full head of silver hair and had evidently kept himself in shape. His face was stubbled, whether by design or because he had more pressing issues on his mind, it was impossible to tell. Though a cursory glance told them that despite the loss of one of his sons, the man still cared about his appearance. When at home most people opted for comfortable loungewear. Edward, however, was dressed in chinos and a linen shirt.

Jemima knew that if she were in this man's shoes, she wouldn't have cared about personal grooming. It would have been a huge achievement just to put one foot in front of the other.

Harrowing images of the Andrews family flashed before Jemima's eyes. Having arrived at their house unannounced, it had been impossible not to recognise the absolute heartache and bewilderment those parents were endeavouring to cope with. They were at their wits' end, yet their daughter was alive. Whereas earlier that day, Edward Trevelyan-Goode had lost one of his sons, an innocent young man whose life had seemingly ended because he was mistaken for his twin.

What's more, it was conceivable that Emyr's death was possibly brought about as a direct result of Edward's own actions, when he engineered a deal to keep his other son out of prison. It was impossible to imagine how Edward could ever sleep easy again. Yet even with blood on his hands, the man looked as though he was ready for a photo shoot.

They had barely sat down before Edward spoke. 'You'd better have a damned good reason for dragging me down here! You do realise that my son's dead? It's only a few hours since I had to identify his mangled body. My wife and I are grieving. We're devastated. Have you found the monsters who abducted him?'

'Firstly, I'd like to offer my condolences. I can't begin to imagine what you're going through,' said Jemima. 'But I asked the officers to bring you in because of what happened with your sons.'

'Sons? That's plural. Emyr should be your sole focus. He was a good person. Never did anything bad throughout his entire life. Then for some reason he was abducted and now he's dead. And you clowns—' Edward's eyes narrowed as he looked from Jemima to Broadbent and made a theatrical sweeping gesture with his arm — 'you've failed to find the people responsible.' He leaned forward, closing the gap between them as he jabbed his index finger and all but spat out the next three words. 'Shame! On! You!'

Jemima allowed the man to finish his rant before she spoke. 'You are not under arrest, but this interview will be recorded and conducted under caution.' She then switched on the tape recorder and read him his rights.

Trevelyan-Goode refused legal representation. 'I'm not wasting my hard-earned money on a solicitor when I've done nothing wrong.' He flicked his hand dismissively as though warding off an annoying fly. 'My son is dead and you're treating me like some sort of criminal. I'll have your jobs for this! I don't know who you think you're dealing with, but I'm not some idiot that you can bully. I'm a respectable businessman. With contacts. People with influence, who can make or break the likes of numpties like you. Mark my words, you'll both be out on your backsides before the day's over.'

'I very much doubt that.' Jemima's tone was level and she smiled sweetly, holding the man's gaze until he was ultimately forced to sit back in his seat and look away. Knowing that she'd demonstrated that she was not afraid of his threats, she continued, 'I'm glad that you picked up on the fact that I said "sons".'

'You've no right to question me about Zach. That investigation is in the past. He stood trial and is complying with the—'

'Enough!' Jemima slammed her fist on the table. The suddenness of the action caught Edward by surprise, and he flinched. 'You're here to answer our questions. We're investigating a time-critical serious incident. Make no mistake, if you fail to cooperate, you'll be placed in a holding cell overnight. There'll be no home comforts and I doubt you'll get any sleep. We'll continue with this interview in the morning, when I guarantee you'll see things in a different light. The choice is yours. But I really wouldn't recommend spending the night in one of those cells.'

Edward's shoulders slumped as indignance gave way to common sense. 'Fine, ask your questions,' he hissed.

'I'm glad you've come around,' said Jemima. 'And I'm fully aware that Zach was found guilty of a particularly distasteful crime. However, it's recently come to our attention that the judge who presided over Zach's trial is a friend of yours—'

'I don't know where you got that information from, but it's a very serious allegation to make,' interjected Edward.

Jemima was quick to notice a slight twitch in his left eye. The man clearly hadn't expected this line of questioning. 'Before the case went to trial, your friendship should have been declared and Rory Lawson would have been obliged to recuse himself from the process. Now, I don't know whether Zach was aware of the link between the two of you, but there is no doubt in my mind that both you and Lawson colluded to pervert the course of justice. I have yet to establish whether money changed hands. But I will be looking into your financial records and business dealings. Though, in any case, the fact that you are known to each other is enough for us to bring charges against you.'

'What a ridiculous allegation!'

Jemima ignored the man's bluster. 'Have you spoken to Lawson recently?'

'No comment.' Edward's voice was strong and steady, but his body language had changed. He'd crossed his arms and dropped his gaze as he did his utmost to control a rising sense of panic. As a successful businessman and a poker player, he was used to bluffing his way out of trouble. Though losing a business deal or a few thousand quid on a hand of cards was nothing compared to the very real possibility of losing his liberty.

Despite the fact that no money had changed hands, Edward had bought Zach's freedom. And it hadn't come cheap. When he'd weighed up the available options, he had thought it was a relatively low-risk strategy. It wasn't such a big deal awarding Tristan Lawson a contract as architect for the new development. If only he'd known at the time that he would ultimately be sacrificing one son to save another . . .

Edward and Rory went way back. Their relationship had been forged and strengthened within the confines of the Marquess Club. It was one of the few places in the country where gentlemen were free to be gentlemen, where they didn't have to worry about negotiating the minefield of modern life. Political correctness was left at the door. The club was a networking and socialising space where like-minded individuals could speak freely, collaborate, help one another out and enjoy themselves.

Exclusivity at the Marquess Club was maintained by restricting membership. Potential new members were proposed by existing members, and their suitability discussed on an individual basis. A case had to be presented at the annual meeting and a secret ballot held. If any existing member dissented then the person was denied membership. Sometimes there were no new members admitted in a year. And any new members who were admitted were required to sign a non-disclosure agreement to ensure that secrecy was maintained.

The overarching principles of membership were absolute discretion and always ensuring that whatever deals were done within the confines of the club were agreed to the mutual satisfaction of any member who was an interested party.

Jemima had lost count of the people she had interviewed over the years. Throughout that time, she had witnessed all sorts of behaviour and various attempts at covering up and deflecting attention away from information she was determined to uncover. No matter how skilled a negotiator or seasoned a poker player Edward Trevelyan-Goode was, he was no match for her.

From the moment she had spotted the uncontrollable twitch of his left eye, she knew that she would break him down. Edward might very well come across as confident, but he was a man on the backfoot. And, unless others on the team identified a credible suspect, this man was her best bet at furthering her understanding of Rory Lawson.

Jemima was as enthusiastic and relentless as an attack dog. Having just tasted blood for the first time in over a year, she relished the chance to ramp up the pressure. There was no way she'd let go until she found out everything she needed to know.

But as this thought raced through her mind, a niggling seed of self-doubt embedded itself and began to grow. A year was a long time to have been out of the game. There was no denying the fact that her instinct was not as sharp as it had once been. Was she calling this wrong? Was she allowing her contempt of misogynistic behaviour to cloud her judgement?

Settling back in her seat she stared long and hard at the man in front of her. Everything about him, especially the threats of having them thrown off the police force, suggested that at the heart of the matter was corrupt behaviour by men who believed they could get away with anything.

An institution such as the Marquess Club would be the perfect place for clandestine deals to go down, where surreptitious agreements happened to ensure the best interests of certain people. It was one thing greasing the wheels to further your own ends — that sort of thing went on inside every institution up and down the land, which was despicable, but also the way business worked. But when a member of the judiciary was involved in the corruption, it became a matter that couldn't be overlooked.

Given what she already knew about Lawson, it was likely the man had numerous enemies they had yet to identify.

'We have a witness placing you, Rory Lawson and Tristan Lawson together at the Marquess Club shortly before Zach's trial. It was a prearranged meeting where you awarded Tristan a lucrative contract. However this goes, you're going to be charged with perverting the course of justice, but your cooperation will be noted when it comes to the prosecution.'

Edward pursed his lips and shook his head vehemently. 'It didn't happen.'

'Stop wasting my time. We'll sequester your business records and will prove the link between you. You'll both be charged with perverting the course of justice and will face a hefty prison sentence.'

Edward began to sweat profusely as his composure crumbled. He suddenly looked like a rabbit caught in the headlights.

'But this investigation is not about you and Rory Lawson perverting the course of justice. That will come later. At this moment in time, we've more pressing matters. Rory Lawson was abducted earlier today and we're—'

'Abducted! You mean like Emyr?' The man's complexion paled, and his mouth dropped open.

'Just like Emyr. He was taken early this morning, about the same time as your son, and we've no idea who has him. We don't get many abductions in these parts. Yet we have two on the same morning, and the common factors in both abductions are Zach and you. As Zach and Emyr were identical twins, it's possible that Emyr's abduction was a case of mistaken identity.'

'And Zach was their target?'

'Yes. From what I've heard, Emyr wasn't the sort of person to make enemies,' said Jemima.

'He didn't. My sons are as different as chalk and cheese. Everyone likes . . . liked Emyr,' said Edward. As he corrected the tense in which he referred to his deceased son, it appeared that the full force of bereavement hit him once again. His belligerent attitude faded. He swallowed hard and blinked rapidly to dispel the tears that were ready to fall. Distractedly wiping his eyes with a crumpled handkerchief that he hurriedly extracted from his trouser pocket, the man's breath caught in his throat. When he continued to speak, it took a noticeable amount of effort to keep his raw emotion at bay and his voice level. 'Are you telling me that those girls that Zach filmed are responsible for Emyr's death?'

'No. We've spoken to them and are certain they had nothing to do with either abduction. But we need to know who Lawson's enemies are, and if Zach has other enemies too, because it's possible that if Emyr's abduction was a result of mistaken identity, they could still come after Zach.'

'No. No. No. We can't lose both of our sons. Zach's no angel, but I don't want anything to happen to him.'

'In that case, tell us what you know. It's the only way of ensuring that they don't come after him.'

'He'll never forgive me. He'll see it as a betrayal.'

'Better that than he's abducted or ends up dead,' said Broadbent.

Edward closed his eyes and sighed. The air was thick with anticipation as both officers waited silently for him to decide. When he eventually spoke, Jemima had to force herself not to let out a sigh of relief.

'I admit that I know Rory from the Marquess Club. We've both been members for years. It's like any club. There are cliques. It's only natural when certain interests align. I joined to further my career. You can connect with people who make things happen. It opens doors that would otherwise remain firmly closed. There's an unwritten code that we look out for one another.'

'In other words, backhanders and bribes,' said Broadbent.

Jemima swiftly kicked her partner's ankle. He stifled a yelp and winced at the sharp, unexpected pain. They were just starting to get somewhere with Edward, and she didn't want the man to clam up because of Broadbent voicing his obvious disapproval of what went on inside the club.

'I wouldn't quite put it that way,' said Edward. 'It's the general cut and thrust of business. The way the world works.'

'Are you part of Rory's clique?' asked Jemima.

'Far from it. We obviously know each other and occasionally might have a drink or supper together. We joined around the same time and were quite close at first. But that was years ago. Lawson and I are very different people. As we found our feet, we drifted apart. It's hardly unusual, as we don't share many interests. Rory joined an elite group. They're the upper echelon. Very selective and secretive.

'We hadn't spoken in months until he approached me about his son. He'd heard on the grapevine that I was looking for an architect for my latest development and he wanted me to consider Tristan. That's why we had dinner together. Lawson instigated it. It took a week or so for us to arrange a date and time we could meet. It was far from easy as we're all busy. And during that time, we had a date for Zach's court case. I told Rory that perhaps we shouldn't go ahead with things, but he insisted it was a way in which we could both help our kids, and no one need know about it.'

'Do you know the names of the other members of this elite clique that Lawson's a member of?' asked Jemima.

'There're only three others. Sean Richardson, Thomas Pargan and Michael Chaloner.'

'What do you know of them?'

'Very little. Sean and Rory met at university. They've been friends ever since. I believe Michael runs a modelling agency, and Thomas Pargan has a string of casinos. I've often wondered what they have in common. They're quite a disparate group. Yet they've remained close for as long as I can remember.'

# CHAPTER 22

There was a knock on the door and Gareth appeared. There was no mistaking his eagerness to speak to them as he was out of breath and clearly agitated.

'I'd like you both to step outside. There's been a development.' His words were rushed, insistent.

Having told Gareth to interrupt them if he found anything of significance, Jemima was pleased that he had seemingly discovered something so quickly. She heard the urgency in his voice, but being preoccupied with how she would progress Trevelyan-Goode's interview, she failed to spot the obvious. She paused the interview and exited the room with Dan.

Once outside, she got her first proper look at Gareth and saw tears streaming down his face.

'What's happened?' She'd not seen him cry before and dreaded whatever he was about to say as she knew it would be something awful.

Gareth wiped his eyes on his sleeve and stifled a sob. 'I-it's th-the guv. I d-don't know h-how it went down, b-but Kennedy's been shot.'

Jemima's jaw dropped and she felt the ground shift beneath her. She suddenly felt cold and numb as though ice had replaced the blood running through her veins, and began to shake. No longer in control of her own body, she staggered towards the wall and leaned against it, desperate for something solid to stop her from collapsing. But even that wasn't enough to keep her upright. Her body suddenly felt too heavy for her legs to support, and with her back against the wall she sank to the floor.

Broadbent had paled but wasn't prepared to accept what Gareth had told them. 'Not funny, mate! Not! Bloody! Funny!' His voice rose with each word. 'You're out of order!' He grabbed Gareth's shoulders and shook him. Their faces were so close that there was not even a couple of inches between them.

'I-it's the t-truth! I had a call from one of the team and needed to go back to the court. I was on my way when I heard a shot. It sounded close so I ran in the direction it came from. I found him. I was the one who found him.'

'How bad was it? Was he conscious? Did he say anything?' Jemima had so many questions swirling around in her head.

'It's bad. At first, I didn't realise it was him, and when I got closer, I honestly thought he might be dead. I called for an ambulance straight away. He was so still, barely breathing, but he must have recognised my voice, because he whispered, "No police. Not safe. Get outta here".'

'What the hell did he mean by that?' The words came out more forcefully than Jemima had intended, and she immediately realised that she needed to dial it down a bit. She'd thought that something was up with Kennedy, and from what Gareth had just said, it seemed the DCI had concerns about some of their colleagues.

'I've no idea, but I didn't call it in. I know I've gone against protocol but the DCI's the boss.'

'Shiiit,' hissed Broadbent. He slammed the heel of his hand onto his forehead. Like all of them, he was having difficulty keeping a lid on his emotions. He paced back and forth, thinking of all the things he'd like to do if he ever managed to get his hands on the scumbag who had shot Kennedy.

When Jemima found the strength to stand, she grabbed hold of Gareth's shoulder and looked him directly in the eye. She could see how distraught the younger officer was and wanted him to know that he had her full support. 'Listen to me. You did good, Gar. It was right to listen to Kennedy's warning. If I'd have been in your shoes, I'd have done the same.'

'Thanks. It just feels wrong not doing things by the book. If it'd been anyone other than Kennedy, I'd have called it in and secured the scene. I know that because of my actions we could have lost vital evidence. Especially things that could identify whoever shot him. I've probably buggered up any chance of a conviction further down the line.'

'Don't worry about that for now. We've more pressing issues. Did the paramedics say anything?'

'I didn't speak to them. When I heard the siren, I moved back into the shadows. They worked on him at the scene then transferred him to the ambulance. He's on his way to hospital. He'd lost so much blood. I honestly don't know if he'll m-make it.'

'He'll make it all right. It's Kennedy you're talking about,' said Jemima. 'We've got to get up there. We've got to be with him.'

The news had knocked her for six. It was as though the world had shrunk, and nothing else existed. Ray Kennedy was more than just her boss. He was her friend and mentor. She respected him more than any other police officer she knew. The man was the moral compass of the team, the glue that bound them together. He had stuck his neck out for her on more than one occasion. He was like family.

Jemima had realised that something was wrong with him today. He had been distracted and acting oddly. Yet she hadn't stood her ground and forced his hand to get him to open up to her. She regretted it now. She should have pushed him harder, backed him into a corner and insisted she was going nowhere until he told her what was wrong. What if she could have helped him? What if she could have prevented this?

Yet as things stood, she had no idea what '*this*' was. Had Kennedy somehow become embroiled in the case they were investigating? Had he got too close to the people behind Lawson's abduction? Had it made him a target? Or was it something else entirely?

There were so many unknowns. So many unanswered questions. Nothing made sense.

'Have you spoken to anyone else about this?'

'No. I came back for you and Dan.'

'Good. Don't say a word to anyone.' Jemima was determined that no more would be said about Kennedy's shooting until they were safely outside the station.

Lawson's fate suddenly seemed inconsequential. From the things they'd learned through the course of the investigation it seemed the man was as corrupt as they came. In normal circumstances, she would have put every effort into finding him. But this latest turn of events was anything but normal.

Jemima needed to be at the hospital. She wouldn't let Kennedy suffer alone. She wanted him to know how much he meant to her, how she valued his friendship. How she appreciated everything he did for her. More than anything, she wanted Ray Kennedy to know that she wouldn't rest until she had found out who had done this to him. And once she had done that, she would hunt the bastard down and make them pay.

The team had suffered too much. They'd already lost Ashton through a senseless act of violence — a young officer with great potential, a good, intelligent, kind man. It was unthinkable that they could soon lose another member of their team.

'Gar, go get the car keys. The three of us are off to the hospital.' Her voice was low.

'But what about the case?'

'Right now, I don't give a fuck about the case. Kennedy's our priority. He's worth a thousand Lawsons. Dan, go and charge Zach and his father with perverting the course of justice. They're both to be placed in the holding cells until we return. I'll go and have a word with the custody sergeant, explain the situation and tell him to make sure that Edward and Zach are not allowed to communicate with each other. I don't want to give them any opportunity to get their stories straight.'

She distractedly ran a hand through her hair as she thought through her next steps. 'Once I've sorted that, I'll go upstairs and tell the others to keep working the case. They can ring me if there are any developments. I'll meet both of you in the car park in five minutes.' She held her palm up to stop Dan and Gareth from leaving before she said her next piece.

'Before we leave the building we each need to book out a firearm.' She saw the look of consternation on each of their faces. 'Hopefully we won't need to use them, but it's better to be prepared than to be facing the barrel of a gun with just a taser or baton.'

They both nodded their agreement, reluctantly accepting her reasoning.

* * *

Dan was already in the driver's seat when Jemima came outside. The engine was running and he was tapping his fingers on the steering wheel in his impatience to get going. Gareth was in the rear seat. There was no inane banter or talk of any kind. Both men looked grim, each lost in their own thoughts. Jemima had only just reached for the seat belt when Dan pulled away. The tyres squealed as though he was taking a bend on a racetrack. This was one occasion when he was determined to drive as fast as possible.

'Ring Sally,' ordered Jemima. 'We've got to make sure she knows.'

'I've tried already, but she's not picking up. I've left a message asking her to call me. I kept it vague, but told her it was urgent,' said Gareth.

No one spoke for the rest of the journey. They all knew there was nothing more to be said. They couldn't help Kennedy — that was up to the medics, but even they couldn't work miracles. The only thing the three of them could do was to wait for the medical team to do everything they could and pray that it would be enough.

Kennedy was already in theatre when they arrived. It was a good sign. At least he was still alive. They raced towards the operating theatre as fast as they dared, mindful that they shouldn't be going so quickly. Hazard signs had been placed along the length of the corridor leading to the operating theatre to prevent people from slipping on a spillage. As she glanced down, Jemima noticed that the warning signs were keeping them away from a trail of blood, of which there was a significant amount. She knew it had to be Kennedy's.

As Broadbent glanced sideways, he groaned and pulled up sharply. Jemima had been so focused on Kennedy that she'd momentarily forgotten about her partner's phobia. They all had secrets. Dan's was that he had an extreme reaction to blood. It was something he had been determined to hide from his colleagues. Yet, working as closely as he did with Jemima, she had soon discovered his aversion to it.

They both knew that should his extreme reaction become public knowledge it could jeopardise his chances of career progression. Given the nature of the job, Dan, like the others on the team, was frequently required to attend crime scenes where blood had been spilled. Jemima had been shocked when she initially realised how much it affected him. Her first thought had been that he was trying to pull a fast one. After all, no one liked seeing the sights they routinely encountered. But she had quickly realised that Dan wasn't just passing the buck because of a reluctance to do that part of the job. His aversion to blood manifested itself in a physiological reaction.

Due to the location of the hazard signs, it had been necessary for them to make their way along the corridor in single file. Gareth happened to be directly behind Dan and hadn't anticipated that he would suddenly stop for no apparent reason. As a result of his forward momentum, he was unable to stop in time, and ended up bumping into Broadbent, who had suddenly doubled over.

'What the hell!' Gareth held his hands out to try to remain upright. 'Why'd you stop?' In all the years they'd worked together, he hadn't realised that Dan had a phobia of blood.

Hearing Broadbent's groan, Jemima skidded to a halt and doubled back to grab hold of him before he hit the floor. Thankfully he hadn't fainted and was only off balance. Otherwise, he would have ended up covered in Ray Kennedy's blood.

'What's up with him? He just stopped without warning.' Gareth couldn't make sense of what he was seeing.

'There's nothing wrong with him. We just react differently, that's all. We're all worried about Kennedy. I couldn't even find the strength to stand up when you told me the news,' said Jemima.

'There's got to be more to it than that. He managed to hold it together to get us here.'

'Leave it, Gareth!' Jemima snapped. Gareth recoiled, and Jemima immediately regretted the harshness of her tone. The three of them needed to be united. Not holding out on one another.

It was obvious to Gareth that something was up with Broadbent, and that Jemima was covering for him. Over the years he had accepted that Dan and Jemima were close. They'd been partners long before he had joined the squad. And until now, that hadn't seemed to matter. He and Dan had become closer following Ashton's death. They'd opened up to each other and supported each other through a very tough time.

With Jemima on maternity leave, Dan had worked closely with him. Yet it was clear that they still had secrets. And even at a time like this when Gareth thought they were all in it together, there were things they weren't prepared to share with him. This wasn't a team united by tragedy. This was them and him.

'Suit yourselves,' muttered Gareth. His facial expression and tone of voice left them in no doubt of the sense of betrayal he currently felt. He stepped around them and continued down the corridor in search of the operating theatre.

'Look away. Take deep breaths,' whispered Jemima. She needed Dan to get himself together. As irritating and inconvenient as it was, she knew that she had to support him. 'You can't let this get the better of you now.'

'I know. I'll be OK. I'm sorry.' He swallowed hard. His eyes were closed as he battled the rising sense of nausea. His skin had taken on a greenish hue, and beads of sweat had erupted across his brow.

'No need to apologise to me. But you owe Gareth an explanation. We need to be united. This is no time to put up barriers.'

As the distance between them increased, Gareth could hear them muttering. The despair that had engulfed him the moment he had realised that it was Kennedy lying in a pool of blood suddenly seemed less acute. It wasn't that he felt any less helpless — Kennedy's fate was out of his hands, and he was standing a few feet away from where the man would either be saved or take his final breath. There was nothing he could do but wait. But whatever secret Jemima and Dan were keeping from him was another thing that had blindsided him. They obviously didn't consider him to be an equal, and he was absolutely bloody furious.

'Don't say anything to him,' pleaded Broadbent. The thought of Gareth finding out about his weakness diverted his attention from the spilled blood, and he was soon strong enough to stand unsupported.

'We don't have a choice. Look at him. Gareth's not going to let this go. Right now, we need one another more than ever, and he knows we're keeping something from him. Think about it from his perspective. He'll feel so betrayed. I would, and so would you. I've kept your secret, Dan. It's not my place to tell him. But I'm asking you to let Gareth in. For all our sakes. We've got to stick together, and he deserves to know.'

A door opened behind them as a cleaning operative trundled through with a mop and bucket in tow. The man obliviously set about his work, cheerfully whistling a tune as he systematically cleaned the spillage. Soon there would be no evidence that Kennedy had been wheeled along this corridor.

Jemima looked from Dan to Gareth. Even from this distance, Gareth's body language suggested that he was angry. The three of them had to be able to rely on one another, and Broadbent's secret was about to tear them apart. No matter how badly it played out for Dan, she couldn't allow that to happen. Secrets had their place. Everyone had them, and sometimes they were kept for a very good reason. But this wasn't one of those occasions.

Dan had nothing to be ashamed of. He had worked hard to overcome his aversion to blood. Having regular sessions with the force psychologist had made a significant difference. But the attack on Kennedy had come out of the blue and had inevitably catapulted each of them back to the time when they had lost Ashton in the line of duty. It was no wonder that any coping mechanisms Dan had put in place had been forgotten about. They were all at a low ebb. Emotions were high. They had been working flat out all day and were running on empty. If any of them had been forced to face their fears they would have been unlikely to react well.

'You have to tell him, Dan. No matter the consequences. You must.'

Dan knew she was right. He'd let his guard down in a moment of weakness, and now had no choice but to try to resolve the situation and hope that Gareth wouldn't shoot his mouth off back at the station. Taking a deep breath, he steeled himself for what was to come. 'Gareth, mate, I need to tell you something.'

Jemima decided to leave them to it, as it was best not to get involved. It was up to Broadbent to explain what had happened. Once his secret was out in the open, she'd apologise to Gareth for snapping at him. And hopefully once he was fully apprised of the facts, he'd appreciate why she'd been so short with him, and they could put it all behind them.

She headed towards the double doors leading into the operating theatre, took a deep breath and bunched her fists before finding the courage to look through a small glass panel. Only yards away, there was a team of gowned-up medical staff focusing their attention on the small area where Kennedy lay. There was a significant amount of blood on the floor, and she could see they were transfusing him to keep him alive.

There was a lot of chatter. From the tone of the voices, Jemima ascertained that they were keeping one another informed of various facts, though she could not make out what they were saying. She could tell just from looking at them that these people were used to working as a team. Their work was so critical that any mistake could cost a life. Yet despite the high-stakes environment, everyone carried out their tasks with no apparent hesitation. It was comforting to know that Kennedy was in competent hands.

Looking beyond the cluster of bodies surrounding Kennedy, her eyes came to rest on the significant amount of machinery crammed into such a small area. To need so many pieces of vital equipment suggested to Jemima that the odds of him making it out of there alive were even longer than she had originally thought possible.

These people were doing everything in their power to save him. But only time would tell whether their skill and efforts would be enough to make a difference. As she wiped away her tears, Jemima took comfort from the fact that as they hadn't given up on him, Kennedy must have a fighting chance of survival.

An alarm sounded on one of the machines, indicating that something was wrong. As a member of the team reached for another machine, others stepped away. The gap it created gave Jemima sight of the monitor displaying Kennedy's vital signs. Digits displaying his blood pressure were dropping at an exceptionally fast rate and his heart rate had flatlined.

'Guys!' said Jemima. Even to her own ears, her voice sounded weak. Vulnerable.

Within seconds, Dan and Gareth were at her side. They huddled together, suddenly desperate for support and comfort, helpless as children watching what might very well be Kennedy's final moments play out in front of them. What felt like hours was actually no more than minutes. But the impact on each of them was startlingly profound as the three police officers, who had sworn to protect life, stared on impotently, wholly reliant on the efforts of the crash team to save their guvnor's life. It was a routine these medics had performed on numerous occasions but the onlooking detectives were fully aware that each time they faced this scenario there was never any certainty of the outcome.

Twenty minutes later there was a noticeable change in pace, and as one of the medical staff shifted position, they saw the monitor displaying Kennedy's heartbeat, back to rhythmic peaks and troughs. It was round about the same moment that the three of them noticed that they had been standing there holding hands.

Any embarrassment was immediately outweighed by the relief that Kennedy was still alive. Jemima giggled. She couldn't help herself, and the inappropriateness of her reaction set the others off too. They let go of one another and stepped away from their vantage point, feeling like naughty children but welcoming the unexpected feeling of elation that broke the tension of the last hour.

When they had finally managed to compose themselves, Jemima was the first to speak. 'Is it sorted?' she asked. There was no need for clarification about what she was referring to.

'Yeah, we're good,' said Gareth. 'But you should've told me, mate. I wouldn't have thought any less of you.' He punched Dan's arm, and Broadbent smiled sheepishly.

Jemima was relieved that her sergeants had sorted things out. She knew it was a conversation that Dan had always hoped to avoid. The forced admission would have dented his pride, but she was confident that Gareth could be trusted to keep it to himself. If anything, it should strengthen the bond between them. She hoped that Dan saw it that way too.

It wasn't long before a woman came out of the operating theatre. Jemima sensed she was about to relay good news, as she readily made eye contact and smiled at them.

'How's he doing?' asked Jemima.

'And you are?' The woman tilted her head, her brow furrowing as she arched her eyebrows.

'We're police officers.' Jemima extracted her warrant card and held it out for inspection. 'The man in there, Detective Chief Inspector Ray Kennedy, is our guvnor. He was injured in the line of duty.'

'I won't lie to you, it was touch-and-go in there. Mr Kennedy lost a significant amount of blood. The bullet lodged in his abdomen and nicked an artery. A few millimetres difference and he'd have bled out before he got here. We managed to remove the bullet. He suffered a cardiac arrest while we were working on him, but we've stabilised him. The good news is that with close monitoring and some proper rest, it's possible for him to make a full recovery. We'll be moving him to ICU shortly. You'll want an officer standing guard?'

'Yes. We'll organise shifts,' said Jemima. She knew that Kennedy would be on a locked ward with only a few other patients. 'Can we see him before he's moved?'

'Not yet. There are still things to be done and he wouldn't know you were there. Anyway, I must go. Try not to worry. He's a tough cookie, and he's survived the hardest part.' The doctor stifled a yawn. 'Sorry, long shift, and I still have a lot to get through.' She squeezed Jemima's shoulder to offer her support then turned and walked away.

Being informed that Kennedy's prognosis was no longer as bleak as Jemima had initially thought brought a sense of relief and she felt her shoulders relax as some of the tension left her body. Ideally, she would have liked to have seen the DCI for herself, but she knew that would be for her benefit not his. And as there was nothing that any of them could do for him, her thoughts moved to the circumstances that had led to him being shot.

She had allowed her emotions to get in the way, had failed in her duty as a police officer. Her top priorities should have been to ensure that the crime scene was secure and to recover any evidence. Kennedy might very well have told Gareth not to go down the official route, but that was surely the ramblings of a critically injured man. The bottom line was, as the senior officer aware of what had happened, she should have alerted the crime scene officers and identified potential witnesses and interviewed them.

This was Jemima's first day back at work and when it had mattered the most, she'd acted like a member of the public. She'd let Kennedy down big time, being so caught up in her own feelings. Instead of fixating on the medical team as they worked on Kennedy, she should have been out there doing everything she could to find and apprehend the person who shot him. It was weak and shameful to have given in to her emotions. And when Ray Kennedy regained consciousness, there was no doubt in her mind that he would give her a dressing-down.

She shook her head in despair. 'I've fucked up.'

'What d'ya mean? I've already told you, he warned me not to get the police involved,' said Gareth.

'That's as may be, but I should've secured the crime scene. The least I could have done is to have gone there and combed the place for evidence. And I'm sure we can trust Jeanne Ennersley. She's as straight as they come.'

'We don't know that for certain,' said Gareth.

'I suppose not, but it doesn't sit right with me. We should be doing something. Where was Kennedy when it happened?' asked Jemima. Having been so caught up in events it had only just occurred to her that she didn't even know this basic fact.

'In an alleyway. The one that runs along the rear of the Marquess Club.'

Jemima couldn't believe what she'd heard. 'Let me get this straight, there was an attempt on Kennedy's life, yards from a club that's likely to be linked to our case? We've got to get a search warrant for that building. I'm making a call.' Her phone had been set on silent since just before she'd gone into the interview room to speak to Edward Trevelyan-Goode. And with the subsequent turn of events, she had forgotten to change the setting. As she took it out, she saw an icon notifying her of a voicemail message. She pressed play, held it against her ear, and her eyes widened as she listened in horror.

The message was from Kennedy. He spoke quickly, and she could hear the fear in his voice.

*Huxley, I'd hoped it wouldn't come to this, but you have to know what I've found. This case isn't what you think. It's so much bigger. The key card you found is for a place called the Marquess Club. I'm there now, in the alleyway at the rear. I'm staking it out.*

*If anything happens to me, I need you to ring this number.'*

Ray Kennedy recited it carefully.

*It's for a friend of mine. His name's Frank Rutherford. He's ex-military. No one knows him at the station, and no one must ever find out about him. He's fully briefed and will know what to do.*

*Apart from Dan and Gareth, you can't trust anyone. There's a network of corrupt officers. Sally's one of them. She had me fooled, but whatever she says, do not trust her. I'm not sure who the others are, so watch your backs. Hopefully I'll know more soon. I'll keep this line open . . .'*

There was a rustling sound as Kennedy presumably placed his phone in his pocket. From then on, the sound was muffled. As Jemima strained to hear, she thought she could make out the sound of footsteps. Seconds later, she heard a female voice. It was Sally's.

*'You should've left it alone, Ray. Then again, you've never known when to back off. I love you, Ray. More than I've ever loved anyone. I hoped we could have been for keeps, but your bloody principles make it impossible to carry on. It's the end of the line for you. I can't allow you to walk out of here. There's too much at stake. Powerful forces at play.'*

*'Sally, put the gun down. You don't have to do this. You know I love you too.'*

Ray Kennedy was pleading for his life.

*'I know, my darling. It breaks my heart. But I have to end this now.'*

At the sound of the gunshot, Jemima almost dropped the phone. Sergeant Sally Trent, a serving police officer and Kennedy's long-term life partner was the person who had shot him.

# CHAPTER 23

It was as though there was a seismic shift. Yet another occasion when Jemima's cognitive functions struggled to keep up with her bodily requirements. As her surroundings swam before her eyes, she gasped for air. Somehow, she had forgotten to breathe.

The DCI's warning had been so chilling that a rising sense of panic took hold and threatened to overwhelm her. Earlier in the day she had been a woman returning to work after an extended break. Now she found herself in charge of a high-profile, complex case without the support of her senior officer. And after spending most of the day running in circles, she had just learned that a fellow officer — someone she had considered a friend — had tried to murder DCI Ray Kennedy.

Jemima had sensed that something was wrong at the station. But even she couldn't have guessed how bad things were. She had no idea what they were up against, but whatever it was, this was no ordinary case. Her team was no longer just investigating the abduction of some potentially dodgy judge. They had been parachuted slap-bang into the middle of a war without any prior warning of what they were about to face.

She had heard Sally shoot the DCI — proof of his assertion that they couldn't trust anyone. Normal rules could no longer apply. They were now in uncharted waters.

This latest turn of events required her to put any immediate fears she had aside. She needed to lead by example, encourage Dan and Gareth to up their game and demonstrate that she had what it took to lead them through this godawful mess. As she glanced at her two colleagues, she experienced a moment of hesitation. She wanted these men by her side. Yet as things stood, there was a significant risk that one or all of them would not make it through to the other side.

What she was about to tell them would change things for ever. Having trusted Sally like one of their own, they were currently oblivious to this treacherous turn of events. But they needed to wise up if they were to stand any chance of coming out of this unscathed.

'Lads, you need to listen to this. But not on speakerphone.' She shoved the device into Dan's hand. He and Gareth huddled together and were shocked into silence by what they heard.

'No wonder I haven't been able to get hold of Sally,' said Gareth.

'What are we going to do?' asked Dan, looking to Jemima to lead them.

'First off, I'm going to ring Frank Rutherford, whoever the hell he is. Fill him in on what's happened to Kennedy and find out what he knows. Let's face it, we're out of our depth. If there are more corrupt officers, we've got no way of identifying them. So we're better off collaborating with this outsider. Kennedy trusted him and in my opinion, the DCI's a pretty good judge of character.'

'Not with Sally,' muttered Broadbent.

The implication hung heavily in the air.

'I don't see we've any other choice. We need to ensure that there's not another attempt on Kennedy's life. He very nearly died on that operating table — he's hanging on by a thread. Whatever's going on here must be big. Sally wouldn't have broken cover in such an extreme way if there wasn't a lot at stake. And it's not as if we can report this and wait around for the IOPC to investigate the matter.' As Jemima uttered the words, she could sense her confidence returning. She was usually good in a crisis. She somehow had the ability to thrive and make sensible decisions in situations that would floor more than ninety-nine percent of the population. Whatever they did from this time forward, they had to go all in. Formulate a plan and stick to it. This was no time to doubt herself. If they were to keep Kennedy alive and ensure their own safety, she needed to act decisively.

'This voice message is all we have. Once this goes public, it puts a target on each of our backs. We're at a disadvantage from the off, because we've no idea who we're up against. Or what reach they have. Right now, it's conceivable to think they could even go after our families to try to shut us down.'

'Ohhh shit! Caro and Harry!' Broadbent's eyes widened as the implications of their current predicament sunk in.

Even Gareth looked paler than usual. And that was saying something. He sighed heavily but kept his fears to himself.

'Apart from Kennedy voicing his suspicions about the existence of other corrupt officers, we don't know who else, if anyone, is involved. We must be careful. I'm not about to risk anyone else getting killed. We lost Fin last year — we're not gonna lose anyone else. I say we follow Kennedy's advice and keep this circle tight. Agreed?' She looked from one to the other, willing them to back her. She knew them both well enough to spot the flickers of hesitation and self-doubt play across their faces. For a few seconds it occurred to her that she might have overestimated their resolve.

Gareth was the first to react. Straightening his stance, he cleared his throat. 'Let's do it.'

'I guess we don't have a choice,' said Dan, with no pretence of bravado or enthusiasm.

Jemima dialled the number Kennedy had given her. She didn't have long to wait as it connected almost immediately.

'I'm Inspector Jem—'

'Jemima Huxley,' said a male voice.

Jemima was taken aback. Ray Kennedy must have already spoken to Frank Rutherford about the need to involve her in whatever it was that was going on. The first thing she noticed was that Frank Rutherford's voice was calm. The second was that for some inexplicable reason, she instantly trusted the man.

'And you are?' She needed to ensure the identity of the speaker.

'Frank Rutherford. I've heard a lot about you from our mutual friend.'

'How do I know I can trust you?'

'Ray's told me something about you that he hasn't told anyone else. He said you'd be angry with him, but that when you thought about it, you'd realise that you could trust me.'

'What did he say?' asked Jemima, dreading what she was about to hear.

'You attend counselling sessions because you cut yourself.'

Jemima felt a lump rise in her throat and swallowed hard. There was no perceived judgement in this man's tone. He was merely reiterating a highly personal fact known only to a handful of people other than her father and Lucy. One was Nick, the husband who had abandoned her. The second was the therapist, who would never have divulged the information or consider breaking patient confidentiality. Finally, there was Broadbent, and Jemima trusted him with her life.

'Wow! Kennedy doesn't pull any punches.'

'Ray said it was the only piece of information he could think of that would convince you that he trusted me. He swore he hasn't told another living being.'

'I believe that to be true,' said Jemima. She had known the DCI for long enough to know that he wouldn't have relayed such personal information about her unless it was essential. She wasn't entirely comfortable that this stranger knew her deepest, darkest secret, but now wasn't the time for introspection.

'Since you're calling me, I take it things have gone south?'

'Kennedy was shot earlier this evening. I've evidence that Sally was responsible.'

'I warned him to play the long game and not go off all gung-ho. We don't know enough about what we're up against. Tell me, is he alive?'

'They've just finished operating. He took a bullet to the abdomen. It was touch-and-go, and he's still unconscious.'

'Which hospital's he in?'

'The University Hospital, in Cardiff. They're arranging a bed for him in ICU.'

'Well, he can't stay there. If he does, I won't be able to guarantee his safety. Sit tight. I'm on my way. I'll arrange for him to be moved to a secure facility and be with you within the hour. This is Operation Knotweed. Stay vigilant, and whatever you do, do not leave his side.'

'But—'

The line went dead.

Jemima turned her attention to her colleagues. 'We're all agreed we do whatever it takes to protect Kennedy?'

'Goes without saying,' said Broadbent.

'Absolutely. What did Rutherford say?' asked Gareth.

'We're not to allow the medical team to move Kennedy. He's coming to get him.'

'But he needs specialist care. He's barely survived surgery.' Gareth's eyes were wide with concern.

'And what the hell is this Rutherford planning on doing?' Broadbent's question was one that Jemima had been asking herself. She had no idea how Rutherford planned to give Kennedy the care he required. The only thing she knew for certain was that the DCI had placed his trust in this man and had asked Jemima to do the same. And right now, as crazy as it sounded, this was their only viable option.

Jemima called a doctor from Kennedy's bedside and explained that they had just been made aware of another credible threat to his life, insisting it was necessary to have an officer stationed beside Kennedy. The doctor was far from impressed and there was a tense stand-off as the medic was unwilling to agree to this precautionary measure. Any other person might have given in, but Jemima wasn't in the mood to take no for an answer.

Gareth took up post at Kennedy's bedside. It was the first time he had ever been required to guard someone from a potential threat. Back in the day, as a uniformed constable, it had been a routine duty to watch over suspects in the interview room. But they were always unarmed and usually posed no threat. Now there was a distinct possibility that if the wrong people had learned that Ray Kennedy was still alive, someone might come to finish off what Sally had failed to do. And if that were the case, anyone could be a potential assassin. It could be someone disguised as a hospital porter. A doctor. A priest. A little old lady . . . Well, perhaps not a little old lady. He smiled wryly, acknowledging the fact that he was letting his imagination run away with itself.

Still, every few seconds, his fingers moved towards the holster to check that his weapon hadn't somehow been spirited away. He just hoped that if it came down to it, he wouldn't freeze and would have the balls to do whatever was required.

Jemima and Broadbent guarded the doors at either end of the corridor. As she glanced in her partner's direction, she could see from his rigid stance that he was as nervous as she felt. She had never longed for the arrival of a man she hadn't yet met as much as she did now. The waiting, watching, anticipating was almost unbearable. She wanted Rutherford to walk through the door and relieve them of some of this pressure.

In normal circumstances Jemima wasn't inclined to offer her trust lightly. It wasn't unusual for a police officer to be naturally suspicious of others' motivations. After all, they spent their lives dealing with people who often lied through their teeth and went all out to hide their true intentions. So it was no easy matter to place her trust in Rutherford, a man whom she had never met, or even heard of until an hour ago.

But it was clear from Kennedy's message that he trusted him, and as the DCI's life was hanging in the balance, it was only right to comply with his wishes.

If there was any negative comeback on this further down the line, Jemima would have to deal with it as it arose. Though given the implications of what she now knew, her only concern was to get through this situation and bring the guilty parties to justice without losing anyone she cared about.

Sally was clearly prepared to kill anyone who got in her way. It was chilling to realise that someone you trusted and thought of as one of your own could so ruthlessly turn on you. She had duped all of them, including her life partner. Yet it was obvious from the voicemail message that there were other unidentified people out there who were equally dangerous. And that was more worrying, as it meant that they had no way of assessing what they were up against.

Kennedy's message and the subsequent attempt on his life had thrown everything up in the air. Professional and even personal relationships forged over the years had been revealed to be shams. The uncertainty of not knowing who you could trust was terrifying. It meant that the three of them could no longer operate in the way they had been trained — if they showed their hand to the wrong person, it could cost them their lives.

As Jemima kept watch she tried to figure out which other officers Kennedy believed to be corrupt. And it quickly got to the stage where her head felt mashed. There were some people at the station she didn't particularly like, some officers who coasted through their shifts without putting in the effort, people who sailed up the ranks, who quite frankly didn't deserve to be in the force, let alone make a successful career out of it. But it was one thing to think badly about someone and quite another to establish that officers were corrupt, and even more of a leap to think that someone you worked with day in, day out would try to kill you if it was in their interests to do so.

Jemima's thoughts were broken by the sound of approaching footsteps. She tensed, suddenly on high alert, waiting for the inevitable arrival of whoever was heading towards the other side of the door. At the sound of low voices, she realised that there was more than one person, which meant that the odds were immediately stacked against her.

As her heart rate increased, beads of sweat erupted across her body. She had faced down some dangerous people in the past. Fought hard. Taken beatings. Given as good as she got. Yet somehow this was different. She'd believed in herself back then. Known that she was tough, capable and formidable. But that was then, and this was now.

There was no denying that a year of being a full-time mother, changing nappies and playing kids' games had turned her soft. She'd lost her edge along with her agility, and her fitness level was at an all-time low. She took a deep breath as she fought a rising sense of panic. Despite the self-doubt and the fear, she needed to focus. Think clearly. Act decisively. She had to face whatever was about to happen.

She removed her weapon from its holster. The metal felt cold to the touch. Pointing the barrel of the gun downwards, her heart rate ratcheted up at an exponential rate. It occurred to her that if this was the moment that a hit squad was about to descend upon them, they might not have sufficient ammunition to defend themselves.

When her phone pinged, notifying her of a text, Jemima almost jumped out of her skin. Her finger twitched on the trigger, and she came close to accidentally shooting herself in the foot. Fortunately, her reactions were sharp enough for her to relax her hand at the last moment. She grabbed it from her pocket and saw the message: *Operation Knotweed. Heading along corridor towards you. FR.*

Jemima breathed so loudly that it took her by surprise. She'd been so uptight that she hadn't even realised that she'd been holding her breath. She retreated a short way from the door, turned and gave Dan a thumbs-up.

The door swung open and a team of four men and two women entered the corridor. Each was tall, muscular and clad in army fatigues. Although hidden from the sight of any casual observer, telltale bulges beneath their clothes left Jemima in no doubt that these people were armed and ready for an enemy ambush. It was like the arrival of the A Team.

'Jemima Huxley?' asked the first man through the door. He held out a hand in greeting.

'That's right.' Relief washed over her and she smiled for what seemed like the first time in ages.

'Frank Rutherford.' As he gripped her hand and pumped it enthusiastically, she felt heat radiate throughout her body. Jemima immediately understood why Kennedy trusted this man. He exuded confidence and capability. Just the sort of person to have on your side in a crisis.

'Well, Jem, as we don't know what we're up against, I suggest we get things moving. My team are one hundred per-cent trustworthy. I've an armoured private ambulance wait-ing outside with a doctor ready to take care of Ray. We're going to transport him to a secure location, where he'll get the necessary medical care to nurse him back to health.'

'How will you get him out of the hospital?' It was a valid question.

'That's for us to worry about. Once we're on our way I suggest that you and your colleagues return to your duties.'

'But—'

'But nothing, Inspector. I appreciate that you've lots of questions, but now is not the time to ask them. We've more pressing issues to deal with.'

'Where are you taking him?' Jemima knew even before she asked that Rutherford would not provide an answer to that question.

'The less you know, the better. Play dumb if anyone tries to pump you for information about Ray. Now let's get the man out of here. Which room's he in?'

'Follow me, I'll take you there.' Jemima marched ahead, the sound of military boots following closely behind. She hoped she was doing the right thing by letting Rutherford take Kennedy to some unknown place. Given the severity of his recent injuries and the subsequent surgery, it didn't seem wise for him to leave the hospital. At least here there was specialised equipment and highly skilled medical staff on hand to give him the best possible chance of survival should he take a turn for the worse.

However, it would be easy for anyone to enter the building and make another attempt on his life, and there would be little, if anything, they could do to stop them. Kennedy expected her to trust Rutherford, and that was what she would do.

Having reached the door to Kennedy's room, Jemima stepped aside to allow them to enter. Gareth immediately sprung to his feet, weapon at the ready, eyes wide, face etched with concern. He instinctively moved to place himself between them and Kennedy knowing all the while it was a pointless gesture, yet determined to do everything he could to protect his DCI.

'From Ray's description, I guess you must be Gareth?'

'That's right.'

'You can stand down, son. Your watch is over. I'm Frank Rutherford, and we're the rescue squad.'

As Jemima and Broadbent appeared in the room, she nodded to Gareth. His shoulders dropped and his stance became more relaxed. He let out a sigh of relief. 'Phew! I don't know what I'd have done if you were the enemy.'

'If our mission was to kill him, you wouldn't have had time to react. I'd have dropped you the moment I opened the door.' The comment was said in a joking manner, but there was no doubt in any of their minds that Rutherford was telling them the truth. He nodded to his team and they got to work gathering up Kennedy's notes, prising open a medicine cabinet to take supplies and ensuring that the patient was ready to be moved. 'You said Sally shot him?'

'That's right. I've a voice recording of it going down.' Jemima extracted her phone and played the message.

'I'll deal with her. She won't be a problem. By the time I've finished with her, I'll know everything.'

Jemima's blood ran cold at the implication. Sally Trent would be no match for a man who was used to getting information from the enemy. And that was precisely what Sally had become.

'What the hell are you doing? Step away from my patient!' The shouts came from a doctor trying to gain access to the room, only to be restrained by a member of Rutherford's team. 'Take your hands off me!'

'Stand down, Parker,' ordered Rutherford.

The man let go and stepped back.

'Orders from the top,' said Rutherford, in a firm, authoritative voice. He addressed the medic and extracted some official-looking paperwork. 'We're charged with moving this patient to a secure facility. It's a matter of national security and will happen with or without your approval.' As he spoke, his eyes didn't waver from the doctor's face.

Jemima had no idea whether the paperwork was genuine. But if it was a forgery, she had to give it to the man — Rutherford was very convincing.

'Mr Kennedy has only just come out of surgery,' countered the doctor. 'These next few hours are critical.'

'I appreciate that. We have a highly skilled medical team standing by, and it's imperative this man is moved to a secure facility. Believe me when I say that every second wasted here puts the lives of everyone inside this hospital in extreme jeopardy.' Rutherford looked at his watch. 'Time to go, people.'

The team lost no time following his order. As the brake on Kennedy's bed was disengaged, Rutherford took the paperwork from the doctor's hands.

'I'll be in touch,' said Frank.

In the time it had taken Jemima to reassure the doctor that everything was as it should be, Ray Kennedy was long gone.

# CHAPTER 24

The day's events were becoming more surreal by the moment, and Jemima had a feeling the surprises would keep on coming.

Broadbent was at the wheel once more, and it was clear that the stress of the last few hours was getting to him. He prided himself on being a calm and safe driver, but as he signalled right and pulled away at a set of traffic lights, he all but skidded around the bend.

They had just exited the hospital grounds and were about to draw level with the All Nations Centre when Jemima's phone rang. Her immediate thought was that it must be Frank Rutherford, despite only having parted company with the man ten minutes earlier. But, glancing at the number, she realised that it was coming from inside the police station. Her first thought was that it would be Steve Morgan calling to say that they had made a breakthrough on the case.

She accepted the call and immediately knew something was up. It sounded as though all hell had broken loose. Numerous voices were shouting, and a siren blasted away in the background. It was like a soundtrack to a disaster movie. Broadbent momentarily lost concentration as he glanced questioningly towards Jemima. Thankfully, she was staring straight ahead.

'You're going to hit the kerb!' She grabbed the wheel, forcing it in the opposite direction and avoiding disaster by the narrowest of margins. 'What the fuck, Dan? If you're gonna drive like a loon, then at least keep your eyes on the road!'

The melee at the other end of the line made it impossible to hear anything clearly. But she could just make out the words '*station now!*'. There was no time to press for more information as the line went dead.

'Blues and twos! Floor it, Dan!' She had no idea what they were about to face, but whatever was happening back at the station, it had to be serious.

Broadbent was already flicking the switch to engage the flashing lights and siren. The tyres screeched against the asphalt.

'What the hell's going on?' Gareth's usually gentle voice was raised and anxious.

'No idea, mate. With the day we're having, I dunno how much more I can take. The world's gone bloody crazy. I'm just hoping I'm asleep and I'll wake up soon to discover this was just an effing nightmare,' said Broadbent.

They pulled into the station car park and Jemima was out of the vehicle before Broadbent had a chance to cut the engine. She raced towards the entrance, her imagination in overdrive, not knowing what she was about to face, certain that it would be some sort of catastrophe she had failed to consider. Gareth was hot on her heels.

The first thing she noticed as she flung open the door was that the siren was no longer sounding. It meant that whatever emergency had occurred at the station was now under control, though it was immediately apparent from the sound of raised voices coming from the custody suite that something was still going on.

They made a beeline in that direction, straining to hear what was being said. But, with so many raised voices and the fact that everyone appeared to be trying to talk over one another, it proved impossible to make sense of what they were hearing.

Gareth was at Jemima's side, both heading resolutely towards the melee. Within seconds, Jemima heard feet slapping against the floor as someone ran along the corridor behind them, rapidly closing their distance. She glanced over her shoulder and saw that it was Broadbent.

'What the hell's going on?' He was breathing heavily and sounded as anxious as Jemima felt.

'No idea,' she replied. 'There's some sort of commotion coming from the custody suite. But so far, we haven't encountered anyone.'

'I don't think I can take much more of this,' said Gareth.

'You and me both, mate,' agreed Broadbent.

They were fast approaching an intersection that led to another corridor along which the custody suite was located. As they rounded the corner, she quickly surveyed the scene. A group of officers were milling about, including some of the top brass. Their presence was unusual and didn't bode well. While on duty, superintendents and above generally remained in their respective offices, each located on the top floor. This was an area of the station where officers of their rank rarely set foot.

As far as Jemima was concerned, the role of high-ranking officers was shrouded in mystery. On the few occasions she thought about what they did, she presumed they spent their days playing politics. Shuffling papers. Having a visible presence at events where they would be wined and dined. Schmoozing high-profile people while denying any allegiances. Playing God as they made decisions that frequently had an adverse effect on the more junior ranks.

There were frequent complaints about lack of funding restricting the number of frontline officers. They were routinely informed that difficult decisions had to be made, which inevitably resulted in reduced officer numbers. Whereas Jemima knew that that problem could easily be rectified by getting rid of some top-ranking officers. In her opinion quite a few of them served no real purpose. They were a luxury forces up and down the country could do without, nothing more than highly paid window dressing, out of touch with the realities of day-to-day policing and uncaring of the social problems ordinary people faced. It made far more sense to use public funds to put boots on the ground and employ officers who could actually make a difference to people's everyday lives.

Straining to see above the heads of those gathered in the corridor, Jemima saw that the doors to the custody suite were closed. 'What's happened?' she asked a uniformed officer.

'All hell's broken loose. There's been a death in custody.'

'Do you have a name?' Jemima had a bad feeling about this.

'Don't know any more than that, but they've shut the custody suite down.'

'Standard procedure,' she replied, before heading further down the corridor to find someone who would tell her what was going on. She spotted PC Dylan Chase with his back to the wall, palms flat against the smooth surface, eyes closed. He appeared shell-shocked, yet no one was taking any notice of him.

Dylan had been in post for more than twenty years and was approaching retirement. His hair had greyed and was fast receding, though his face had retained an air of youthfulness with a remarkable lack of lines. Whenever they bumped into each other at the station, Jemima stopped for a chat, and he always seemed pleased to see her.

Jemima had always admired the way in which Dylan undertook his duties. His quiet competence and good grace inevitably dialled down tensions. He brought an air of calm to potentially fraught situations. Yet as she looked at him now, she noticed that he was far from being his usual self. His skin had an unhealthy pallor and he was sweating, despite the temperature being far from warm. When he opened his eyes, they darted about, unable to rest on anything for very long. He appeared confused. More worryingly, his breathing was loud and rapid.

'Dylan, what's going on?'

When he failed to respond, she turned and mouthed to Broadbent to go and find out what was happening from some of the other officers. He didn't need telling twice.

Turning her attention back to Dylan, Jemima gently placed an arm around his shoulder. With Gareth's help, they steered him out of the corridor towards a nearby seat and carefully lowered him into it. As her fingers inadvertently brushed against his skin, Dylan flinched as though he had been struck. He blinked, then stared open-mouthed, as though seeing her for the first time. He looked lost. Completely bewildered.

'I-I called you. I-I'm sorry. I'm so sorry. The custody sergeant was busy. He asked me to check the prisoners. There was no reason to expect . . .' He shook his head in despair.

Jemima squatted down and squeezed his hand. Despite her rising impatience, she understood that his immediate need of support outweighed her own need to establish what had happened before their arrival.

'Go get Dylan a cup of tea, Gareth. Strong. Plenty of sugar.'

Peters rushed off, glad to be doing something practical.

'Don't try to talk. Just concentrate on your breathing. In . . . and . . . out. Nice and slow. In . . . and . . . out. Watch me, if it helps, and we'll do it together.' It felt somewhat ridiculous demonstrating how he should breathe. But Dylan's eyes locked onto her face, and he mimicked what she was doing. And by the time Gareth returned with the tea, Dylan was starting to look more like his usual self.

'Guv.' Broadbent had returned from his fact-finding mission.

Jemima knew even without looking at him that she wasn't going to like what he was about to tell her. She stood, grateful for the opportunity to stretch her legs, gently squeezed Dylan's shoulder and indicated to Gareth to keep an eye on him.

'What is it, Dan?' She guided her sergeant away from the others.

'Edward Trevelyan-Goode's dead. They found him in his cell. Professional Standards have been informed and they've closed the custody suite.'

'Suicide or murder?' The way things had gone today, it was impossible for Jemima to contemplate that the man had died of natural causes.

'No idea at this stage. They're processing the scene now. But from what I've been told, there's no suggestion of foul play.' Broadbent's lips barely moved as he spoke.

'Who's carrying out the post-mortem?'

'John Prothero's on his way.'

'Good. At least we know we can trust his findings. If Trevelyan-Goode was murdered, John will find the evidence to prove it.' At any other time, Jemima wouldn't have uttered those words. After all, they had never had any cause to doubt the findings of other pathologists. But over the years they had built up a rapport with Prothero and Jemima trusted the man completely.

An icy shiver ran down her spine, and Jemima suddenly wished she was anywhere other than inside this building. Over the years she had become accustomed to feeling unsafe on the streets. That feeling came with the job. But discovering that colleagues you knew, and in some instances trusted, were prepared to murder in order to keep their secrets safe was the worst feeling of all.

'Trevelyan-Goode was fine when we interviewed him. No suggestion that he was ill. He wouldn't have just dropped dead, Dan. He was murdered. I'd stake my career on it.'

'I agree. Sally might've pulled the trigger, but Kennedy's convinced there're corrupt coppers at the station.'

Jemima nodded. It was hard to believe that in a matter of hours she had gone from playing hide-and-seek with her toddler to finding herself caught up in layers of subterfuge she had never thought possible. During her time on the force, she had faced down and fought off many criminals. There had been occasions when her life had been on the line, when she had been injured, sometimes severely, in the line of duty.

The difference was that on those occasions, no matter how desperate the situation had been, she had known that her colleagues had her back.

Whereas now, apart from Dan and Gareth, it wasn't obvious who she could trust. Criminals and murderers were masquerading as police officers, which made rooting them out doubly difficult. She desperately hoped they'd get to the bottom of things and expose the corrupt officers before anyone else lost their life.

'What do we do now?' asked Broadbent. It was clear that his confidence was shattered.

Jemima knew that the burden was firmly placed upon her shoulders. Dan and Gareth were scared. She was too. But as she was the senior officer, they would look to her to step up to the plate and formulate a plan that would end this mess once and for all. Which meant that she had their lives in her hands. It would have been an enormous amount of pressure to handle in normal times, but with the stakes being at an all-time high, and her self-confidence wavering, it was a hell of an ask.

Appreciating that she needed to demonstrate that she was unfazed and had a workable plan, she said the first thing that came into her head. 'You should head up to the incident room. Check on progress. I'm going to see if anyone can shed light on what happened inside that cell.'

Jemima desperately needed to establish the sequence of events that had taken place inside that holding cell. Had Edward Trevelyan-Goode died of natural causes? Or had he been murdered to prevent him from exposing the presence of corrupt officers inside this police station? Throughout his interview there had been nothing to suggest that the man had any health issues. And given the fact that an attempt had been made on Kennedy's life and he had warned her not to trust fellow officers, she was inclined to believe that Edward had been murdered.

# CHAPTER 25

PC Dylan Chase was looking much better when Jemima returned. Between drinking his tea and Gareth doing his utmost to reassure the man, his confidence and composure were returning. She decided to ask him about the events leading up to Edward Trevelyan-Goode's death. She explained that she had been in the process of questioning Edward when other events had caused her to suspend the interview, resulting in him being placed in the holding cell. She just hoped that she hadn't given Chase cause to think that her questioning was anything more than natural concern.

'All I can say is, it was a normal shift until I found him dead inside that cell. Thought the bugger was asleep at first. He was just lying there on the bench. Curled up, facing the wall. I called out to him. When I got no reaction, I went in and checked, but he'd gone. There was no pulse. So, the training kicked in. I hit the alarm button, turned him over and started CPR. I've been over and over it in my head. I did everything I could. I was just too late . . .' He faltered and wiped his eyes with the back of his hand.

'I know it's hard, but you shouldn't beat yourself up about it,' said Gareth.

'Easy for you to say. You weren't the one who found him like that.'

'No, but we lost one of our team in the line of duty last year. We've had to learn to live with self-recriminations. They eat you up if you allow them to, but it doesn't change the outcome,' said Jemima.

'She's right. We feel for you, that's all,' said Gareth.

'Perhaps you're right. Oh, I don't know . . .' He still looked haunted by the recollection.

'Had you looked in on Trevelyan-Goode before that?' Jemima pressed further.

'No. The sarge had everything covered, and I was in and out of the area around the custody desk. I had no need to go back to the holding cells. I took a call from the front desk and was away for about twenty minutes or so. By the time I got back, a new prisoner was being booked in. He was a right state. Must've been drinking for hours. I could smell the alcohol on him, and he was effing and blinding. Banging on about how they had no right to arrest him. He was having a go at everyone. Then he puked his guts up. The stink of it.' He wrinkled his nose and curled his lips, as he replayed the scene in his head. 'It was a right mess.'

'I had a hunch that the custody sergeant would be tied up for a while, so I asked him if he wanted me to do the routine checks on the other prisoners. Just thought I should help out. That's why I was the one that ended up finding him. I wish I hadn't offered now. I'd have been better off getting the mop and bucket to clean up the mess at the desk. Hindsight, eh? If only I could go back in time.'

Chase wasn't going to give them any useful information. Apart from being the officer who found the body and raised the alarm, it was clear that he hadn't seen anything suspicious. Now he was looking much better than when they first encountered him, she thought they could safely leave him.

'Come on, Gareth. Things to do,' she said.

Gareth was looking paler than usual. Which, given his naturally pasty complexion, was concerning. He took the hint and followed her. When they were a safe distance from anyone else, he spoke. 'Any update on the DCI?'

'No and keep schtum about him while we're inside this building. Anyone asks, you've not heard from him and have no idea where he is,' warned Jemima.

'Well, at least the last part is true. It's not looking good, is it?'

'No, and we need to watch our backs. I know we've got no evidence, but I wouldn't be surprised if Trevelyan-Goode was murdered. Which means that at least one officer in this station is a killer. Any of us could be next if we're perceived to be a threat.' She regarded Gareth sternly. 'Get back to the incident room. Anyone asks, tell them you've been chasing up leads on the Lawson case. Keep it vague and say as little as possible. That way you're less likely to get caught out in a lie. I know it's an impossible ask but try to clear your mind of what happened with Kennedy. As far as you're concerned, you haven't seen or heard from him since leaving the station.'

'And how's that going to work? I'm the one who rang Sally. I've left messages on her phone. She's not stupid, she'll know that I'm aware that Ray was shot. And if she knows, then who else has she told? I've most likely signed my own death warrant.'

'I agree it's not ideal.' Jemima's heart sank. With events spiralling out of control she'd forgotten all about the message Gareth had left on Sally's phone. And although he hadn't specifically mentioned that Ray Kennedy had been shot, he had told her that she needed to get to the hospital as quickly as possible.

'Not ideal? Not bloody ideal? This is my life we're talking about!' Gareth's voice rose as a sense of panic took hold.

'Shh!' hissed Jemima. 'I know you're scared, but you have to keep a lid on it.'

'That's all right for you to say. You're not implicated. You weren't the one who left the message. I did. So now I'm the one in the shit. We know for a fact that Sally shot Kennedy. She wouldn't think twice about offing me.'

'You're not on your own. We're in this together, Gar. If anyone comes for you, they'll have to get through me first.' As she uttered the words Jemima knew just how ridiculous they sounded. Gareth was right. That phone message, done with the best of intentions, had marked him out as a threat that needed to be neutralised. If only she'd realised it before Rutherford and his team had taken Kennedy from the hospital. She could have insisted that they take Gareth too. He could have acted as liaison, been her eyes and ears inside whatever operation Rutherford was running. It would have been a beneficial arrangement for all of them. More importantly, it would have also ensured that Gareth wasn't a sitting duck for whoever would inevitably come after him.

'Gareth, you need to calm down. I've no intention of allowing anyone to harm you. You, me and Dan are a team. We're in this together. We'll look out for one another.'

'How?'

'For a start, I've changed my mind. You can come with me. I know I said you should head back to the incident room, but we're better off staying together. From now on, I'm not letting you out of my sight. So, say as little as possible. Keep your wits about you and observe everyone's body language, because the rogue officer, or officers, might be the ones we're about to speak to.'

'Where are we going?'

'I need to speak with top brass. Since I was questioning Trevelyan-Goode, it'd look odd if I didn't try to establish what happened to him. As it is, I'll have to come up with some cock and bull reason for Dan and I having walked out mid-interview. I just hope that I don't raise suspicion with the wrong person.'

There were fewer officers in the corridor than there had been fifteen minutes earlier. The more junior ranks had dispersed, returning to their respective duties while no doubt spreading the word of what had happened in the custody suite. Jemima knew the way things worked and was convinced that news of Trevelyan-Goode's death would be all around the station by now.

Up ahead, Jemima spotted two senior officers standing close to the entrance of the custody suite. They had their backs to her and were talking to a scene-of-crime officer, who was dressed in protective gear.

'It's a good sign that they're following procedure.' Jemima kept her voice low, so that Gareth would be the only one able to hear what she was saying. As they took a few more steps, she saw that the scene-of-crime officer was Jeanne Ennersley.

Jeanne glanced in their direction and subtly nodded her acknowledgement of their presence but continued speaking to the more senior officers without so much as taking a breath.

Jemima noted that Jeanne's voice had a hard edge to it. It was an unfamiliar firmness that she had not encountered in all the years they'd known each other. Whenever they crossed paths at crime scenes, Jeanne had always been friendly and accommodating. Though, as Jemima and the team carried out their investigations with a high degree of professionalism, there had never been cause for Jeanne to become annoyed with them.

Jeanne sighed with frustration. 'I'll reiterate yet again. I am not disputing the fact that at this moment, you happen to be the most senior officer in this station. But this is a crime scene. As you very well know there has been a death in custody, and I will not countenance you or anyone else having access to this area until my team has secured all the evidence.'

'Get out of my way, woman!' bellowed the deputy chief constable. 'As the chief constable isn't here today, I need to get in there and assess the scene myself.' He reached out as though to grab hold of Jeanne and move her out of the way.

'Lay one finger on me and I'll have you charged with assault! And I'll have plenty of witnesses to back me up!' Jeanne's voice oozed assertiveness. She knew that irrespective of his rank, the man was in the wrong.

'You ridiculous woman!'

'I will not be spoken to like that when I am carrying out my duties. If I choose to report you, you'll be in all sorts of trouble. So, if I were you, I'd stop digging while you still can. And for your information, the only person here that's being ridiculous is you! You need to calm down and think very carefully before you do something you'll later regret. Do you want to be accused of tampering with a crime scene? Well, do you? Because that's where this is heading if you think you can force your way in there.' Jeanne pointed at the closed set of doors. 'Now I suggest you turn around and walk away. Do whatever it is someone of your rank should be doing and leave me and my team to get on with our jobs.'

The DCC's complexion had turned an unhealthy shade of purple. And even from more than twenty paces away, Jemima swore she could feel the heat radiating from his body. If the stand-off continued between him and Jeanne, it was possible the man would either have a heart attack or spontaneously combust.

Throughout the encounter, the officer who stood shoulder to shoulder with the DCC had remained inordinately silent. His stance was tense. Yet he had not attempted to support his senior officer's bullying of Jeanne.

The DCC harrumphed loudly. It seemed he might finally be accepting that he was getting nowhere with trying to intimidate the woman into doing what he wanted. Over the years there had been quite a few rumours about the man — none of them good. He was known for being overtly sexist. Indeed, he wore this prejudice like a badge of honour.

Jemima knew for a fact that he had a hand in ensuring that officers who displayed misogynistic tendencies progressed quickly up the ranks, regardless of their abilities. And with someone like that in such a senior role, things were unlikely to change for the better.

Then there was his string of unfortunate PAs. Jemima and others had often commented upon the fact that he worked his way through assistants like a chain smoker through cigarettes. Jemima had coined the phrase for the man's requirements as the 'FACY factor', as apart from hair colour each assistant invariably possessed four attributes: they were female, attractive, compliant and young. Each arrived full of enthusiasm. None had lasted longer than six months.

Jeanne's assertiveness must have come as quite a shock, as he wasn't used to women standing up to him. There were whispers on the station rumour mill that his wife had tried it years ago, but gave up when he knocked that insolent streak out of her. Sadly the woman had been on a hiding to nothing. It wasn't as if she had a realistic prospect of getting justice by reporting him to his mates.

And as for the workplace . . . Well, misogynism was part of the culture. As acceptable and enjoyable as mid-morning tea and toast — which invariably arrived at his desk at ten o'clock sharp, courtesy of his latest assistant.

Jemima knew that in the current climate, men like this must feel that everywhere they looked the world was going to hell in a handcart. Women were getting above themselves. Not only expecting to have well-paid jobs but insisting men defer to them. And the #MeToo rubbish — as they put it — was the thin edge of the wedge. Jemima counted herself lucky in so far as most of the male officers she had worked alongside didn't treat her differently because of her gender. But she had also heard horror stories about those Neanderthals on the force who believed it was time that real men stepped up and sorted things out. Brought back proper standards when a man could be proud of what he was instead of having to walk on eggshells and apologise for having a dick.

As she watched the confrontation playing out between Jeanne and the DCC, Jemima could all but see the cogs turning inside the man's head as he assessed the personal ramifications of his actions. He was astute enough to appreciate that this dreadful woman would most likely report him for all sorts of things if he were to take things further. The only sensible course of action was for him to back off. But that didn't mean he had to go quietly. Certainly not without emphasising the fact that he was the one in charge.

'Get on with your job, and then get out of this station!' There was no attempt at hiding his anger. Yet spitting out the command was the only way he could feel as though he had had the last word.

'Believe me, it'll be my absolute pleasure,' replied Jeanne.

The DCC turned away from her so quickly that he bumped shoulders with the other officer. The man clearly hadn't expected the physical contact and almost lost his balance. As he stumbled towards the wall, Jemima saw his face for the first time and realised that it was Superintendent Deavers.

Jemima was used to negotiating the misogynistic attitudes of some of the force's dinosaurs. Legislation had long since been put in place to prevent discrimination in the workplace, which was all well and good, but just because there was a law in place didn't mean that it would be routinely enforced. The old boys' network was still very much alive and kicking, though it went on covertly and its existence was vehemently denied. And the kicking part was certainly applied — the stalwarts of the old culture did everything possible to kick out anyone who didn't conform to their criteria. White straight men were always acceptable, and if they demonstrated a certain way of thinking, then progression up the ranks was more or less assured. As for anyone else, well, there were quotas to fill.

Not every male officer was of the same mindset, but those who were often the least capable, were the ones who longed for the return of the seventies and eighties, which included some who hadn't even been alive at that time. They longed for the force to return to a time when men were men and women were plonks — there to do the filing, make the tea, and possibly provide some relief from sexual tension.

It saddened Jemima to know that the public's negative perception of the police was exacerbated by the machinations of the outmoded structure of this crucial service. The entire organisation was overdue a drastic overhaul. It was no different from much of the public sector, which harked back to the past and had not moved with the times. Only recently the Met had hit the headlines about routinely failing to deal with misogyny and other issues. As if the Met was any different to every other police force throughout the country.

Jemima was beginning to wonder if the DCC had had something to do with Edward Trevelyan-Goode's death. A death in custody was a relatively rare occurrence. Yet every officer was aware of the procedure that needed to be followed. Any such incident would place the police force under intense scrutiny. And wherever you went there was always someone out there looking to find the next big story. If the DCC was telling the truth and the chief constable was not on duty that day, then as the officer in charge of the station, the buck would ultimately stop with him.

The DCC's face was like thunder as he stormed along the corridor in their direction, glowering directly at Jemima. His eyes looked as threatening as a pair of laser beams. Given the speed he was going they both thought it wise to step aside and allow him plenty of room to pass. The man's anger was so palpable that there was every possibility that if they got in his way, they'd end up flat out on the floor. He'd have the satisfaction of knowing that he'd got two for the price of one, by asserting his dominance over both an openly gay officer and a female one too.

He pulled up sharply alongside her, taking Jemima by surprise. Gareth kept his eyes averted, but Jemima dared to make eye contact.

'Where's that boss of yours?' The words boomed with such force that it hurt Jemima's eardrums. It took a significant amount of willpower to stop herself from wincing. Worse still was the fact that some of the man's spittle had sprayed across her face.

'I've no idea where DCI Kennedy is, sir.' Her tone was level, emotionless. She could play poker with the best of them.

'What do you mean, you've no idea? You're in the middle of a high-profile case and by the looks of it, out of your depth. Yet you've no idea where your senior officer is? This death in custody is down to you, Inspector! You're completely incompetent. In my opinion there's no place on this force for officers like you.'

Jemima told herself to remain calm. Not take the bait. But she wasn't about to let him get away with a remark like that. She cocked her head to the side and with a puzzled expression, asked the obvious question. 'I don't understand, sir. What do you mean by an officer like me?' Her voice was sugary sweet.

'I mean, Inspector, an officer who takes a year off for no good reason. Treating their professional role as though it's a hobby to be picked up and dropped whenever the mood takes them.'

'Let me get this right, sir. You're saying that because I've taken a period of maternity leave, you feel that I'm not fit to be a police officer?'

'Eh?'

'It may surprise you to know, sir, that there is such a thing as the Equality Act, which came into existence in 2010.' Jemima's voice had risen so that others were listening to what she had to say.

'That's—' interjected the DCC.

Jemima wasn't about to let him interrupt. 'As I was saying, sir, it is a criminal offence for any employer to treat an employee less favourably because of their gender. It might be wise to familiarise yourself with that particular piece of legislation.'

Everyone could see that the DCC was apoplectic. With his face now an unhealthy shade of purple once more, it looked as though he was about to burst a blood vessel.

'I was pregnant, sir. Pregnant because I was raped. By. A. Man. Do you have any idea what that was like? No, you don't. And I have no intention of allowing any man to degrade me again. Do I make myself clear?' Her words rang out in the silence that had descended throughout the entire corridor.

It suddenly felt as though the temperature had been ramped up at least ten degrees. Everyone was watching. Listening. Wondering where this confrontation would lead.

Jemima glared at the man, her chin tilted defiantly, an insolent glint in her eye. It was conceivable that any, or all, of these officers could be out to get them, could set a trap to lay blame at their door — or even kill them, should they get too close to the truth of who was behind the corruption. But Jemima was determined that she wouldn't allow that to happen. This wasn't about being treated in a discriminatory way. This was about survival and getting justice for Ray Kennedy.

It took guts to call this despicable man out. Throughout her entire career, she had respected the chain of command, despite the occasions when she had witnessed how some more senior officers covered their own backsides at the expense of the junior ranks. But if the DCC was gunning for her, she was going to shovel the shit in spades. Make everyone present aware that this man had a problem with her, merely because she was a woman.

She needed a public confrontation. It was her best chance of staying safe and remaining on the investigation. No matter how dangerous things became, they needed to remain on the inside if they were to have any hope of getting to the bottom of this barrel of rotten apples. And if the DCC were to take disciplinary action against her there would hopefully be some officers who would stand up and attest to the man's discriminatory words.

The natural expectation was that the DCC would reprimand her then and there. But as he opened his mouth to castigate her, someone cleared their throat loudly. It was not obvious which officer had done this, but it was immediately apparent to Jemima that it was meant as a warning to the DCC that he should think carefully about the next words that came out of his mouth.

And the warning clearly worked. The DCC glanced at someone further down the corridor and huffed. However, he pulled himself back from the brink. Though he was clearly not done, as his following words attacked her in another way.

'From what I've heard, this Trevelyan-Goode shouldn't have been in the holding cell, let alone died in there. You've brought this force into disrepute and I'll have your badge for it. There'll be no police pension for you. Inform DCI Kennedy that I expect him in my office in five minutes. If he's not there, he'll be looking for another job too. Now get out of my sight, the pair of you!'

Superintendent Deavers followed in his wake, saying nothing but wearing a quizzical expression that suggested he was mystified by his superior officer's behaviour.

Jemima was flabbergasted. She'd had little to do with the DCC in the past, but had heard plenty of rumours that he was a misogynist. After this unreasonable, bullying encounter she knew that he was so much more. The man was clearly unhinged. Unreasonable. Possibly even barking mad. He was desperately looking for a scapegoat for this recent turn of events.

But the question she was now asking herself was this: did the DCC have a hand in Edward's death? And was his demand to see Kennedy a cynical bluff to convince people further down the line that he had no knowledge of the attempt on the DCI's life?

# CHAPTER 26

Jemima watched the DCC's rapidly receding form. Shockwaves rippled throughout her body as he all but hurled the door from its hinges.

'Jemima!'

The sound of her name brought her back to the here and now. As she turned in the opposite direction, she saw that Jeanne Ennersley was still in the corridor. She beckoned for Jem to come closer.

Glancing around to ensure that the DCC had indeed vacated the corridor, Jemima and Gareth quickly made their way in Jeanne's direction.

'I've come up against a fair few misogynistic arseholes in my time, but that one takes the biscuit,' declared Jeanne. 'I take it that the Trevelyan-Goode chap was one of yours?'

'Unfortunately, yes. I was in the process of questioning him a few hours ago, and there was no suggestion that there was anything wrong with him.'

'I'm not surprised. On the face of it he looked healthy enough. John Prothero will be doing the post-mortem, so he'll be able to confirm one way or the other. But I'm fairly sure your guy was murdered.'

Jemima and Gareth exchanged a worried look. This was confirmation of what they had both dreaded. There was a killer in the station.

'Are you able to tell me how he died?'

'Oh, it was sophisticated. Nothing as obvious as slashing his neck. Or strangulation. My initial thought was possibly natural causes. Perhaps a cardiac episode. Prevalent in many men of his age. But as I was photographing the body, I noticed that the hair on the nape of his neck was rather dishevelled, which seemed at odds with the rest of his appearance. Anyway, I took a closer look and that's when I saw a small mark. Miniscule, really.'

Jemima could tell from the tone of Jeanne's voice that the woman was feeling pleased with herself. 'A puncture wound?'

'Exactly. And one that would be easy to miss.'

'Excellent work, Jeanne.'

'Now, I can't categorically confirm that that's what killed him. That's well beyond my particular skill set. But I'm fairly confident that when John's taken a look, he'll tell you that it was made by a hypodermic needle, and it's not the sort of place you'd inject yourself.'

'So, you think someone injected him with a poisoned substance?' asked Gareth.

'Not necessarily. An empty syringe would do the trick. If you introduce an air bubble into the blood stream, it can cause cardiac arrest. No drugs needed, and a far greater chance of getting away with murder, if no one spots the puncture wound.'

Jemima and the rest of the team had investigated far too many murders. She'd heard of this method of killing someone. Yet, in all the crime scenes they'd attended, it hadn't once been the method used to end someone's life. It was such a simple way to cause someone's death. So easy in fact, that it made it even more likely that any one of them could easily become the killer's next target.

'Where in the cell was the body found?'

'The corpse was prone on the bench. But I understand that efforts had been made to resuscitate him. Whereas lividity showed that he'd spent a significant amount of time on his side up until they turned him.'

Jeanne's account appeared to back up what Dylan had told them about finding Trevelyan-Goode on his side, facing the wall.

'Was there a syringe at the scene?'

'There was no evidence of one,' confirmed Jeanne.

'Which means that someone visited that cell and killed him. And only a serving police officer could have gained access to that area. Which means we have a killer among the staff.'

'That's my reading of the situation. So, I suggest you watch your backs.' Jeanne nodded pointedly at both of them.

'Was there any sign of a struggle?' asked Jemima.

'None that I could see. Nothing obvious out of place. His clothing wasn't disturbed.'

'Which means he felt comfortable enough with whoever killed him, as he didn't perceive a threat.' Jemima articulated her thoughts. This latest information gave her something to work with. She just needed to establish which officers Edward had had a connection with. And she had a feeling that status was everything for a man like Trevelyan-Goode. He wouldn't have willingly socialised with any officer of a lowly grade. He'd already told them that he knew powerful people. People who could get them kicked off the force. Even the likes of a DCI wouldn't be able to pull that one off, which pointed to anyone of the rank of superintendent or above.

'And I don't know whether I'm making something out of nothing, but when I arrived, there was a hell of an argument going on between the custody sergeant and the DCC,' said Jeanne.

'What were they arguing about?'

'I'm not sure. We arrived a few minutes after we got the call, which was probably a lot sooner than anyone expected.

We'd only been told that there was a death in custody. No other details. But I tell you, it was all kicking off. I was under the impression that when it came to the custody suite, the custody sergeant ruled the roost.'

'He does. No one gets in or out of there without his say-so,' said Jemima.

'Well, I'm telling you, the DCC was having a right go at him. At one stage, I thought he was going to hit him. I've a bad feeling about this. Something's not right. You'd all better watch your backs.'

'You too,' said Jemima. 'You've already pissed off the second-highest-ranking officer in this station.'

Jeanne smiled. 'It'll piss him off even more when he realises it's not just Professional Standards he has to worry about. You see, I've already alerted the Independent Office for Police Conduct. There are IOPC officers on their way here as we speak. Oh, and if you need an independent witness for any employment tribunal further down the line, then I'm up for it. My phone has been recording since I heard him kick off with the custody sergeant. I have an audio file of everything that man said.' Jeanne's grin almost reached from ear to ear. 'I'm telling you, your DCC had better find himself a hell of a big umbrella, because he's about to have a whole heap of shit raining down on his head.' She laughed loudly and headed back towards the crime scene.

They were buoyed by Jeanne's words. Jemima had no reason to doubt that she was genuinely on their side. Leaving Jeanne to get on with her work, they walked to the incident room in silence, looking out for any signs of trouble. Leaving that section of the station behind, it appeared that it was business as usual. Officers were going about routine activities. It was a far cry from where they had just come.

Jeanne's revelation about the recent events in the custody suite had reinforced the feeling that it was no longer safe inside the station, at least for Jemima, Dan and Gareth. Having worked closely with Kennedy for many years, there was no doubting their allegiance, which put a target on each officer's back. It was a strange, unsettling feeling, not knowing who to trust. In the space of a few hours, they had gone from being ordinary police officers, to finding themselves centre stage in a deadly conspiracy. For the foreseeable future, this building was no longer a safe space. Every step they took felt like moving deeper into enemy territory, where they had to operate in a state of heightened awareness.

There was no sign of the DCC or Superintendent Deavers. Jemima guessed that the former was busying himself with finding ways to cover his own arse. Either that or trying to engineer a situation whereby Kennedy's closest trio could be eliminated, in a manner that made it impossible to be traced back to him.

Entering the incident room was like stepping back in time. Everyone was busy. It seemed so normal. Then again, apart from Broadbent, none of the others were aware of what had happened to Kennedy. And remarkably it seemed that news of Edward Trevelyan-Goode having recently been murdered inside the building hadn't yet reached them.

'How's it going?' asked Jemima, surprising herself by how normal her voice sounded.

'I think Aadi and Victoria might be on to something,' said Broadbent.

Before she had a chance to say anything, Jemima's phone rang.

'Hold on, Dan. I'd better get this.'

It was Father Mason Roy. And although it would not be work-related, she felt compelled to answer it, as she knew that Mason wouldn't have rung her without a good reason.

'Sorry to call you, Jem. Are you dealing with that judge who went missing earlier today?'

Mason's question took her by surprise. 'How do you know about that?'

'He's all over the media, Jem. I mean TV, radio, social media. It's gone viral. If you're trying to find him, you need to take a look.'

# CHAPTER 27

Jemima covered the mouthpiece of the phone as she instructed Gareth to switch on the TV and select any channel. There was no need for him to ask which one as they were all running the same story. It became immediately apparent that this was a well-executed plan. Whoever was behind this was leaving nothing to chance, as social media platforms across the world were going crazy too. The story was everywhere. Yet what they were about to see was nothing like they had expected.

Jemima hastily thanked Mason and put the phone down before he had a chance to respond. The fear and confusion of the last few hours faded to insignificance as she rushed across to join the other officers who had all abandoned their respective tasks to gather around the TV. As a camera panned over the area, it gave viewers the first look at part of a scene that many would find unimaginably depraved.

It was a rare moment inside the incident room when no one spoke, moved, or hardly dared to breathe. It was possibly the most compelling live TV broadcast since the original moon landing. There was no question that Rory Lawson was alive. But the man, who until yesterday had been held in such high esteem as a senior member of the British judiciary, was restrained and completely naked. He was upright, his back against a board that went from floor to ceiling. His head was fixed in place with a leather strap while his wrists and ankles were manacled so that his feet were about eighteen inches apart, placing a great deal of strain on the muscles of his legs. His arms were aloft, hands approximately thirty inches apart. The position in which he was firmly secured ensured that he had no chance of hiding his torso. The man was a pitiful sight. Scrawny, pot-bellied, balding, wrinkled, his shrivelled genitalia displayed for all to see.

The camera slowly panned around a surprisingly large, windowless room. Given the equipment on display and the padding on the walls, the obvious assumption was that this was a room where people came to encounter extreme sexual experiences.

As Broadbent took in the scene, he couldn't help but voice the question they were all thinking. 'What the hell's going—'

'Shh!' Jemima was in no mood for interruptions or distractions of any kind. 'Turn the volume up, Gar.'

Moments later, a woman's voice was heard, though the narrator remained hidden from view. *'Firstly, let me assure you that this is not a hoax. We have commandeered the airwaves. This is a live broadcast playing on whichever TV station you have tuned into. We are also livestreaming on YouTube, TikTok and Facebook.'* A link for each site was displayed across the screen. It was a clear indication, if any were needed, that this operation had been meticulously planned.

> *'We are members of the newly formed PASA — People Against Sexual Abuse. We have come together out of desperation and the realisation that the laws of our so-called civilised society are woefully inadequate. Our country, like many other Western democracies, masquerades as being just and fair. British politicians are forever proclaiming that our justice system is second to none. Yet the harsh reality is that many of our laws are archaic and unfit for purpose.*

*'It is not our intention to cause unnecessary distress to anyone. My fellow victims and I have planned this operation to bring to people's attention the plight of vulnerable people across the globe.*

*'Victims of sexual abuse deserve better. It is time for change. Time to shine a bright light into the shadows. To expose paedophiles and others guilty of sexual crimes. Name. Shame. Drive them out and give them nowhere to hide. These monsters should be prosecuted. And if a jury finds them guilty, it is a reasonable expectation that the perpetrator will serve a prison sentence commensurate to the crimes they committed.*

*'Some would call what we are doing here vigilantism. Sadly, it is. But we feel compelled to take this drastic course of action because of the corruption of our justice system.*

*'It is a sad fact that each day in every country across the planet, sexual abuse and violence against women and children occurs. It happens in the home. It happens in the workplace. It happens on the streets. And it needs to stop.*

*'I do not claim to speak for everyone who has fallen victim to sexual violence, and readily acknowledge that this plight is inflicted on many individuals regardless of gender. However, I can only speak my own truth. And urge others to do the same.*

*'Do not cower.*
*'Do not suffer in silence.*
*'Men like this one—'*

The camera zoomed in on Lawson.

*'—have made you feel worthless. You are not. Your life is precious. You are valued. Find strength in what we are doing. Take back control. Join our cause. Because if you have suffered any form of sexual abuse, then our cause is your cause. Stand shoulder to shoulder with us. Take strength from what we are doing. We can change the balance of power by saying enough is enough. Name and shame your abuser. Drive them out of the shadows. Give them nowhere to hide.'*

There was the sound of footsteps as a woman in army fatigues came into focus. Jemima's immediate thought was that she looked familiar. But before she had a chance to recall where she had seen her, the woman introduced herself.

*My name is Matilda Lawson. And the man splayed help-lessly on this equipment is both my father and my abuser. You should not feel sorry for him. This room, which is filled with unimaginably depraved equipment, is a room that my father and his friends regularly visit. It is a room they designed. A place where they abuse the vulnerable. Where nothing is off limits. A playroom where they can fulfil their sexual desires.*

*'Some of you will know this man as Judge Rory Lawson. He has spent many years as a so-called respected member of the British judiciary presiding over criminal cases in the High Court. A man who has acted with impunity, as his office has placed him above reproach. Yet, this man is himself a criminal of the worst kind.*

*'He hides behind his judicial paraphernalia, and sees himself as issuing fair and reasonable sentences for those defendants whom the jury have found guilty. That's how you'd like everyone to think of you, isn't that right, Daddy dearest?'*

*As Matilda turned to face her father, her voice hardened. 'Come on, Daddy. You're an erudite man. Always ready to impart your wisdom. The voice of reason. The truth seeker. The setter of punishments. Now is the time for you to say something. You've a far bigger audience now. It's not just the courtroom hanging on your words. Offices and households across continents will be watching. Wondering. Listening. You're not usually shy, so don't start now.'*

It was apparent that someone else was operating the camera, as the lens zoomed in for a close-up on Rory's face. Apart from a split lip and some slight bruising to the skin of his right cheek, there was no obvious sign of injury. Tears streamed down his face, though it was unclear whether they were the result of pain, humiliation, or both.

*'It seems that my father doesn't want to tell you his side of the story. So, I'll tell you mine instead. I was six years old when this man Judge Rory Lawson came into my bedroom and ended my childhood. Until then, I'd thought that monsters only existed in fairy tales. But when he eventually pulled his trousers up and walked out of the room as though nothing had happened, I knew that my father was the biggest monster of them all.'*

Matilda drew breath and paced about.

The tension in the incident room was palpable. After some gasps and the odd expletive, no one spoke. As his daughter revealed details of her upbringing, the plight of Rory Lawson faded to insignificance. Jemima suddenly felt dizzy and realised that she was holding her breath. Her own rape had been traumatic enough, and extremely difficult to come to terms with. But what Matilda Lawson was describing was on a whole new level. Her heart went out to the young woman. If what she was claiming was true, then she had suffered immeasurably.

Jemima surreptitiously wiped away a tear with the back of her hand. This tragic tale wasn't about her. This was no time for her to allow her own experience to cloud her judgement. Or distract the rest of the team. But listening to what was being said, it was impossible not to visualise the scene and feel the woman's pain. There was a part of Jemima that wanted to reach through the screen, draw her into an embrace and hold her tight, reassure Matilda that she understood and empathised. But the truth was, she and many others could only begin to imagine the horror and depravity this poor woman had endured. Her life from prepubescent child onwards must have been a living hell.

Jemima's reverie was broken as Matilda continued to speak, and the emotion in her voice became more noticeable with each word. The woman was clearly reliving her experiences as she laid her soul bare.

*'There is no justification for what my father did. This man—'*

She jabbed her finger into his chest and Rory Lawson flinched as though he had been prodded with a red-hot poker.

*'—This despicable specimen of humanity, kept on doing it. His sexual assaults on me happened as regular as clockwork. I've lost count of the number of times he raped me. Week in, week out, for twelve years.*

*'Some of you will ask why I didn't report it. Tell another adult. Perhaps my mother. Or a teacher. Well, here's the shocker, my mother knew all about it . . . I recall one occasion when she walked into the room. Daddy dearest had me pinned to the bed. He was his usual sweating, disgusting self, grunting away. I was ten years old and had learned a long time ago to lie there and let him get on with it. If I managed to do that, it was less painful. I'd always turn my head to the side so that I didn't have to smell the alcohol fumes and stale food on his breath. I'd close my eyes and try to block everything out. Force myself to think of this happy place I'd created in my head. A world where I was all grown up, strong and in charge. Somewhere where Daddy Monster didn't exist.*

*'On that occasion, it seemed to be going on for ever. He was rutting like a demented stallion. It was brutal, relentless and I thought my ribs would crack from him pressing down on me. Either that, or he would split me in two. I remember that I could only take shallow breaths, which made me feel light-headed and I thought, "That's it, I can't breathe properly. I'm going to die . . ."'*

Matilda's breath caught in her throat.

*'That's when I heard the door creak. As I opened my eyes, I blinked away my tears and there was my mother. There*

*was a fraction of a second when I had a glimmer of hope,*
*but that faded almost as soon as it began. She was standing*
*there open-mouthed, staring at us. I thought she'd go ballistic*
*— drag him off me, make him stop. But she did nothing.*
*Just stood there and watched him continue to rape me. This*
*piece of shit was angry. He yelled at her to get out. And*
*instead of doing something to help me, she turned around*
*and scuttled out of the room.*

*'I have the parents from hell. My father the paedophile*
*rapist, my mother complicit in the abuse I was forced to*
*suffer. I'll never forgive either of them for what they put me*
*through. I hope they both die painful deaths and rot in hell.'*

As tears streamed down Matilda's face, she gulped loudly
as she fought to contain her emotions.

*'When I was planning this, I promised myself I wouldn't*
*cry. I didn't want to give the judge and his drunken enabler*
*the satisfaction of seeing me like this. I wanted them to see*
*that no matter how hard they tried, they hadn't broken me.'*
*'Do you want to take a break?'*

The question came from an unseen female.

*'No. I'm fine. Keep filming. This isn't just about my pain.*
*What everyone needs to understand is that this about all*
*the other girls that my father and his friends have abused.*
*There are a pack of these animals. Powerful men who meet*
*in secret and abuse children. We only found out about it*
*recently. Otherwise, we'd have taken action before now. You*
*see, I thought I was the only one he'd done this to. But I was*
*wrong. I didn't know about the other men. Or that my father*
*was abusing other girls. But they've had this paedophile club*
*thing going on for years. And because of who these men are,*
*they've had an endless supply of girls to inflict their sick*
*fantasies on.*
*'Anything you want to say to the world, Daddy?'*

Matilda prodded her father with a cane.

'*Go to hell,*' growled Rory Lawson.

*'I'm already there, Daddy. I've walked among the flames for as long as I can remember. You saw to that. For those of you who may have missed the start of this broadcast, I guess you're wondering where we are. Well, this room is a specially designed torture chamber. We didn't create it. This hideous room exists courtesy of my father and his friends. They designed it. You might think that it's abhorrent that I've stripped my father and splayed him on this contraption. After all, it's a disgusting thing to do. But I'm begging you not to turn away from the screen. It's important that you see his vulnerability. This is a small part of what this man and his friends do to their victims.'*

The camera zoomed in to show the equipment.

Jemima was transfixed to the screen, loath to drag herself away. The live feed was horrifically, shockingly compelling. But she knew from the off that she did not have the luxury of being a passive looky-loo. As the officer in charge of finding Lawson, she couldn't afford to waste time. More importantly, it probably wasn't safe for her, Dan or Gareth to spend much time inside the building given Kennedy's attempted murder and his warning them not to trust anyone at the station.

The recent brutal encounter with the DCC was proof that the man was already gunning for her. He was a misogynist, but Jemima appreciated that such a prejudice didn't necessarily mean that he was corrupt. At best, he had the means to make life awkward for her. Worst, he could arrange for some awful accident to befall her and the rest of the team, ensuring that crucial evidence was not catalogued correctly or went missing altogether. The safest thing to do was to stay out of his way until she'd sorted out the Lawson situation, identified the corrupt officers and found Sally Trent. Any one of those tasks would have been more than enough to handle. But three in a day was a hell of an ask . . .

Frank Rutherford and his team would do a far better job of keeping Kennedy safe than they could ever hope to do. So, for now, it was best to put the DCI out of her mind and concentrate her efforts on locating Lawson, whose life was clearly hanging in the balance. Under normal circumstances, a victim was a victim, but as more revelations came to light about the judge, the greater the revulsion she felt for him. In truth, Jemima didn't care if the man ended up dead, but what she didn't want to happen was for his daughter to end up serving a hefty prison sentence should she take the ultimate revenge against him. And that was the only reason Jemima was determined to do everything possible to find and rescue the man before it was too late.

Matilda's anger against her father was heartbreakingly poignant and understandable. But if she was to take things too far and killed him while broadcasting her personal attempt at justice, there would be no coming back from that. And Jemima had a sickening feeling that that was how this scenario might play out. The young woman was at her wit's end, having suffered immeasurably at the hands of her father. What Rory Lawson had repeatedly done to his daughter would have been enough to drive anyone insane. And for Matilda to know that she had escaped his clutches only for him to go on and abuse other vulnerable girls would have been a further slap in the face.

Jemima was certain that Matilda had taken this drastic course of action because it was the only way she could think of to prevent her father and his like-minded friends from continuing to abuse vulnerable people. Society had let them down. The law was lacking.

It was a brave yet reckless step to have taken. If they managed to arrest Matilda, the broadcast demonstrated that at the very least she was guilty of false imprisonment, which meant that she would have to face charges. If the allegations against her father proved to be true, then taking legal action against Matilda seemed harsh and punitive. Her actions shone a spotlight on a shocking situation. And with the allegations against them it meant that there would be an investigation into her father and the other men too. Hopefully that would lead to criminal charges being brought against them. But given Rory Lawson's extensive knowledge of the law, it was easy to imagine that the man would utilise every available resource and exploit every legal loophole to lessen the charges against him. His career was effectively over, and his reputation shot, but that in itself would not be a commensurate level of punishment for the evil deeds the man had committed.

Matilda's actions were those of a desperate person, of someone who believed they had nothing to lose. There was a realistic possibility that Matilda saw this as her end game. And if that was the case it was conceivable that having revealed the most personal details of her life to the entire world, it was her intention to kill her father and possibly even herself.

Jemima was unequivocal in her belief that the world would be a safer place without men like Rory Lawson in it. Of course, she would never dare voice such an opinion. Nor would she stand aside and allow his life to be sacrificed, as it would ultimately go against everything her role as a serving police officer stood for. She would do everything humanly possible to ensure that there would be no loss of life. But if Rory Lawson were to die, she would not shed any tears. Matilda, however, was another matter. Jemima wanted the young woman to come out of this with some sense of vindication and a future to look forward to.

Now she knew who had abducted Lawson, Jemima needed to switch the focus of the investigation and quickly reallocate her resources. A quick search should provide details of any vehicle registered to Matilda Lawson. If the make and model matched the one that had been tailing the judge, then they would be able to use numberplate recognition cameras to try to follow the path that vehicle had gone on to take. However, if the initial search showed that the vehicle had not belonged to Matilda, that would kibosh that particular line of enquiry.

But before she reallocated resources Jemima needed to see the images of the other men Matilda Lawson claimed were co-conspirators along with Rory Lawson. Apart from the need to bring these men in for questioning, there was a distinct possibility that they could already have been abducted. And if they were currently going about their daily lives, putting their names and images out there had immediately made them targets for members of the public to seek them out. Some people could feel the need to approach them and make a citizen's arrest. Others might very well decide to take matters into their own hands. Especially since Matilda had already made a public appeal for people to join PASA's cause. It wasn't unrealistic to think that within a short space of time, there could be numerous angry mobs roaming the streets, preparing to mete out their own form of justice.

As Jemima considered the possible implications of this broadcast and the chaos it could cause, her thoughts were disrupted by Matilda's next statement.

*'These are the photographs of the men who, along with my father, regularly come to this very room to indulge in their perverted, immoral and illegal sexual fantasies.'*

The camera panned around to another wall where images of five middle-aged men were displayed. Along with their names. It seemed that every officer in the room must have scanned those faces at the same rate as a collective gasp filled the air.

Three of the men — Sean Richardson, Thomas Pargan and Michael Chaloner — were names given to them by Edward Trevelyan-Goode shortly before they were forced to cut short his interview. Though it was apparent that the man had been economical with the truth as he had sought to protect himself and another. But Matilda's actions had seen to it that their names and faces were now out there for everyone to see. Two familiar faces were displayed on the screen. The first was Edward Trevelyan-Goode. The second, Superintendent Peter Deavers.

'Gareth, get a message through to the team at the courthouse and tell them to get over here. We'll need every available officer to help locate where the broadcast is coming from,' said Jemima. 'Once you've done that, find out if Professional Standards have arrived at the station and make them aware of the allegations against him.'

'Right you are, guv.' Gareth picked up the phone. With events moving so fast, concerns about his own safety disappeared from his mind.

'Dan, you're with me. We're going to find and arrest Deavers. He was with the DCC, they were heading back to his office. We need to act quickly. Prevent him from having contact with anyone else until Professional Standards can arrange for him to be transferred to another station. There's no way these allegations against him can be ignored. There's always a chance he might be innocent, but they'll have to investigate the claims against him.'

Arresting Superintendent Deavers was a controversial move. Especially if he was still in the company of the DCC. Both men outranked her, and it was obvious from their most recent encounter that the DCC did not hold her in high regard. Despite the fact that arresting Deavers was the right thing to do, the DCC could make it impossible for them to do so. Jemima hoped that the team from Professional Standards would arrive soon.

Having witnessed the two men together today, it was reasonable to think that they might be friends. And as this thought occurred to her, Jemima recalled that someone had mentioned that they had gone through training together. Which gave even more credence to the possibility that there could be a significant amount of loyalty between them. The DCC may very well do everything in his power to prevent them arresting Deavers and allow the man to make it out of the station before Professional Standards arrived. And as Peter Deavers knew the operational playbook by heart, he would have no trouble staying a few steps ahead of them. If he went to ground, they might not find him again.

# CHAPTER 28

As they ran up the stairs to the next floor, Jemima could hear Dan breathing heavily. She was nowhere near as fit as she used to be, but Dan had no excuse. He needed to cut back on the pies and pints and regularly put in a few hours at the gym.

'Day from hell, or what?'

'Yeah, and I've a feeling we've got more surprises to come,' said Jemima.

They approached the corridor housing the various offices of the top brass, and there was no mistaking the sound of raised voices. Even from this distance, it was apparent that one of them was angry and the other fearful.

'Is this true, Peter?'

'Of course not!'

'Don't treat me like a fool. I've overlooked your mistakes in the past, but you've run out of rope. Friendship only goes so far and I'm not risking my career or my pension over this. You're on your own, Peter. You'll get no support from me.'

Jemima suddenly felt more hopeful. It sounded as though the DCC wouldn't make it difficult for her to do the right thing. As they both skidded to a halt outside the DCC's door, she quickly decided to knock instead of barging in.

'Enter!'

She opened the door and they stepped inside. A quick glance showed that Matilda Lawson's broadcast was still playing. Across the room, the DCC had Deavers pinned against the wall. The senior officer's anger was palpable. With faces no more than centimetres apart, spittle sprayed from the DCC's mouth across the forehead of his one-time friend.

'Where's she broadcasting from?' growled the DCC.

'I've no—'

'Don't give me that crap. I swear to God, unless you tell me where she's holding Rory Lawson, I'll knock you through this fucking wall! You're a nonce, Peter! A fucking pervert! Your life's as good as over. But Lawson's daughter doesn't deserve to go down for this. And I'm going to make sure we get to her before she goes too far and kills the sick bastard. She and every other woman that you lot have abused deserve a life and justice. Now, where's she broadcasting from?'

'The Marquess Club, just off the Boulevard de Nantes.' The words were uttered with none of the man's usual bluster. He'd clearly realised that there was no way out of this appalling situation of his own making.

Before Jemima had a chance to say anything, there was the sound of hurried footsteps heading along the corridor. Two women, who Jemima recognised as internal affairs officers, entered the room.

'This is Superintendent Peter Deavers.' The DCC released his grip. 'Read him his rights and get him out of my sight.'

'As for you, Inspector—' he turned his attention to Jemima — 'get your team together and head over to this Marquess Club. I just hope you get there before Matilda Lawson gets herself into more trouble.'

'I will, sir. But there's something you all need to know. DS Sally Trent attempted to murder DCI Kennedy earlier this evening. Gareth Peters found him in an alleyway at the rear of the Marquess Club. She shot him and we've got audio evidence of it happening.'

'We'll need that evidence,' said one of the internal affairs officers. If she was surprised by this revelation, she hid it well.

She was already making a call as she spoke. Moments later she informed the head of Internal Affairs of the need to locate and arrest Sally on suspicion of attempted murder.

'Did Ray survive?' asked the DCC.

'Yeah. They operated on him, but it was touch-and-go. He almost bled out. If it wasn't for Gareth, we'd be arranging his funeral,' said Jemima.

'You should have come to me sooner.' The reprimand was implicit in his tone.

'With all due respect, sir, Ray Kennedy warned us that there was a network of corrupt officers operating in this very building. We had no way of knowing if you were one of them,' said Jemima.

The DCC's jaw slackened, clearly taken aback by Jemima's statement. She and Broadbent left the room before he had a chance to respond.

Jemima felt a glimmer of optimism. From his genuine response, it seemed as though, despite being objectional, the DCC was on the level. And as Internal Affairs were already in the building and had arrested Superintendent Deavers, she was beginning to think that their collective plight was not as bleak as it had appeared to be an hour earlier.

* * *

It took the best part of fifteen minutes to round up every available officer to carry out a search of the Marquess Club. Splitting the team into two groups of six, Jemima, Broadbent, Peters and another three officers headed up the stone steps at the front entrance of the imposing building.

This establishment catered for a very particular class of clientele. The security guard at the front entrance was dressed formally, his tailcoat and top hat at odds with the general standard of dress usually seen on a Cardiff street. The man seemed less than impressed. And though he was clearly troubled by their appearance he managed to retain an air of dignity. 'You've no business at these premises.' The statement was made directly to Jemima. 'This is a gentlemen's club.'

'Oh, believe me, there are no gentlemen at this establishment.'

The man's face darkened. Jemima had the sense that he was hoping that good manners and etiquette would prevail so that he could avoid an unseemly altercation. She knew without doubt that he would not put up any physical resistance to prevent them from entering the premises. He was there for show, as undesirable visitors did not visit the Marquess Club.

'Unless you want to be arrested for obstructing police officers going about their duty, I suggest you step aside and allow us to enter,' said Jemima. Her matter-of-fact tone made it clear that she was in no mood to be messed about. She looked the man directly in the eye, holding up her warrant card for him to see that the threat was a genuine one.

She watched as the realisation of what was about to happen hit home, and his haughty expression faltered. Jemima guessed that in all his years as a doorman at this gentleman's club he would never have encountered such a situation. As consternation played across his face he swallowed hard, his Adam's apple bobbing prominently against the collar of his immaculate white shirt. In other circumstances she might have felt sorry for him, as given the status of the club's members, she could appreciate that he genuinely couldn't imagine why the police would have cause to enter the premises. After all, until Matilda had broadcast her plight across the airwaves, the thought of Rory Lawson being a paedophile hadn't crossed any of their minds, and it was possible that this man was unaware of current events. Having quickly weighed up his options, or rather the lack of them, he nodded his acceptance, stepped aside, and reached out to open the door.

Jemima glanced around. The world might have moved on, but this establishment had retained many of the values of the Victorian era. The air was heavy with the smell of tobacco, despite smoking having been banned in enclosed public spaces more than a decade earlier. It was a clear indication, if any was needed, that within the confines of this building, the law of the land was of no concern to the management of the club nor its members.

Every so often, Jemima's nostrils picked up a different, more subtle aroma. And as her mind raced to put a name to it, her eyes fixed on the copious amounts of highly polished wood. Only then did it occur to her that it was the smell of beeswax, something she had not encountered since the death of her grandmother, who had insisted that her cleaner apply it regularly to the wooden furniture in the dining room.

'What do you think you're doing? You're not members of this establishment. You have no business being here.' The man appeared from a room further down the dimly lit hallway. He was clearly a member of staff as he wore a uniform of similar colour to the doorman. His voice was haughty, self-important, contemptuous. Before any of them had the opportunity to respond, he continued, 'I suggest you turn around and get the hell out of this club. Before I call security and get you forcibly removed!'

Jemima was in no mood for his bullshit. Instead of doing as she was told, she quickly closed the distance between them. 'And your name is?' She arched her eyebrows.

'That's none of your concern. Now get—'

'Oh yes, it is, because if you try to obstruct me or any of my officers, I'll have you carted off to the police station and you can spend the night in one of our cells. Now cut the attitude, sunshine. Or else you'll soon be experiencing a different side to life. You won't be breathing in tobacco and beeswax. You'll have to contend with the usual cocktail of vomit, piss and shit. Do I make myself clear?'

The man's eyes widened as he tried to make sense of what he was hearing.

'Well? I'm waiting. Are you going to make life difficult for yourself? Or are you going to cooperate?'

'I-I'll c-cooperate.' His voice was suddenly devoid of belligerence. Having been threatened with incarceration, common sense prevailed. Even the most obtuse or entitled person would appreciate that this was not the time to play the privilege card.

'What's your name?' demanded Jemima.

'Dewi . . . Dewi Curzon,' he replied.

'Oh shit!' muttered Gareth.

'What's the matter?'

'Sorry, guv, but with everything that's happened, I'd forgotten all about this until now.' His usually pasty complexion reddened as he rummaged in a pocket and eventually pulled something out. 'When I came across the DCI in the alleyway, he was holding this. He must've thought it was important as I had to practically prise it from his hand.'

As Jemima glanced at the object in her sergeant's hand, her heart rate increased. It was virtually identical to the one she had seen earlier that day. A distinctive black key card with the letters *PM* embossed in gold. But whereas the one in Rory Lawson's study had displayed the number 1, this one had the word *MASTER* emblazoned across it.

'Where did you get that?' asked Dewi.

'Why? Do you know what it's for?' asked Jemima.

'It's the key card that allows you to access the Platinum Members' area of this establishment. Only a very select group have been allowed to join. They each have a numbered key card. They're the upper echelon of members. The place is sacrosanct. Even staff aren't allowed inside.'

'Show us where the entrance is,' demanded Jemima.

Dewi's jaw dropped. From the shocked expression on his face, he had found Jemima's order an inconceivable demand. 'But no one's allowed—'

'Take us there now! Then give one of these uniformed officers a list of names and contact details for each of the Platinum Members. After that, take yourself into the main reception area and wait there. We'll need to interview you once we've finished searching the premises.'

# CHAPTER 29

The door to the Platinum Members' room appeared much like the others they had passed along the dimly lit corridor, with two obvious differences. Firstly, there was the plaque that identified the room as being for the exclusive use of Platinum Members. Secondly, there was a keypad requiring a pin number, locking the room to those without knowledge of the access code. However, upon inspection, there was nowhere for a key card to be inserted.

'I thought you said this key card allowed entry?' Jemima looked accusingly at Dewi.

'No, what I said was that each of the Platinum Members has one of those key cards. But I've no idea what it's for. This door has always had entry via a pin number.'

'Just open the damned door!' demanded Jemima. She was quickly losing patience with this man.

'I can't. I don't know the code. They don't give it out to other members. Let alone to the likes of me. They're important people. They wouldn't allow just anyone to enter that room.'

'Shall I break it down, guv?' asked one of the uniformed officers. He had come prepared with a battering ram and was keen to put it to good use.

'You can't do that!' shouted Dewi.

'Oh yes, we can,' said Jemima. 'You've shown us where the room is, so we no longer require your help. Now, take yourself back to the reception area and wait there to speak to one of my officers.'

Jemima stepped aside to allow the youngish constable sufficient room to swing the device. As she stood and watched, a memory of Broadbent about to do the very same thing flashed into her mind. They had been standing outside a property named West Winds on the outskirts of Leighton Meadow, the village where Jemima had now lived for almost two years. It was the last case they had worked together before she went on maternity leave. A property and a case she and the rest of the team would never be able to forget.

Metal smashed against wood, resulting in an inevitable splintering as the door separated from the frame. A shiver ran down Jemima's spine as the door swung inwards, revealing a darkened space. Jemima blinked rapidly, exhaling forcibly as she did everything in her power to drag herself back to the here and now. This was not the time to dwell on the past. Especially since she had no idea what they were about to face. Until they entered the room there was no way of knowing if this was going to turn out to be a complete waste of time. Instinct suggested she'd made the right call. Then again, she'd been out of the game for such a long period.

Her fingers instinctively feathered her weapon in readiness to react to any threat that might present itself in the next few seconds. They needed to see what they were walking into. Yet for the moment, the only light inside the dark space bled in thin strips from the edges of hefty curtains, drawn together, presumably to retain privacy.

Gareth shone a torch around, revealing that the room was empty.

'Find the light switch,' she ordered. 'It's gotta be near the door.'

One of the PCs ran a hand across the wall and located it. Everything became visible. Given the supposed exclusivity of this area, which was accessible to only a few of the club's most prestigious members, the room was surprising dingy and spartan, clinging to the grandeur of a bygone age. It was in need of attention and a significant upgrade as everything about it was well past its prime. A dark wooden boardroom table, far too large, with hefty chairs around it, filled much of the available space. The carpet, which in places added reds and greens to brighten the dour choice of furniture, was patchy, faded and threadbare in places where feet had trodden throughout the decades. And although the space appeared superficially clean, dust motes floated in the air.

'Three crystal decanters containing liquor of varying hues sat upon a sideboard, though there were no glasses into which the drinks could be poured. To the side of this was a bookcase, which appeared to have been purposely built and covered that area from floor to ceiling.

'There's nothing here.' Gareth's shoulders slumped with disappointment.

'Nothing immediately obvious,' agreed Jemima. She surveyed the area carefully, determined not to miss anything that could lead them to the whereabouts of Rory Lawson and his captors.

'It doesn't look as though Lawson's being held inside this building,' said Broadbent.

'We don't know that, Dan. We've only just started searching. I'm sure this room has some significance.'

'Well, Kennedy was holding onto that key card as though his life depended upon it,' said Gareth. 'And we now know from Dewi Curzon that only the so-called Platinum Members have those keys, and this room is their exclusive domain.'

'Exactly, and there must be a reason for that. Let's face it, this isn't the most welcoming of spaces. It's shabby. Austere. There's got to be a reason for that group of men to want to gather here in secret, and I'm convinced it's down to what we saw on that live stream. You don't put a keypad on a door just for the sake of it. They're ensuring that no one else can enter this room, which suggests there's something in here that they want to protect. We just haven't found it yet.'

'Yeah, I guess they could do whatever they want once they're locked away inside this room.' Gareth nodded as he began to cast a more critical eye over the space.

'Exactly. Which makes me think there could be a hidden entrance to allow them to get into that torture chamber without raising suspicion,' said Jemima.

'You think that that room is somewhere inside this building?' asked Broadbent.

'It must be. We don't yet have a list of names for the Platinum Members. But those that we know of have this club in common. And why is this room off limits to everyone else? Look at it. It's a dump. It's possible there could be a hidden doorway. I know we'd all rather forget about it, but we've encountered it before,' said Jemima.

Dan and Gareth exchanged a worried look. Just the thought of a hidden doorway brought back a whole host of unwelcome memories they had each spent the last year trying to put to the back of their minds.

'And as far as I can see, there's only one possibility. That built-in bookcase must be disguising the entrance. After all, Lawson used a bookcase to hide the safe in his study. So why not use one to hide the entrance to a hidden room? We'll know soon enough once we start emptying those shelves,' said Jemima. 'But before we make a start, let's get one thing clear from the off. If we find a hidden entrance, no one takes any chances. We came far too close to losing one of our own today, and I'm determined it's not going to happen again. We play it safe and watch one another's backs.'

'Amen to that,' echoed Broadbent.

Jemima's radio crackled to life. An officer from the team in the alleyway where Kennedy was found made contact. 'Guv?'

'What is it?'

'There's a forensics team processing a crime scene out here, so we ended up having to approach the rear of the premises from the other end of the alley. Anyway, the upshot is there are two doors fairly close together. One of them looks like a bog-standard type of fire door. There's a notice above it identifying it as an emergency exit ordering people to keep the area clear. Pretty standard stuff for any public building. The other door looks sus. It's about five yards further along.'

'Still part of the same building?' interjected Jemima.

'Absolutely. Thing is, there's a substantial hasp on it but no padlock.'

'Are you able to open it?'

'No. We've tried. There's no give in it.'

'It must be locked from the inside,' said Jemima. 'Any sign to suggest it's another emergency exit?'

'No, guv. Is it OK if I send someone around to get the battering ram so we can force entry?'

'I'll send Blethen out with it now. He'll meet you at the far end of the alley. But if you manage to force the door, then make sure to have your wits about you. We're not dealing with an ordinary perp. His daughter's a trained soldier. She'll be prepared. If this is where Lawson's being held then we could be facing an ambush. So, I don't want anyone playing the hero. Lawson's no innocent victim.

'We're searching for a way in, at this end. Keep this line of communication open. We both need to be aware of progress,' said Jemima.

In the time it had taken to have this short conversation, about a third of the books were already off the shelves. The rest of the team were working fast. They'd organised themselves into a chain to remove the tomes and stack them efficiently on the table.

Being a few inches shorter than the smallest of the male officers, Jemima's line of sight picked up a different perspective of the shelving unit. And as the latest handful of books came off the shelves, she was the first to spot the mechanism into which the key card slotted.

Relief washed over her as she called for the others to stop what they were doing. She'd made the right call. There was a hidden room inside this odious, misogynistic establishment. But they had yet to establish if this entrance would lead them to the torture chamber, and to Rory Lawson.

# CHAPTER 30

There was a noticeable tremor to Jemima's hand as she placed the key card in the slot. From the moment she had arrived at the station that morning, everything had been worryingly unpredictable. She'd had concerns about returning, but that was because her comfortable routine was being upended.

Nothing could have prepared her for what she and her team had faced in the last few hours. Since coming on shift they had been metaphorically tossed from pillar to post, forced to hold their nerve and adapt to extreme circumstances, with the level of danger they faced ramping up with every passing second.

Being a seasoned officer Jemima knew all too well that she needed to display confidence in front of the team. Act decisively. Lead by example. But there was a niggling seed of doubt that she was out of practice, and possibly no longer up to the job. Her heart skipped a beat and she hardly dared breathe, hoping she could let go of her insecurities and not let anyone down when push came to shove.

There was a time not so long ago when she would have blocked out the fear of the unknown and put any concerns for her own safety to one side. But things were different now. Perhaps it was because this was her first day back on duty, and she was still readjusting to the dangers her chosen career posed. Perhaps it was because Ray Kennedy had almost lost his life that day. The sickening dread that lurked in the pit of her stomach was possibly a combination of these factors. But it was also that she had so much more to live for now. For the first time in her life, she had everything she wanted. She was happy with her boys, whom she loved more than life itself.

There was a click. The locking mechanism disengaged and the cleverly disguised door swung open, revealing a wide staircase leading down to a lower level. The area was well lit, the walls on either side displaying hundreds of framed photographs. There were so many of them that it was difficult to focus on any single image. But when Jemima stopped to examine them she wanted to rip these men to pieces.

The walls were covered from top to bottom with a showcase of the Platinum Members' memorabilia. Young women, some only teenagers, stripped naked. All terrified by what was being done to them. Some were strapped to the various contraptions displayed on the recent broadcast. Others were photographs of them as they were being raped, and the faces of the men carrying out these attacks were there for all to see. There were images of Rory Lawson, Peter Deavers, Edward Trevelyan-Goode and others, their vile acts captured and immortalised to enable them to relive the moments whenever they should choose.

'Bag these up, and don't allow them out of your sight,' ordered Jemima. The sickening explicit images left nothing to the imagination. She was damned if this group of perverted sadists were going to get away without facing the full force of the law. Between the photographs and the forensics they'd collect from the torture chamber, there would be sufficient evidence to prosecute each of these men. The only way they would avoid a trial is if they pleaded guilty. And if they chose to contest the charges, they would not have one of their own masquerading as a high court judge to ensure that they got off with only a few months community service. Though, whether impartial juries could be selected for these men who had already been outed in such a public way would inevitably be a big ask. There would always be people who had not watched the broadcast, but the shocking nature of its content meant that it would remain a topic of conversation for a very long time.

As they continued down the stairs, Jemima noticed that the air was slightly unpleasant. She guessed that the odour was most likely stale air combined with sweat, fear and sexual activity, but the thought went out of her mind as someone spoke.

'I was wondering how long it would take you to get here!' The woman's disembodied voice came from somewhere below. 'Come on down. We're unarmed and will not resist arrest. But I should warn you, that everything you do or say will be broadcast.'

Jemima and the others recognised the voice as being that of Matilda Lawson. She, Dan and Gareth drew their weapons as they arrived at the open doorway to the torture chamber, though when they saw what they were facing, they holstered their firearms.

Rory Lawson was still splayed across the contraption, looking haggard and defeated. His daughter and another woman sat cross-legged on the floor, with their hands held aloft. Somewhere in the distance came the sound of the officers in the alleyway, still attempting to gain access to the building.

'As you can see, we pose no threat to you,' said Matilda. 'I have used a minimal amount of force to take this action against my father. Everything we have done has only been done to bring their crimes out into the open. Given the men we are up against, we had no other option but to go down this route. We want to give evidence. Even if it means that we serve custodial sentences. Whatever happens to us from now on will be worth it as long as these men are sentenced and serve an appropriate amount of time behind bars. They are monsters hiding in plain sight. Duping everyone with their fancy clothes and their high-flying careers. We just want the evidence of their crimes out there so that people can see that they have destroyed hundreds of lives, and will keep on doing it until they are stopped.'

'I hear you, and I guarantee that we will look at all of the evidence. This won't be swept under the carpet. You have my word on it,' said Jemima.

'I'll hold you to it.' Matilda stared at Jemima, as though appraising her. 'You'll soon realise we have no weapons. What we've done wasn't about violence or revenge. It's only ever been about justice. Something every one of their victims deserves.'

Jemima was impressed with the calmness of the women. Matilda's accomplice identified herself as Rachel Knowles, who was a social worker and herself a victim of sexual abuse. Both women complied with every instruction as they were arrested and cuffed.

'We went into this knowing that we would be arrested for abduction and false imprisonment,' said Rachel. 'You might want to tell your team in the alleyway to stand down. We've barricaded the doorway, and I'd be surprised if they could gain access that way.'

'For God's sake, do your job and free me from this contraption. Allow me some dignity,' growled Rory.

The three officers ignored the man's loud protestations. After the recent revelations it was impossible to care about his needs. He was not the victim here. There were others far more deserving of sympathy.

'You've seen the photographs hanging in pride of place on the way down,' said Matilda. 'If they're prepared to display those abominations, I can only begin to image what they're keeping locked up in that safe.' She pointed at one of the walls.

Jemima looked across, wondering what Rory had hidden in the safe in his home office.

# CHAPTER 31

For much of that night it was all hands on deck, and despite everyone's profound tiredness, a new sense of urgency prevailed. The case had mushroomed so rapidly that it was all but impossible to keep pace with the revelations they had uncovered.

The discovery of the hidden room at the Marquess Club had resulted in hundreds of pieces of evidence that had to be catalogued, bagged up and transported to a secure evidence locker. With the other sex offenders still at large, the race to find them was on. These men had wealth, privilege and connections. They would find it relatively easy to go to ground, not just fleeing their homes but possibly leaving the country altogether. And if that should happen there was little chance of ever bringing them to justice.

Then there were the victims too, whose brutal ordeals had been displayed like hunting trophies in a sickening collage of depravity. So many images of young women and teenage girls in agony. Degraded. Terrified. Possibly even wishing for death. And all to satisfy the desires of a pack of sadistic monsters, barbaric men who thought nothing of taking whatever they wanted to repeatedly reinforce their feeling of omnipotence.

What had started out as an abduction had quickly spiralled, revealing a rottenness of unimaginable proportions. With so many crime scenes needing to be processed in such a short space of time, forensic officers had been drafted in from other areas.

Given the recent events at the station, it was impossible for Rory Lawson, Matilda and Rachel to be taken there. Instead, they were transported to the South Wales Police Headquarters at Bridgend, along with Jemima, Dan, Gareth, all the evidence from the latest scene and the evidence collected throughout the day.

Since his arrest, Peter Deavers had been taken to a station at another police authority, where he was being held under an assumed name. From the moment the internal affairs officers made the arrest, his case would be dealt with by them. It was the only way forward, as there were obvious allegations of corrupt officers still being at large in the station.

'I'm knackered,' sighed Broadbent, splashing cold water over his face in an attempt to reinvigorate himself.

Gareth stifled a yawn. 'Me too.' His eyes were watery and bloodshot. Both officers were in a restroom at the Bridgend Police Headquarters. It was a station neither of them was familiar with. 'Still, we've gotta keep going. We owe it to Lawson's daughter and Rachel. All the other victims too.'

'Yeah, I agree. Bet they've had years of sleepless nights, and a lot of nightmares whenever they eventually drop off. Puts my tiredness into perspective,' said Dan. 'We'd better get going. The clock's ticking.'

When Dan and Gareth entered the room they had been allocated, they found Jemima sorting through a box of evidence.

'This from the Marquess Club?' asked Gareth.

'No, it's the contents of Lawson's home office safe. I haven't looked at the DVDs yet, but these photographs certainly explain why he went to so much trouble to stop anyone finding them.' Jemima handed each of them a selection of graphic images of girls and young women.

'The bastard deserves to be castrated,' growled Broadbent. 'Isn't that—'

'One of the bedrooms at Lawson's house, and I think that's Matilda,' interjected Jemima. The photograph showed Lawson having sexual contact with a young girl. The child's expression was blank, suggesting that this was not the first time she had been forced to participate. It was a look of hopeless acceptance that this was how her life was.

'One thing's for certain,' said Jemima, 'if he makes it to trial, he'll go down for life.'

'Can they give him that long a sentence?' asked Gareth.

'I think she means that they'll be queuing up on the inside to finish him off, Gar. And in my opinion, whoever does it should be given a medal.'

'I'm off to interview Matilda and then Rachel. I want one of you to come with me, and I'd like whoever stays behind to take a look at those DVDs. As things stand, we've more than enough evidence to charge Lawson, but first thing in the morning, we're going to have to get a specialist sex crimes unit involved. We need to identify as many victims as we possibly can. They deserve support and justice. Which one of you will interview with me?'

'I think Gareth should go with you,' said Dan. 'I'm not in the right frame of mind to speak to them. I'm just so angry about what Lawson has done that I'm unlikely to be impartial. As far as I'm concerned, Matilda and Rachel have done the world a favour. If it was up to me, I'd let them walk without charge.'

Jemima accepted Dan's concern without question. She knew from personal experience that he sometimes let his emotions get the better of him. But of course, you'd have to have a heart of stone not to feel sympathetic towards Matilda and Rachel. If Lawson's daughter was telling them the truth, then she had suffered horrendously. And it was perfectly understandable that she had felt that no one would help her. Her father's status and mother's complicity had seen to that. Jemima planned on showing her the photograph in the hope that it would back up the young woman's allegations. She too wanted Matilda and Rachel to walk away from this without having to serve a custodial sentence.

'Oh, and Dan, I've spoken to Anita Formby and told her to caution Emilia Lawson and bring her in for questioning. Find an interview room to stick her in. I'll speak to her when I've finished with the others. That woman's got a lot to answer for. She knew what her husband was and could have stopped him. Instead, she turned to the bottle and looked the other way. As far as I'm concerned, she's complicit in her husband's crimes and has played a role in ruining countless lives.'

Dan just wanted to go home and forget that today had ever happened, but before he could return to his wife and child, he would have to view whatever depravity was on the DVDs that Lawson had squirrelled away for safekeeping.

# CHAPTER 32

With the formalities out of the way, Jemima took a long look at Matilda Lawson. The slump of the young woman's shoulders, dishevelled appearance and haunted expression was a far cry from what would be expected of her as a captain in the British Army. Yet after everything she had suffered over the years, along with the pain and humiliation of broadcasting her story to the world, her fortitude still managed to shine through.

There was no doubt in Jemima's mind that most people would have been broken beyond repair if they had suffered years of such horrendous abuse. But it was evident that Matilda was drawing on her military experience to push through. She was on a mission and was determined to see it through to the end. No matter the cost, this was her own personal battlefield, and the fight would be on her own terms.

Despite her all too apparent exhaustion, the young woman was keen to keep the momentum up and tell her story. Everything else was an unnecessary distraction. She nursed a cup of tea, from which she took the occasional sip, but which must have already gone cold.

'You do realise that you have the right to legal representation?' asked Jemima.

'I don't trust anyone to represent me. This nightmare has gone on for as long as it has because of my father being a judge. He's got contacts everywhere, influential people who'll do whatever it takes to discredit me and shut me down. I wouldn't put it past him to have someone try to kill me. That's the sort of man he is.'

Although Matilda's allegations were alarming, Jemima was struck by the way in which she spoke about her father. The statements were made in a calm, matter-of-fact tone. There were no histrionics. No show of emotion. This woman believed what she was saying.

'I saw some of the statements you made during the broadcast.'

'That's good. It was the only way I could think of getting the truth out there. Hopefully so many people would have seen it that it will be impossible for my father and the others to hide.'

'For the purpose of this interview, I'm afraid I'm going to ask you to tell us everything about what your father did to you and any involvement your mother had.' Jemima hated to ask her to relive the trauma again. She knew from experience the cost of dredging up such awful memories.

They sat in silence as Matilda gave a heartbreakingly detailed account of her father's sexual assaults. And apart from Matilda's voice, there was no other sound in the room. When she had finally finished speaking, Jemima opened the folder on the table in front of her and extracted the photograph.

'I'm sorry to have to show you this, but I need you to look at this image and tell me if you recognise anyone or anything in the photograph. For the purposes of the tape, I am showing Matilda Lawson photograph exhibit number N223, which was taken from inside a locked safe in Rory Lawson's home office. The image shows a young female masturbating an adult male.'

Matilda's body immediately went rigid as though it had been zapped with an electric current. She clearly hadn't expected to be confronted with the image. Her feet propelled her chair backwards, away from the table, as her composure crumbled. Beads of sweat broke out across her brow. An anguished howl rose from the pit of her stomach and she folded her arms across her midriff, clasping her sides tightly and rocked back and forth, sobbing inconsolably.

'Interview suspended. Switch the tape off, Gareth.' Jemima rushed to comfort the woman, who accepted without protest the unexpected show of support. She buried her head on Jemima's shoulder and allowed her to take her weight as all her pent-up emotion spilled out. 'Get her another cup of tea, Gareth. Lots of sugar. And a box of tissues wouldn't go amiss.'

It was almost twenty minutes later when Matilda was sufficiently composed to continue with the interview. She identified the two people in the photograph as being herself and her father, explaining that it was one of many that he had taken in her bedroom on an automatic timer.

'During your broadcast, you mentioned PASA?'

'That's right. We're a group of activists. People Against Sexual Abuse.'

'I'll need a list of members,' said Jemima.

'That's not going to happen. I came out with my story. I've no doubt that Rachel will tell you hers. As for other members of the group, it would be down to them as individuals to decide whether to approach you.'

'Your request for people to join PASA could be interpreted as a call for vigilantism.'

'That was not my intention.'

'Nevertheless, others could interpret it as such. Which means it could go against you when the case goes to trial.'

'I'll take my chances. PASA is a self-help group. We sit. Talk. Listen. Support. We certainly don't advocate using violence. Our aim is to bring about societal change, raise awareness of what's happening all around. These predators get away with abusing people because they have anonymity. If we expose them for what they are, it's our belief that we can stop some of these assaults from happening.'

'It's a great sentiment. If that's what happens.'

'What do you mean?'

'Are you aware of another abduction that occurred at about the same time that you took your father?'

'No. Someone snatched another sex offender?'

From the expression on Matilda's face, Jemima sensed the woman was telling the truth.

'Not exactly. As far as we can ascertain, it was a case of mistaken identity, leading to the death of an innocent man. However, the person we believe to be the intended victim is linked to your father.'

Matilda's hands shot towards her mouth as she gasped in horror. 'That's awful! B-but it g-genuinely has n-nothing to do with me. Nothing like that was ever discussed in any PASA meeting. We didn't tell anyone what we were planning to do.'

'Will you give us a list of PASA members?'

'No. I'm sure you'll have ways of finding out who they are, but there are no circumstances under which I will ever willingly reveal that information. After all, there are a lot of people who hold grudges for one reason or another. It doesn't necessarily follow that it was linked to our cause.'

Jemima appreciated that there was no point in following this line of questioning. Emyr's death was not her case. It was down to Glen Buchannan to follow up on that. Though she doubted that given Matilda's military training, he would ever be able to get her to talk. Plus, there was always the possibility that she had been truthful when she said that she knew nothing about it.

'Rachel and I abducted my father because it was the only way we could get him to face justice. We used minimal force to get him to come with us.' She covered her eyes. 'What will happen now?'

'Your father's crimes are more extensive than you realise, and we have enough evidence to charge him. When we have finished questioning him, he will remain in custody. I will strongly recommend that he should not be allowed bail.

Though, considering the charges against him, I would be surprised if it were an option.'

'Good. I want him to answer for what he's done. I knew from the moment I took this course of action that I'd face a trial too. And I want to have my time in court. For every sordid detail to come out. To tell everyone what drove me to do this. It's the only hope for everyone who has suffered at the hands of men like him. I'll take whatever punishment I'm due as long as I get justice for what he's done.'

'You're right, you will be charged for abduction and false imprisonment. There's no way around that. But I'll see to it that you're bailed,' said Jemima. 'Given the high profile of your actions I'd be surprised if the case didn't go to trial, but when I'm called as a witness, I will make sure that everyone knows that you were driven to take such extreme actions because of a profound failure within our justice system. I've no way of knowing for certain, but my best guess would be that any sentence imposed for that aspect would be a non-custodial one. As for the call for people to join PASA, I haven't got a clue how that will play out, and there's a distinct possibility that you'll be questioned by the officer investigating that other abduction. But you're free to go for now, pending further questioning. You'll be informed of the date when you will have to attend a plea hearing.'

'Really? I can go? What about Rachel?'

'We'll be questioning her soon.'

'In that case, do you mind if I wait?'

'That's fine.' A sudden thought occurred to Jemima. Something she had never thought she would consider. 'Look, Matilda, it's none of my business, but if I were you, I'd seriously consider contacting this solicitor and ask her to represent you.' Jemima wrote down the name Prudence Dwight on a piece of paper. Over the years, they'd had many a run-in with the woman. She was at best formidable, at worst terrifying. Undoubtedly one of the best in the business, her fee reflected her level of competence.

'How would I know she's not in my father's pocket?' It was a reasonable question under the circumstances.

'That would be for you to assess. All I can say is that as a police officer I'm certainly not a fan of Ms Dwight. That said, I have a great deal of respect for the woman, and I'd be surprised if she's in anyone's pocket. Put it this way, if I was in your shoes, Prudence Dwight would be the first person I'd call. I'm sure she'd have your back.'

Having released Matilda, they went to check in with Broadbent, who was still viewing the DVDs and scribbling away furiously.

'How's it going, Dan?'

'He's a sick bastard. As far as I can tell, when he started abusing Matilda, Lawson photographed the encounters. But a few years down the line it appears that he moved on to videoing them.'

'Leaves little to the imagination to guess what he spends his time doing in that study of his,' said Gareth.

'Yeah, anyway, what I was about to say is that you need to take a look at this. Now where is it? Give me a few secs.' Broadbent ran down his notes with his forefinger until he found what he was looking for. He selected a particular section of the DVD currently in the machine and pressed play.

'He's positioned the camera so that it's picked up in the wardrobe mirror. Allows him to get a better all-round view.' As they watched the scene play out the bedroom door opened.

'That's Emilia Lawson!' Jemima watched open-mouthed as the woman stood there, staring at her husband as he raped their daughter. It was clear that Matilda was terrified. Yet Emilia did and said nothing at all.

Yet again, Jemima realised that she'd forgotten to breathe, she was so reviled by what she was watching. Dan stopped the recording, and she suddenly became aware that her hands were painful — she had been bunching her fists so tightly that her nails had almost punctured the skin on her palms.

She couldn't understand how anyone could allow their child to suffer such violent, repeated abuse. It was inconceivable. A despicable abdication of parental duty that went against the nurturing instinct. It was undeniable proof that throughout much of her childhood, Matilda had not received love or care from either of her parents.

'Has Emilia Lawson arrived at the station yet?'

'No. Shouldn't be much longer.' Dan glanced at his watch.

'Well, when she does, that bitch is going to be charged and locked up,' growled Jemima. She marched out of the room with Gareth in tow. All she could think about was how she wanted to rip the woman's face off.

# CHAPTER 33

Rachel Knowles was unapologetic about the role she had played in Rory Lawson's abduction. Then again, there was no reason she should have had any regret for her actions. She had helped do what the law-enforcement bodies should have done — exposed a predatory sex offender along with an entire group of like-minded men.

Jemima soon learned that Rachel was Matilda's fiancée and was very protective of her. It was heart-warming to see that someone was finally giving Matilda the love and support she deserved.

'How did you learn about what was going on inside the Marquess Club?' asked Jemima.

'I'm a child protection officer. The kids I deal with have been at the bottom of the heap for their entire lives. They've learned the hard way that they can't trust adults. Even some- one like me, who's actually fighting their corner and doing everything I can to look out for them. Long story short, it was a lucky break. I was visiting a community centre when I overheard a hushed conversation. A teenage girl was telling some of the others about the club. How there was this group of rich men who bunged them some cash and gave them lines of coke. All they had to do was have kinky sex.'

'And what did the other girls say?'

'Some of them were keen to get involved. *Fifty Shades* has normalised BDSM for so many people. And I suppose if you're a teenage girl with few life choices, finding your very own Christian Grey would be a dream come true.'

'I suppose it would,' admitted Jemima. She knew the desperate lengths some people went to, to try and improve their lives.

'Anyway, I mentioned it to Matty, and we decided to stake the place out. The girls are taken in through the doorway in the alley. We've seen the same woman delivering and collecting them. I've no idea who she is, but I've got a photograph of her on my phone, which might help you identify her.'

'Your phones are being looked at as part of the investigation, so we'll find the photograph you've referred to. Did anyone else use the rear entrance of the club?'

'Not while we were staking the place out. The men use the main entrance. When we saw Matty's father go inside we kept up the surveillance for a few weeks, just to make sure that he was a regular there. Once we realised that he was, we knew he'd be involved with it.'

Rachel was charged and released pending further investigation. As Jemima walked with her towards the reception area, they heard raised voices.

'That's Matty!' Rachel picked up her pace.

Jemima followed hot on her heels to find a constable doing his best to defuse an argument that had the potential to become a physical confrontation.

'Stay back, I'll sort this.' Jemima placed a firm hand on Rachel's shoulder. Still, Rachel hesitated momentarily. 'Rachel, if you both want to go home tonight, I suggest you do as you're told. You're not going to be much comfort to Matilda if you're banged up overnight. Now back away and leave this to me.'

Common sense prevailed and Rachel stepped away from the confrontation. Jemima on the other hand had no choice but to step into the fray, as the argument was turning uglier by the minute and the lone constable was clearly out of his depth. Jemima did the first thing she could think of — she stuck her fingers in her mouth and whistled loudly. The piercing sound shocked everyone into silence. As all heads turned towards her, she recognised the man who was verbally abusing Matilda. It was her brother Anthony.

'Dr Lawson, I suggest you calm down and step—'

'You've arrested my mother and it's all her fault!' interjected Anthony. Spittle sprayed from his lips with the force of his words. He jabbed a finger towards his sister, who flinched, despite there being no physical contact.

'Dr Lawson! Your angry outbursts are not helping anyone. Especially your mother. I'm the one who asked for her to be brought in for questioning. This is not Matilda's doing. Now I suggest you moderate your behaviour. Otherwise, you run the risk of being arrested too, and I don't think you'll want that to happen, as it could very well affect your career. Your mother is facing some serious charges, and it is likely that she will remain at this station overnight.'

'But she's ill!'

'I assure you that as a matter of routine we'll have an independent doctor examine her and assess whether she is fit to be interviewed. But under no circumstances will you be allowed to see or speak to her until she has answered our questions.'

'And what about my father?'

'It is my understanding that your father was examined by a police doctor and was found to have received only superficial injuries. I intend to interview him shortly, after which he will be placed on remand in a prison outside of this area, where he will be housed in a vulnerable prisoner unit.'

'Why would you do that?'

'Because should anyone learn of his identity, he will be at risk of attack.'

'Surely he'll be bailed? I'll stump up the money.' The anger, only seconds earlier prevalent in Anthony's voice, had disappeared as the reality of the situation started to sink in.

'Given the nature of his crimes, I'm afraid that won't be possible. Now I must go. And I suggest you go home. There's nothing you can do here for either of your parents. And as I've already said, leave your sister alone, because I'd hate to have to charge you with interfering with a witness.'

Jemima and Gareth found Broadbent just ending a call. From the lines on his forehead and the slump of his shoulders it was easy to see that like them, he was running on empty.

'Any developments?' asked Jemima.

'Just more of the same depravity on these DVDs. Oh, and Emilia Lawson's been checked out by the on-call doctor and is fit to be questioned.'

'About time.'

'Oh, and one of the inspectors popped his head around earlier to say that they're taking Lawson to Bristol after we've finished with him. His brief's turned up. Even though he's more than capable of representing himself, seems as though he feels the need for backup.'

'He's not going to be firing on all cylinders, is he? He's had a lifetime of being the one in control, always making the decisions, having people hanging off his every word and never questioning him. Since waking up this morning, in most people's eyes, he's literally gone from hero to zero. So, right now, he needs someone who has his back,' said Jemima.

'When you put it like that . . .'

'Let's get on with the interview. We don't want him hanging around here any longer than necessary.'

'Mind if I sit this one out?' asked Gareth. 'There's so much riding on this, I don't want to let you down. And I haven't eaten for bloody ages. I could do with grabbing a coffee and a snack.'

'Fine by me. Dan?' Jemima turned to face her partner.

'Yeah. Bring it on,' said Dan.

'Once I've done that I'll chase up on Matilda and Rachel's phones. See if the image of that woman supplying the girls is good enough to help identify her,' said Gareth.

Rory Lawson and his solicitor were deep in conversation as Jemima opened the door. The conversation died mid-sentence. The solicitor glanced up and placed his hand on Rory's arm and, as he turned to face them, Jemima was surprised to see that it was none other than Vernon Foley. The man was a shark if ever there was one. Their only previous encounter with him had happened just over a year ago when he had represented a client who lived on the edge of Leighton Meadow, the village Jemima now called home.

He smiled, and Jemima felt that same sensation of distrust and revulsion that she had back then. He was wearing a suit that was way out of most people's price range. She also noticed that he still wore his hair in a topknot, not that she held that particular fashion statement against him.

With the formalities out of the way, Foley was the first to speak. 'I trust that my client's abductors have been formally charged? They have destroyed the reputation of this good and honest man with baseless allegations. Their actions cannot go unpunished, as they have made it impossible for him to continue with his chosen career. Be in no doubt that we will be seeking a sizeable amount of compensation for their slanderous accusations.' As Foley stopped to draw breath, his eyes narrowed, no doubt to emphasise his seriousness and the enormity of his client's trauma.

'Let's not go there, Mr Foley. When we entered that basement there were numerous photographs of your client displayed upon the wall. Each documenting the sexual abuse that went on at the club.' She returned the man's stare.

'I have not seen these photographs, but my client has assured me that although they might be viewed as distasteful, they do not show any illegal act taking place. The young women in the photographs were indeed just that. Young women, over the age of consent. And it is my understanding that they did indeed consent. There was no coercion involved in any of those sexual encounters.'

Jemima chose to ignore the solicitor's remarks, determined not to allow the man to steer the interview away from their intended line of questioning. 'I understand that you have been examined by the on-call doctor, who has confirmed that you are fit for interview, and that you have received refreshments since your arrival at the station, Mr Lawson.'

'As a matter of deference, you should address my client as Lord Lawson,' interjected Foley.

'Please be quiet, Mr Foley.' Jemima's voice was icy and authoritative as she held up her hand to silence the man. 'I will not allow you to disrupt this investigation. And I will continue to address your client as Mr Lawson, as he is not here as a member of the judiciary. He is being interviewed in a private capacity, as allegations have been made against him. During the course of the day we made considerable efforts to discover what had happened to Mr Lawson. And when it was established that he had been abducted we concentrated our efforts on finding him and resolving the situation in a peaceful manner—'

'My daughter's a troubled soul, Inspector,' interjected Lawson.

'Please allow me to finish, Mr Lawson. As I was about to say, our enquiries led us to discover some evidence of a troubling nature.'

Broadbent opened a folder and extracted a series of photographs, while Jemima studied Lawson's expression and body language. The most noticeable changes were a slight slump of the shoulders together with a nervous twitch of the eye, which he was unable to control.

'Having interviewed your daughter, she has confirmed that these are images of the two of you. I believe that she was approximately ten years old at the time. It is apparent from the graphic nature of these images that you were sexually abusing your daughter.'

'You had no right—'

'We had every right to enter your study and open the safe, Mr Lawson. And as you know, there wasn't just photographic evidence. There were the films that you made and subsequently downloaded onto DVD. Quite the collection, too. All, as you are fully aware, recordings of you sexually assaulting your daughter.'

'What do you have to say for yourself, Mr Lawson?' asked Broadbent. The tone of his voice was surprisingly measured, considering the fact that he would happily hit the man into the middle of next week.

'No comment.' Any hint of assertiveness had disappeared from his voice. Lawson knew that he didn't have a hope in hell of coming out of this unscathed.

'Moving on,' said Jemima. 'When we were notified of your abduction it was our immediate priority to establish who had abducted you. And given your role as a judge, it was necessary for us to consider the possibility that your abduction could have been linked to a trial you had presided over. Which is why a number of officers spent a considerable amount of time examining court records and trial transcripts. And as a result of that work, we came across a troubling matter in a case you recently presided over.'

'What's this rubbish you're talking about?' Foley's voice was raised slightly. The man had remained silent as they'd presented the evidence of Lawson's systematic abuse of his daughter. But this latest line of questioning had clearly not been anticipated. It was the first time that Jemima had seen him thrown off guard.

'I've no idea what you're alluding to. Please enlighten me.' Lawson sounded weary.

'We have reason to suspect that you are guilty of malfeasance in public office.' As she put the allegation out there, Jemima's eyes did not leave Lawson's face.

He did his best not to show how her words had unsettled him. Yet Jemima spotted the flicker of uncertainty in his eyes and a nervous tic at the side of his mouth. She had to hand it to him — he quickly regained his composure. So much so, that had she happened to blink at that moment in time, she would have surely missed it.

'Really, Inspector? That's an outrageous allegation,' countered Foley.

'Having examined court records and the transcript of one trial in particular over which you presided, it has come to our attention that you failed to declare a conflict of interest whereby you should have recused yourself from the proceedings.'

'I-I've n-no idea what you're alluding to,' said Lawson.

'Then let me enlighten you,' said Jemima. 'You presided over the trial of a young man named Zach Trevelyan-Goode.'

'If you say so.' He shrugged his shoulders and shook his head as though genuinely unaware of what was being alluded to. 'I've presided over numerous trials throughout my career, far too many for me to be expected to remember them all.'

Jemima noted that Lawson had regained his composure. It demonstrated a remarkable strength of character, given the pressure the man must be under. She had fully expected him to bluff it out. After all, he was unaware of the tragic events that had befallen the Trevelyan-Goode family throughout that day. And he had no knowledge that they had a recording of Tristan confirming that his father had helped broker a deal with Edward to land a lucrative contract, the timing of which clearly demonstrated a quid pro quo between the patriarchs to benefit their respective offspring. Under normal circumstances both men would have refused to acknowledge any such deal. And Lawson would have been confident that Edward would not divulge any compromising information.

'Zach is the son of Edward Trevelyan-Goode. Like yourself, Edward is a member of the Marquess Club. We interviewed Edward earlier today under caution, whereby he confirmed that you colluded with each other to ensure that Edward awarded your son Tristan a lucrative contract, in return for you ensuring that Edward's son Zach would not face a prison sentence should a jury find him guilty at his upcoming trial.'

'He's lying!' Rory's complexion had paled, and although the denial was as forceful as he could muster, there was a noticeable tremor to his voice.

'I put it to you that you are the person who is not telling the truth. You see, we also have a recorded interview with

Tristan, who informed us that you set up and attended a meeting with Edward, which is where the deal was brokered.'

'You'll be hard-pressed to prove this in court. Tristan was obviously distressed and not thinking clearly. He would have been out of his mind with worry about me. As for Edward, I'm sure he'll recant his statement.'

'I can assure you that he won't, Mr Lawson. You see, Edward Trevelyan-Goode died earlier this evening. As such, his statement will stand. And as I'm sure you're aware, your actions perverted the course of justice. Which means that there will be calls for every case you have presided over to be re-examined. You have turned the justice system in this country into a complete travesty.'

'That's enough, Inspector,' said Foley. It was apparent that the solicitor felt compelled to defend his client, but his rebuff was lacklustre, and he was already putting away his notepad and pen. He knew that there was no coming back from this. It was impossible to adequately defend the indefensible. His client would be placed on remand and would serve a hefty prison sentence.

Moments later, Jemima read out the list of charges that Rory Lawson now faced and he was returned to the custody suite, where he would be taken to a waiting armoured vehicle and transported to Bristol to be housed on the vulnerable prisoner wing.

The final task of the day was to interview Emilia Lawson, who had been conferring with a solicitor. With the formalities out of the way, the interview began.

'Firstly, Mrs Lawson, I can confirm that after his earlier ordeal, your husband is safe and well. He was examined by the on-call doctor, has rested and received refreshments. He was later interviewed, but I will not go into specifics about what was discussed. Though I will tell you that following the interview, Rory was formally charged and will shortly be taken to a prison, where he will remain on remand until a trial date is set.'

Emilia Lawson closed her eyes, grimaced, but said nothing.

'Emilia, why did you do nothing to stop your husband from sexually abusing your daughter?' Jemima leaned forward and stared at the woman.

Emilia's eyes were still closed as she repeatedly shook her head. It was as though she was attempting to rid herself of the words she had just heard.

'Really, Inspector! You are clearly distressing my client with your unfounded allegations. You may very well have the evidence to charge her husband, but it seems to me that you are skating on very thin ice when it comes to Mrs Lawson. I suggest you present your evidence or move on.'

'Emilia, we interviewed Matilda earlier. As you will no doubt be aware, she alleged that your husband sexually abused her throughout much of her childhood—'

'She made it up,' interjected Emilia. 'She was always making things up. It's the sort of child she was. Always wanting sympathy and attention. She's ill. It's a mental illness.'

'We both know that Matilda didn't make it up,' said Jemima.

'Yes, yes, of course she did!'

'There were numerous photographs taken from the safe in your husband's home office, which prove that the abuse took place.' Jemima laid them out on the table. 'As you will see, the abuse took place in your daughter's bedroom.'

Emilia recoiled and howled. 'Stupid, stupid man.'

'These photographs do not prove that my client had any knowledge of the abuse. You can see how distressed she is,' insisted the solicitor.

'I agree that these photographs do not prove Emilia was complicit. However . . .' Jemima nodded to Broadbent, who placed a laptop on the table and selected the part of the film they wanted to play.

Turning the screen to face both Emilia and her solicitor, the latter watched in horror, while Emilia kept her eyes closed and placed her hands over her ears. There was no denying that Matilda's mother had known about the abuse. No denying the fact that she had chosen to ignore her husband's evil deeds and consigned her daughter to a life of pain, terror and humiliation. Yet even when confronted by the irrefutable evidence, Emilia still refused to look at the recording and kept repeating that it was all lies.

The woman was clearly in denial, despite the evidence against her being irrefutable.

As Jemima and Broadbent went in search of Gareth, they found him in conversation with another officer.

'Did you look at the photographs on Rachel's phone?' asked Jemima.

'Yeah. The woman escorting the girls to the club was Sally Trent.'

'You've gotta be kidding me!' Dan couldn't believe what they'd just been told.

'There's no doubt about it. There're at least five shots of her. It's Sally all right. That master key card that Kennedy was holding gave her direct access to the building from the alley. Apparently, that door our lot were trying to open led to a small passageway. Inside that was another steel door that required a key card to be swiped. They must've installed it to get the girls in and out without any other members realising what was going on.'

'Kennedy must've taken it and when she realised it was missing, she would've known that he was on to her,' said Jemima.

# CHAPTER 34

Jemima returned home that night to find the house in darkness, which was unsurprising as it was almost two a.m. and everyone was asleep. She turned the key and opened the front door as quietly as possible, wincing as it swung inwards when the hinges squeaked. It was the noise it always made. Not so noticeable during the day when other sounds drowned it out, but amplified to teeth-clenching proportions by the silence of the night.

Having shut the door, she stood for a moment, straining to listen for any sign of movement coming from the upper floors. It was how she imagined a burglar might feel. Eventually satisfied that she had not disturbed anyone, she bent down to remove her shoes, the heels of which she knew from experience ricocheted against the floor tiles, and went to the kitchen to pour herself a glass of orange juice.

Throughout the journey home, she'd realised that her tongue kept sticking to the roof of her mouth. She hadn't had time to grab a coffee or even thought to have a sip of water for many hours. As for food, she'd hardly eaten anything throughout the day. Yet as hungry as she was, she was determined to wait until breakfast. If she ate something now and went straight to bed it would undoubtedly lie heavily on her stomach and she'd struggle to get to sleep. At this hour it was better to have a growling stomach than a full one.

She climbed the stairs, placing her feet tentatively on each of the risers for fear of making a sound. Reaching the first-floor landing she poked her head around the open doorway and listened in the darkness to the sound of James's steady breathing. She smiled for what seemed like the first time in many hours. Satisfied that her boy was safe, sound and contented, the next stop was her room, which she shared with Finlay. The plug-in night light allowed her to see her son as he lay on his back snuffling away, oblivious to her presence. She kissed two of her fingertips and gently touched his forehead, then undressed and got into bed. Within minutes of her head touching the pillow, Jemima was fast asleep.

She woke to the sound of Finlay doing his utmost to attract her attention. Daylight was streaming through the flimsy curtains and the toddler was wide awake and raring to go. He had reached a stage where everything was fascinating and fun. There were so many things to explore. So many new experiences to be had.

The little lad wanted his mother's attention and was determined to get it. Gripping the bars of his cot, he bounced up and down, clearly enjoying himself. 'Mumma! Mumma! Mumma!' he squealed, and gave a heart-melting broad smile along with the cutest of giggles when he saw her open her eyes. He swayed precariously as the mattress dipped where his feet landed, though he somehow managed to maintain his balance. Letting go of the bars, he held out his hands, imploring her to scoop him up. Drowsy and bleary-eyed, Jemima was unable to resist doing just that.

Breakfast was a rushed but joyous affair. The kitchen filled with chatter and laughter as everyone set themselves up for the day. James insisted on telling his cousins some jokes, which were as corny as those in Christmas crackers. The younger children laughed uncontrollably, spurring James on to tell them more. It gave Jemima a warm glow to see her adoptive son so at ease with his extended family. Lucy had made them feel welcome, and Jemima really felt as though this was where they belonged.

Jemima ate the last scrap of food from her plate, cleared the table, placed things in the dishwasher and switched it on. It was the least she could do when Lucy and Eloise, the children's nanny, would inevitably do the lion's share of housework now that she had returned to work.

'Mum, will you help me with my homework tonight?' asked James.

It delighted Jemima that within the last year the boy had taken to calling her Mum. It was something she had hoped he would feel comfortable to do. She had long since thought of him as her son. Now, whenever she heard him say that word, she felt as though her heart would burst with joy.

'You know how it is, James, I can't make any promises. But I'll do my best to be back home at a reasonable time. And if I am, you'll be my top priority and we'll do your homework together.'

'OK, Mum.' He smiled, kissed her cheek and trotted out of the room to clean his teeth.

It was barely eight o'clock and Jemima already felt guilty about the very real possibility of letting her eldest child down yet again.

As she was on her way out of the door, her phone pinged. It was a text to say that the Cathays Park station was temporarily closed. Investigations into the death in custody were still ongoing and would be for days. The custody suite was still off limits, with prisoners being housed and processed in nearby stations. There was also the allegation of police corruption which needed to be investigated. Not to mention the fact that Sally Trent was still at large, presumably still in possession of the firearm with which she shot Ray Kennedy.

Overnight, Internal Affairs had also decided that every officer working out of the Cathays Park station had to be interviewed to enable them to establish whether they were linked to the corruption. It didn't seem to matter that

Jemima had only returned to work yesterday. She had to face the same scrutiny as everyone else.

The crown court had also been shut temporarily while records of every trial Lawson had presided over were examined. His actions were unprecedented, and once news of his active role in perverting the course of justice became public knowledge, it would open the floodgates for appeals. Someone was bound to leak the story to the press, if the hacks didn't get wind first that something was up. Some of them spent their days sitting in the public gallery to get the lowdown on any newsworthy cases. Breaking the story of a corrupt judge could be the scoop of a lifetime.

Jemima was told that an appointment would be made for her to attend an interview at the Cardiff Bay police station. Until they were satisfied that she had nothing to do with the alleged network of corrupt officers, she would not be allowed to return to work. When her phone rang later that morning, the display showing the call to be from an unknown caller, her immediate thought was that it would be someone from Internal Affairs. She had guessed wrong.

'Huxley? Frank Rutherford.' Wasting no time on small talk, his voice oozed assertiveness.

Jemima felt her heart miss a beat. She knew that Rutherford wouldn't have called her if it wasn't important. Either Kennedy had taken a turn for the worse or he wanted Jemima to do something.

'How's Ray doing?' There was no confident tone to her voice.

'Relax, Huxley. You should know by now that Ray's a tough cookie. I'm just calling to tell you that he had a good night. I've got the best people looking after him and he's on the mend. Of course, he'll need to rest. But who wouldn't if they'd taken a slug to the gut? He's only human after all.'

'That's a relief. I've been so worried about him. Is there anything I can do to help?'

'That's why I'm making contact. Ray's going to need some of his home comforts. I'd go myself but I'm a bit

273

tied up at the moment and I can't spare any of my team. I thought you could pop in sometime during the day, after work maybe?'

'Actually, I'm free now. They've closed the station while they're investigating the corruption allegations. So I'm at a loose end, waiting for a call to find out what's what.' Doing something for Kennedy was an appealing thought.

'I'd advise you not to go by yourself. My people checked out his house yesterday and there was no sign of Sally, but my resources are stretched to breaking and I haven't had eyes on the place overnight.'

'Don't worry. I'll give Dan and Gareth a call. If she's any sense, she'll be long gone. There'll be plenty of people keeping an eye out for her. I just hope someone finds her soon. She should be locked up. Ray deserves justice. After all, he's spent most of his life fighting to get it for other people.'

'Call me cynical, but in my experience, justice is often elusive,' said Frank.

Jemima couldn't argue with the man's sentiment.

'Apparently, Ray's got a travel bag he keeps packed in case of emergencies. He's got a similar mindset to me in that respect. Never know when I need to move quickly. Anyway, I believe it's under his bed. He'd like you to call at his house to pick it up for him and wants you to get his laptop too. Oh, and there's the cat.'

'The cat! That's a joke, right?' Jemima had had no idea that Ray Kennedy had a pet, and she certainly wasn't keen on cats.

'No joke. Apparently, it's a neutered tomcat, named Bilko.'

'Bilko?'

'One of his favourite shows. Phil Silvers? A bit before your time. Before mine too, if I'm honest. Perhaps you've seen the Steve Martin film?'

'Can't say I have.'

'Anyway, the reason behind the name's not important. He told me to tell you that the cat's very affectionate, once

274

he gets to know you. He likes to have his head rubbed and he's partial to sitting on your lap and having his back tickled.'

'And you're telling me this because . . . ?' Jemima had a sinking feeling that she already knew the answer.

'Because Ray's hoping you'll be kind enough to adopt the cat. Under the circumstances he can't take care of the animal and he wants to know that it'll go to a good home. Somewhere where it'll get attention.'

'And he thinks that's with me?'

'He said your sister was considering having a cat. Thought it'd be good for the kids to have a pet.'

'Really? I wasn't aware they were in touch with each other.' Jemima suddenly wondered what else was going on behind her back, between members of her family and her work colleagues.

'Apparently so. Anyway, the cat carrier is in the laundry room. As is the cat food, litter and litter tray. I can tell you now, it'll be a weight off Ray's mind to know that you'll have the damn cat. He dotes on it. I suppose it's the nearest thing he'll get to having a child. So, can I tell him you'll sort it?'

'First things first, I don't have a key.'

'Ummm, Ray might be a good copper, but he's still an old fool. Third flowerpot to the right of the front door. Key's underneath.'

'Seriously? That's asking for trouble.'

'Afraid so.'

'That part of the request shouldn't be a problem. But about the cat, can you ring me back in ten minutes or so?' Jemima had no reason to think that Ray had lied about Lucy's desire to have a cat. But given that the animal would ultimately end up living in Lucy's house, it was best to have her agreement first. The children would be up for it — they were always going on about wanting to have a pet.

It was almost twenty minutes later when Frank rang again, and in that time, Lucy had confirmed that she was more than happy to offer a home to Bilko. Jemima couldn't help but think it was yet another crazy day.

'What's the verdict?' asked Frank.

'You can tell Ray to stop worrying. Bilko's got himself a new home. Can't say I'm overly enthusiastic, but my sister's over the moon and I know the kids will be delighted.'

'It'll be a weight off his mind. He's got more than enough to worry about at the moment.'

'I suppose you're right. So, how will I get his case and laptop to you?' asked Jemima.

'I'll collect them from your sister's house. Ray's given me the address. How does ten o'clock tonight sound?'

'Like you've already made up your mind,' said Jemima.

'Later.' Rutherford disconnected the call before Jemima had a chance to respond.

Jemima checked her watch. The morning rush-hour traffic would have eased and it was the ideal time for her to make the journey to Kennedy's house and collect everything he needed. The sooner she picked up Bilko, the more time he would have to settle in and explore the house at his own pace. To gain some confidence in his new surroundings before the children returned home from school and nightly chaos ensued. As children, Lucy and Jemima had not been allowed to have a pet. Their father had been amenable, but their mother had forbidden it. Jemima realised that it was that lack of experience around animals that made her question her competence around them. Common sense told her that she would adapt. After all, how hard could it be? However, it concerned her that there was a possibility that she wouldn't bond with Bilko, and she didn't want to let Kennedy down.

She selected Dan's number, drumming her fingers impatiently on her thigh as the call went unanswered. When the answer machine kicked in, she left him a message telling him to meet her at Kennedy's house. It was the same when she tried to contact Gareth. For whatever reason, neither of her sergeants were answering their phones.

Concerned that it might take her a long time to locate Bilko and encourage him to get into the cat carrier, she decided not to wait until she heard back from at least one of them. Instead, she picked up the car keys and headed out.

As Jemima pulled into Kennedy's street, she kept an eye out for Sally's car, breathing a sigh of relief when she finally reassured herself that it wasn't there. If the woman was going to front it out and feign innocence, she would have made contact soon after Gareth had messaged her to say something was wrong. But as she'd not chosen that particular course of action it was safe to assume she had put an escape plan into play. Returning to the house she had shared with Kennedy was the riskiest option available to her, and Sally had already proved how resourceful and duplicitous she was. After all, she'd had everyone fooled. Even the seasoned detective she shared a bed with.

The terraced house was set back from the pavement, with a boundary wall of decorative stone and a low wooden gate that needed painting and the hinges of which required some oil. The front garden was small but attractive and suggested that either Ray, Sally or both enjoyed pottering around keeping the place in order.

Jemima stood still and listened hard for any sign of life coming from inside. Finally satisfied that there was none, it was time to find the key, which was where Frank Rutherford had told her it would be. In fairness, it was underneath a hefty pot, with a well-established lavender bush adding bulk and weight. Nevertheless, Jemima was surprised that after everything Kennedy would have encountered throughout his career, he still risked leaving a key to his home that could be discovered with relative ease by any would-be burglar, which in turn would invalidate any insurance claim should the worst happen.

Stepping into the hallway, the smell of cigarettes was all-pervasive. Jemima wrinkled her nose in disgust. Having never smoked she disliked the smell. Ray Kennedy was a non-smoker too, and it seemed unfathomable that he allowed Sally to smoke inside the house. No amount of air freshener could successfully mask the overriding odour.

She locked the door behind her, pocketed the key and got her first look at the inside of Kennedy's house. She was surprised to discover that the interior was bright and modern. It was not what she had anticipated given the age of the property. The ceilings were smooth, the walls painted in shades that were bang on trend. It appeared that Kennedy had an eye for style, which wasn't at all apparent from the clothes he wore to work.

Having already decided that her first objective was to find Bilko, she headed to find the utility room where the cat basket was kept.

Jemima couldn't help but gasp when she saw the full extent of the kitchen. Light flooded the space from a set of bi-fold doors that gave access to the garden, which was a plot far larger than Jemima's house in Thornhill had sat on. The room was enormous and incorporated a living area. The space extended to the full width of the property with skylights adding to the light and airy feel. The floor was tiled in a herringbone style and the entire far wall featured wood panelling, providing texture and interest to what would otherwise have been a bland space. It was painted in a deep accent colour, which drew the eye towards it and offset the high-gloss units.

A substantial island with bar stools at one end and an induction hob at the other was the centrepiece of the workspace. An extractor, which Jemima guessed would have cost a small fortune, was suspended above the hob. A small number of plates and bowls were stacked neatly, waiting to be put away, evidence that until recently life had continued as normal. Enormous salt and pepper mills located not far from the hob suggested that either Ray or Sally took delight in preparing food. That observation was also borne out by the surprising fact that there were four ovens built into a wall of kitchen units.

Jemima was still puzzling over why Ray and Sally would need four ovens when she spotted the door to what must surely be the utility room. Unlike the doors to the lounge and the kitchen, this one was closed. With her thoughts still preoccupied with the surprising things she had just learned about Ray Kennedy's lifestyle, she walked towards the closed door and absentmindedly pushed down on the handle, while still looking over her shoulder, marvelling at the top-of-the-range appliances. Realising that the door would open towards her, she stepped back and gently pulled it.

All of a sudden, a searing pain shot across the side of her face as a frying pan hit her with tremendous force. It propelled her head sideways, changing her centre of gravity. Jemima's legs gave way and she crashed to the floor, narrowly missing the edge of the nearby work surface. There were seconds when pain blocked out all thoughts, but miraculously she did not lose consciousness.

Years ago, as a novice kickboxer, Jemima had learned to cope with pain. When practising a martial art, discomfort and injuries were an inevitable consequence. Especially in those early days, when her knowledge, ability and concentration levels were no match for those of her opponents. It had been a steep learning curve. One which tested her physically and mentally. Through sheer grit and determination, she had trained hard to become the best she could possibly be. Fully appreciating that if she wished to perfect her skills, she needed to rise above the pain. These were lessons she would never forget. Every blow she received had increased her resilience, made her more focused and taught her not to give up.

Nature showed that a wounded animal was often at its most dangerous. And as she found herself spreadeagled across the floor, wondering what the hell had just happened, that is precisely what Jemima had become. She had let her guard down and allowed herself to be caught unawares. It was a stupid, rookie mistake and she was paying the price for not being vigilant. With her heart hammering nineteen to the dozen and her vision blurred by tears of pain, she sensed more than saw someone about to dodge past her legs.

In that moment, instinct and training kicked in. No one treated Jemima like this without being paid back in spades.

Over the years she had taken down formidable adversaries, sustaining her fair share of injuries in the line of duty. But that was when she had been in peak physical condition. Recently, fitness and training had taken a backseat. Motherhood had taken priority and she had let her training slide. But she refused to allow her attacker to get away scot-free.

Despite being down, Jemima was not out. Since opening that door, the smell of stale cigarettes was even stronger. Which could only mean that Sally was the one who had attacked her. And after what that woman had done to Kennedy, Jemima was determined that there was no way she was going to allow her to leave the house. She owed it to Ray to be the one to bring her down, to give him peace of mind that the bitch was no longer free to take another shot at him.

Though Jemima was out of condition, there was no doubt in her mind that Sally was in a worse shape. The woman chain-smoked and to Jemima's knowledge had never been keen on exercise.

Jemima's legs shot up with surprising speed, clamping one of Sally's legs mid-calf, in a pincer movement. In a seamless swipe, she thrust herself sideways in the opposite direction to which Sally was going.

It was the right call, and the result was inevitable. Sally's arms flailed about like a bizarre windmill. But her efforts were to no avail as she was going down. There was a tremendous crash as she knocked some crockery off a work surface and plummeted to the floor. The ceramics shattered, littering the previously pristine floor tiles. Sally landed heavily with a thud, grunting as the wind was knocked out of her.

She had clearly not anticipated Jemima, or anyone else for that matter, turning up out of the blue, which meant the woman wasn't prepared for a physical confrontation. She'd obviously improvised when she heard someone open the front door and, Jemima had to give it to her, using a frying pan as a weapon was a stroke of genius.

After Sally's attempt on Ray's life, Jemima appreciated that the woman would do whatever it took to evade capture.

Until yesterday, she had successfully masqueraded as plain old Sally. DS Sally Trent, who smoked far too many cigarettes and had passed up any chance of promotion to continue with her work at the Sexual Crimes Unit.

That particular posting now seemed like a sick joke. Having spent years witnessing the devastation that resulted from these crimes, Sally should have stopped these men from destroying countless lives. Yet instead, she had repeatedly delivered victims to their door.

She had befriended Ray's friends and colleagues. Fooling them all. They had all seen what she wanted them to see. None of them had thought her capable of such duplicity or treachery.

Despite being injured, quick thinking and incredible fortitude on Jemima's part had turned the tables. Though to capitalise upon the advantage she needed to push on, which was easier said than done as her jaw throbbed relentlessly, and the pain was making her feel sick. But if she was going to fully incapacitate Sally, it was now or never.

Jemima knew that Sally liked being in control, but that physically, the older woman was no match for her.

However, Sally soon proved to be more resilient than Jemima had expected. Recovering quickly, she began to push herself up from the floor.

Jemima was having none of it. She wanted the woman to remain prone, and to ensure she stayed there, she practically belly-flopped on top of her. As her torso slammed onto Sally's it crushed the older woman's chest against the tiles.

Sally grunted as air was forcibly expelled from her lungs. Gasping for breath, she reached out and ran her fingers across the floor until she found what she was after and manoeuvred a lengthy shard of ceramic towards her. The shattered plate was part of the dinner service she had chosen when she'd first moved in with Ray.

Jemima was oblivious of her opponent's makeshift weapon. 'You're going nowhere, lady.' The words were so low they were almost a growl, and Jemima's mouth was so close to Sally's ear that her lips almost brushed the lobe.

Sally writhed like a bucking bronco, but lacked the core strength to eject the younger officer.

'Gerroff me! Lemme go!' she squealed. She knew that Jemima would not release her. Her only hope was that she could manoeuvre her arm into such a position that she could stab her with the makeshift weapon.

'No way. You shot Ray. How could you do that? He's a good man. He loved you!' Jemima had never experienced such a burning sense of rage. Throughout her career, she had hunted down and arrested some of the most abhorrent people. On each of those cases, she had inevitably felt anger and revulsion at what they had done to their victims. Yet she felt pure hatred towards Sally. The woman had tried to kill Ray, the man she professed to love. However this played out, Jemima would never be able to forgive her former friend for that.

'He left me no choice. You're deluded if you think I set out to kill Ray. It needn't have got to that stage, but the stupid sod just kept pushing, sticking his nose into things that didn't concern him. That was Ray all over. Once he got wind of something he was like a dog with a bone. Wouldn't let things lie. Shooting him was the hardest thing I've ever done. I loved him. I still love him. We'd mapped out our future growing old together.'

Jemima couldn't believe what she was hearing. 'You don't know the meaning of love, you evil bitch!'

'You've no idea what our relationship was like. Ray was the love of my life!'

'Yeah? Why'd you shoot him then?'

'I had no choice. You know what he's like. Saw himself as the guardian of morality. He'd stick to his beliefs, even if it meant that he had to sacrifice his own happiness — or even his life.'

Jemima was sickened by the rubbish Sally was spouting as she tried to justify her actions. This was a woman she had trusted. Someone who helped victims of sexual assault. She had even been the person Jemima had trusted when she had been raped. To eventually discover that Sally Trent was closely linked with a group of men who raped young women and underage girls felt like the most heinous of betrayals. It made Jemima question her own judgement, as she had not seen what had been right in front of her face. She could only imagine the devastation Kennedy must have felt when he discovered what his partner had been up to. It was no wonder the man had seemed so out of sorts and distracted in the time leading up to his shooting.

'How could you betray those girls, Sally? It's obscene. You work with victims of sexual abuse. You helped me when I was raped.'

'Peter made me do it.'

'Peter Deavers?' Jemima repeated the name as she thought she must've misheard. 'What the hell did he have on you?'

'Nothing. It was my brother, George. He's a teacher. He'd been to the pub one night and ended up having sex with a girl who turned out to be underage. Peter saw them and started to blackmail me. George said it was a one-off. But Peter had photographs. My brother could've lost everything. His wife. His kids. His job. I couldn't let that happen to my family.'

'So you sold out all those young women to save your brother's marriage?'

'Yes.'

'How'd you get the girls?'

'I've got contacts in children's homes, and there're always kids who've been trafficked. It's not that difficult.'

Jemima couldn't believe that Sally was trying to normalise her actions. It was sickening to realise that the woman felt no remorse. She grabbed a clump of the woman's hair and yanked her head back. 'You're nothing but pond life, Sally. You're going down for this,' she hissed.

Sally yelped, but the pain made her more determined than ever to get away. She circled her arm and drove the spike into Jemima's leg, catching her mid-thigh.

Jemima screamed and let go of Sally's hair. She glanced down, saw that Sally still had hold of the weapon and was about to stab her again.

Jemima took the only option open to her and launched herself sideways. Fortunately, the initial wound had missed the major artery, but there was no guarantee that any further impact wouldn't hit the mark, and if that were to happen, Jemima might very well die right there on the kitchen floor.

Both women rose steadily, eyeing each other like a couple of wildcats readying themselves for a fight to establish dominance. Sally had managed to capitalise on the element of surprise, but now it would be a wholly physical confrontation, and despite her injuries, Jemima was far more likely to be the victor.

Jemima did her best to block out the pain. It was easier said than done. Her jaw was throbbing and she couldn't fully put weight on her injured leg. Under the circumstances, these were both distractions she could do without.

Placing one hand on the island to take the pressure off her leg, she eyed her opponent. She was aware of the danger Sally posed and needed to either disarm or incapacitate her. This confrontation had to end as quickly as possible. She was losing blood. The injury wasn't a fatal one, but it was incapacitating nevertheless. The more time that elapsed without getting help, the weaker she would become.

Sally's eyes momentarily flickered towards the front of the house, betraying her desire to make a run for it.

Jemima needed to act swiftly. As she looked for something to help her bring Sally down, the only potential weapon she could see was the peppermill. Jemima swiped it and gripped it in the way she would a baton. Being taller than Sally, she would naturally have a far greater reach, allowing her to use the implement as a cosh without fear of being stabbed. As police officers, they had both been trained to use batons, and knew how effective they could be.

As Sally's gaze rested on Jemima's hand, she knew that she had lost the advantage. Understanding that she needed

to make a run for it, she lurched towards the door, striding as fast as she could.

Jemima swiped with the peppermill. It caught the woman on the shoulder. Sally dropped the ceramic shank as a pulse of pain shot through her upper body. But she kept on running, skidding to a halt as she reached the front door.

It was locked.

Jemima had caught up with her before she had a chance to open it, and this time she was determined that she was going to end things. As Sally turned the lock, Jemima hit her across the ribs with all the force she could muster.

The blow propelled Sally sideways against the wall with such force that it knocked her unconscious.

# EPILOGUE

The crowds lined the streets, cheering the runners on, shouting out words of encouragement. It was the Cardiff half-marathon and the first time that Jemima, Dan and Gareth had entered such an event.

'Come on, Dan! Keep up. Get those legs moving,' shouted Jemima. Her pace was steady, but slower than she had hoped for.

'You can do it, mate! Don't let the side down,' said Gareth.

'Bugger off . . . the pair . . . of you,' panted Dan. He distractedly wiped his forehead with the sweatband around his wrist. The one encircling his forehead was heavy with moisture and had stopped being effective a while ago. It was unlikely that he would ever be as fit as the others, but he had no intention of giving up and was determined to cross the finishing line if it was the last thing he ever did. And the way he felt now with less than a quarter of a mile to go, he thought that it might very well be his last few minutes on earth.

Up ahead something caught his eye — a small lad in his mother's arms.

'Daddeeeee! Daddeeeee!'

It was Caroline, Dan's wife, and their son, Harry. The little boy wriggled and pointed, desperate to get free and join in what he clearly viewed as fun. The sight of his family spurred Dan on. He forced himself to smile and rose a hand in acknowledgement as he strode past, matching his colleagues, pace for pace. It was just the motivation he needed to keep going and see it through to the end.

For the last six months the three officers had trained for this event. Jemima had taken it easy to start with, due to her leg injury, courtesy of Sally Trent. However, she had got used to endurance training during her years of kick-boxing. And although she was out of practice and not at peak physical fitness, she had improved week on week.

Gareth was as lithe as a whippet, but nowhere near as fast, though his diet was far better than Dan's, who until recently never held much with exercise, and had long since started to develop the dreaded middle-aged spread.

So much had changed since Jemima's first day back after maternity leave, and it was safe to say that the squad would never be the same again.

Sally Trent had been hospitalised and treated for a fractured skull. There was an inevitable investigation into what had happened at the woman's home, and Jemima had eventually been exonerated. Bruising on Sally's body tallied with Jemima's version of events and blood spatter on the wall confirmed that Sally's head had collided with it.

Jemima had also spent the rest of the day in the hospital, being treated for concussion and having her leg wound assessed, stitched and dressed.

Sally had remained in hospital for about a week and had been guarded for the entire period, as it was not known whether someone would try to kill her to prevent her from revealing what she knew about police corruption and the predatory sex offenders who were Platinum Members of the Marquess Club. As it turned out, Sally had remained resolutely tight-lipped and had refused to answer any questions put to her.

Jemima had given a statement about what Sally had revealed to her during their confrontation at the house.

However, as Sally had not been cautioned, and there had been no other witnesses to the events which had taken place, it was Jemima's word against Sally's.

Efforts had been made to follow up on Jemima's assertion that Sally had claimed she was being blackmailed by Peter Deavers, who supposedly had incriminating evidence against Sally's brother, George. However, there was no evidence to suggest that Sally had ever had a brother, as records showed that she had been an only child.

When Sally was fit to be discharged from the hospital, she was placed on remand under an assumed name.

Glen Buchannan's investigation into the abduction and subsequent death of Emyr Trevelyan-Goode continued for many weeks, until he received an anonymous tip. The information turned the case on its head, and it was eventually discovered that Emyr had indeed been mistaken for his twin. The abduction turned out to have no connection to Matilda Lawson or to PASA.

It was eventually discovered that Zach Trevelyan-Goode was in a relationship with another young woman. However, on this occasion her brothers had learned of his notoriety and had decided to teach him a lesson before he had a chance to harm their sister. They knew that he lived in the village but were unaware that he had an identical twin.

The brothers hadn't planned to kill Zach, or even physically harm him. Their sole intention had been to humiliate him by filming, then posting a compromising video of him online.

Six months later, the police station at Cathays Park remained closed. No one was even sure if it would open again. The anti-corruption team had rooted out nine officers of varying ranks who they believed were linked to the alleged corruption. The most serious offender was Superintendent Deavers, who as well as being a Platinum Member of the Marquess Club was also believed to have murdered Edward Trevelyan-Goode.

Ray Kennedy had fully recovered but had decided it was time to retire on a full pension. Though Jemima knew that her friend and mentor was not about to take things easy. In recent months she had learned that Frank Rutherford was Kennedy's cousin, and Ray had agreed to join his private security firm, offering protection for high-profile individuals.

Revelations of Rory Lawson's corruption and other criminal activities had embroiled Cardiff Crown Court in a scandal that would never be forgotten. There were months when the entire building had been shut while investigations concerning the extent of the corruption took place. Every case he had presided over had needed to be scrutinised and as word had got out, so appeals flooded in.

When Jemima, Dan and Gareth were eventually cleared by the anti-corruption team, they had been relocated to the Cardiff Bay police station. But the changes didn't stop there. In the previous week, Jemima had been promoted to Detective Chief Inspector.

There was also to be a new way of working, as Jemima and her team were no longer restricted to the South Wales Police. With all the changes that were underway, Jemima's team would investigate major incidents occurring through-out south-east Wales. Which meant that they would also investigate crimes that occurred in the area covered by Gwent police force. It would be a huge undertaking, but Jemima had no doubt that with Dan, Gareth and whoever else joined the team, they would meet any challenge that faced them.

**THE END**

# THE JOFFE BOOKS STORY

We began in 2014 when Jasper agreed to publish his mum's much-rejected romance novel and it became a bestseller.

Since then we've grown into the largest independent publisher in the UK. We're extremely proud to publish some of the very best writers in the world, including Joy Ellis, Faith Martin, Caro Ramsay, Helen Forrester, Simon Brett and Robert Goddard. Everyone at Joffe Books loves reading and we never forget that it all begins with the magic of an author telling a story.

We are proud to publish talented first-time authors, as well as established writers whose books we love introducing to a new generation of readers.

We have been shortlisted for Independent Publisher of the Year at the British Book Awards three times, in 2020, 2021 and 2022, and for the Diversity and Inclusivity Award at the Independent Publishing Awards in 2022.

We built this company with your help, and we love to hear from you, so please email us about absolutely anything bookish at: feedback@joffebooks.com.

If you want to receive free books every Friday and hear about all our new releases, join our mailing list: www.joffebooks.com/contact.

And when you tell your friends about us, just remember: it's pronounced Joffe as in coffee or toffee!

**ALSO BY GAYNOR TORRANCE**

**JEMIMA HUXLEY CRIME THRILLERS**
Book 1: THE CARDIFF KILLINGS
Book 2: THE BRIARMARSH CLOSE KILLINGS
Book 3: THE CAERPHILLY MOUNTAIN KILLINGS
Book 4: THE LEIGHTON MEADOW KILLINGS
Book 5: THE MARQUESS CLUB KILLINGS

www.ingramcontent.com/pod-product-compliance
Lightning Source LLC
Chambersburg PA
CBHW020302200626
46814CB00006BA/2047